CW00662746

A Tree for the Birds

A Tree for the Birds

Vernon RL Head

JACANA

Other titles by Vernon RL Head

The Search for the Rarest Bird in the World (Jacana Media, 2014)

The Laughing Dove and other Poems (Staging Post, 2015)

First published by Jacana Media (Pty) Ltd in 2018

10 Orange Street
Sunnyside
Auckland Park 2092
South Africa
+2711 628 3200
www.jacana.co.za

ISBN 978-1-4314-2565-5

Cover design by publicide
Editing by Henrietta Rose-Innes
Proofreading by Megan Mance
Set in Sabon 10.5/15pt
Printed and bound by CTP Printers, Cape Town
Job no. 003335

See a complete list of Jacana titles at www.jacana.co.za

Dedicated to
Mom, Tykie and Vlad

In memory of
Dad

IN HIS NINETEENTH YEAR, he sat afloat – at last – on the Great Dancing Road. An African river, deepest on Earth; a glittering place. Sacramental waters danced on sandy banks. Somewhere, the rain chanted. Chrisnelt stared into the current, thinking of the dead.

Pastor Kadazi sat at the prow, shaking his head and grinning, big teeth shining on a fat-pink tongue, bald head iridescent, the back of his neck a neat ladder of folds filled with sweat. Pastor Kadazi did not like the River. It was beyond his control. Everyone on board except Chrisnelt wore gold neck-chains, like rows of metallic scales. Expensive silk designer shirts fluttered, the way gills do on dying fishes. Chrisnelt's old Coca-Cola T-shirt stuck to him like skin. Everything was hot.

The wooden speedboat moved urgently away from the City: a treeless, desiccated landscape of lost opportunities. Water was in a hurry, determined to be like it always had been, on its way from the sky to the ground, then onward to the distant coast. The spray smelt rich, the river was brown and alive. The big shadow of the boat pushed against the ripples. Stainless-steel bolts rattled on the wooden deck, as did the men's sleeping pistols and machine-guns. Chrisnelt was alone inside himself; oddly hollow. He looked down at the deck, tapped it with a heel. Wood was always a message from a tree.

The men were making their way northwards toward

a remote farm of chickens and chicken shit. Pastor Kadazi's farm was situated on the left bank of the River, approximately one hundred and fifty kilometres from the City – a three-hour ride in a fast, determined boat; a monthly route of much chicken business.

The speedboat roared, continuing upriver. 'The boundary is where the future begins,' whispered Chrisnelt to his notebook. He repeated it twice, like a hymn. It was his special sentence. If he could afford a tattoo, he'd have those words written in deep black on his right arm, on the delicate inner side, from the armpit to the palm, where the veins bulged. He'd keep it close to him, pressed to the body, as one would hold a promise.

Leaves gathered one by one against an edge of the hull, making a raft of yellows, browns, reds, purples and fading greens, mixing things. The raft got bigger and bigger all the time: a shadow of the boat, swelling, until suddenly swirling away on a journey that would never end: the tumbling remnants of a tree, strangely regrouped by chance, remembered for an instant.

'Chrisnelt, do you see the little birdies?' said Pastor Kadazi, pointing with his huge arm, wiggling thick fingers. All the men looked.

'Yes, I was just going to show you, very interesting, Pastor. They are weaverbirds, *tisserand oiseau*,' he said. '*Mizingi*,' said Chrisnelt in Swahili, enhancing the glamour of his performance, compensating for not knowing the Lingala word.

Pastor Kadazi liked it when he spoke this way; it made the self-taught preacher feel instantly well-travelled. Chrisnelt had observed Pastor Kadazi doing big business and big politics with visitors in other languages, throwing foreign words around like grand possessions. Flattery was useful in Pastor Kadazi's world.

Pastor Kadazi instructed the speedboat to stop. The five men rocked in the surge of engines, the wooden hull bobbing like a twig in a stream, freshly out of place, waiting for the current to take it away forever. Chrisnelt was obliged to look at the ubiquitous weaverbirds yet again, this time through Pastor Kadazi's binoculars. The men watched him watching.

Pastor Kadazi laughed. 'I see the soft yellow-orange ones now, very bright and pretty,' he said. 'Soft like scrambled eggs. Maybe tasty?'

The men laughed. Chrisnelt laughed for them. He laughed very loudly for them. And Pastor Kadazi's great belly wobbled under the sheen of his shirt. His Rolex hung from the wrist, the face facing down, time and the telling of time irrelevant. Next to it, a raffia bracelet linked a row of white cowry shells, the raffia the bright green and yellow and red of a national flag, tight to the arm: part of his flesh. The two adornments hung there, valued by different worlds in different ways, each bejewelled in its own ignorance of the other. Pastor Kadazi's arm clinked.

'I would stick to chicken, Pastor, more meat,' said Chrisnelt, patting his stomach.

'I will show you my beautiful chickens,' said Pastor Kadazi, holding out his hands as if picturing a prize fish. He nodded.

'Chickens don't count in birdwatching,' Chrisnelt had said, boarding in the mud that dawn, to much laughter and flapping of elbows. Crude rooster calls had rocked the boat. Railings had squeaked and cushions had clucked. Thighs had swayed above the stink of the shore.

Mirror-sunglasses on all the men twinkled, the spray from the speedboat casting rainbows above the water. A dragonfly shimmered on the new heat; was part of the heat. Glistening, it lifted, escaping the no-man's land of reeds and birds. It was a translucent pause inside a moment of contemplation, unsure, bouncing above the current. Chrisnelt watched it move, carrying bits of sun.

'Dragonflies are special, living a life of two worlds. One of water, the other of air,' said Chrisnelt to the men. 'It is said when they change from aquatic hunter to creature of the sky, they carry the memory of water in their wings, the way the moon lingers in daylight as a little pond on the sky.'

'You are not right in the head, never have been,' said Pastor Kadazi, glaring. 'Shut up and think about my tree.'

'Dragonflies are the ultimate ambassadors between worlds,' thought Chrisnelt, very quietly.

The dragonfly hovered over Pastor Kadazi's head. He swished it, as one would an annoying fly, his wide hand tinkling with jewels. A thin man at the steering-wheel – eyes stained by bad moments – grabbed the dragonfly from the air, making a crunching fist. Angel wings splintered. Purple ooze dripped onto the deck and the wood absorbed a stain forever. The thin man leaned forward, flicking parts of insect off his fingers, wiping a thigh. 'Shit,' he said.

'FASTER!' shouted Pastor Kadazi.

'Yes!' said all the men.

The thin man pressed a thumb down on a red button on the console next to the steering-wheel; the boat thundered, and the rear shook in storms. The man had missing fingers on his left hand. The islands of reeds rocked with unsure edges. The speedboat rushed on. The River did too. Nausea surged in Chrisnelt's throat.

'Yes,' he said in a soft echo.

'Still a long way upriver, before we get to my chickens,' said Pastor Kadazi.

'Yes.'

'Yes.'

Chrisnelt watched the reeds stretch into the distance as they left them swaying behind. He searched for trees. Deep in his mind. Deep. Private. He searched for memories of tragedy and friendship, and the image of his father. They came irregularly, the speedboat bouncing along. Images rose like a turning world. He saw a great tree, a fluttering canopy under a sun of dreams.

He blinked. He came back to himself. He saw the yellow birds again, filled with energy, swinging on winged nests, free to roam, awake in the wake of ripples.

'When we get to that tree, you'd better make sure it lives,' said Pastor Kadazi.

Chapter One

THE RAIN CAME TO CHRISNELT as the softest stars, large drops landing in the street of dust. His imagination took each drop into his heart, bouncing and glittering in every colour. He counted the seconds between drops. He counted the drops becoming muddy dents and swelling brown circles in the sand. The patterns were slow and rhythmical, a breathing thing of delight. He began to run in leaping arcs below the heavens, his little arms outstretched, his thin fingers splayed like feathers and his pink nails twinkling. Around the tree he went in gentle wetness toward happiness, as only seven-year-old boys can go. And his long shadow rippled upon footprints and across the old walls of rust in a tail of joy. He laughed, following the spoor-line of his best friend, who was no longer on the ground, but now high in the middle of the brightest mango tree.

The tree was the only greenness in that world of corrugated iron and homemade bricks the colour of burnt earth: the rancid hue of soils passed through the bowels of an insect.

A tropical street in the late afternoon is often cooler than a house in those parts. The mists from the River at the edge of the City found their way between houses, up alleyways, over roofs and into the wide streets, whereas houses simply held heat. And so it was always good to have a veranda: a place that gave shade and a wooden stool or two. There were intermittent verandas along the street. Each was fringed with palm fronds held on the arms of ancient tree-trunks bleached like bones, standing rhythmically and pattering swathes of shadow here and there in the dust. Wood had become scarce, no longer coming from the forest, a forest that seemed to get further and further away with the passing of every season. All the houses were very low, some sagging, some swelling at the sides as the dry walls crumbled, like rising ribs revealing lungs.

Chrisnelt's street was a typical street, his house a typical house, although one of the few to have a wooden deck below the overhang of the veranda, and the only house to host bats in the eaves near the front door, swinging like little black flags of welcome. The Malotikas loved bats, as they loved all wild things; it was just their way. Mainly, it was Mr Malotika's way, since his youth far up the River. Along the house-fronts on both sides of the street lay concrete culverts filled with sewage, flowing with flies. Dogs drank occasionally from these edges, as did the little birds after bathing in hot sand that seemed to bubble. Below the house, buried like a corpse under the linoleum, lay the hard mud of a previous house made by unknown owners, and below that, the crushed pieces of a forest that was now charcoal.

Yet within the dirt, and deep inside all the browns – as with anything fertile – lay hope and life, and the unknown. From a street of hardened sand near Chrisnelt's house – a two-minute sprint for an energetic child with big feet and eyes filled with notions – a marvel of leaves had slowly pushed up to the sky, or so his father told him. The mango tree had arrived unobserved by almost everyone, a relic (all seeds are relics) from a meal once tossed as waste.

With unfathomable resilience, it had fought its way to the light, shaped by goodness, looking for a future away from the darkness cast by walls; avoiding rush hours of storming feet, dodging the sacks of charcoal dragged monthly by tired men to the sooty doorways, and bending deftly away from the wheels of wooden carts. Once it had been trampled by a stumbling drunk who vomited upon its first leaf, and twice pissed on by a dog. It always bounced back. It knew only to rise, and to continue rising, constant, instinctive, on the route that all trees take: the profound stretch toward the inevitable edge of the sky – or so Chrisnelt was told by his father. And as it went up, so it went down, great roots singing all the time as they drank, down into the vast depths that held the song of the River, which, in turn, held everything else. Eventually the tree grew beyond harm – higher than the tallest man, with a trunk fatter than any belly – and became part of the street: a wild thing from nature finding a place in the City of shading walls. Chrisnelt remembered this story very often.

Once, during a particularly hot summer, sitting under the tree with his best friend No, soft pollen fell on his feet. Then they heard whistles coming from above; undulating, battling within the grinding from old trucks, and under the honk of taxi-cars, and below the shrieks and moans of wandering people. The whistles came from inside the tree's tiny flowers, and they made a poem, a private lullaby for this special boy and his friend. Chrisnelt and No seemed to be the only people to hear it: the buzzing wings of insects and the rattling legs of ants that shone like glass. The sprays of creamy flowers erupted in waterfalls right before their big gazes. Glistening creatures from the world of feelers, carapaces and pincers came to feed, playing on twirling leaves and dangling petals of scent, alive in all their senses. And everything swelled into bulbous green, blushing finally into red, becoming the gift of fruit.

Chrisnelt's laughter became louder, intermittent giggles bursting out in between and here and there, every time he had a deep thought. He pranced and ran, being sure to plant each foot in the prints made by No. The summer raindrops – as it is in the tropics – continued to dance with him, bouncing and ululating. One by one they came down, some tickling his cheeks, some dribbling off his pointy chin, some hesitating, clinging to him like friends do. His thin shadow, and the thick shadow of the tree, held hands as he circled it again and again. He circled some more. Everything glistened. His wide eyes glowed. 'I'm a bird and I'm looking for a tree!' he said at the top of his voice.

No had loved birds since he could first crawl, watching them on the veranda in all their intricate colours. He would lie next to Chrisnelt there, spitting bits of masticated corn at the sparrows that looked like tiny toys, the birds hopping closer and closer, often sitting on his outstretched fingers, once even on his nose. No loved birds so much, he squeaked and chattered like them before he could talk. And when he could walk, he flapped like them too. Chrisnelt learned to love them as well. He loved everything No loved. The love was wild and true like wilderness.

'If you close your fingers tightly and point your arms, you can make wings and fly like a fast pigeon ah, with all its colours. And if you wiggle the tips you can dive like a sparrow,' said No to Chrisnelt on a quiet day, watching a distant flock of white birds against a white cloud.

'You can't fly like me yet Chrisnelt ah, I have already taken off into the sky up here,' said No (pronounced Noh, with the 'h' floating off the tongue). No always wanted to be first. Chrisnelt would have the idea, No would then take the lead. He was very brave. Chrisnelt would often hide behind that bravery. They had been neighbours since birth. They'd shared the adventure of standing for the first time, holding each other up, with a single gurgling cry. It had been a grand day back then for both families; the parents had clapped and the two boys had fallen into each other's arms, the strong arms of No, the weak arms of Chrisnelt: four legs and one fat body of folds wobbling on the green linoleum floor.

'I'm coming, but first I've got to finish my circles,' said Chrisnelt, always hesitant, but certain of the way. An odd leaf fluttered prematurely to the ground and No shuffled higher and higher above the din, climbing on creaking branches made of chuckles. This was the game called Catch Me, a variation on another game played by other boys. The difference was that it was in a tree, and Chrisnelt was secretly never really interested in the 'catching' part, preferring the talking and laughing part. It was always played on sticky afternoons, once the time of chores had passed, during the lull in the City when cooking-fire smoke hung low, and parents were tired and kind to children in Dee Dee Street.

'Ninety-eight, ninety-nine, one hundred raindrops,' said Chrisnelt, still running around the tree in circles, flapping his arms.

'Ye, ye, always counting things, ah,' said No, as he climbed. 'You and your stupid numbers,' he shouted, in a rustling triangle of infinite leaves, high above the ground: 'Hurry up, cluck, cluck, cluck.' He climbed higher, flapping his arms as if they were wings. 'You know what your mother will do if we're late again, and I'm sick of watching you get that punishment stuff ah. I'm sick of hearing those psalms she makes you read over and over.' He could almost climb no further. 'Makes me late for dinner, ah. And anyway, I've found new things in the distance to see here. Cluck, cluck.'

Chrisnelt pretended to ignore him, as usual, continuing to count and dream and laugh, the moving air of his leaps and tilting sways cooling him in the heat.

'Wait,' he said sharply, suddenly becoming cross. He stopped momentarily in the mud with his hands on his hips. 'You know the last time you didn't help me down, and I had to use the damn rope of this swing' – he pointed with his longest finger at the pendulous object – 'and, and that damn tyre-seat grazed my leg.'

'I'm going to ask your father to build you a ladder, Chicken Shit!' shouted No.

They both stopped to look at a huge, iridescent rooster. It jerked along. Past the tree it rocked, puffed up and proud, following two white hens greedily, its head waving loose bits that shone like a crown of princely jewels. It scratched for things like boys scratch. Chickens on the street were indeed most uncommon, being valuable animals kept behind high fences, owned by those with money, fancy gates, big houses and shiny cars that hissed, and Chrisnelt was in two minds as to whether he should give chase for his mother's big cooking pot.

Above the tree, the rooster, the hens and the boys, grey

clouds became a single cloud of black. It was a shifting cloud of mysterious shape, familiar in the afternoons, made of warmth that seemed to come from far away: strange and foreign scents fell from it, always different, always new. A flock of sparrows flittered out of the tree, cascading on wings that looked like question marks; they chirped in unison, disappearing into a distant yard edged with high walls. A moth stirred as a streetlight began to flicker. The mango tree changed into a new green.

'My Tata made this swing because you begged him, not me, *you*, and *you* never use it,' said Chrisnelt. 'You always go straight up there, and you never wait for me. That's why I never come all the way up.' He'd never had the courage to climb to the top of the tree, not once in any of their games.

'I begged him for *you*, ah,' said No.

'No, you didn't, liar.'

'Yes, I did. It's supposed to get you off the ground so that you can come up here to the *top* of the damn tree.'

'Liar.'

'Sit in it and your bum will sit in water anyway. It's like a bucket that thing,' said No. 'Especially after the rains. And it's full of bloody mosquitoes, those ones with the black-and-white legs that like to bite me and not you, ah.' He scratched a thigh, dangling a twitching leg. 'Besides, up here you can see the World.'

Chrisnelt laughed loudly at the words 'bloody' and 'mosquito', then No got the joke and laughed too. All the time – deep behind the laughter – Chrisnelt knew of the World from his father's long stories: stories of a great Forest owned by the River that fed all the leaves with the deepest water on Earth. He knew stories of the endlessness of the green and the power and fury of the waters – it was these stories that fed his private landscape of unexplainable dreams, isolating him in thoughts, coming to him most nights in images that screamed until dawn. Chrisnelt was often detached from the reality of the City, finding solace in a world inside clouds, made of raindrops, rivers and fantastical oceans. He knew deep down – very deep – that he was not the same as other people.

'You know, Chrisnelt, I can actually see the River and right at the back, where it bends, where it's almost dark, I can see the Forest and all the different colours, ah,' said No.

'I'll see it one day. Tata will take me. He's told me all about it,' said Chrisnelt. 'He's told me about the colours too.'

'I am telling you, it goes on and on in every colour. And down here, nearby, on the left, other side all the rust of these bloody houses – if you look between the TV poles – I can see one damn big, white house just down our street, ah.'

Chrisnelt looked up at No. He hesitated, then took a deep breath and began to climb, the image of the house becoming stronger, the intrigue of it tugging like ropes attached to his quivering arms and gangly legs. 'Okay, I'm coming, you idiot.'

'It's one monster of a one, with pigeons on it.'

Chrisnelt pulled himself up onto the first branch, using the leverage of the seat of the swing, and he fell to the ground with an embarrassing thump. He got up and tried again, propelling himself with a bit of a jump. And again he fell. His knees burned. He tried again, his haste fuelled by the fact that No had not seen him fail. This time he reached a sturdy place that held him. He grabbed a higher branch. Up he went in sweat and fear and soft gasps.

'I've seen that one, okay,' lied Chrisnelt. 'Even from down here you can see it, you know.'

'It's got a roof of white scales like the ones on top of that church, and there's a gold tip and a flag,' said No.

'I saw it, before you, even without the swing.' The lying continuing as he clung to the trunk; he wanted to be ahead, first to discover something for once. He breathed heavily, and then he really did see it, from the middle branch on which he wobbled – 'That thing looks just like the altar in Mama's church. The one with the big wings and crosses. You can see it nicely from down here. It's not far away, anyway.' They laughed and teased, as they always did. No chucked a handful of twigs on top of Chrisnelt, who would not climb any higher. This was as high as he'd ever been. The rain was trickling off the leaves, making dots below the tree that began to turn into minute muddy streams.

'Maybe it's so white because of pigeon shit, ah,' said No, soaking wet.

'Well, it's not chicken shit,' said Chrisnelt, secretly marvelling at its whiteness that glistened like teeth. The great house of marble glowed in all the darkness. Lifting his eyes slowly, he looked for the first time beyond everything he knew. At the edge of his world, a faint line hinted at greenness, and from within it he was convinced he could hear the songs of birds. They inhabited the edge, linking it to the City. He watched the bending River, and it shone like his uncertain dreams.

More clouds came together on top of a big blue cloud, and all the weight started to slowly sink upon the City in sweltering heat. That new shadow beat above them like a heart. The rain fell harder and faster. A sweet smell of chocolate buns and glazed croissants filled the air, floating up from the dust like the memories of all the bakeries ever visited by boys. Chrisnelt looked up, and then he looked down. He had one foot on the seat of the swing. He dangled unusually, upside down, before sliding back to the ground. For a moment he saw the sky as a reflection of the City. The vision reminded him of his own face floating on the water in his zinc bath at home: an upside-down dream that came every night before bedtime.

A flock of sparrows burst from the tree. The sky-reach of thunder rumbled. Lightning began to flash in the distance. Down came more rain. The culverts on both sides of the street gushed brown and slippery, carrying plastic bags and rolling Coca-Cola cans. Deeper noise boomed. Everything seemed to shift and crack. 'I think you should come down, No. I'm wet,' said Chrisnelt, his fingernails turning purple. He hopped back onto the sand, stepping away from the tree.

'Yes,' said No in annoyance. 'I'm coming, ah.' More leaves began to fall in untimely flurries; but the falling was slow, in the humid embrace of air that slows down time, a special time that comes only with the thickness of a West African storm. One more sparrow darted from the tree, and then another.

A loud bang split the sky, shaking everything. Chrisnelt fell back, slammed in the chest by the brightest white light, the violence of the punch tearing at his body. Breath ripped itself from his delicate lungs. He could not find air. He could not find anything. It was as if he were under water, in the deepest water he had ever known, water so hot it pulled at his skin, his eyes becoming fire, his hair blazing in pain, his finger tips crackling, and his toes curling like the ends of burning matches. Was this the great, boiling pot of so many of his nightmares, in which chickens screamed? The water was very strong too, pulling his arms further apart than they had ever been. Rain came in a burst, and then it went away. He felt himself melt, swirling. He clenched his fists, and then he found coolness. The shockwave from the lightning took him into a deep sleep. He sank into the soft mud.

After some time – perhaps mere moments – he pushed his hands into the earth. He sat up slowly, bending each part of himself carefully. All about him was ash. The brown dust of the street had become silver dust. And the clouds from high above had come to rest on the ground in plumes, so it seemed, until he realised it was smoke. Pieces of wood lay scattered across the street: breathing chunks of fire below the heavens. He raised his big head, his fragile ribs flexed, propped on shaking elbows. Before him was a circle of shining footprints, his footprints – made only a few minutes before, in the boys' final game – shimmering in a glow of unspeakable horror.

The mango tree was gone: taken suddenly, as dreams can be. His street had become a blazing sun before him, wilder than all the wars he'd ever imagined in stories. The tree was an inferno. It howled, its own winds gushing and shrieking from every branch. This was a world without any water: a world of irrevocable death.

He lay dazed in his silence and shock, burying cries so deep inside his gut they would never end; his tears so lost they would never begin to fall. His eyes watched and his mind glowed with searing loss. In the silence, Chrisnelt bore witness to a night of the hardest new charcoal. He had never felt more alone. He was all that was left in the City, he thought. 'An explosion has killed the world,' he whispered. He vomited from his greatest depths.

The tree glowed orange-yellow-red in beating pulses. And then the fire stopped. Higher up, black wood shifted into black crosses, leaking smoke. One of these crosses, near the very top – where leaves had once danced – was the outline of a boy, his arms and legs now charcoal branches, his reaching fingers now charcoal twigs, the bulge of a torso now a roasted bough below a fixed scream of white teeth. And in the stink of burned flesh, all he knew was that No had become part of a tree.

People came like rats in the silver night, crowding along the sides of the houses. Along the walls, giant culverts of silver rain had formed. A very large lady approached, more frantic than the others, lumbering as fast as her body could afford.

'Get out of my way. Get out of my way!' Mrs Malotika shouted, pushing the crowd apart. Chrisnelt's mother had run all the way up the street from her home, followed by her husband, who was flanked by two squealing girls.

'Chrisnelt, Chrisnelt, aah, aah, aah, Lordoo, Lordoo,' she moaned. She almost collapsed on top of him, draping his curled-up shape in all the wet cloths she could carry from the house. She'd seen the tree explode from her veranda, her son tumbling through the air in terrifying puffs of white. Her fat arms shook, her face shining – a film of rain and perspiration, mixed with dread. Her huge breasts heaved. She'd not run that fast since her youth, before marriage and pain.

Mr Malotika was silent, scooping up his son in one movement. The twins – Divine and Nipcia – continued to squeal at his sides. Together the family carried Chrisnelt home, away from the smoke and the eyes of people. Chrisnelt turned his head; through a gap in his father's powerful arms he looked back at No, frozen like a terrifying doll high in the sky of torment. The crowd was swarming the tree, trying to peel him from the high reaches, until the pyre fell.

'I don't know, Lordoo, I don't know anymore, Lordoo,' said Mrs Malotika, searching for some sort of redemption in the sky. And the rain began to come again. 'My boy is cursed. First the terrible blood that flowed at his birth, and the pains in my stomach before that. And the talking in his sleep every night. All the screams. All so loud, so loud. And he is scared of everything, poor child. NOW THE HEAVENS HAVE SPOKEN. They ... He ... has pointed!' She wailed louder than anyone had ever known.

'Quiet, Mama, none of that now. There is too much of that these days. Time to be still with him, that's what is needed, please,' said Mr Malotika firmly. He was always firm, and he saved words for important things. He had the gift of teaching – a calling, which was unlike the things that called to his wife at church.

'Tata, he's shivering,' said Nipcia and Divine together, in tears. Each held one of his drifting hands, his fingers shining, covered with silver scars.

Chrisnelt closed his eyes, sleeping in the heat of scorching shapes that would forever haunt his mind. The rain continued to fall, the fine drops like diamonds in the early-evening light, holding the dusk in mist. The street was awash with white ash floating in the puddles like a froth of madness.

Up ahead, a man stood in the middle of the street, his brilliant white suit phosphorescent, his white hat rimmed in silk, puffed with many plumes. The tips of these feathers – plucked from chickens' wings – picked up the haze from lighted windows. Alongside him, a white Mercedes-Benz waited, exhaust puffing, body shaking, eyes glaring gold. He was the Spirit of Extravaganza to all those who watched from the pavements.

'It's the God himself. He has come to Dee Dee Street,' said Mrs Malotika with a yelp. Chrisnelt's eyes had opened again, jarred by the bumpiness of Mr Malotika's gait. The white shape smiled, stretching its arms toward the family. Behind them, the crowd grew, following in awe: a dark wave of silent faces layered in soot.

'Pastor, my Pastor,' said Mrs Malotika. 'Lordoo goodness.'

'Hello, Pastor Kadazi,' said Mr Malotika softly, his unconscious son in his arms. He approached the pastor, feet squelching in the mud, the boy's body in his arms. Chrisnelt seemed suspended like an apparition above the street, clothes dripping. Mrs Malotika and the girls hid in their shadow.

'It's much appreciated that you are here in front of our home, and so quickly,' said Mr Malotika.

'I was almost next door, visiting, as I always visit at dusk, even in a storm,' said Pastor Kadazi.

'This horrible moment is without our words now,' said Mr Malotika.

'Let me look at him,' said Pastor Kadazi.

'Oh Lordoo, thank you.'

'Thank you,' said the bystanders.

'Lordoo.'

'My wife is most grateful that you have come. She has asked for a long time that you will come to our house,' said Mr Malotika.

Chrisnelt opened his eyes, and he listened.

'Pastor, oh, oh Pastor,' sobbed Mrs Malotika, her great waist vibrating. The girls sobbed too, in sympathy for everyone, and also in fear, pulling at Mrs Malotika's skirt, and at Chrisnelt's long fingers dangling in the raindrops.

'Oh Pastor,' said the bystanders. Many more had gathered. The rain kept falling.

'Lordoo.'

'Mr and Mrs Malotika, this street has called all of us. Such is the power of the fires from above. Praise the Power. Praise the way of Strength against Weakness. Praise the Light. Praise the Lord Man. I shall save this pathetic child. I shall cure his weakness and fear. I shall take the demons out right now. I shall use these very hands and place them inside him.' Pastor Kadazi sparkled before the gathering people: it was crowds he loved and lived for, crowds that had made him what he wanted to be. Crowds and more crowds – the bigger the better – shaped him and his great wealth under the glow of God.

'We are here to help with the pains that have beset you.

We will bless you and make you right,' he said, staring directly at the boy. And he continued – many long and slippery words – in Lingala, then in Kituba, in English and in French, and then also in a mixture of Swahili and French, which some used. He wanted to make sure that the many peoples of that City understood him; his words needed to show his power to all the faces in the rain.

Mrs Malotika stood in front of the family now. Still cradled in his father's arms, Chrisnelt looked through the tails on her wayward head, the long strands of her braids dancing. She shook, whipped into a terrible frenzy of Belief, obscuring his view. Then she stepped aside, and he could make out Pastor Kadazi clearly. He had never seen him before: a black face with black eyes and the deepest stare. A vast man of dangerous height and hands, floating in lies. He stood under the protruding wooden eaves of the Malotika house, and below him gushed the street of rain.

A terrifying cry cut the street, like knives scraping on bones. Cry after piercing cry. It was Mrs Matombo and the other Matombos – No's family. Past the many faces squashed tightly on the pavement, Mr Matombo ran – helplessly, shattering the light and the wetness, stumbling up the hill, screaming, arms outstretched. He ran in an isolation no father should ever know, disappearing into the rising silver. And in the distance he bellowed beyond solace. Some people went to comfort him, but most were silent and still. Mr Matombo was running to the remnants of his son; in many ways he would never stop running.

The Malotikas and the Matombos had been neighbours for many years. Mr Malotika could not go after his friend now. His own son lived; and he needed to keep living for his son. He stared straight at Pastor Kadazi for his family's sake, and perhaps also for the forsaken faces of the Matombos. His eyes surrendered tears. His back and his stomach ached.

Pastor Kadazi grabbed Chrisnelt like he grabbed chickens, except not around the neck. Some would say the sacrificial child bleated like a goat. Some would say he clucked. The truth was he was silent in the hardest, most frozen silence that was possible in the dying moments of a storm. Pastor Kadazi raised him up to the spitting raindrops, hands high above his head, chanting all the while. He held him there, above the white feathers of his hat, and began to rock backward and forward, the boy sobbing on the edge of delirium.

'Skies of the Lord Man. We pray that You will take the evilness out of this child. Such skin-and-bones needs a chance to grow a life. Bless him. Clean him, Lord Man,' he called out and upward, swaying in his own glow. 'Help and bless all these people of the City. Clean them too, Lord Man, show them the way to my church. Tell them what a beautiful church of riches it is for them. No more pain in the soot for them, Lord Man. Tell them to vote with love.'

Chrisnelt lay suspended. Pastor Kadazi plunged his hand inside the boy's singed clothing, squeezing him gently, and then shook him as one might a doll. Chrisnelt was alone inside the petrifying heat of that night. And he pissed himself.

CHAPTER TWO

HE DID NOT SPEAK FOR ALMOST twelve months. He foamed at the tight edges of his mouth in the early mornings when the birds sang, and he would only eat when not directly observed by the family, when the shadows pushed through the windows like growing leaves and roots. He made grunting noises and whimpered frequently and tugged at his eyelids. He stared at everything inside the house with the longest, most penetrating stares and – in the confines of intimacy – rubbed his groin and stomach, and scratched at the hollow in his chest.

His eyes grew redder in his big throbbing head, and Divine and Nipcia suggested this was key to the blinking problem. (In fact, the blinking allowed for a closing of eyes – a moment to reflect; Chrisnelt made maps in his mind, pictures of the entire world: blizzards and lightning storms, the many shades of rivers finding seas ...)

His neck became very thin, showing winding green veins that thumped like distant drums. To everyone who visited, Chrisnelt seemed a delicate thing, teetering precariously: big hands, thin wrists; big feet, thin ankles; big heart and the body of a dry, snapping twig.

Mr and Mrs Malotika had kept Chrisnelt and the girls away from the funeral because they didn't want to upset the children any further, and besides, the boy was not well. The girls remained with their brother under strict instructions to look after him all the time, even when he went to the toilet.

'Mourning is an honourable thing, and it comes in many forms, and sometimes these forms are not of this City. They come from the Forest and the River in the minds of the displaced, who have witnessed their way of life die,' said Mr Malotika softly to his wife, in a tone that sounded a bit like a sermon. He bent down to look at his son, holding the boy's face in his hands. 'A drought is coming here,' he said. Outside, the City creaked in the dust; a single dog staggered in the shivering heat, and the mud shifted into loose sands. The Malotikas walked out the front door and up the street to where the mango tree had once been.

They were the only ones in attendance: a gathering of two – not counting the small man who dropped off the envelope, placing it on top of the charred stump. 'Mr Matombo asked if you could say these few words,' he said. 'You are the only people he wanted to come to this.'

The couple stood in front of the scorched patch of street, where the ground was stained a darker brown. They looked at each other in surprise. The Matombos had told them there would be people. They had certainly expected Pastor Kadazi. Mr Malotika shook his head slowly. He knew the people only walked in the sun in the City if they had to go somewhere, otherwise it was a place where people sat in shady recesses, like those recesses in the heart that wait for pain. It was a hard city, even harder in the heat, only flinching at midday – the unbearable moment – when time came out of hiding to cross all the faces, searching for shade. Eyes watched eyes.

Faces waited for faces to do things. Nothing was done.

The mud had become very hard – the long dry season had begun stretching everything into cracks. Light shattered in the sky, the heat chasing the birds far away. The street seemed lonely. A smell of thirst was on people's skin. In the harsh light, the only movement was the clear bottles of water glittering in crates, lining the walls of stalls in the distance. Twelve noon. The hot air from the deserts in the far north had come as it always came and the air was brown.

In the two weeks since the storm, a story of footsteps had hardened in the earth of Dee Dee Street. Stampeding, slipping and sliding footsteps were cast in the mud below the stump, all on one side, where people had tried to push it over. Two deep prints were impressed next to a hole, dug by a heavy person in an attempt to set the deepest roots free. New footsteps on top of old spoke of people come to gossip, or just on their way to work. Underneath it all, a child's footsteps circled faintly, in a subtle ring.

'Perhaps his death was too real,' said Mr Malotika to his wife. 'Too raw, too close to our pasts, when we lived free under the sky. People don't like to be reminded of a lost past, even if they can't quite remember it all.' He opened the envelope and read a farewell, the words meandering, ending like a path in a forest: 'We have gone back to our village of trees. No shade in this place.'

In time, the stump would become a seat on which Chrisnelt would sit, most days. A place to think, polished by wear, shining under the sun and the moon. But for now, in his sadness, Chrisnelt stayed inside. On the first day he lay under the kitchen table, transfixed by the front door, not even moving when a splatter of hot fat landed on his big toe. On the second day, he rolled into the living room, coming to rest against the one wall that always got hot by nine o'clock: he lay against that warm wall with his back to the family, the heat of the mud bricks somehow more necessary than the soothing coolness of the floor. On the third day, he chose another wall. On the fourth, he stared at the light fitting in the living room all day long, until finally it burst into light at seven in the evening, whereupon he cried out and closed his eyes, not opening them until morning. On days five and six he could be found on his stomach up against Mr Malotika's chair, refusing to be moved. And on all these days he never said a word. It was only on the seventh day that things evolved into something resembling hope.

'Pass me my book, Mama,' said Mr Malotika from the couch, his shoes kicked off after a long day, his socks stained, a scent of heavy work sitting in the air above his head. Mrs Malotika was hurriedly preparing for church.

Books were Mr Malotika's passion. They were everywhere in the house: next to his bed, by his chair in the living room, next to his bowl on the kitchen table, on the timber bench on the veranda, even next to the toilet. 'I was never allowed a pet as a boy, only a book,' Mr Malotika often said, when Mrs Malotika looked at him, waiting for conversation, or when the children wanted him to go out and play with them. Chrisnelt knew books, and had even pretended to enjoy reading them, just to be near the man he worshiped, near all the wise words and smiles that flowed from that kind face like rain.

'This one?' she said, picking up the closest book on her way to the bedroom, stepping over her drooling son, shaking her fat hands in the air in torment to dry her nail polish. It was purple, with small hearts in the middle of each shining nail.

'No, that one,' he said, pointing to the book on the floor near Chrisnelt, who lay staring at the ceiling, his arms and legs outstretched, his moaning soft, his dribbling soft as the patter of rain on leaves. 'My work book, yes, that one.'

The book was long and green with a hard, velvety cover that creaked. Against the green shone a silver row of trees, the glint catching his son's eye.

'What's it about, Tata?' Chrisnelt's hoarse squeak was almost inaudible, the first words he'd uttered for days – and the last he would utter for almost an entire year.

Mr Malotika sat up and stared at his son. 'It's about trees, and the rainy seasons of our region, and how things grow, like the crops and forests and gardens, and the work of water. It's about all the things that make a lumberyard a living lumberyard,' he said in excitement.

On hearing her son's voice, Mrs Malotika hopped back into the room, her stockings half on. 'We'll get you some books, my child. If it'll make you feel better and heal your head.'

Chrisnelt nodded, rolling back onto his back.

Mr and Mrs Malotika put out the word urgently. They knew now that it was only reading that calmed Chrisnelt, settling the many questions in his complicated mind: questions that had become very loud on the pieces of paper that lay everywhere in the home. They could see, with a certain amount of astonishment, his desperate searching for No in the little pictures of leaves drawn between the words. At the Church, and at Café Gourmandine, at the patisserie where she worked, Mrs Malotika spoke of the need for the books. Mr Malotika called for books at the lumberyard, at the tavern, and at the place he taught adults to read the newspapers.

At the beginning of his sickness, Chrisnelt started with the largest books of many pictures, then moved on to the very small books with stories of jungle paths and soaring city highways that rushed all over the world. When it was time to sleep, he bent himself into a little ball, covering his legs with sheets of folded paper that carried new poems, the paper claiming each stanza because they would never be read. When it was time to eat, he would not use his hands, insisting – with a violent squawk that did not qualify as speech – on slurping up stuff from above the flames that licked the cooking pot, face buried in the smoke. His parents indulged him patiently.

The books came from all over. ('Such is the way of books,' Mr Malotika had said.) Many came from other parts of the City: from every crack in the dryness; even from sullen people who worked for the government in the Library of Liberation that did not admit children; from the many religious places; two from a prison; and once one came from a lady who arrived by mistake, thrusting out a glistening thing that later was revealed as a book offering holidays on an ocean of ice.

Intrigued, Nipcia and Divine observed the steady arrival of the books. On the first morning, in the wet air released by the tropical heat after the time of heavy rains, in the steam that rests everywhere – on the sticky skin, curving blouses against breasts and generally flustering minds – a young man stepped under the overhanging roof at the veranda entrance, flushing a bird from the eaves near the bats. He was new in manliness, freshly shaven, perhaps for the first time. Mrs Malotika was not home – she was seldom home then, too busy with her church work – and the girls opened the door shyly. He was tall, and he looked strong. His smile shone like the smiles in the advertisements on the poles near the big shops.

He held out a pile of books wrapped in serviettes from Burger King and said: 'This is for the sick boy who needs books. Our soccer team wishes him to get well. We're scared of playing games in the rain now.' He paused, and ended in a rehearsed tone: 'My mother says we must all be thankful for the knowledge.'

On the second morning of books, a Japanese man knocked on the wooden door, while peering through the side window. He was new, having just arrived, as foreigners constantly do, to take up the government lease on the house vacated by the Matombos, who had disappeared. ('The world is a government lease,' was a common refrain of Mr Malotika's: 'Africa is One Big Lease.')

'Hello, hello,' the man said in English, speaking to the closed door. 'I come from next door. I Mr Nagasaki. I hear about boy. I bring book, I hear he like book, make him feel better in head. I sorry. Tell parent I come to meet sometime, okay.'

The girls did not speak good English, but they understood faces, and they knew the fold and shift of skin near eyes that had come from far away. They said thank you with hand gestures, as was often done in the City of many languages.

'Here Chrisnelt,' said Nipcia when the visitor had left, 'another book.'

'*Here*,' said Divine impatiently, taking it from her sister and placing it in front of Chrisnelt, like some sort of experiment.

He extended his fingers slowly. He took it, reading the spine: *Life Inside the Deepest Roots of the Tallest Trees.* He peered up at them briefly from under giant eyelids, and then he was gone inside the pages, the bruises on his head quieting into the colours of happy flesh.

'Dr Divi,' said Nipcia with a smile.

The next few book mornings – it was always mornings in the beginning – were rather busy for the girls. Sometimes two or three deliveries came on a single morning before they had to walk to school. In his room at the back of the house, Chrisnelt lay motionless, alone on the floor in his unusual, peaceful detachment, eyes deep in a book.

'I can't eat breakfast anymore, there's never time,' said Nipcia. (She was too fat and Divi too thin – they'd always been that way.) But secretly, the twins had begun to enjoy very much the opening of doors, meeting people from many districts of the City. It was only after two months, on the day the noisy truck arrived, that they started to get irritated.

There was a tremendous rattling of ceiling beams; palm fronds leaked moths from above, the bats shuffled outside, aluminium pots on shelves dislodged and bounced, and a cloud of plucked chicken feathers wafted from under a kitchen stool. A crystal vase, patterned with cherubs tangled in vines, shattered and lay in prophetic shards that twinkled like diamonds. Everything combined to fill the morning with bizarre music and movement, a cacophony, much like the screams, laughter and drumbeats from the barracks near the end of the City. The roughness of the street – corrugated, like all the serrated surfaces and edges of that district – made the great wheels of the flatbed truck vibrate, reverberating up into its steel carcass, causing a war in the girls' ears. An enormous shadow slid across the façade of the Malotika home, draping the roof too. And then the dust: it billowed through the open windows, into the kitchen and the living room in a vast cloud; down the passage it rolled, through open doors, filling all the rooms. Even the water in the toilet bowl was instantly coated in a layer of dust. And Chrisnelt's grey room, right at the end of the house, changed forever, transfigured in a blizzard of fertile brown.

A long pause was followed by the tap of considered steps, the floorboards outside creaking lightly. The girls opened the door, coughing, waving their arms about, trying to focus through the blur.

Chrisnelt raised his heavy head from the floor. He could smell it all: the man standing at the door, short like a rusty little nail. An odour of dirty oil and grease came off the thin man, along with the sweet, lingering scent of freshly sawn wood. His arms hung full of books, his face wide, his smile filled with many big teeth. He was made of many tones of khaki: his tea-coloured skin, his eyebrows, moustache, watch-strap, shoes, trousers, shirt and tattered cap. The children were not sure if he was dirty or clean; he seemed part of the dust and the sand.

'You must be Divine,' he said to Divi.

She smiled at him. *Your name is always to be said slowly and with a proud smile, girl,* Mrs Malotika frequently told her, explaining that she was fortunate to own the most popular girl name in the City, a name of considerable status due to its reference to the Heavens of Powerful Thunder.

'My name is Chaminda Ushantha Patabendige Warnakulasuriya. I'm a good friend of your father. It's indeed a great pleasure to see you. We work together at the lumberyard near the River, sometimes. I hear much about you!' He shifted his smiling gaze to Nipcia, not wanting to be rude: 'And very much about you too, Nipcia. *And* about you, boy,' he ended his greeting emphatically. His kind eyes, sagging slightly, were a special golden-green that was both fierce and tame.

Without entering the house, he gently placed the books, wrapped in vegetable leaves, at Divi's feet, and looked at Chrisnelt. 'Here are the things I promised for you. It's *all* my books. Your father told me how you read. And from so young. Very good. Very good for this place. Very important for life. Your father tells me how you always watch the sky. Big sky!' He laughed generously, looking up at the stained ceiling. 'Maybe this one' – pointing to the top book – 'is a good one for you. All about the birds in the sky ... and the other things that want to fly too: all the plants.' He laughed again, and turned, waving goodbye – he loved children, had loved all the children of his earlier years: a time of learning long ago, back on the distant island of Sri Lanka.

Vernon RL Head

Strangely still, momentarily forgetting to close the door, the girls watched him go. He went away with the dust, remnants of dried mud clinging to his sleeves like toys above a crib; his armpits and his back a collection of deep-brown triangles pointing down to legs like arrows, a collection of fantastic patterns and smudges. He leapt up into the high seat of his truck, disappearing like magic.

Chrisnelt peered out the door, having raised himself and slithered forward on all fours. The rattling began again – a new vibration, now connected to thoughts of friendship – and the truck was gone in a wave of sand. Chrisnelt took a gulp, gazing down the street. He glimpsed the back of the wobbling truck, which was carrying a pile of planks so freshly sawn they leaked dried leaves from the thin edges of bark. A special man was lost in the brown.

The visit by Chaminda Warnakulasuriya triggered a deeper silence in Chrisnelt that reached into the furthest reaches of his head, on the far side of his eyes, and he moaned softly for two days, proffering squeals when touched; the bumps on his forehead shone again in ever wider blue bruises, like purple thoughts. He read constantly, furiously, his eyes redder than ever. His parents summoned the doctor, who also brought books, just in case: one was bright red, like fresh blood.

'It's not malaria or yellow fever, and although the eyes are red, there's no bleeding there, so we don't need to worry about that,' he said as he prodded the boy, who lay splayed near the wall like a corpse. 'No need for my usual emetic. I do think he just needs to rest and stop banging his head against these walls. An understanding of death takes time, you know,' he continued, having up-to-date

34

insight into all the events of that street, and indeed the events of the City. 'Death takes time,' he repeated, looking over his spectacles at Mr Malotika.

There was also the problem of Chrisnelt's sleeping arrangements. He refused to sleep in his own bedroom. It simply was not an option. The room was as important to Chrisnelt as the mango tree had been, keeping his memories of friendship, his images of No. It had been a place of fun, which had found its way into the walls in deep scribbles, carved with No in their most preposterous games. These four walls – one with a door onto the short passage, and another, with a circular window at its centre, leading onto a tiny yard – could be read like an ancient book. Any suggestion of a night in this room of memories was met with yowls of unspeakable fear.

So it was that he spent all his time in the living room, reading in a dim light that made swaying piles of pages stretch upward, bending their way to the pock-marked ceiling, stained from past rains. Here, the landscape was transformed into one of books. It had become an urgent place, almost desperate: a scene of a boy's frantic journeys, on his way to the far reaches of his mind. It happened like a cure.

The flow of books started to slow down, trickling to one a month, and eventually they stopped altogether, and there was stillness on the green linoleum floor. The City had begun to lose interest in the Boy and the Burning Tree. The last book, almost an afterthought, came from Pastor Kadazi via Mrs Malotika. It was a promotional gift more than anything, with his gold-framed photo on the cover, his white smile the same colour as his suit, his hat a forest of the most elaborate white feathers. (It was said, Mrs Malotika told her family in confidence, that many years previously, Pastor Kadazi, while sipping champagne on a high, intercontinental aeroplane edged in ice, saw an exotic fur hat advertised in a duty-free magazine and decided to have it replicated in chicken feathers for the heat of Africa.) That book came with a tinsel bow, because Christmas was approaching.

'Chrisnelt, shouldn't you ask Tata before grabbing those?' said Divi, passing a wide bamboo spoon through the potato soup, shaking her head in the ripples of light from the fire. Her brother had clasped a handful of pens – disturbing a kitchen spider that had been resting on top of the pen jar – and some fell to the floor like rattling twigs. He grunted, settling back on his tummy, the linoleum squeaking against his skin.

'You don't even look at Tata. You just reach and take. It's rude. And they aren't yours,' said Nipcia. 'I always ask.'

The Pen Shelf was an important shelf, displaying newspapers in a neat pile, cooking pots that were too new to cook with, coloured drinking glasses made from plastic that looked like rainbow glass, and the box-of-matches bowl that was reached for on special nights when candles were required at table. A shelf of special things that needed to be asked for by children.

'Not everything is for you, Chrisnelt,' said Divi.

But Chrisnelt just reached, in a way that was obligate, like the way he reached for soap in the zinc bath.

'It's okay this time, girls,' said Mr Malotika steadily, watching his son write: the darting nails flickering, the little arm rocking, bent and tight, the words flowing like water across the pages of a notebook. In between the words came tiny pictures of trees and birds. As Chrisnelt wrote, he read, his lips pulsating with the words, fluttering, forested. He seemed peaceful when he had the books open in front of him.

That particular evening, Chrisnelt's eyes ached from the many months of reading. He lay observing the flames studiously – he was never too far from the kitchen fire. Shapes danced deep inside the heat, and at the very centre of each flicker he thought he could see life. There was tremendous brightness in the moving light, and revelations in the crackling of coals and the hotness stroking his face.

Divi handed Nipcia a box of matches: the girls often played with them while cooking, when no one was watching. But Chrisnelt was watching now, in the deepest possible way – the fire controlled him – as Nipcia placed the head of one unlit match against another. Divi lit a third. The first two matches roared into a single flame at the instant the third touched, sealing them together forever in a single, new, longer match of bending black charcoal.

Chrisnelt marvelled at the transformation. Something was born inside him, a new world rising. Now he understood the death of No clearly: this was the image of his best friend, waving hello, burning and bending in resurrection at the top of the mango tree. No had become the skeleton of the tree.

For the next week – the final week of illness – Chrisnelt lay on his side. He had read every book, and now an idea was coming. At night he looked at the sky through the glass window, remembering the rains he'd played in with No, all the rains he'd known during happiness. And he looked at the stains the raindrops had left in the dust: messages from the clouds.

He had looked high and low in every recess of every book. Some books were manuals; some were scientific dissertations, or theses on bizarre things like the history of the Caesar Salad. There were colouring-in-books and novels; many were in strange languages, and one or two smelled as if they might be alive. There were Bibles of varying sizes, translations of the Torah, the Quran, and scriptures with elaborate pictures from other sacred ways that shone in the distance. He'd read everything he could find that hinted at a knowledge of rain, and how it gave the land life; everything he could find about the things that grew from the gift of water. He'd reread every sentence with the words 'green' and 'water' and 'rain' in it, at least five hundred times. His idea was rooted in the miracle of growth.

Sometimes – in between the words – memories of rain came to him during the day, the sun taking the rolling drops across the room in gleaming shafts that became thorny branches. But it was at night that he stared the hardest into his past, eyes blazing, eyelids vibrating like bird wings. He observed water wander: curves and turns of wetness darting left and right, swinging into zigzags for a moment, becoming great looping waterfalls, finally linking and speeding up in rushing jerks, spewing glittering breaths across the horizon. He thought of all this rain, and he thought of the grinning wet face of No as they played under all the happy storms of the past. He thought of the new knowledge he'd acquired with his reading and writing: the dancing words, the truths of all kinds of thinkers, those who lied and told the truth by accident, those who wanted to tell the truth but could not find it (which was itself the truth), those for whom the truth came only because of innocence. This was his delirium. He kept seeing No's smiling face. And then the fixed face of bleached teeth and charcoal.

He remembered images of birds, No's beloved birds: the colourful tails, the sparkling eyes, the power of wings, the loud beaks, all of them in the air, that in-between world of truth. The rains and the birds were a connection to the sky. The rains becoming rivers, reaching from the sky to the land and the land to the sky. His idea formed like a bridge of feathers; he could feel something clearing inside his lungs and his head. A way forward. He gave a rare blink.

He began to invoke calculations, releasing numbers and more numbers onto pages, more sums, more dashes, no full stops, many equal signs; long numbers with many zeros, pulling him like a vast wind, the air and clouds twisting in blinding flashes of the hottest light. It showed him a new shape in the Universe: that of a great new tree. His fever was strongest then.

He tossed and turned. He saw the gentle circles he'd made running round the mango tree, before the lightning came. He saw birds scattering from that tree. The shape became clearer. A single shape, now, strong, perfect. He looked again and again at the stains of water on the dusty glass, at those memories. Drops framed in dust, stuck, petrified. They had once been living: dancers, jugglers and acrobats. The rain fell as death had fallen, but when it fell life also rose, always, in vast determination, somewhere, somehow, because of it.

Chrisnelt lay under the table predicting the voyage of each raindrop as it entered his disturbed thoughts, and its time of landing on the ground. He sweated. He saw water and the way it made renewal. He saw birds and their command of the endless air and the commonality of land. He saw the path of rain before it even fell from a cloud.

Vibrations of taxi-cars in the street outside became vibrations of past downpours on the roof of the Malotika house. It stirred him further – the metallic tinkle on corrugated iron above the living room signalling soft taps on palm-frond shingles above the veranda – causing dreams to slide him onto his back in convoluted wonderment. He counted every sound into numbers and he shook. He counted the names of birds – he had learned the scientific names of over one thousand species during that year. He quivered, his fingers fluttering like feathers. Sometimes he shat the most foul-smelling shits. He knew, with absolute certainty, as a proof is known, the total number of raindrops that had arrived in the City in every storm. It was as if the heavens spoke to him in drifting facts. He needed water. It was water that would feed the roots. He needed to watch and understand birds. It was birds that knew the secrets in the clouds. It was the sky and the water that would bring his friend back. No had changed into a tree that day; a single tree. Chrisnelt resolved, right there and then, to grow a special tree, a new tree that would reach very high, and he would find his friend in the leaves at the top.

He sat up, drenched and weak. Nausea had made his

face pale; his eyes were swollen. His thin neck creaked, as did his thin fingers. Dementedness had left him. He began to draw on the floor. His drawing quickly grew up onto the one wall of the living room, and then he stood on a chair, continuing the drawing. It spread onto the ceiling. Mrs Malotika shrieked as she turned from her cooking to see the rapidly expanding image. It all happened silently, in a few minutes. 'You've gone mad,' she yelled, 'oh Lordoo, you've gone mad!'

Mr Malotika, who was buried in his newspaper, looked up and said nothing for a moment, raising his hand, as if to signal to his wife not to come thundering out of the kitchen. 'Let him finish,' he said, after a deep pause. 'We have paint, and we have cloths for wiping stains. Let him finish.'

The girls scampered from their room to see what the shouting was all about. 'CHRISNELT,' shouted Nipcia.

'Oh my God,' said Divi, her head in her hands.

'A tree,' said Nipcia.

'Quiet, girls.'

'It looks like ghosts, and screaming faces,' said Nipcia.

'I can see raindrops.'

'I can see eyes.'

'They're leaves.'

'I can see fingers.'

'Those must be branches that are also arms.'

'Quiet, girls!'

Chrisnelt teetered on his tiptoes, the chair rocking. He drew with fury, his little arms reaching up, the pen busy, making a horrendous scratching sound. Bits of paint fluttered to the floor like the burnt wings of moths. When the ink from one pen became exhausted, he dropped it, continuing uninterrupted with another. Pens lay scattered. The fine lines shone, winding into an exorbitant tree, like an apparition, draped on the three flat surfaces of the room. In the canopy showered raindrop-shapes that were clearly also leaves, and in the middle of everything twirled a powerful current of twigs around the light fitting that exploded like the sun.

'I'm going to grow one,' shouted Chrisnelt, as he finished, hopping down.

That afternoon, after things had settled, and Mrs Malotika had been calmed by her husband with a short chat outside on the veranda, Divi said: 'Chrisnelt, do you think when it stops raining in your mind you'll talk to us normally again?' She could hear the remote dripping sounds echoing from the back of his mouth.

'And anyway, why do you blow on the glass and then make big circles, you know Mama is going to make us clean that as well. And all the sounds of pages turning in here, it reminds us of school, and we are sick of falling over these damn books and standing on your sharp pens, they're all over the place,' said Nipcia, leaning on Divi, showing the boy an inky blue hole in the sole of her foot.

'Sorry, Nipcia,' said Chrisnelt, to everyone's amazement. Mr Malotika almost fell off a kitchen stool in the background, dropping a croissant he'd begun to eat.

'You're soaking wet with sweat, yuck,' said Divi to Chrisnelt, pulling a face of disgust.

'You need a good bath, boy,' said Mr Malotika. 'It's been a while.'

'You stink.'

'Yes.'

'Like the heat stinks when it lifts the air to my nose,' said Nipcia.

'I'll go now, Tata, even with cold water, but I've got a lot to do. I need to grow a tree. Very tall and strong and full of No's birds.'

'All this reading has oiled your brain,' said Mr Malotika. 'I am glad you are feeling better. Books! Much learning in them. Many juices for the body.'

'He should go back to school now Tata, like us, every day, even Saturdays,' said Nipcia, settling back into annoyance, yet relieved at her brother's recovery.

'After a long bath with salt,' said Divi.

'And he must clean this room,' said Nipcia.

'I'm not doing it.'

'Girls, leave the boy. His education is not your concern. He's younger, yes? You'll always have each other; he has no brothers his age. He has lost things,' said Mr Malotika, signalling to the twins, eyebrows creased in a code they had come to know. Chrisnelt had secretly learned this language, catching it with glances, and he smiled slowly from the other side of the room, for the first time in a long time. He scribbled a cluster of loose numbers all over a page of a notebook, surrounding them with the little outline of a tree.

'Raindrops,' said Chrisnelt softly.

Mr Malotika clicked a button on the radio, soft foreign music played, Chrisnelt began to draw and write more things. The girls went to cook dinner in the kitchen.

'And how come he doesn't come to school tomorrow and learn when we learn, Tata? It's not fair,' said Divi, in the heat that wrestled with the cooking smoke.

'There are many ways of learning in the City,' said Mr Malotika above the Brazilian, Dutch, French, Russian, Spanish, English and Chinese tunes that jostled for space as he turned the dial of the radio. 'This is a world of different ways becoming one way.' He looked down at his son, who was reading on a crackling mat made of plaited reeds from the River, held together with plastic rope. 'Look! Inside our house the books of the world have made a single tree.'

He was sick for many months. And then, seven weeks before Christmas, Chrisnelt became restless, rustling papers, prodding his chest with a pen, running fingers across the slippery floor, feeling for the rhythms of the bumps hiding in the earth, even licking one particularly large bump near the door. He slid a thumb along the stippled surfaces of the walls, tapping the indentations, stroking his legs and arms, counting the fine hairs on his calves that told of growth. As the world rose with the sun, in the energetic sunshine, birds sang. He got up off the floor, dusted his short pants, tucked a pen behind an ear, glanced at the dirty window pane once more, and then had a long bath. He went outside for the first time, wearing his favourite T-shirt. He looked up. He looked out along the street. In the distance was the charred stump of the mango tree.

'I'm going to look for a seed,' he said.

Chapter Three

IT WAS LATE AFTERNOON, when parents are tired and always kind to little boys on Dee Dee Street.

Nipcia, Divi and Mr and Mrs Malotika waited for Chrisnelt to leave, not wanting to derail his new momentum. They stood dead still as he walked to the front door, sighing as he shuffled past, his lips shaking and mumbling but his face clear. They let him go, then rushed after him, tripping over books in the suddenness of it all. He did not look back. They held each other like families hold each other near Christmas. A flock of white egrets cast a shadow over the house, a fixed and shifting scatter.

The City simmered. The dry season had been long, and all things remained very brown: the longest dusty brown in living memory. The sky and the land seemed to be a single creature of warm air that gripped the City in the strongest grip. Chrisnelt did not run up the street as he always used to do, that two-minute sprint of an energetic child filled with notions. He walked down instead, in the opposite direction to the stained earth where No had burned. The sun shone on the back of his red T-shirt, illuminating the slogan COKE ADDS LIFE in flamboyant white swirls. All he could think about was growing a tree. His thoughts were urgent. They came with desperate longing. He had to be careful with them. They were strong, and they could make him cry if he was not as brave as a boy can be.

He wasn't sure where he'd find the seed, or what it

would look like; but he knew it was out there, waiting for him. He began to look like enlightened people look: eyes calm, brain busy. He walked slowly. The steps – sliding in the dirt – made his sisters feel sadness yet again, as they watched him in the distance.

'We will let him go, girls,' said Mr Malotika, resting a hand on each of their shoulders, his wife holding him around the waist, squeezing gently. Another flock of white egrets flew over the house, on the air that rushed to the River.

'He seems so small with that big head, Tata,' said Divi.

'He seems so lonely,' added Nipcia. And they heard him whistle faintly in the language of busy birds.

'Eight years of life. It is all about seeing the world differently, finding a place,' said Mr Malotika.

Chrisnelt stretched out his arms parallel to the dusty pavement, making wings, descending down the gentle street that – at its centre – rose like a lump might do in the throat. He knew he couldn't go too far: 'Always within a ten-minute walk of home, please,' was the instruction, and 'Always stay in Dee Dee Street. Ee Ee is not safe.'

But he needed a tree. And he could feel new strength in his limbs and in his head. He knew more about his world and his City now: a land of many worlds coming together, many thoughts becoming a single thought, shrinking space so that shadows sometimes appeared to be one terrifying shadow. The piled pages of his books had helped him understand this shadow that swayed like the tallest tree on the green linoleum landscape of his searching. All the time the searching for the story of trees.

He ran his fingers – which had grown longer, the nails

extending into points, except for his thumbs, which had become quite wide and flat like spades – along every boundary wall he saw, as if they were sentences in Braille. The texture of sun-dried bricks was creamy, singing to the touch, and he could scratch lines with his nails, releasing tiny, whispering avalanches of ochre. The concrete blocks of the higher walls were the hardest, making chalky squeaks like terrified mice. The painted wall – there was only one along the entire street, so high you couldn't see the house hiding behind it, so blindingly white it tugged at the roots of his eyes – that wall was dead silent.

The sky above was flat, rippling with brown waves of heat. The walls repeated too, again and again, as did all the corrugations on all the roofs. It was only the birds that changed: he followed their songs in relief.

Walls and more walls. Then he arrived at a wooden wall. He liked it. 'Made from the limbs of a tree,' he said very loudly, almost as a pronouncement. He pulled a piece of paper from his pocket, rolled it into a hollow tube and dragged it across the slats of the fence, releasing the *doo-doo* sound of escaping doves. Another fence, a few paces further on, reminded him of the large woven basket full of bananas and pawpaws on the kitchen table at home. Through the weave of twigs was filtered a lattice of yellow light, making cavorting shadow crosses across the dust, right up the walls of the houses on the other side. On one twig, which had managed to extend a root to the ground, grew a single bud that wanted to become a flower.

And it was on this particular wooden wall that Chrisnelt observed a bird. He viewed it afresh, the way No would have seen it, or Chaminda Warnakulasuriya.

Clearly. And – more importantly – in the way No would have wanted to continue seeing it.

Chrisnelt decided to begin a bird list there and then; to count the various species he might see, like he counted numbers into memories of rain. '*Yes*,' he said to the sparrow – urgency dancing with conviction – and named it loudly: 'House Sparrow, *Passer domesticus*, with your grey crown and blushing cheeks. That is what the books say. You'll be my number one, even though you're common, and you will sit as a picture at the back of my notebook.'

Silence came then, as silence always comes after an intimate gaze upon wilderness. Silence pushed him onward.

'Ten minutes of walking has arrived,' he said.

He'd been counting the time in his head with each step and now it was up, according to the rules of his home; he shouldn't go any further. He could see the stern face of Mr Malotika.

Chrisnelt pondered things, looking around. One side of the street leaned in darkness, the other stretched in glowing purples, the dust making the edges of everything blue in the most unusual changing shapes. The smell of evening was not too far off, the light growing dappled with soft cricket sounds and the solitary burp of a waking frog. The end of Dee Dee was at hand, and he was on the street by himself. He did not want to turn left into Ee Ee: it would be for the first time. Fear came to him quickly.

A black-and-white lady flushed from a shadow. She was a nun from the world of sermons. He hated sermons. Or perhaps she'd been flushed out like a hidden idea. She was different to other nuns he'd seen. She had a secret on her face. He stared at her black body and white breast, her black head with its shiny-sharp beak that creaks. 'Pied crow,' he said.

He did not mean to be disrespectful, but she gasped, and nearly knocked him to the ground with a frown. Dust took over her lower parts as she ran hastily on toward him in the crackling sands.

And then, instant revelation: a wreath of flowers of many colours swung into view, hanging from her left hand; flowers from an exquisite garden that only fantastic dreams could have formed. She pushed past him. 'Please get out of my way,' she said as she went.

Chrisnelt had only recently begun to read about gardens, particularly in one book made of rainbows, immediately expanding his mind with all the possibilities of life waiting in wild places. The book was called *Golden Edens: Handbook of all the birds & some of the common plants of West Africa*. It was a treasure of inspiring instruction that had been on top of Chaminda Warnakulasuriya's pile, filled with melodies and wings and curses. The one and only book for a boy who now wanted to keep a bird list, and who was determined to grow a friend from a tree. The only book from which feathers and pressed leaves fell when opened.

Chrisnelt could not take his eyes off the wreath, transfixed by its beauty. Apart from the waterfalls of tiny flowers on the mango tree, they were the only blooms he'd ever seen in the flesh.

'A garden on a floating ring,' he said to the back of the nun's head. 'What a circle of colours! What shapes! More beautiful than in all the books.' Pink balls on curling springs bobbed, orange hat-shapes bristled, yellow spoons wiggled on the greenest stalks, and some protuberances on the outer rim looked like explosions of the most intense sunrise. The wreath shook in tantalising exuberance; Chrisnelt was convinced that inside that ring he'd seen a seed pod. He had to follow.

He, the nun, and the ring, turned into Ee Ee. He tried to pluck a flower, but the nun was too quick, grunting as she pushed forward. They'd entered a crowd, a throng of people moving in the same direction. Her grunts became loud. She pushed deeper. Chrisnelt pushed behind her. Her head became a shaking shadow of bright petals.

'Please, Lady of God, may I have one of those flowers with a seed!'

She disappeared into the crowd. It was tight, swelling like clouds can swell and rain can push. He felt very small. A little boy behind a little lady who kept disappearing, absorbed into a mutable animal of hundreds of faces, flushed and pushing forward in the heat. Everyone sweated. Everyone pushed. The dust rose above all the heads, the people surged, the crowd growing all the time in a hum of much excitement and many languages. The men wore smart suits and smarter hats; the women – draped in many colourful silks, glistening in the heat – chattered to each other. Some sang hymns in this river of souls. Chrisnelt noticed that almost all the people also carried wreaths, floating high above their heads. He squealed and tried to grab, but he was too short. He leapt and he fell. He tried again. Men shouted at him. He pushed, they pushed.

Then the nun reappeared, squeezing her way to the front. Chrisnelt, squashed in the throng, closed in behind her. The current flowed. He watched the circle of flowers hovering high above the nun like a halo from dreams. He knew that inside the biggest flower waited special seeds.

It was a helpless trance. His mind left him, drifting into a place of wonder and hope: perhaps he could get the biggest of those flowers, dry it in the sun, unlocking the biggest seed from its heart. What a tree would come after rain! He thought of all the flower trees – the most beautiful in the books, always filled with the most birds. They smelled the best, and it was written that they sang when climbed. That's what the books had offered: the Orchid Tree, the Flame Tree, the Tree of Rhododendrons. (Bird number two glided over him then, Rock Dove: a purple-silver flash on the ridge of a distant roof.)

The nun had disappeared again. Chrisnelt panicked – she'd become his guide in this crowd. He sank to the ground, coughing in resoluteness. Crawling would be his easiest way forward in the tightness. The air was very hot. His head throbbed and he couldn't see much. He squeezed through skirts and dresses, thick like curtains; some stank of perfumes that made him sick, and others gave off the sweetness that comes from dust on unwashed skin. He rubbed against legs; hard shoes kicked. He tugged and pulled with little arms. He squeezed his head and neck into a gap, then pulled through his shoulders and knees. His short pants tore. A man swore at him, right in his face, another spat on his head, prodding with a walking stick that had once been an umbrella in ancient rain. A stomach rumbled, and a large fart fell from a fat man who was very slippery to the touch. And still Chrisnelt crawled, quicker all the time, coughing ever more determined coughs, fragile bits of the Coca-Cola logo aglow in sweat on his tattered shirt, lungs burning, all the way to a bizarre destiny shaped by the singular need for the beginnings of a tree.

He parted two legs in front of his face. Light – the brightest white – slammed him in the eyes, the way lightning had once done. His head popped out between elbows and jacket flaps into a clearing, the burning sun at a low enough angle to blind everything for an instant. He took a fresh breath. There she was, just to the left, in the open, a few arm-lengths away. She was bent over, placing the ring of flowers at the base of a high wall.

The long stone wall went all the way down the street, then bent away to the left. Along its entire length, they lay in rainbow rings. Wheels and wheels of petals, the colours whizzing like the firecrackers of New Year's Eve, Diwali, St Patrick's Day, Freedom Day. The pinks had become brighter pinks, yellows soared with the power of the heat, oranges rushed in cartwheels, and there were reds, pale blues and sprays of intermingled whites that burst concoctions of confusion for the mind. Kneeling, Chrisnelt could hardly make out the wall behind the glory of soft flowers.

The crowd came forward in groups, bending in their finest clothes, moaning in reverence and tears, gently placing circles against the wall. It was a scene he could not have imagined, or even read in any of his many books: a throng of people in homage, placing gift upon gift. A world praying to a wailing wall, a wall of great importance, holding unfathomable sadness.

A short distance to his right, where the crowd was most

dense, hung two wide gates of corrugated iron, painted white and held shut with chains. Above was an arc of wooden planks, spanning the sky on two sharp spikes that sprouted tendrils of steel, all also painted white. On the hewn wood, in flamboyant twirls, shining in gold paint: *Grace's Private Burial Home.*

The chains began to rattle, dribbling away like a stream of water, pulled from elsewhere. The gates creaked, grinding open, making wings of sand in the dust as they swung. And a roar of vehicles came from within.

Chrisnelt recognised Pastor Kadazi, deep in the back of the first car. The side window was down, and it was dark inside except for the white hat of tumultuous plumes. Behind the white Mercedes-Benz, followed one, then two, three, four, five, six, seven black cars – one longer than any car Chrisnelt had ever seen – parting the crowd with sharp hoots. They disappeared down Ee Ee Street, leaving only blue smoke, flailing arms and a crescendo of cries and screams.

'Who has died in there, sir?' asked Chrisnelt, pulling the hand of a man standing next to him.

'It's the death of the Governor. So many funerals … and now the Governor,' said the man sadly, waving to the distant cortege of dust.

Freed from the crowd, Chrisnelt rose and stepped forward alone: one step, then another. He fell to his knees. He reached out to pluck his prize: a single bulbous flower, the one that had caught his eye: the biggest and fattest, white-blue-pink-orange mixed together like the snow cones in the shop that sold ice from Paris, France. It was becoming a fruit, which must surely hold the seed, just as his books had said. The silver baubles inside the bloom seemed to whisper to him, twitching in the late afternoon breeze that was lifting the City toward evening. He wiggled his long fingers, and he plucked.

But it was stuck: the stem was fastened to the circle, and to the other flowers too. The more he pulled, the more the entire wreath shook. He sat on his bottom and tugged with both hands, his feet braced against the thick arrangement. The world shook. Something snapped, and he tumbled backwards, rolling in the dust in between the many feet, below skirts and dresses; for a second or two he didn't know where he was, the back of his head aglow where it had thumped the hard earth. Leaning on one shoulder, he looked at the flower. Its underside offered an embossed message in capital letters. He read: *MADE IN CHINA*.

The nun had gone. The crowd had eased, beginning to disperse. The wall grew higher in the bending shadows of lies, and Chrisnelt looked more closely at the lurking circles. All identical – or perhaps there were variations: some predominantly pink, some yellow, a surprising number mostly white. But essentially, they were all the same, the same circumference, the same number of blooms, the same bushy-fatness, the same ratios of colour, as if made by a single man of mysterious formulae.

He waved his hand at the thousands of busy insects crawling across the colours. In an electric fizz of bodies that flushed up into his face, everything stung; his eyes swelled in a cloud of green metallic flies. Below all the flies, and below the plastic, a damp stain of leaking sewage spread. And Chrisnelt cried, rolling into a ball.

'You okay, boy?' said a man in a gold suit, having placed his flowers against the wall. 'You look very upset. It's a sad day. We too loved the Governor. It's important to love him in my family. There was work if you loved him. And now we will have a new Governor to love. It will be okay.'

'Yes,' said Chrisnelt, on his knees. 'THESE ARE ALL LIES.'

'No. Very cheap, good quality at Casino Supermarché, or even from Good Market of Heaven. And cheaper if you buy them in packs,' said the man, his face shining in the heat as if it were part of his glistening suit. 'You must tell your mother that it is okay for a child to bring a wreath too. I'm sorry, boy.'

'Yes, Sir,' said Chrisnelt softly, helpless in his disappointment. He was alone.

'Next time. There will always be a new Governor.'

'Yes, Sir.'

Chrisnelt wanted to run away; was about to run. But his big head needed to run more than his little body. His thin neck and thin limbs wanted to run the least. His body made him linger and turn. Through a crack between the gates – with a new kind of glance, a glance of realisation – he saw the stumps of dead trees.

The sun was going away, as it always does in tropical Africa: in a sudden blink, without the luxury of lingering light. He knew that he'd better hurry home. But the crack in the closed gates held his gaze.

A remarkable land of green, free for the eyes to run and the mind to skip, the hands to stretch forever, collecting all the colours of all the petals … It was the only open space he'd ever seen. Until then, his world had been houses and the squashed spaces they made between rusting walls. The field rolled into the distance in many minute hills, hills rippling into hills that would never end. Some had crosses; some had hard slabs of stone pointing upward in the shapes of hands and strange churches; some were just hills. He could make out the polished stumps of felled trees between these hills. But on all the hills, on every single one of them, there were swathes of living flowers stretching to the sky. And he knew immediately, the hills had been shaped by dead bodies, and the bodies had been made into an eternal bloom.

The gates rose high, the wall even higher. Pied crows squawked, gathering on a nearby roof to roost. (Bird number three.) The crowd was gone. Chrisnelt was alone. He turned and began to run: bounding back up Ee Ee, right into Dee Dee, heat holding him inside a haze of dust the colour of mangoes. His nostrils and mouth filled with air, his ribs heaving between disappointment and hope, his shirt disintegrating, his shorts in shreds, the clapping sound of his bare feet finding the way home like the sound of drums. The street had grown silent, as it always did before dinner. He swooped along, like a lonely moth dancing toward a dangerous heat.

Just before he reached the front door – his delicate chest rising and falling – a sparrow, startled by the clatter, lifted above him, twisting in its ascension to the dusk, and shat on his naked shoulder. He wiped himself with his hand, drawing a white smudge down his side, and inside the white came the fresh colour of green, and inside the green, his fingers rolled a warm seed along his skin.

CHAPTER FOUR

THE SPOT OF LIGHT CAME through the glass circle in the bedroom door, swelling a brilliant sun on the wall. The room and its walls of scribbles were no longer terrifying to Chrisnelt; instead the words now danced in instruction. He sat up, rubbing his eyes, and reached for a clear plastic pot next to his sleeping-mat. Picking it up with much care, he held it to his chest. It swayed on his ribs, cupping mist from the soil at its edges, and in the middle swirled the pale green stem of a little plant. 'It's just like a finger,' whispered Chrisnelt.

He lay with the precious thing. A week of waiting had gone by, the air heavy above the house, holding soporific heat. Every dawn, he'd turned on his sleeping mat to look at the quiet pot, only to turn back into sleep. At night, when the world was at its most silent, except for the sounds from the barracks and the screams that sometimes came from dreams, he'd turned repeatedly, each time seeing only soil. His bedroom had become a place of deathly stillness, except for his restless turning. But now his seed – from a bird to the sky to his shoulder to a pot – had become a life.

'A great tree is coming, Tata!' Chrisnelt ran down the short passage into the living room, the pot in his hands. 'A great tree is on the way up to us,' he said proudly, aglow with hope. He showed Nipcia and Divi, who both shook their heads, continuing to cook and clean.

'Planting and growing are two different things,

Chrisnelt. You'll have to find the right place for such a tree,' said Mr Malotika, smiling from between the pages of his newspaper. 'What about the yard outside your room? It's small and empty, sheltered from the street and the noise, and you can get there straight from your door. No one will disturb you there.' He looked at the girls, making signs with his eyebrows. 'It can be your special place to grow. Just yours. But you'll have to fix the soil around that big rock. It's like linoleum out there,' he laughed.

'I've already made a hole, right next to the rock. It's been filling with sand the whole week, Tata,' answered Chrisnelt. 'Even sand has been wanting to hold this tree.'

'Trees need rivers, my son,' said his father wisely, 'just as much as they need the sand.'

Mr Malotika spoke in prophetic tones that dripped like silky water. That was his way. That was how he'd been trained to teach, and how he'd become used to talking – even to people at work, or in the tavern, and occasionally when in bed with his wife.

His newspaper rustled in front of his face like a warning flag, the headline bold and big, white shaping black: 'NEW RIVER-BRIDGE IDEA BOMBED. MANY HOPES DROWNED.'

The open area at the back of the house was a yard of three corners and three rather high sides. The corners came by chance, as did the sides: one side was the Malotika house – specifically, Chrisnelt's bedroom, which spanned its width in an extension of ancient mud blocks, supporting a roof of palm fronds, under which a ceiling proclaimed the private area for his sleeping mat. The other two sides consisted of the neighbours' corrugated-iron fences and walls, patterned with much rust and neglect. These formed a triangle open to the sky, this framing only apparent if one lay on one's back, dreaming of a world of trees and their birds, looking up at the drifting clouds that never spoke – or at least, had not done so for some time.

This stark and neglected place – though fertile with the opportunities that cracks can give – had come about because of an obstacle, much like a road changes direction when it comes up against a wall of mountains, or a port spreads along a coastline, or a city stops abruptly, brushed by the most powerful River on Earth. The yard had been formed by a rock: big and black and uncommonly smooth, polished by time and great distance, having rolled down the River many millions of years before. Its surface now of the finest satin, it shone when the light was right. It had come to settle here, just for Chrisnelt, or so he imagined, and over many hundreds of years, a city had grown around it. Because it was so heavy and hard, houses had come and gone, unable to shape or shift it, framing it with walls in strange homage.

For Chrisnelt, at his young age, this remnant of the River was simply a friend; he could lie on its flat top, looking up at the sky, waiting for clouds and birds. Lying on those black curves, he often flew, very quietly, with the swallows in the mornings, tugging on the tips of their familiar tails. An entire flock of newly arrived travellers from the far south, coming from the edge of the continent where the oceans meet, he'd been told. Their feathers were worn, tattered from time and endurance. They soared in their thousands on the incoming breeze, a sprinkling of tiny shadows below the sun. Lesser-striped Swallow, number four for his list. Chrisnelt lifted his arms wider than they'd ever been; his fingers wiggled, his legs straddled tomorrow, his thoughts raced in a new, high wind just below the whitest clouds. Dust billowed in the tropical sky and he drifted with the birds, their beaks pricking him in song, their wings tickling his dreams. The sharp chatter of their calls pulled him along on threads of joy, and below he saw the City as only a boy can, nestled in the words from his books and from Mr Malotika's extemporaneous tongue.

Roofs lay scattered across the horizon like playing cards; in the endless shimmer of the sun, houses clustered tightly around brown lines of moving people, which widened into boulevards of hooting taxi-cars; in turn widening, in the centre of things, into vast plazas between government buildings of concrete, pock-marked with occasional flags and sculptures of past presidents covered in rust, which, in every instance, boasted a ribbon of pigeons coming from the head, and spatters of white expelled from the arses of birds.

All of this – all the walls everywhere – was owned by the River: shaping the City with a giant arm resting in a curve, rippling, its waters flowing over rocks like sinews hold bone. The arm held the City's past because it belonged to the River's body that lay across all of West Africa, stretching right back to where people had begun, in the deepest Forest inside the breathing body of the Continent. The River, deepest on Earth – almost two hundred and fifty metres deep in parts – was a living thing that never ended, not even when it reached the sea. It had been there since the first peoples of Africa, and continued to be there now for these peoples of foreign dust, who had come from every island. ('Our world is a world of islands,' said Mr Malotika every dinner time, almost like a prayer.)

Chrisnelt soared in wide circles, just below the speaking cloud. He gazed to his left: rising high into the air above the City was a great stem, bursting into a canopy of glittering leaves and chirping sparrows. At the base of that mighty tree stood a boy in fluttering shade, leaning on a rock, framed by a triangle of corrugated iron.

Chrisnelt clung to the swallows with all the strength his dream could give. He looked down onto the River below him now – The Great Dancing Road – and it was not only water on its way, but also a hero of the myths told by fathers. The River was a famous player in the life of the City, just as famous as Gako the footballer, or the powerful Governor of the Province. The River was a symbol of community, an irresistible route to a better place. It was all the churches of every religion. It was the blood, and his tree was to be the heart.

Chrisnelt rubbed the rock with his fingers as one might stroke a pet. 'Rock, you and I are going to make a garden, so this tree isn't lonely. No one should ever be lonely. Tata once told me of the Forest that was here. And you were here then too. Aren't I right, Rock? You must have been?' He patted the rock, his little body draped across it like a shadow. 'Tata always says: "This was a green place then, the greenest in all the world; the trees so high, they touched the clouds, and so close together, one tree became the next in leaves that never ended." What do you say, Rock? You were here. "Back then the birds flew between

the leaves, instead of having to fly so high above them."
That's what Tata said. Right? And, it was all because of
you that the first huts began to make the first circle in the
first clearing. Tata said the rock would not be moved by
the roots of trees or the hands of people. The rock was a
place of lots of light. *You* would not be moved, hey Rock?'

That rock spoke to Chrisnelt like no rock has ever
spoken to any little boy of humid dreams: 'Yes, I was
smoothed by my journey in the waters of the River, by my
gorgeous tumbles, curling in foam toward the future. And
also by the juices and heat of all the people upon me, by so
many resting hands, deliberating, bodies in pain catching
their breath against my sides. People wandering, looking
for the light, drifting across all the islands of the world –
and then they found me, and looked up. And on seeing the
clouds for the first time in the clearing, those deep forest
people knew instantly that, without rains from above, no
River could have come about to bring me – an island in
my own right – here to make a clearing. And without a
clearing there would be no home for them.'

Chrisnelt opened his eyes. 'You slept here all this time,
waiting just for me, Rock.' The warm rock absorbed the
sun as it absorbed Chrisnelt. His spine clicked, adjusting
to the world of high blue and deep white lines on the sky.
The weight of midday waking him, sitting on his puffed
cheeks, the sweat beginning to come. He wiped his brow,
sliding slowly down the smoothness, and knelt next to
the tree.

In the shade that was forming on one side of the rock,
a green sprout prodded the heat, roots slowly tugging the
hard sand, a leaf beginning to flex with laughter and play

somewhere inside the tip. He'd been bringing water from the toilet bowl every few hours, pouring it gently from his cupped hands, fingertips dripping like rain, the dark stain around the stem fading always within seconds. He was very grateful to the rock for its shadow. The phantasmal greenness bent toward the darkness in relief, leaning beyond the boiling air and the white glare.

'From the sky to me. Now to the ground, becoming a tree. It was as if I did not need to dig, as if this yard were waiting, just like you were waiting, Rock.'

Books moved from the living room to his bedroom in armfuls, fluttering in gusts of air, as the family hastily reclaimed order in the home – Chrisnelt loudly directing events. Eventually they settled, forming a wall two books thick – stacked one upon the other, titles carefully placed the right way up so that Chrisnelt could easily read the stories on the spines. Even the girls helped to carry the lighter piles, Nipcia remarking: 'Thank the "Lordoo". Finally, these things are going to be out of the way.'

Within a day of the little tree being planted, Chrisnelt was observed rustling up and down Dee Dee Street, searching for anything that grew. A latent brilliance was dawning in his eyes, which glistened now with clarity and health. Although he also had a strange squint: one eyeball looking up for birds, the other looking down for living leaves, together the eyes forming images that might have been from other worlds. And once again his parents let him go freely, confident he was healing his mind in the sweltering dust.

'Sickness can delay the forming of an almighty brain,

as surely as tragedy can hasten it,' said Mr Malotika to Mrs Malotika in his usual gnomic manner. They were in Chrisnelt's room while their son was out hunting for a garden – Mr Malotika smelling the air that books breathe, neatly adjusting the edges of various tomes, gazing upon the rising façade of literature, inhaling the languages and facts that hovered before him. Books on the subject of plants lay open on the floor near the sleeping-mat like giant, resting moths. 'He and I share a love,' Mr Malotika said, stroking the bumpy texture of the special, new wall. 'We share a love.'

'I worry about the sun on him. His tongue swells like a sponge in his mouth, his nostrils stretch like tents, and his little lips are cracked like the pavements,' said Mrs Malotika, vividly. 'He is very delicate in the head. And he is always running to the toilet.' She was looking out through the small glass window in the bedroom door. 'He has made little holes everywhere in that yard and filled them with weeds. This boy? And he's even polished that rock,' she said, shaking her huge head of hairy tails.

'Leave the boy,' said Mr Malotika. 'It's very good that he's out in the fresh air. It's good air after all – in between the cooking times, when the bad smoke comes.'

'But *this* air is like other people's wet breath; and he's digging in the street drains. They're full of sewage-mud and rubbish from people's dustbins. You see how it's all thrown' – she shook her arms, the flab gyrating as she spoke, nearly knocking a tower of books to the floor – 'and he's bringing that muck here.' She pointed – her fat finger bending against the hot glass – at the scattered world of weeds and smells of new life in the yard. They looked at each other as parents often do: smiling, shaking heads in helpless understanding.

Not too far from the front door, half buried in a muddy ditch, Chrisnelt yelped and stood up suddenly, hands aloft, waving a long elastic thing attached to a weed of many colours; the snap of the extraordinary plant made a loud twang. Chrisnelt spluttered in the goo. 'Here's the soil-maker, that's what I read,' he chanted, 'here's the Maker!' He was most excited by the find, and so close to home. To add to his good fortune, his bird list had grown ten species stronger.

He opened the front door and scurried toward his bedroom, leaving a trail of brown toe-prints. The girls screamed and jumped up and down as he passed, as did Mrs Malotika, almost dropping a bale of baguettes. The thing was two metres long, pink, glistening like a strand of spit, and most uncooperative. It dangled and wriggled in huge loops, its one end buried in a small bush of roots and leaves and a single flower that looked like a daisy. In one fist was the end of an earthworm, in the other a weed, and no one was sure when the one thing ended and the other began.

'I think I'm going to faint, Mama,' said Divi.

'Me too,' yelled Nipcia, 'and the tip winked at me!'

Chrisnelt giggled, disappearing in slime, skidding down the dark corridor, winding through his room, then out into his garden of light and new scents.

He would come and go all day, and even into the beginning of night, right at its edge, sometimes eating dinner while walking up and down the street just before the high lights began to buzz with insects. He spoke in humming sounds to himself, uttering poems – some short and jerky, some wild like tendrils and long like tall trees – and elucidating to his hands the merits of garden maintenance and other such technical stuff.

On one such walk of discovery, he found a neglected box of plants on a crate outside the gendarmerie, which was strategically situated next to the lucrative Ministry of the Interior's Storage Depot for River Sand. Mid-morning crowds swarmed as usual, the dialects of villages and the languages of regions fighting for independent air. The City was now a new world of cities, just as the Continent contained all continents.

From not too far off, he watched the flowers in the box as one might a play on a church-school stage. The golden marigolds and tall green shoots moved, swaying in the heat, part of the crowd that did not walk past so much as flow; such was the humidity. 'How neglected they are,' he said to himself and to a fence nearby, meaning the plants and not the people. The box was filled to the brim with cigarette butts, the flowers appearing to float on strange soil. So beautiful, he thought: *as if the grains of sand have each swelled into tiny drums awaiting tiny hands to beat songs upon them, so the bees might dance.* Then he looked more carefully: some of the butts had lipstick stains, others teeth-marks; one or two were black like soot, and one, attached to chewing gum, leaked blood. Chrisnelt became quickly disgusted, concluding that this was indeed a giant ashtray of everybody's waste. 'Cigarette butts are not pretty drums!' he said. Duty-bound to rescue the plants, he pulled at them gently, and they surrendered, leaking dust.

'Put that down, you little thief! Stealing government

property means death,' shouted a man, his machine-gun prodding Chrisnelt's back. 'I arrest you in the name of the Governor and all that is holy, little scumbag.' The officer was drunk, swearing in a haze of *pétrole*, a home-distilled alcohol of the City: a substance of huge importance in both military and policing circles.

'It's a misunderstanding,' said Chrisnelt. 'Please, don't shoot me. I'm just saving these plants – see.' He pointed with his free hand, the other holding the marigolds above his head like a shield, the root-dust scattering everywhere. Everyone laughed, including a man Chrisnelt recognised as a book-deliverer. The policeman laughed the loudest, grabbing the back of Chrisnelt's neck and shaking him: 'And now you go to jail forever for stealing weeds.'

Chrisnelt fell to the ground, limbs seizing, his brain shutting down, the corners of his big eyes welling with tears, darkness fighting with light. He lay there, deep below all the legs and laughs. A man with a crocodile under his arm shook it in his face, another with a wiggling bucket of catfish and the worst of breaths spat a cigarette butt onto his chest, the other policemen came outside to join the fun. Chrisnelt curled up into a ball and shivered. Eventually people became bored with him. He lay still in that throng. With darkness, he was able to limp home in silence, all the time clutching the green stems and golden flowers, their roots intact and waiting.

'Why are you crying again, Chrisnelt?' asked Mrs Malotika, arriving at the front door at the same time as he, her arms full of yesterday's bagels in a plastic sack.

'It's nothing, Mama,' he said. 'Just my gardening work. Making me tired. But I won't give up.'

Four weeks of digging and raking with his bare fingers had made Chrisnelt's hands ache, but they had also become quite muscular, with tiny bulges between the joints. The little tree had become strong too, the stem thicker, leaves wide under the sun, side branches beginning to unfurl, more leaves hinting at their presence. It was just like him in shape and disposition, hurrying upward with energy, committed to being something of significance in a very unimportant corner of the world, waiting for clouds and their rain.

Mr Malotika had spoken many times of the quiet people of faithful footsteps who talked to trees, people of the deepest forests to the north at the beginning of the River and of all rivers, where water waited. These people could understand what trees say when the wind blows through the highest leaves. Different trees with different leaves spoke different languages in the wind, yet as a limitless forest, they spoke together, as it should be. Leaves shaped words that were sentences, and there was indeed much to be said.

'For these same people, flowers on the forest paths would slowly turn if looked at, facing up from the mud, smiling in the rush of raindrops and the warm afternoon light. At a simple touch of a finger, or if trodden on by mistake, those flowers would patiently return to the ground, which, after a time, would become a flower again,' said Mr Malotika. He was sitting on the rock next to his son, playing with his wooden wedding band. He often twiddled it with his thumb when he spoke about trees.

'Tata, if I talk to my tree, perhaps it'll grow faster? Christmas is coming in a few weeks and I want the tree to be big and bright like a friend for us then,' said Chrisnelt.

'Perhaps it will, but you'll have to do a lot of talking,' laughed Mr Malotika. 'Never underestimate the power of words, my son, especially near Christmas.' Mr Malotika laughed again.

'I've been talking to it, Tata, even at night. I've been talking to the rock too, asking for more gentle shade,' said the boy with a smile. 'Look at all my other plants. I haven't wasted any space. I've even put the ones from Chaminda Warnakulasuriya along the fences; I think those will climb up the sides one day. The bigger one has leaves that seem to grip the metal.'

'I like what you have done with this pond, my son – you have made a perfect circle next to the rock,' said Mr Malotika. 'Where do you get the water in this drought?'

'From the toilet, Tata,' said Chrisnelt.

Mr Malotika laughed. 'Is that where this stink comes from?'

'No, that's from the damn goat dung,' said Chrisnelt, not wanting to say the word shit. 'I made a mixture with it from a recipe in a book, but I think I've used too much.'

'We've had complaints from Mr Nagasaki, the Mukendis, and from Mr MacDonald, that new Scottish man from across the street with the unusually long nose, who always wears long socks on hot days.'

'Sorry, Tata, but it's going away now. I had to sleep in the passage for a week, just so I could breathe, you know. And you should've seen the flies.'

'I know, and I did.'

'Those flies turned into lovely worms in the end. It's helped the garden. There's so many colours. Most of the plants come from the street drains. Except for that bush.' He pointed to the marigolds. 'And now I'm getting butterflies, big green ones and a black one too,' said Chrisnelt with excitement. 'And birds are coming because of all this green, I think. I've added five more to my list, including a kingfisher.'

'That one is probably because of this pond, and the frog that sings at night,' said Mr Malotika, dipping a bare toe into the middle, making a circle that rippled all the way to the edge, disturbing a newly arrived dragonfly with its wings of water. He cleared his throat and said to his son slowly, as seriously as he knew how, and in a deep tone: 'You're creating a special thing here in this crack between all these walls of our City; it's a thing coming from your heart. I'm very proud of you.' He paused: 'I know you're still young, but always remember that emptiness and non-emptiness are all part of Nature. And there's a place between the two where life begins.'

Somewhere in the middle of garden-making, Chrisnelt thought he was going to die. He'd been working very hard, searching for plants and finding them in the most unusual places: a creeper extracted carefully from a wooden lamp-post, where it had found a footing in a hole below a poster of the President hugging the Governor; a round, flat bush lifted from under a tin drum, only to be later identified as a fungus (but that didn't matter); a handful of reeds from a gutter in permanent shade, where he had to run from hungry mosquitoes with black-and-white stripes on their legs. It was after that that the dying began from above, when the World fell on his head.

He'd been ordered by his mother – now that he was strong again – to dust the palm-frond fringe of the veranda with a broom, being mindful not to wake the sleeping bats. It was not rush-hour. Not the time when charcoal trucks delivered, or when many people gathered with sacks and the noise of hunger, nor was it the time of lumber trucks. It was peaceful, and safe for Chrisnelt to climb up on a stool placed in the street where the pavement was narrow. But as he lifted the broom, a violent shadow came upon him, crackling from a bus window.

The unexpected tourist bus expelled a map as it passed by in the dust at speed, enveloping the little boy in paper. The gush from the long bus sucked him off the stool, his imprisoned shape tumbling in the air, and he rolled. The map was big, having unfolded to full size on impact, and for the longest while – or so it seemed – he could not see the sun. Tightly wrapped, he was narrowly missed by an on-coming taxi-car. He could not breathe.

'You fool! You little idiot, playing games!' screamed the taxi-car driver, hooting and swerving, exhaust fumes fuming, the bus all the while continuing onward in ignorance.

'Watch how you driving, you the idiot!' shouted someone else, walking up the street, shaking a large pot-plant at the taxi-car. 'You could've killed the boy.'

Chrisnelt was carefully unwrapped by the man with the pot, and he stood up holding his sides and gasping for air: 'I thought I was dead.'

'You okay, boy? You okay, Chrisnelt?' said the man, clutching the flapping map in one hand and Chrisnelt's arm in the other.

In all the dust and khaki, Chrisnelt looked at him and smiled: 'Hello, Mr Warnakulasuriya.'

'It's okay. I think this is yours,' he said, folding up the map neatly and handing it to Chrisnelt, 'and you can call me Chaminda, if you like. That is my name.'

He laid the map out on the planks of the veranda, the shadow of the palm-fronds above giving it an edge like feathers. It was the most colourful thing the boy had ever seen, covered in leaping words and shapes, more colourful than any flower or bird he'd imagined from books or seen in his favourite dreams. He forgot about everything. He forgot about Chaminda; all he could see was the map of genius. It enveloped him again, only this time in a wondrous journey, flying through a paper sky: He stroked the shiny surface, running a pointed finger across the pandemonium, showered by secrets. The map shone in purples, lilacs, pinks and whites; blacks, yellows, browns, creamy shades, and the auburn tones of changing days. There were little images in the shape of circles with arrows pointing to answers, making places for his mind, floating worlds. Bending rivers glowed bright blue, bursting into eternal aquamarine oceans; paths and roads throbbing in red, snaking like delicate, dangerous veins; and before him was more green than he'd ever dare hope was in the world.

'Actually, I was on my way to bring you another little plant for your garden, your father told me you're very busy with it,' Chaminda interjected, leaning over the map to hand Chrisnelt a pot. 'And he has told me about the great tree, too.'

'Thank you very much, Mr Chaminda,' said Chrisnelt, pulling at a leathery frond.

'It's a tree orchid for your tree. I got it when I was chopping down a very tall tree faraway, up the River, beyond any place that knows this place, and I've had it at home for some time. It had your name all over it. There are no flowers yet, just these ancient leaves.'

That night, in privacy, Chrisnelt spread the map out on his mat in the darkness and sprawled across its full width, tumbling within it as he tumbled within the pages of every book. In the shape of a star he slept, the air crisp, wet and cool as he wandered the world of crackling futures, flying high like the highest swallows. Books, birds, maps and trees came together to him then as one true story, held together by a River of waters made by rain. And he tumbled onward over borders, boundaries and the great divides between continents, across all islands, making one big new island beyond the scars left by No.

From that time, maps would find him constantly, the way rainwater finds a growing puddle, or weeds find fissures to make little lines of life in pavements. Maps fell out of the sky: blown from magazines in the reception area of the hotel near the airport; kicked from the floors of taverns; peeled from placemats stolen from the Café Gourmandine; offered from back pockets and truck dashboards at the lumberyard; 'borrowed' from girls'-school geography classes; and on stickers pulled with giggles from taxi-car windows; cut from every newspaper in every dustbin in the street; torn from government propaganda sheets; lifted from the backs of cereal boxes; and cut from the decorative parts of promotional umbrellas that had been fashioned to alter the mind. They were everywhere, even on T-shirts and Coca-Cola cans. He'd find them and his family and their friends and neighbours would find them for him too, bringing them just as they'd brought books, as would people from further out, from the City's beginnings – those who carried heavy crates of crying chickens, and baskets of herbal roots, catfish and forest animals. In exchange, he'd read to them, telling of the marvels of the world, pointing to the mysteries and discoveries, elucidating the spectacular interactions across boundaries of peoples of every colour and every place.

Maps came in books, joining his many other books, quickly becoming the walls and ceiling of his bedroom: floor-to-ceiling and ceiling-to-floor journeys; wide roads and dusty paths, and often mountains to be summited and borders to be breached like great divides in search of ways to make a garden. 'Maps are very thin books of just one page,' he said after he'd stuck a small one on a postage stamp over the last vacant bit of wall. Covering every surface had seemed to take years but – as with the gardening – had in fact been mere weeks of franticness. 'And Tata was right, if you want to make a garden that looks after a tree, then you've got to read lots of books: the very thick ones and the very thin ones too.'

One morning at the breakfast table, from the far side of a map and a high pile of steaming bread and another pile of books, Mr Malotika said to his son in his familiar teacher-voice: 'When a glass is filled with water, catching light from above, holding the picture of one's face uniquely, there's a necessary pause for those who think before taking a sip.'

Nipcia and Divi rolled their eyes at each other and giggled.

'I can see the face,' said Chrisnelt, pausing to stare into his glass, smiling with questions in his one eye and genuine thirst in his other. It had been a hot dawn in the garden: the sun always arrived early.

Mr Malotika went on: 'Bits of the face escape to play in the water, you see that?'

'Yes, Tata,' said Chrisnelt, 'all moving in the light.'

'You see that,' said Divi, throwing a piece of croissant at Nipcia.

'You see that,' said Nipcia as she caught it, surprised at her luck.

'You see that,' said Divi, throwing another piece.

'Not at the table, girls.'

'Sorry.'

Nipcia arranged the bits of croissant like little islands on the wooden table.

'You'd better eat that, girl.'

She looked at her father and began to eat. 'Sorry, Tata.'

'And they throw the colours of our identity about. The smile and the blink and the twitch of the cheek give the water a new life, a hint perhaps of a new future face of one colour, just for a moment. Capturing the past, becoming something new, the water speaking about the lost joy of unity,' said Mr Malotika.

'I've seen water scream near fire, in the hottest colours,' said Chrisnelt.

'Look at your map there,' he said, moving his son's bowl to one side, brushing croissant crumbs out of the way. 'You see all the countries, all in different, scattered colours. They were all once one colour, one endless country in fact, when there were no borders, more or less. Not too long ago!'

'Did the water move them all apart like floating places, Tata? Pushing them together, then apart like the bits of my face in this glass?' asked Chrisnelt, chewing on a hot slice of bread.

'Yes. They were together for a time in the very distant past, and then apart in the water not too long ago, but always moving as one thing. That is the nature of this Earth. That is its way, and always will be. Today they're apart in *other* ways, but we have great powers that can make them move together again. This is the power of water.'

'Perhaps like magic, when many clouds become one cloud.'

'Water!' said Mr Malotika, rolling his wooden wedding band on his finger.

'These days, water's in the toilet or in the long ditches. Very colourful ditches. Full of cans. Very colourful. I can tell you that, Tata,' said Chrisnelt.

'If you tilt your glass, pouring carefully, water will flow from the glass to the floor through the cracks in the linoleum, giving all those reflections back to the roots deep below, very deep, as it always has done before the time of glasses. Water always finds its way in the end.'

'Look, it's raining in here,' said Divi, dribbling water from her mouth onto her knee, which then made a rivulet down her leg onto the floor.

'Look,' pointed Nipcia, flicking a piece of croissant at Divi. 'It's heading for Chrisnelt's foot.'

'Girls.'

'Sorry, Tata.'

'It's in charge of my tree, Tata, and the garden, and my maps. It's in all my maps, even in the ones with deserts on them. Water's at the edges of those deserts,' said Chrisnelt, pointing up at the ceiling with a finger that was a long shadow. There was much forming in his swelling mind of leaves, his eyes blinking, tinged green.

After dinner that evening, Mr Malotika did a thing he'd never done before. He lay with Chrisnelt on his mat in the bedroom of maps and together they looked up at the Earth and its many worlds. Chrisnelt shivered deep inside, his heart beating like it used to beat each time No climbed into the mango tree. He was strangely nervous, looking up at the wide continents drifting across the ceiling and sideways down the walls. He imagined reaching up with his arms, feet grappling; climbing into unknown branches, into the vastness of adventure, in between the new discoveries that hung like big, red-orange, laughing mangoes. All these places in his heart held No.

His father smiled like No then, briefly, in the moonlight. 'Being like this on our backs on the floor is like being inside a book, Chrisnelt,' said Mr Malotika softly, still in a scholarly mood. As they got comfortable, bodies rustling, the sleeping mat wobbled the lamp, and the dull light made shadows move in exotic animation. 'Look! Your maps are alive and breathing.'

On the ceiling, various maps had begun to form big bubbles from the humidity; they curled down at the edges, swaying in the light like leaves and tendrils. 'See how the Sahara hangs next to the Amazon now, and the Great Barrier Reef is swimming up the Alps,' smiled Mr Malotika. A cluster of placemats – cocktails and palm trees against South-Sea-Island sunsets – shone like an escaping shoal of fish as Chrisnelt adjusted the lamp, cottoning on to this game of journeys. 'Tata, and look, Africa with all its greens is dancing with China and ignoring Europe and America,' he laughed.

The two girls lay next to each other on their shared mat in their shared room, listening.

'We also want to play!' shouted Divi.

'Yes, all we do is clean up!' shouted Nipcia.

'You two have bits of bread to find. And the floor needs to be dried.'

'Sorry, Tata!' they shouted together.

Chrisnelt fiddled with the lamp again; a gecko wagged its tail on the Nile, and all the islands everywhere jumped across the room, inhabiting the South Pole, awakening a green-and-blue cricket sleeping on the Eiffel Tower that was in turn balancing on top of one of the pyramids of Giza. An armada of frivolous beetles, congregating in Europe, flushed a mosquito in the Middle East, scaring a spider sleeping on the Red Sea.

In the corners, the maps bent and flexed: maps at right angles to maps, linking new latitudes and longitudes. At one such meeting of walls, Chrisnelt had slit the layers of paper with a kitchen knife in an attempt to make a crisp line; instead, the cut formed an accidental cave, long and delicate. 'Tata, the cave is alive!' he shouted in joy.

'I see it,' said Mr Malotika, rolling on his side to watch. In the thin shadow, a row of antennae tapped languages in Morse code, like he used to watch his father do on the river barges as a boy. 'Over there is a cockroach at the mouth of the Thames, trying to find London, or is it trying to find the sea? It even looks like a glistening boat.

A Tree for the Birds

A cruising yawl in the heart of darkness,' he laughed to himself, dreaming of books.

Chrisnelt stared up at the crack and the movement inside the cave again, at its furthest, deepest edge, and said: 'Tata, from there I can see a beautiful garden escaping on the backs of those greenest of insects, on the other side of the ocean, calling for my yard.'

'To get here, they'll have to run right across the Atlantic and up a very deep river in this Africa, but they'll get here in the end, I'm sure,' said Mr Malotika.

The lamp was like a giant moon; a moth passed. Outside, the garden glowed in the starlight through the door that hung open like a friend. 'My pond is the Ocean, and my tree,' said Chrisnelt, 'is the land.'

'We think you've had too much sun!' shouted Nipcia.

'And too much toilet water fumes!' shouted Divi.

'Girls.'

With his eyes serious for a moment, Chrisnelt said in a whisper that seemed to dribble excitedly through the gaps in his teeth, leaning toward Mr Malotika on an unsteady elbow: 'Tata, I think tomorrow's the day. The garden is beginning to sing and speak. Tomorrow my tree will be ready to take over all of it, and look after it, like the continents look after the oceans. It'll be strong from tomorrow. It's been getting stronger every day with all the help Chaminda has been giving me – so many plants. Perhaps soon it'll even shade the rock, and one day the whole house throughout the hottest months. One day it'll be on one of these maps, and you will see it from above the rainbows. Do you think we can invite Pastor Kadazi, and Chaminda, and the neighbours, and we can bless the tree into health? Mama will like that.'

'I'll speak to your mother,' Mr Malotika said with surprise. 'And it's the oceans that look after the continents, not the other way around. I'm looking forward to seeing how that tree has grown over these past days. And forget about hottest months, tomorrow is supposed to be the hottest day.' He stared at his son carefully. He twisted the lamp again: 'Chrisnelt, see Greenland stretching into the white top of the world.'

All the commotion had finally pulled Divi to the doorway, leaning against the wall, viewing the amusing show on the mat: 'Map, maps! Chrisnelt, your room is one big map, yet you can't even find the hole in the toilet seat.'

'Yes, Chrisnelt, you live in maps and we live in mops!' yelled Nipcia from her room, laughing again.

The living room squeaked with the Nagasakis, particularly the only couch, which was not used to three people: Mr Nagasaki and his two boys, both of whom could swear perfectly in Lingala now. (His wife and daughter remained in Japan, due to a strange affliction suffered by the child.) The rest of the room rattled with the MacDonalds, who'd brought hamburgers and chips on a tray covered by a tartan cloth to apologise for things of which they were not sure; and the Mukendis and the Mohameds, quiet in their humble way when immersed in other people's religious moments. Chaminda stood chatting to Mr Malotika, holding yet another plant in a plastic pot. Below his freshly ironed khaki shirt hung a brilliant blue-silk sarong, the one he saved for the special times, when he wanted to remember the ocean around his island. Altogether, it was a room full of many complicated sounds, resembling a crate of chickens at the market. Mrs Malotika had been careful to make sure Pastor Kadazi arrived last, as he'd instructed earlier that day, while she was assisting him to polish the sculpture of an angel near a creaking pew.

When the white Mercedes-Benz settled against the edge of the timber veranda in the late afternoon, the group inside the house prepared themselves for a grand entrance. But it was not to be. Pastor Kadazi was too skilled for that. Instead he lingered theatrically, sensitive to the nuances of an intimate home, then simply knocked. The door was opened and he entered like a soft mist, in all his whiteness and smiles.

'This is a very good afternoon in the heat,' he said, wiping a glistening face with a white handkerchief, the cowry shells on his wrist rattling like teeth. 'That burning tree in the street then. What pain it caused for everyone. Now. I look forward to seeing this great new tree I've heard so much about.'

'Oh Lordoo,' said Mrs Malotika.

'Chrisnelt is in his garden, preparing things for us,' Mr Malotika announced, handing around a bowl of locally grown nuts and dried plantains. 'He's been taking extra water to nourish the plants all morning in preparation. This is a big day for him, as you can imagine. He's walked a long distance to achieve this progress in life, as you all know. And we thank you for the books and the other help' – he looked directly at Chaminda – 'and the understanding. We are most grateful for the progress over these many weeks. And he wishes to dedicate his tree and its garden to his dead friend. Please follow me.' He rubbed his wooden wedding band more vigorously than usual.

They rose in ceremonial slowness, as the afternoon light leaked across the tops of houses.

A howl preceded the appearance of Chrisnelt in the corridor. Mrs MacDonald dropped her pudding, Mr Mukendi, hurriedly swallowing a nut, gave a burp, and both Mr and Mrs Mohamed put their left hands on their open mouths. Everything ended in an embarrassing moment of stillness. Not even Pastor spoke. Chaminda placed his pot plant on the floor and folded his arms in thought.

There he was, his body retreating slowly like a shadow pulled sideways against the wall. He rubbed the painted surface of the corridor with his shoulder; he wanted to climb into that wall, into the bricks and the darkness, away from all the staring faces, but he remained fixed there; nowhere to hide. He shuddered. Tears wanting to come. Rage was powerful too. He burned inside; he would not *ever* face the searing heat of those faces breathing at his back.

A hasty queue formed, peering down the corridor, trying to see past Chrisnelt, who blocked the way. They shuffled up to him, wanting to unravel the calamity that was consuming his swollen face. They stretched their necks: tall people upward, short people sideways, and very short people downward; the Nagasaki boys on their knees, staring between Nipcia's and Divi's legs. Chrisnelt tried to block the view more forcefully, his outstretched arms swaying, lips quivering, knees wobbling.

At the end of the dark corridor, framed by the little bedroom's open doorways, glowed a luminescent vision so spectacular that Mr Nagasaki sighed aloud, then bit his tongue. It was impossible to ignore the shining green. It seemed endless, rolling into the distance, bursting with leaves and flowers.

The crowd pushed forward, stumbling out into the garden, like a thing with many legs. A miniscule place had become the world, if one truly looked with eyes that fed on beauty. The circular pond reflected a bouncing flock of doves and a drifting cloud immersed in bright blue. The ground around the pond sparkled with leaning fronds and the bending arcs of little ferns; on every surface, leaves nestled against buds and unfurling blooms on their way to the tops of walls and eaves, and the air was alive with butterflies, the chatter of bees and cavorting dragonflies.

'Allah be praised,' said Mr Mohamed. 'A tiny oasis in this desert of rusted iron. And the scent. The scent.' His nostrils swelled as he chewed on a nut, thinking back to the jasmines and ambers, the musk and oud of an Arabian youth.

'This the smell of Hokkaido in Springtime,' said Mr Nagasaki, and his boys sniffed the air. 'Very beautiful smell. Most unexpected so far away across seas.'

'And I've got to say that it's like my grandparents' farm in the bloody valley,' said Mr MacDonald. 'Lovely.'

Far at the back, Chaminda smiled, the pot plant firmly back in his hands.

Pastor Kadazi said nothing. Being at the front of the queue, he reached out to embrace Chrisnelt with a hug of religious wisdom, carefully choreographed for such occasions, a bone-coloured plastic cross studded with rhinestones in his one hand, a golden bible in the other.

Secretly, in his wildest dreams he had never seen such power. Not even the light through a stained-glass window could dance souls like this; no words to paying crowds could be this lucrative.

'It has lost all its leaves, and its stem is turning brown,' said Chrisnelt to his father directly. Then he sobbed and ran out into the street, leaving the front door open. The brown veranda shimmered with bright dust, as did the brown sky, erupting into an orange sunset.

The small tree stood clearly now, for all to see: set off against the black rock, just beyond the pond, held in mosses and liverworts and fluffy balls of weeds, in the precise middle of all that was alive. It was indeed a strong little thing, with a shining stem and wide branches, the shape fresh and vibrant in every way – except for leaves. It had been pushing up steadily, but it was mainly pushing sideways now, the light turning it copper.

'Books can teach new words, but hope can cloud understanding,' said Mr Malotika to everyone, the profoundness heavy, as was his way. He did not chase after his son. That was also not his way.

'I shall continue to pray for him. He has much to offer our City,' said Pastor Kadazi to Mrs Malotika, climbing into his car. The Nagasaki boys giggled.

Christmas Day settled on the City in promotional waves of soap packets, cereal boxes, sales posters, large tins of food and sacks of imported merchandise that would never sell because it was too foreign. Christmas hung extravagantly in bits of gold or green or red tinsel, or a twirled combination of the three, on taxi-car rear-view mirrors and in places where money changed hands. It draped itself over radio programmes and political messages: a photograph of the new Governor on the front page of the newspaper showed him kissing his wife under plastic holly tied to a palm tree. (The only palm trees in the City where those that lined the boulevards to the international airport made of glass curtains, the Governor's house and the City centre. They all had bases painted in the brightest of bright whites.)

Christmas Day was another hot day, as all days had been for a long time. Dust rested above the streets, lapping against front doors like water along the quiet edges of the swollen River. Trees at the distant edges of the City battled against the brown, some falling in muted tones of ochre. The Malotikas' district was the dustiest and hottest, lying in a large hollow of constant, swaying heat. And in their home there was much stillness inside all that heat: Chrisnelt was refusing to come out of his room, and the circular pond had dried up, revealing crinkled black plastic that looked like old skin. Yet the garden continued to survive, sheltered from the street in its own world, in part quenching its thirst from a slow drip from the wash-basin pipe, jimmied by the boy during one of his flights of fancy. The tree was a skeleton, roots starved of rich and constant waters, creaking every time the puffed-up sparrows alighted like voluptuous Christmas decorations, until finally it fell under their weight.

On his way home, Mr Malotika walked past an appliance-and-furniture store. In the big glass window, newly arrived television sets crackled with identical images of a Christmas tree – Christmas was always about a Christmas tree in this City, and had been that way for a long time. For the last few days, he'd been preoccupied with a complex thought about seeds, and how he could help his son. Now, an idea flickered.

'Chrisnelt, I'm home, and I have something for you.' Mr Malotika pulled a small, white Christmas tree out of a box. 'This one doesn't need any water.'

Chrisnelt could see it from the vantage point of his sleeping mat. He lay under a map and two open books, near many blue ballpoint pens. Wire limbs covered in furry plastic strands bounced like monkeys' tails in his father's big hands. In a way this tree is just like me, he thought: all over the place. Everything a bit out of control – his mood, his aspirations, his understanding of what was real and what was not.

'I feel like a tree living in a thin box like that cardboard coffin. It's probably all the way from China or Europe, or who knows from which horizon,' he whispered, looking up at his ceiling. China leant down on him with much pressure near an overlapping Australia that squeezed. The Nile River hung in a new breeze that lingered.

Then his father entered the home, somehow clearer that ever before, the sun following him like a pet. His long shadow extended down the corridor, the smell of dry street-dust casting a haze of intimacy. His wedding band glowed – the brightest, warmest wood. The Christmas tree and his father became one in the light, as No had been absorbed into the charcoal branches. The silhouette of Mr Malotika holding the little Christmas tree danced into his heart. Chrisnelt would never forget this day and this image. It was to become the best memory of his father: a man of love, becoming a tree.

'What you got there?' asked Mrs Malotika, stirring a pot in the kitchen, the walls a bit wet with steam.

'It's a tree,' said her husband. The whole thing shook and shimmered, wanting to be bent into appropriate shapes, yearning for an alpine form: a wide splay, filled with the ice crystals of distant fantasies. The trunk of the tree was a ready-made plastic stand: three sharp, straight roots waiting for the flat landscape of the living room floor. 'It was free,' said Mr Malotika, almost apologetically. 'People from the East are giving them away at the store next to the catfish stall if you buy ten blue plastic chairs; and we need chairs at the lumberyard, especially at this time of year.'

Mrs Malotika shook her head in amazement. 'And now people are giving away trees. Black people getting free, white trees for buying blue chairs.' She continued stirring. 'You two and trees.'

Mr Malotika unearthed glass baubles from his pockets. They shone like ripe fruits and twinkled like seeds, rolling on the floor.

Chrisnelt sat up bravely, emerging from the Forests of Borneo that blanketed his legs, along with pages of new poems and calculations. He was disappointed with Mr Malotika's gift, and cried in his furthest reaches, shaking right down to his toes; but he let no one see. This was not a tree at all, just plastic. But it had come with love, and the colours reminded him of No. 'At least there are colours,' he whispered to himself, 'No's colours.'

Mr Malotika had been clever with the intriguing shapes and colours emerging from his pockets, showing them off like planets and stars and the glistening raindrops that gave life to trees. While making his garden over those many weeks, Chrisnelt had renewed his great love of colours, finding new colours too: the rainbow iridescence on a bird's tilted beak; the brightest tropical petals that called to the transparent ants, whose lungs could be seen rising and falling from above in happiness.

Colour – the joy of many different colours – had been one of gardening's gifts. Colour offered him a vibrant image of No, in the way birdsong offered him No's voice and the smell of water offered him No's hope. It had come to him erratically, with each wild thing he sheltered from the street. Chrisnelt recalled how the hand of Mr Nagasaki had reached over the high wall with a blue plant, the wall too high to see his face; and how Mrs Mohamed had handed him a pink plant, the wall also too high to see her face; and how an unknown hand had handed him an orange plant through the front door when it rested ajar due to heat. Colour was in all the gaps: on all the edges of things, and between the wings of birds and the leaves of the foliage in his daytime and night-time imaginations. It was, of course, all over his bedroom, on the maps of boundaries and separations.

'The World is all about colours if you really look,' he said timidly to his parents that day, shuffling down the corridor, carefully wiping away tears. 'No was right, it's all mingling and changing in colours you know, all the time: the linking and fading colours, the intertwining colours, the kissing colours. You know, when my tree died, it changed through many colours, very quickly.'

'Chrisnelt, help your father with that tree,' said his mother.

Mr Malotika and Chrisnelt sat in the living room surrounded by a loud burst of every colour. 'Can you believe this, a white tree, manufactured of hard plastic so it can stay white all year long? A tree covered in the snows of other continents,' said Mr Malotika with a smile, placing the tree in the corner of the room like an empty basket. 'Remember the faraway snows on your maps, Chrisnelt? Come help me with these Christmas fruits, which might hold Christmas seeds for you.'

'This is our first Christmas with one of these trees, Tata, and now these colours too,' said Chrisnelt, holding up a particularly purple glass ball, with a ring of silver snowflakes that twinkled on the widest part.

'Yes, I think it's time we had one. Just once, anyway. And those are the fruits of knowledge.' Mr Malotika smiled, patting his son gently on the shoulder.

Late-afternoon pinks released by dust came through the glass pane facing onto the street, casting a black profile of the white tree on the evening wall.

'The tip looks like a spear,' said Chrisnelt. 'All it needs is a fresh piece of chicken and a fire.'

'You'll have to wait for your chicken like everyone else, I'm still busy here,' shouted Mrs Malotika in the distance.

'It's more like a prophetic finger,' said Mr Malotika. They began hanging the decorations on the limbs of the tree. Mr Malotika rubbed his wooden wedding band.

Inside the festival of twirling colours, Chrisnelt lay sprawled on the floor, legs and arms twisting. The evening sun stretched bronzy across the ceiling above them and the moon lifted its silver head onto a nearby roof, wobbling

Vernon RL Head

hadedas into song. Clicking bats rustled, as they always did at dusk. Chrisnelt turned a deep orange bauble in his fingers. It reminded him of the many mangoes he'd picked with No. The colours changed.

'The curve of the glass holds light like a butterfly wing, Tata.' He watched orange butterflies dance above and below the snowflakes that patterned the surface, the butterflies becoming smaller and smaller, spinning off the edge of the Earth into clouds of glitter. 'So many came on the day when the first flowers opened. And at night it was the turn of moths.'

Wrapping tinsel around the base of the tree, and threading a cable of tiny lights between branches, Mr Malotika said: 'You know, I spend my life slicing many trees into planks, and you seem to spend yours trying to grow a single one.' He laughed. Then, more seriously: 'Maybe there's hope for the world. Time for a new tree. If there's one thing I know, trees aren't planks. And there are too many fake trees like this one.'

'That's for sure.' Chrisnelt turned the orange decoration again, looking for the butterflies. 'It's all actually a *single* colour, making one beautiful thing, like a flowering weed pushing up through the dust at the back of the house.'

'Africa's like a Christmas tree,' said Mr Malotika, 'all dressed up in dangling fruits, little lights twinkling here and there for the world to see, a steady base packed with gifts for the world to take. In fact, it *is* a Christmas Tree' – the thought becoming even clearer – 'a white, plastic, imported Christmas tree that has replaced a living tree that once burst with the purest green.'

'Well, this looks like a mango to me,' said Chrisnelt,

90

and more butterflies escaped above the line of snow. 'Except for the snowflakes, Tata.'

'And what's the most foreign thing you can think of, Chrisnelt?' said Mr Malotika. 'And you can't say a Coca-Cola can.'

'SNOW. That white place at the top of the world is the furthest from us.'

'Exactly, that's what I mean. How long do you think snow would last on a mango tree in this street?' Mr Malotika pointed at the Christmas tree. 'Behold the white plastic before you. Beware of the white snow as it falls on the trees of Africa,' he said theatrically, with the intrigue of a magician. He looked out the window. His son followed his gaze: high in the deepest of skies, deeper than even the deepest ocean on any map, an international jetliner cut a line of white ice on the pacific heavens. 'That's a golden thread for some people far away,' said Mr Malotika.

'Girls, dinner is nearly ready,' shouted Mrs Malotika, summoning Nipcia and Divi from their homework in their room. 'Hurry up, these tree-men are getting hungry with all the tinsel-talk and bauble-things.'

Chrisnelt was still holding the mango-bauble. He hung it in the tree, and it swayed in a trillion butterfly wings. 'I think of No so much, Tata. I think of his tree and how it'll grow for us one day. I've looked at all the maps and I've read all the books, looking for a way. You know that on every single map, it's always green at the edges of rivers? So many trees.'

'I've told you before about the Matombos and their tribe up the River, in the heart of the forest, the tribe that speaks to the trees when the wind blows through the leaves. I've told you why I thought No loved birds and that mango tree. But I've never told you why his parents came to the City,' said Mr Malotika, pressing a white switch in his hand. The tree became dancing stars in between baubles of butterflies of every colour dodging snow. 'You see these lights? That's why they came.'

'They came for Christmas?' asked Chrisnelt.

'They weren't even Christians in my book!' shouted Mrs Malotika. 'They never came to any of Pastor's rallies, and they never had a proper damn funeral for the boy.' Her great girth rubbed against a protruding chicken leg that was turning white in the steam. Nipcia and Divi nodded beside her.

'No, they came for the light,' said Mr Malotika.

'For these little lights?' asked Chrisnelt.

'For the lights of the City. For the powerful lights screaming out across this whole bloody place. That's what for. Just like everyone else here. Lights that give an illusion of an education, under their song of bells and steeples and choirs. That's what for.' He switched the lights off, little wraith fires reflecting in his eyes. Then he switched them on again, and some sort of twinkle mechanism made them flicker very fast, like hopes.

Mr Malotika went to the drawer next to his chair and came back with a letter in an envelope: 'I wasn't going to give this to you now, but it's yours to keep. It's from his funeral day.'

Chrisnelt opened it and read, breath and mind hopping erratically from sentence to sentence: '... *and so we are taking a piece of charcoal back to the Forest ... to the new leaves and warm soils ... the coming of cleansing waters from the River ...'*

'You know, Chrisnelt, if you want to see a real tree of truth, the biggest in the City, I should take you to the one at its heart. At the rising place, where all the streets meet all the boulevards in the very middle, where once, long ago, a small clearing held the huts of a village that made its own rain and sunshine. That Christmas tree has lived there for almost one hundred years now. It stands very quietly, only telling the truth at Christmas-time. I call it Africa's Tree. My own father told me that the city officials back then, the elders from many places and tribes, had met before his birth – in a time of bizarre blizzards, when things were decreed by white people – to plan the careful planting. You see *that* one, and it'll help you grow your tree.' He rubbed his wedding band.

CHAPTER FIVE

BEFORE, CHRISNELT HAD NOT known anything about special trees, or the history of trees. About the arrival of foreign trees; the disappearance of local trees; the commonness or rareness of trees; the trade in the trees of tradition; the movement of caged trees with chains; the way trees made spaces in forests of legend; or the way absent trees made bleeding holes in the history of every land. From the many maps and books and the counting of birds – which required a patient way of seeing – and from experimenting with plants, their collecting and their watering, had come a powerful connection with the image of a tree. Once, when he put his face close to the picture of South America, he thought he could smell the rain-forest leaves and the great river brushing up against roots, and the same happened when he put his face to Africa. He was inseparable from anything to do with trees and their roots looking for water. And he arrived at a knowledge of trees purposefully, with a vision involving vast forests and the music they made with their rivers.

Yet in all the deliberateness, there was a strange process of osmosis that occurred in his huge watery eyes and at the tips of his wet, wiggling fingers. It was not knowledge that a ten-year-old – however gifted – could have hoped to gain from formal education, through reading or even by trial and error. And it made him unusual, unlocking green times, black times and white times in his mind. All was new and foreign, like snow falling slowly on the widest tropical leaves. All was fertile.

The day after Christmas was as it always is: quiet, lazy, and a bit uncomfortable around the swollen stomach area. There is only so much chicken a growing boy can eat, even when given the wings, which were his favourite parts.

'This is a home of abandoning acolytes!' shouted Mrs Malotika. 'None of you've come to church with me, none of you, not even once. And it's Christmas! Pastor did not expect you' – she stared at Mr Malotika – 'or you' – she stared at Chrisnelt – 'but even *you*' – she stared at her daughters – 'didn't come, and he was giving away new hats for the heat. It's all this damn tree talk. Pastor is right about you, the abandoning acolytes of this City.' (Mr Malotika always said to his children: 'Mama's Faith is to be admired like any achievement'; and, 'It is what it is.' And that was the end of that.)

Chrisnelt had begun to water his garden furiously, anticipating the visit to 'Africa's Tree'. In many ways, the thought of it was his best Christmas gift ever, even better than the sparrow skeleton in cotton wool No had once given him, saying: 'After it died the ants came and planted its body in the sand, leaving this memory for you on Christmas.' When they'd shown it to Mr Malotika, he'd said: 'If you took all the leaves and fruit off that mango tree of yours, it would look just like this. Every living thing leaves a skeleton behind, even rain with its patterns in the hard mud.'

'Gardens only come after houses have hearts,' said Mr

Malotika that dawn before he went to piss and whistle, his private custom before heading up the street to the lumberyard and his other work obligations beyond. Reaching for the wooden handle, stepping onto the veranda, his lunch bag of croissants in one hand, he added, '… just like footprints only come after people. That's the way of our world, Chrisnelt.'

Chrisnelt lay in the living room, reading thoughts about footprints and gardens in one of his many notebooks piled high above bibles and other such volumes – which had begun to accumulate again, as books do. The pages of that particular notebook were awash with numbers and words meandering like lost clouds. It was from his first weeks of gardening, and was filled with sketches resting next to geometric formulae, and poems interpreting predictions, and diagrams of the shapes cut by rivers into the earth. It contained family songs and stanzas sprouted by the boy, and drawings describing the mathematical way veins spread in leaves, miraculous journeys revealed only when held up to the sun.

He'd been lying there reading and watching his mother cook special things for New Year's Eve, which was still a few days away; he was thinking of his father, and when he would be home, so they could plan the trip to Africa's Tree. 'Glowing coals make food and family-time,' he said inside the pages of the notebook, the crisp paper edges tickling his face, plucked chicken feathers floating about in white wisps. 'Walls hold things separate, but glowing coals make homes in the City. Coals are my happy memories: many little fires and firesides. Black, then burning, coals emerge, and then there will always be ash, and stillness, waiting for that white dust to end it all at daytime,' he concluded, his youthful fingers working the page, his other pen clicking in his free hand.

'When do you think Tata will be home, Mama?' he said, watching the coals and Mrs Malotika at her cooking stove. Now he was drawing giant Christmas trees, forests of them filled with birds. The fire played, the kitchen walls rippled red and orange. The smell of smoke danced with the smell of family. The living room became warm, then hot. The red light deepened the heat until sweat came. Nipcia and Divi shouted at each other – something to do with homework and the heat. It had been some time, a long time, longer than ever before. Shadows entered the kitchen, then left, leaping into the shapes of roosting birds. The many crows settled, taking black onto the rattling roofs. The many sparrows settled too. An owl howled. Bats scratched on the metal corrugations.

'He's gone to a meeting at Pastor Kadazi's house to sort out an order of charcoal,' said Mrs Malotika.

Chrisnelt lay there in the living room – rolled in a ball on his father's chair – in the cavern of that night, every sound foreign, and through the deeper craters of the following day sounds becoming more foreign, screaming inside his tumbling head. He would not be moved, not even when Nipcia said, 'I have to dust here, you know I have to always dust here, idiot. And it's hot, so hurry up. Tata is often late.'

Not even when Mrs Malotika said: 'I'll go and see down at the lumberyard, sometimes he's got to go up the River suddenly, and it's that crazy time, and with all this heat. And I'll also go and speak to Mr Warnakulasuriya.'

The next day, Chrisnelt ran out and up the street to sit on the mango-tree stump that was starting to grow smooth from memories. He sat in silence like a stone. He sat there under the dust, in the morning haze from the River. He sat there in the heavy stickiness of midday, when birds only flew if they had to. And he sat there in the flailing light that began to turn in bell-like tones, smelling like fires that never ended. He swayed there for hours, before plummeting down a hole of dread that made his ears ring, and he felt the stump shake below his arse. This was the horror that comes with despair; this was the pit of terror. He was alone. He shat his pants, and the shit ran hot down his leg and between his toes.

'Chrisnelt, come back home,' shouted Mrs Malotika, clutching a torch as she searched for him, not really knowing what to do, the street light flashing on and off and confusing her sense of depth. He kept appearing and disappearing. 'You can't just sit there looking like an upside-down bat. You're making the girls cry more than I can manage right now. Come home.' Behind her, the two eyes of Pastor's white Mercedes-Benz burned for her as he arrived, sending Chrisnelt's shadow shooting away from reality and hope.

He raised himself like a rooster on the stump, extending his arms and fiddling his fingers, finally letting out a scream into the night. Perched on the very edge of things, disappearing into darkness that shattered every day he would ever know, he wept. The wailing that followed folded the entire street down onto his lungs, the tremendous pressure of the pain so heavy he fainted, tumbling off the stump.

He did not awaken until the cold hands of Pastor Kadazi resurrected him with life-giving waters previously used on his mother and sisters, who had also wailed. These waters were held in a tin bathtub brought into the street by Mr Nagasaki and Mr MacDonald; Mr Mohamed stood filling and refilling a plastic Coca-Cola bottle from the bath, with gurglings and bubblings, and handing it to Pastor Kadazi.

The Pastor poured the sparkling liquid, chanting: 'Chrisnelt, wake up. Come back. These are the waters of the River, and they are blessed to wash away the Evil. Come back to your mother and to the street. This street has claimed too much pain. Come back.'

'Come back,' said Mr Mukendi from behind.

'Come back with these waters,' said Mr Mohamed.

'Come back,' said Mr Nagasaki.

'The Waters.'

'Come back.'

'Lordoo, Lordoo,' said Mrs Malotika. And together they lifted him, carrying him aloft on shoulders and heads, down the street – Pastor Kadazi at the front of the procession, muttering many languages behind his plumed hat – back into the house and onto his mat, water flooding the linoleum floor, the wide puddle spreading before disappearing into the cracks.

Some said he had gone up the River to the Forest. Some said he had gone down to the sea far away, across all the steaming cataracts and cliffs and out to the flat sheets of water that lived beyond the bluest waves and whitest foam. Some said he was at the bottom of the River at its darkest depths, tossed like a doll that had outlasted itself. During all of the talk in the street, within its walls that seemed to bend with questions, the Malotika house stayed low, lower than it had ever been. The roof sank in the heat, a pitched tent of corrugations filled with despair. The older palm fronds shook with tears; the newer fronds buzzed like flies, especially when crows sat there in their hordes, eating bits of decaying meat. The house leaked strange smells of sadness in those hot days and nights; each day, matting was hung on the veranda to dry, dripping piss.

Mrs Malotika sat next to her son, wiping his face, shooing flies, the tin bath of soiled water next to her. As was her hope. Chrisnelt had slept for two days and two nights; never had she seen such shaking of his delicate body. Nipcia and Divi had been taken to the Mukendis' home so she could care for Chrisnelt properly. He did not eat. He only drank, occasionally, staring at the water as it shattered the image of his face in the cup. He was too weak to be moved, his screaming too loud to be controlled. Mrs Malotika remained there, holding him, all that time. His ribs were extended and his fingers gripped her dress. He cried into her fat thigh, and said: 'Where does all the blood go after leaving the land, Mama? Will it go to the sea? What if it never rains again? No healing of the world. No cleaning of the blood.'

'There is no talk of blood now, child, you are not talking sense,' she said softly. 'No talk please.' And she too continued to cry in her own way: 'Oh Lordoo.'

Chrisnelt looked up at his mother, her wide nostrils dripping, her cheeks shining. Her blue lower lip quivered as she patted him all over.

'Tata said time' – he cried again – 'falls from the sun and the moon onto the back of clouds, carried in a billion, trillion raindrop clocks that never stop ticking; and that tomorrow's happiness runs to the ground in water from the clouds, before mixing into the drains. The power of water controls everything. Mama, we must find it before it finds the sea. It has his blood. Maybe he is floating somewhere waiting for us, and he is together with No!' Surprising her, he sat up, breathing out sharply.

'He is gone, Chrisnelt, and we don't know more. That is the way of all of this. It must just be that he is gone,' she said slowly, rocking his body against hers. They sobbed together. 'Pastor will come in the morning, Chrisnelt; and he will tell us what to do. You should sleep some more, my child.'

'If he's with No, he's with a tree. Then he will be with my tree and the waters it needs.'

'Still.'

'I can't be still, not tonight, not ever.'

'Still.'

He looked down the corridor, where the white limbs of the Christmas tree fizzed; the tiny lights went on and off and on and off, flashing like a fleet of scattered ambulances.

Dawn was sudden, like the inevitable wave that finds every ancient bay; or perhaps it came like the river current, rushing to a coast of sins. It rustled with the sound of distant birds, calling deep in the darkness that comes before the future. Chrisnelt had been awake all night, writing a poem.

He usually wrote poems about his surroundings. His mind

unwrapped every part of the family house for inspiration, the poems extolling loudly like treasures that could talk, gleaned from simple things: brown walls that stroked the air, open doors that sang, wooden roof-beams that yawned, the fire-shine that would hide until dawn, the black cooking-pot of chickens that cried, the dark grey-green charcoal that coughed and its lazy dust that got lost, the sounds of his sisters arguing about homework, a golden leaf that blew in on the breeze from a distant place of pilgrims, all brittle and cracked. His poems were deep: deep like the River in his father's stories, which he would dream about forever. Deep like the roots of great, green forest trees. Deep like his special gaze – sometimes he did not blink for hours, his thoughts holding poems up to his gaze, fixing answers and images of pure brilliance. Chrisnelt had discovered poems without knowing what poems were. They arrived instinctively: revelations held in groups of ideas, that in turn held hands in phrases and winding sentences; these poems flowed in tides and waterfalls, they fell cavorting from his fingers in mighty rains. Sometimes a poem would be written in three languages, hopping about the page, like a map of the entire world without borders. And in every poem was the word No.

Now – for the first time – he wrote a poem solely for his father, and he would take it to Africa's Tree, the living light in the darkness of the City.

CHAPTER SIX

CHRISNELT FOLLOWED THE MOVEMENT of people down his street. It was that strange moment before dawn when yellow window-light and orange fire-light waits for the sleeping sun on the wings of resting flies. No birds called yet in that sky. The distant River trees still held the birds in a special agreement made of quietness and night; he knew this from his father's stories. Many people squashed him in the throng.

'Going to work in the deepest dark is the same as working in the deepest dark. That's the work that's poisoned Africa. That's foreign work,' Mr Malotika had always said, waiting for the day. Chrisnelt walked in silence, disturbing his thoughts with rapid blinks. Wednesdays always held the sweet smell of bread under the mist. On this Wednesday it only held mist. He wiggled, much in the way a little fish might, as it follows the flow of a stream, hoping to find a quiet pond. And his tears fell like raindrops onto the dust.

He was alone among the busyness of the ants that early morning; and he was as small as an ant, having turned ten, heading quickly to eleven. His head bobbed big and round on a thin neck. He was smaller than everyone his age, yet his head had become bigger; his legs and arms hung thin, shining waxy in the night. All of him was indeed ant-like. His big eyes ached, especially when thinking moments came, and they came all the time.

The year was a few days from ending, and much was ending; much had changed. He'd written a poem two hundred thousand and three words long, ending with the word 'change'. He had just completed it that very night. He'd had to use twelve pens and his fingers were swollen and red, one finger bleeding at the edge of a damaged nail, the cuticle inflamed, the nail chewed unusually: chipped into tiny facets, as one would whittle a piece of wood. A new pen rested now in the miasmic warmth behind his ear. The poem – a roll of paper wedged into the waistband of his brown cotton pants – bent and crackled as he walked, his little feet making the sand squeak. Dryness lingered, except for that which was mist.

The crack
The split
The gap
The life
There is no street without walls
The praying hands
The preying hands
There is no street without walls
The lines of leaves in a rhythm of trees
The row of shadows that breathe
The lines of leaves in the dream of trees
The route for roots
The rush

He chanted lines of the poem softly to the rhythm of his steps. It changed from poem to song and then to poem again; such is the mind when walking. His lungs sagged in his chest, heavy with melancholy. He swallowed repeatedly. His ribs hurt, bruised from days of stillness on his sleeping mat. He knew this poem by heart. He knew all his many hundreds of poems by heart; some were made of lines of numbers that rained like storms in his changing mind. His head thumped, pushing sweat out of his skin. His eyes thumped, pushing memories. And in all of this, he continued forward in earnest, deep within the shadows that always followed him. Deep like the deepest river on Earth. He was in a hurry to be in the centre of the City.

Chrisnelt rounded the corner of Dee Dee Street, and smelt it, just for an instant: water. Mud rippled – a tap had been left on in the street overnight, fighting with the dust, changing its dance, reminding itself of its past – and a strong smell pushed ripples of stench across the roofs. There was no camaraderie under the corrugations that lay upon the City before him. Nobody seemed to care about where water came from or where it would go. The mist wrestled with the wet street. The tap hissed like a snake, the pipe protruding from a high wall shuddering, rachitically deformed into a twisted curve. He turned it off and walked onward. *Water in pipes should only be used when really needed. When water is in pipes, it's borrowed; when it's released it's returned to a journey.* He recited the lesson silently, thinking of all the oceans his father had placed in his head. He could not stop himself from thinking of his father constantly: all the words he used, his demeanour, his odour, his ceremonial ways. 'Where does a stain of blood go on the land when it rains?' he said to himself.

He was determined – more determined than he'd ever been in all his years of life; he walked with big, new steps, the steps of a boy wanting to hasten his way to the place of men. To Africa's Tree.

'Perhaps I'll get a big seed from its lowest branches. I *will* grow my tree, that's for sure,' he said aloud, stamping his feet in a patch of sand: dust puffed like a little cloud.

On the opposite side of the street, he could see his mother through the glass front doors of Café Gourmandine, framed like a painting; she had left for work very early, unable to sleep, and also due to the traditional demands of the season. Chrisnelt had watched her get dressed. She'd been singing a hymn softly, the way people sing when they're thinking sad things. She had not seen him sitting in the dark with his pen and his many papers, or known of his pending departure into the night. She could not see him now.

Mrs Malotika, wrapped in a pure white apron, was leaning over a long table, beating flour in an incantatory rhythm, her big wooden spoon thudding dully. Next to her, Mrs Savi Koubaka (one of the many givers-of-books), in similar attire, clutched an urn of something, pouring salt like rain, and other people carried trays of things, and pots of other things. All that was white shone golden as they made croissants, baguettes, bagels and doughnuts under an African glow. Chrisnelt marvelled at the strength of his mother, at her quietness as she worked, her resilience, her purposeful posture, twisting the way a winged sculpture might twist from stillness into life. The scent of bread so strong, it held the boy in a comforting kind of heat, just for a moment. He thought of the black pot at home: the glowing coals, the smoke and the family songs above the soot. He could see his father becoming a Christmas tree.

'Chaminda will show it to me. He knows the centre of the City.'

The earth squeaked again as he walked away from his mother. He turned another corner. The street, widening now, was packed even more tightly: more ants, with occasional trucks and slow cars in the shadows, reminiscent of the rattling beetles in dreams. New shadows searched for the deeper dark of side streets, and the blackness reached for him too, and for his tears. The narrow dirt lanes reminded him of his home street, peopled with sleeping mounds that heaved under matting or corrugated-iron sheeting; some mounds as small as dogs, some even the size of chickens. He became very scared – this was a new part of the City. He had never been this far before, not even with Chaminda, not even when they looked for weeds together. He peered down a particularly dark street and said: 'He said his house was this way. I must just find the hill, and keep counting the streets.' The poem crackled in his shorts. He recited line after line.

The street lights were high now, in a wider street rising from pavements of stones set in ancient river-sand. Each light grasped the mist, so that its connection with the pole was uncertain in the haze: a sky necklace, linked by power lines. From the cables hung pendulous bats, with abandoned red-white-and-green tassels of celebration fluttering in between. It was a mixed street of houses, shops and stalls of varying heights, none more than a storey tall. They formed long walls on either side, funnelling the mist like water in a pipe, and showing him his path forward.

Below the necklace of lights, the houses coughed the smoke of breakfast fires. Shops fought with the dark loneliness of night. Stalls framed vacant space, carving skeletons in blackness. Chrisnelt did not enjoy this time of no birds. Instead of mist he wished for raindrops to help him think as he walked; he would have wanted to count them, to share with them his memories, his considerations, and he would have wished to then share his tears with the drains. But there would be no rain for him now. Two tears fell, one from each eye. He closed his eyes. He could see No, alone like a tree in a desert of pebbles. He could see his father, alone: a tree in a field of ice. Just then, a single bat flittered across a hole in the mist, playing with the stars under its wings. He walked on, looking for Chaminda.

The mist was persistent, steadying the world of the City. It was not ordinary mist, such as holds ordinary cities. This was his River Mist, alive every day at this time; water waiting to claim the land where it once sifted leaves and carried rocks, in the time of wild green, the time of forest. The mist clasped the City tight in exorcism each day before dawn, searching between all the dead wood and dead walls, in the corrugations that lay silent as carrion in the night.

Chrisnelt opened his mouth wide. He stuck out his tongue, splayed his fingers and extended his arms to collect the mist. He ran, faster and faster still, as fast as he had ever run. 'I'm coming!' he shouted up to the emptiness. 'I can see you. I can see my new and special seed ahead.' His skin shone brown and blue and black, flickering silver here and there.

He knew the hot mist of the City. It had always been intimate with him. It sat on things, like when a friend sits just looking at you, smiling. He'd come to understand it. No had often spoken to the mist. 'Come inside, Mist, there is space on the mat. Tell us about the River,' he said one night as they lay together in his room, letting the mist in with a big smile. Chrisnelt had been scared of the mist then, but No had made him feel safe. In truth, he did not love it like he loved the liberation of rain. Yet the smell and touch of the mist – that Mist – had always brought him the image of the River, every dawn of his life. In recent times, the mist would come in through his always-open door, into his room of maps and books, delivering scents from his private garden: The Bedroom of the World, the Garden of the Rock, the Mist of the River, together. 'That's a *real* prayer-group,' he shouted as he ran on. The running seemed to stop the crying. 'The rock will be at its shining, black best now. And my plants will drink for sure.'

The mist was an emissary hinting of distant change, an apparition of wild waters – the tides of the coast, the vast currents of the oceans; searching for an endless, pristine world that did not know the obligations of a continent. At the end of the gush of it all there might indeed be a seed, some sort of chance for hope. A seed for No.

'I'm coming, Chaminda!' he shouted, disappearing into a hollow of thicker, wetter mist.

Chrisnelt was not accustomed to walking on cobbled stones, their shining coldness biting his heels in the dark like rats; but he continued onward. 'This is the twelfth street now, I should turn left. I can feel the hill coming in front. It can't be too far. He said it was after the twelfth.'

Africa to North America sways in new captives
The drumming fingers

Are like wooden oars
Paddling the rains on a blotting sea,
Stretching blurred paper messages on a river of other
people's ink.

He ran and he chanted, and he could see the great
Christmas tree rising in brilliant green, at the back of his
mind and the very front of his dreams. There in the middle
of the City.

The mist cooled him. It cooled his pain and allowed for
clarity, showering him with gifts like seeds opening, damp
and fresh.

The knitting of seeds into beads and wild birdsong
Before a tide of waves on a sky of lost oceans ...

He chanted more lines of his long poem, a poem made
of other poems, many of which his father had helped
him write. And he stopped. He stood, toes gripping the
cobbles, the pace of his heart never more present in his
ears. 'Trees!' he cried. 'A line of trees, and so high! So alive
and free!'

In Chrisnelt's part of the city – his street, and the street
next to that – the only vestiges of green had been the
mango tree; a row of low bushes, which No used to crawl
under when talking to sparrows in the heat; and a glimpse
of the distant edge of the River, that one time. Other than
that, it was a landscape of corrugated-iron houses, walls
and ditches. It was a sad fact that the only majestic trees
Chrisnelt had ever seen – except perhaps, temporarily, the
tree of his garden – belonged to books, maps and midnight

dreams. In his sleep, he rose into those highest treetops, sleeping on giant golden leaves warmed by the sun and the moon; the branches scooping him up to the beat of drums that hung as seedpods from every twig. The leaves and the nesting birds would help him catch raindrops before they turned to snow and ice. He'd slept there almost every night, often next to No's shadow, rocked by the mist.

But now here were real trees. Free trees. He could barely make them out: a row of thick stems, so dense they seemed to come together as a primordial thing, lining the edge of a canal. The upper parts swayed gently above the water on its way to the River. The bottom parts seemed clearer, firm and still. 'Wild trees!' he said loudly. 'In water!' The trees were so high they held mist and clouds of egrets, cormorants and herons in dark magnificence near the top. He could hear more than see them, the birds beginning to squawk, unsettled before sunrise. There was no green yet, only a blackness flickering in six-billion-seven-hundred-and-twenty-two-thousand-nine-hundred-and-twelve-and-a-half dots of life – he counted the leaves aloud with his eyes closed. They were alive to his arrival. The topmost dots ululated in unison with the mist and the birds, anticipating the ecstatic new colours that would come with the sun.

If this had been any other moment in his life, any other day, he would've stayed. He longed to stay, to live right there forever. He would climb up for seeds, to show No how brave he'd become; dig down for seeds, to display his new strength and determination. Then maybe he would dive in and follow the stream all the way to the River and the Forest: swimming and searching and diving, singing and chanting his poem. Down to where roots made up the bottom of the stream and the reeds sang with frogs. 'I can't be too far from the edge of the City,' he said. 'I can smell the freshness …'

But he was scared. The idea of an edge, of a possible beginning, was more than he could handle alone. He was pulled in many directions, wanting to snap into bits.

'I CAN'T STAY,' he said very loudly. 'Chaminda, I'm coming! I'm coming, Tata and No!'

He turned back onto the street of cobbles, under the necklace of lights. After some time, he found a side-street with no name. This was the street he'd been told about, familiar on the map inside his mind: 'Rue de Rue,' he said. 'Chaminda says that's your name, and you become a stream in the rains, don't you?' From there, he found a path that led him to a smaller track between fences. At the end was a gate.

He opened it slowly, then climbed a metallic hill of crushed Coca-Cola cans (and every other type of can imaginable), flattened by time. Silver scales, like an immense shoal of tiny fish in the moonlight, covered the ground; plastic packets rustled, making bushes of translucent shadows shake in the language of jellyfish. The legs of a blue plastic chair stuck out of the silver like the legs of a dead hippopotamus. The ancient antennae of rusted radios and television sets – machines he'd never been allowed to engage with, on the strict instruction of his father, who regarded them as temperamental mouthpieces for others, filled with the demons of sovereignty – wiggled in a unison of reeds next to a gleaming bog. The gentle slope sparkled in fecund steel and plastic and the stolen past; the used and the useless. It was the City Dump.

At the top of the hill was a small, low house made of wooden boards. The house rocked under the stars as a well-captained boat might do in a river current. A flag fluttered on the tip of a long branch that extended above the ridge line of the roof like the sail of a yawl.

The house glowed in those early hours before sunrise: the deadest and most alive time of his life. Lit windows greeted him as he approached, offering bright eyes. Even the front door was a window: a modified car door, green glass glowing, surrounded by a polished-green frame, green hinges and a curly green handle. Either side of the front door, the walls scattered windows of every size, some high and thin, some wide and low, some fitted at strange angles.

'Twelve windows and a door,' said Chrisnelt – he could not help counting. It looked like each window had been found on the hill of silver over much time; each told a story of a different house or strange structure somewhere else, of the importance of the powerful apertures in walls, of their resilience, of their reincarnation and their need to give light. Shimmering in the light of a breakfast fire within, the beauty of the many windows was inescapable, their shapes strangely comforting, even with the dread he carried. 'They are like glass baubles from a Christmas tree,' he said. One car window had a white frame and a white rubber gasket holding deep, blue glass, so that a blue beam burst from it like a waterfall; one frame was of wood, painted gold, with filigree textures, the glass tinted so that an orange shaft leapt from it in a pirouette. One window was a conglomeration of little windows, each pane a different colour, a precious stone edged in lead, each a scene from a distant place. This window was pointed at the top, as if two hands had come together, holding stars in the curve of warm palms.

'*Nellie*' was scratched freshly into the front door, hand-written in cursive currents with a knife. It would be re-scratched every year, once rust came for it, and on that morning it had been given new life. The shining name was that of Chaminda's dead wife, tragically killed by tentacles while bathing in a beautiful bay at the edge of their island far away, sending him to Africa forever, and to the freshness of foreign trees.

'Chrisnelt, what the hell you doing here?' shouted Chaminda from the distance of the kitchen, dropping a plate of carrots. A pot of Sri Lankan tea spluttered somewhere in that kitchen – a place sometimes called the lounge, and regularly called the bedroom, after long days on the road. 'The day is still considering itself, still only waking and stretching. And you're appearing here like a ghost? You frightened the hell out of me!' He reached for the tea, offering a cup to the boy.

'No thank you, Chami.'

'Come in. Come in quickly from that dark mist. What's your father going to say, hey?'

'He's gone. Dead. Mama thinks he went up the River days ago, and he doesn't ever miss the Christmastime, and now he has missed it,' said Chrisnelt softly. 'That's what Mama says.' The tears held the light.

Chaminda put his arms around him tightly for some time. Chrisnelt shook like a little earthquake.

'Take me to the centre of the City. I have to go, and

I don't know how to get there,' he said, eyes tight with tension, long arms hanging at his sides. He hovered in the doorway, his front aglow like a Christmas decoration, his back still in darkness and the memory of river-trees.

'Chrisnelt, I can't. I must prepare for work: a long journey for a big order of charcoal. You know this time of year. I'll get fired, boy. We go in a few days, when I'm back? When you are stronger? What's this all about?'

'Please,' he begged.

'I'll get fired.'

'I'm dying in my head.'

'I was almost fired last week. It was only your father who saved me from that damn Pastor.'

'Going there was Tata's gift to me.'

'Chrisnelt.'

'He gave it to me in a promise.'

'I'll get fired, or worse. That man has a temper.'

'Chami. It's all I have, the sight of it. The branches. The great height. The memory of Tata. He said it will help me forever.'

'Sit, eat some fish first, it's *ngolo*, and take some *fufu*, and then I'll think.'

'Please.' Chrisnelt cried like he had never cried. He collapsed on the floor, rolling into a ball of helplessness.

'We go after you eat,' said Chaminda, on the floor now, holding the boy tightly. And he slowly wiped the tears. Tears came to him too.

'This is all so hard, Chami.'

'It'll be alright in the end. Your father was a wise man. I know it's *that* tree you must see, and its powerful beauty. It's the heart of this City in so many ways,' said Chaminda.

They sat up carefully, together, and moved to the dining table as one. Chaminda wiped away more tears, and sat opposite Chrisnelt in the pose of a Buddha. He knew it was not a time to talk: his young friend would do all the talking, if required. Chrisnelt began to shiver. Chaminda knew the shaking and rubbing of hands was a sign of distress, and he did not want to add to it.

Chaminda knew the world Chrisnelt lived in: a place of greater dimensions than he could ever understand. He'd never met anyone who burned inside like this boy burned. He'd come to know this after much time spent with him in his emerging garden, at the beginnings of that doomed little tree. He was prepared to grant a request now, especially as it came from Mr Malotika, and especially as it was clearly of huge importance to the world. He was sure of that much. He appreciated rareness in the world, and this boy had rareness: it flicked in bits of heat from the child-man-eyes in front of him. They'd always been child-man-eyes. Significant eyes. Always, since that very first day he saw him in his pain.

There was a long stillness. From the back doorway – draped with old shower curtains, tied with naval rope below drooping flags from cargo ships that represented ports and harbours across the oceans – they looked onto a part of the rubbish dump previously hidden from view. It was a living hill because it would always grow: during the day it grew loudly; during the night it grew surreptitiously; during the droughts it grew in great clouds of dust; during the rains it grew involuntarily; during the time of sickness it grew to the sound of wails; during the time of health – a time of plenty that had lasted a decade – it grew with profound excess, like a brash shirt is layered with a white silk suit dripping in gold chains.

Chrisnelt's legs had stopped shaking. His chin had stopped dribbling liquid. He no longer felt alone. He began to eat. He had to – he had not eaten properly for many days. Chewing violently, as if for survival, and taking deep breaths between bites. Tears still hung in his eyes, but cheeks that had ached from crying now ached from chewing. He sniffed deeply. 'I can smell vegetables. I can smell them living out there at the back.'

'That's my private vegetable farm in all its glory,' said Chaminda. 'It's an important place to me, like your garden's been to you. No trees, though.'

'Tata said that a farm isn't ever a garden, only a factory of green conveyor-belts making food. Like a factory making Coca-Cola in cans.' He ate and thought of carrots, of vegetables – anything except the face of his father. 'If I plant vegetables in my garden, they'll become *plants*, not just vegetables anymore. That's the power of a garden.' The face of his father came to him right there and then; his father pointing to gardens in books in the mists of his mind. He could see the pointing, the turning of laughing pages, and the endless gardens with trees that soared. 'I will *not* forget him. That's why I must go to the centre of the City.' He ate and he cried.

Chaminda chopped carrots and then he chopped some onions, as he always did before the day began. He could not take Chrisnelt anywhere in the dark until he had chopped his vegetables. Besides, he needed to feed this weak boy, whose eyes sagged so tragically, the cheeks below glistening purple in crescent moons. 'The mist from these always cleans my eyes before dawn,' he said, slicing the biggest, whitest onion. 'All the way from Asia originally, but living here in Africa now. Not so happily.'

'You've made a green island hidden on a hill of muck,' said Chrisnelt, finishing his plate of food, licking his tears.

'It does remind me of my island back home. It's like a monument in that way.'

'A monument?'

'Yes.'

'Like a statue?'

'More like a living reminder. Your father helped me plant these vegetables, you know. Those are his green rows in the sand, Chrisnelt. And they're now little living walls in this bloody City. He said there was nowhere better to plant things than right here, on this dump of waste. It's the highest place in the entire City now. It's my mountain.'

'Tata helped you like he helped me with my garden. With all his words and ways. This City is the flattest place in the world, that's what he said to me, except for the great Christmas Tree, which lives higher than anything.' More tears wanted to come, but they did not.

'We go, Chrisnelt?'

The night stayed with them a little longer, clinging to limbs and the other moving edges of the City. The mist had gone. Heat was coming back up from below, as if the ground had stored it through the tropical night.

'Yes please.' Chrisnelt blinked, the poem crackling as he rose. The vegetables reached over the hill in long, green lines.

'Stay close to me. This is a dangerous place,' said Chaminda.

Chrisnelt followed down the hill. Under their feet, the hollow sound of cans sliding into the dust. Plastic bags clapped like coughing lungs. And above, bats adjusted the sky, mirroring the ground, a faint hue of orange tingeing everything in the firmament.

'First, I have to take you to the Great Dancing Road, Chrisnelt.'

'The River?'

'Yes.'

'The real River?'

'Yes, the big one.'

'Tata always called it that – the Great Dancing Road.'

'I learned it from him. We go there? It's only great roads that'll take you to the real centre of the City. This is going to be a long walk, but he would have taken you there first.'

'Okay, Chami.'

'One day you'll grow that tree of yours, Chrisnelt. I know it in my soul. But when you see the middle of the City, you must also know from where the City once came. Its edge. Your father spoke of it a great deal. All trees have a history.'

'Okay.'

'Stay close to me.'

No speaking, that is what defined the walking. Much breathing, that is what followed. A strange owl called – new for Chrisnelt's bird list. The list never slept. It was like the dreams of trees, sheltering the memories of birds. Chrisnelt chanted his poem again, this time inside himself. He added the owl, inside himself too.

It took more than two hours, the boy silent at

Chaminda's side, dangling like a limb. It was a very tiring walk for a small boy. The same owl called, as did a rooster. The sound of Chaminda's big steps slipped here and there. Desperate men surrounded them: dead-end men who started work in the pitch dark, filling the streets with a litany of sad destinations, pathetic as vomit on kerbs next to taverns, because the City only took, never giving. The mist, having thickened earlier, left relics of slime now, a smear that would soon dry. The people everywhere struggled forward. The City was sick, and only pure heat each day could make it rise. The stink was its wake-up call.

Chrisnelt struggled to keep up. He would not give up. He made his biggest steps, almost leaps. They walked on, along thin streets and then thick ones, always slowly, downwards, following the tumbling stains of mist. Chrisnelt stared ahead, his lips moving constantly, mouthing the words of his poem to the back of Chaminda's head, as if each stanza held his father's breath, giving direction like a friendly old map.

'What's it about this time before daylight that pulls us, Chami? What's it? The sky's holding something.'

'You're becoming eleven, and you mustn't stop asking these questions. Your father would want you to never stop,' said Chaminda sternly. 'It's like the instant before you light a candle, Chrisnelt. When that match is fire between your fingers, the warmth sparks your young mind to think about what you're about to see. Even though you know your bedroom, even though you know what was there when you went to bed the night before.'

Much was dark up ahead. Chaminda was taking the

boy to the outermost extremity of the City before taking him to its heart.

'Wait a minute Chami, I need to catch my breath,' said Chrisnelt, embarrassed. He simply could not keep up. They rested, not speaking for some time. 'Okay, we can go.'

They continued for a long while. Chaminda walked more slowly, Chrisnelt leaping from step to step, more determined than ever.

They heard the drums. Chrisnelt heard them first, and they came to him as deep church bells. Chaminda heard different, mutating sounds: an ancient scream, a call strangely muffled in resounding hollowness: pathetic echoes from deep in the past. Chrisnelt did not know real drums, only bells. Chaminda could see it in his eyes.

'That's the sound of drums near the edge,' said Chaminda. Beyond the calling drums whispered a vastness of water. 'Do you hear the River coming? Look.'

Chrisnelt looked like he had never looked before. Above them stood black trees, similar to the trees that had aroused his hopes earlier that morning. Within the tumult of their leaves glittered pieces of the River on the clicking backs of frogs.

Chaminda stooped, pushing steadily down a bank of filth through the heavy, dark undergrowth, parting bushes for the boy, flushing a scurry of American cockroaches, and cosmopolitan larder beetles and smooth woodlice from Europe. He came out onto a flat stretch of mud that defined the end of the City. He reached back up to guide Chrisnelt toward him, but the boy fell and rolled. He shrieked in pain, and a puff of mosquitoes rose – the

musical ones with black-and-white stripes on their legs –
in a tiny cloud above his head.

'You okay?'

'This is very slippery in the darkness,' said Chrisnelt,
wiping the mud off his hands, onto his shorts, his face
covered in black mud, the mosquitoes following him.
'Sorry.'

'You okay?'

'YES. These mosquitoes are my friends anyway. No
said they sing.'

'How it looks like skin, this mud,' said Chaminda.
'Look at the sheets of it out there.' And it did: like an
outer membrane of a beast stolen from its own identity.
'You'll know beasts one day, especially the ones that
seem tame. Be careful of mud. It stinks and rots in front
of the River like a rejected carcass. It's the very last bit
of the City. You see it? It rests here, waiting.' He pointed
upriver to the place it all had come from, all the water
and all the mud. On both banks, the tallest trees held the
Forest far away.

Looking at the shining mud, Chrisnelt imagined the
edge of Africa sliding slowly into the oceans of the world.
He could see his many maps, and how the Continent
was shaped like a pile of throbbing chicken organs: a fat
gut, a big liver, all deep in the dark of old reds, wobbling
restlessly at the beginning of purple, near a heart muscle
of pumped energy, leaking constantly. Leaking. Always
leaking. And upon those organs hung bits of white fat,
persistent growths of excess.

He could see, too, how his precious map of Africa –
his newest map – had such clear edges against the blue of

water. Africa's big edge, at the beginning of all the blues, where it welcomed the entire world. Now he looked at the mud before him on the bank of the River.

'Maybe all the beaches and sparkling bays and rocky shores and river mouths are all just mud and dead skin now, Chami? Like this, peeling from a lost skeleton,' he said, sinking into the muddy bank.

Chaminda listened without surprise. He'd heard such prophetic words from the boy before, as if they had come out of him from spirits. The owl called again, this time from far up the River, on the other bank. 'I'm scared, Chami.'

'Me too, sometimes. Just stay close.'

'I can hear the drum sounds again. They're nice. But I'm still scared.'

'They're there with the owls and the trees.'

'And now there's one here,' said Chrisnelt. 'Listen, in between the frogs.' The fear helped him with his sadness.

'I hear.'

But there was indeed a living River beyond the mud – the Great Dancing Road of glory before him in that earliest of mornings. He looked up at Chaminda and smiled for the first time in a long time.

This great and powerful river of so much water, this Great Dancing Road, must have fed the greatest Christmas tree in the world, he thought; no wonder it grew to be so high. And water tugged the stench away, pulling away pieces of mud in dark puffs like leaking blood.

'It's loud now. Down here. You hear it? That deep howling down here now? Sounds like it's coming from a hole.'

'I've never seen a hole, except for the one I dug for my tree,' whispered Chrisnelt. 'I've read about caves, though. Some are on my maps, especially the craters made by shooting stars. And there's one that's a slit filled with green insects on my wall.'

'Again!' Chaminda paused to listen. 'Down there, beyond these bushes.'

Chrisnelt stayed close against his side. 'Yes.'

'You wouldn't have seen a real a cave before, or even a great hole, it's a thing not known to you in that street, or in this flat City. A cave has got an ancient roof of stone, and it's a magnificent window and a magnificent door too. It's a chance to see inside the earth. My Nellie gave me this gift when she died. I dug her the deepest hole under a great cliff of dead coral.'

'The drum again.' Chrisnelt could feel himself shake. He adjusted his feet, so as not to slip again.

'The far ones are calling too. Maybe talking across the waters?'

'And now the one in the hole with the frogs.'

'Just here.'

'Behind the bushes,' Chrisnelt crackled, his poem shifting in his pants. He chanted silently in his head: *Holes in the earth. I guess the tallest trees need the very deepest holes in the Earth.*

He slipped in the mud, getting up, holding tightly onto Chaminda's shirt. He was still very scared. All he could think about was a tree that fluttered with the many faces of No; that gripped with steady branches that were his father's hands. He said to himself: 'And the roots will be golden down to the middle of the world.'

'This is good. You know the River will always give if you listen and look. This is good, with this calling drum right here. This is very good for us now,' said Chaminda, clearing his throat above the clicking of frogs and the beating of drums nearby: 'Once there was the Plateau of the Rivers – *Tassili n'Ajjer* – in the far desert directly to the north, near the end of Africa before it gives itself to Europe.' He pointed upriver into the changing dark, his hand shaking ever so slightly, his finger making an arrow into the silver shimmer that was slowly turning golden. 'Before that land of Europe begins, far away, is a place where caves hold paintings of herds of cattle, crocodiles and dancing peoples who lived before the time of deserts.

Yes, thought Chrisnelt; before even the time of maps or the need for maps, when rivers made caves, linking the rain to the land and the peoples; before the time of all the walls on Earth.

'And I've got to tell you of these people, who had no perimeters, no lines on the ground, who had only openness and who sang in an expanse; and who eventually came to live one day between here and the desert, who were guided from the dry lands, coming into this wetter world of great trees and shade.' Chaminda pointed out beyond the River into a distant blackness that was becoming green: 'Those people had the fish gods as their guides. Hear the River, Chrisnelt, and the trees and their birds above the frogs, and hear the caves in the Earth in the sound of the drums.'

To the left, leaning out of the river, was the front half of a rusting steamboat, broad and flat like a scow; the teak-wood frames of two abandoned little cabins stood on its hopeless deck, broken space holding other, smaller frames of missing doors and missing windows; and a funnel pushed through everything, hollowed by smoke, a reverberating route for a pigeon that clattered and then escaped up and away from the river. The steamboat offered a pointed shadow in homage to the moon, the stars and the hesitating glow of day. And the shadow stood still, unaltered by the unfathomable ripples of the river or the changing shape of the muddy bank that leaked away constantly, like the edge of a continent. A small crocodile smiled unblinkingly before dipping under the water. A Coca-Cola can bobbed against the hull. Chrisnelt noticed the pattern the nails made in the metal. Just like the footprints No and I used to make on our street, he thought.

'All river edges can be streets, I guess,' said Chaminda, as if reading Chrisnelt's mind. In the distance, long barges rocked next to other boats, moored for the night. Inside people slept.

'Yes.' Chrisnelt held Chaminda's hand now. He was shaking.

'And all streets can be rivers.'

Chaminda parted the bush. They stepped down, closer to the water's edge. A man sat there on a chiselled stool, hunched over a log, the water touching his toes, the mud and his feet becoming a single, slimy thing. He was dressed only in a dirty cloth wrapped around his waste. Above him was a floating rock, protruding from the bank, and below it was a hole. It was his sleeping place, it seemed. The man tapped the log with two sticks – the log echoed constantly, breathing through thin, dark slits – and the sticks seemed to dance delicately in the humidity, pushing moths about gently near the trees. The man looked up, startled, as Chrisnelt and Chaminda quietly approached. 'Go away,' he said in a language only Chrisnelt understood. 'Go from here. This is a private time before the City wakes.' Leaves fell on him as they approached.

'We'll be quiet,' said Chrisnelt from behind Chaminda. 'We'll be dead quiet.'

'We're just watching the River come toward the City. It's very beautiful and full of knowledge,' said Chaminda, his eyes flickering.

Frogs sang in a new silence. The distant drums continued, as did the distant owl. The man's grey head moved slowly, his eyes shining white like eggs. To Chrisnelt's questioning face, he answered: '*Bekeke wa alando.*'

'He says it's the log of the *bolondo* tree,' explained Chrisnelt to Chaminda, pointing at the drum. 'He's speaking Wangenia. Tata spoke it' – the man spoke on – 'and he says this thing is carved very carefully, with the quiet removal of the red heart-wood of souls at the deep centre of the log. His exact words. He must be from the far north-east, beyond that, where the River stretches into another part of Africa. That's where Tata came from,' whispered Chrisnelt. 'What a sound of the inside of the Earth. What a deep sound coming from a tree.' He looked at Chaminda with tears in his eyes. He knew then that trees could talk; his tree would speak one day too.

'Yes, the talking drum, as I've said,' said Chaminda, smiling at the man.

In the near darkness the man spoke slowly to Chrisnelt, all the while beating his drum. Moths danced, coming and going freely, lifting one by one from the river, as if called;

then floating up to the trees, high among the sleeping birds and leaves. The man spoke at length, pausing to breathe between words and sentences, his voice part of the voice of the drums. Chrisnelt listened. The water rippled evanescently.

After much time and talking, darkness leaving the glittering world, Chrisnelt translated for Chaminda: 'Mr Botowa's name is Peter, here on the bank. He says his ancestors are to be found under the water, far upstream, resting on the floor of this river. Above them lives the Great Dancing Road of fishes, taking Africa to the sea, as it always has done. All the fish we eat come from his ancestors. Many ages ago, his people wanted to come down the river, from the edge of the forest to the start of the sea, the place that makes all the clouds of the world and all the first fishes. They wanted to move from one beginning, one freedom, to another. Isn't that right, Peter?' Chrisnelt looked questioningly at the ancient drummer. 'But their great pirogue lay deep below the angry waters, in the clasping mud. It was made of very heavy wood, inhabited by the spirit of a stubborn ancestor. One unknown man was brave enough to go on the water, walking on its furious surface, and then down into the water to speak to the ancestors and retrieve the pirogue. But before embarking on his journey, he coloured his body with black earth, and he coloured ropes of forest tree-twine black too – these would be used to haul the pirogue up from the depths. He told the people that if the River turned black, it would mean that he had died, and they should flee back into the forest.

'After some time, the pirogue rose to the surface and

everything in the water turned white, even the water was white. And all that got wet turned white: the wet trees and the wet birds, and the people dressed in wet, white mud. And although there was a boat for a journey, the water was too white to find fish in. The people could not move with empty bellies. But then the bright clouds came, healing everything with great smiles from another time; they delivered the rains, and unfathomable numbers of raindrops washed off the mud. Fresh fish flowed from the sacramental sky, filling the River, making the view clear again, green against the lighted trees: trees translucent like crystals. From that time onwards, anyone catching fish would colour themselves black, preparing for the coming of the whiteness – and praying for the eventual green.'

Peter extended a cupped palm, his black skin caked in mud. He wanted money for his story. 'We have none,' said Chrisnelt. And Peter spat a yellow patch in the mud.

'This is where I buy my fish, near here anyway, just round the bend,' said Chaminda. 'The *ngolo*, the *ngola*,' – Chaminda used the Lingala and then the Kituba names, mouthing syllables musically to his friend of glorious words. 'They are brought here in barges as food for this City, fresh from upstream places, wriggling in slippery crates. An eight hundred kilometre journey in the heat – they live for long in all this sweltering! Just like the people. And the chickens. I usually come here once a week for the fresh stuff. It's a big market, and I look at all the slippery mud and mess. But now I'll be reminded of the drums and the caves.'

'Money,' said Peter to Chrisnelt.

From behind a curve in the bank came a young woman

waving her arms, humming softly. She was feeding a giant catfish that seemed to follow her, swimming with a slow sway, its top fin protruding out of the water. She was shaped by sepulchral light dropping from the trees, her heavy eyelids cloistering her from this world. She broke bread in the dawn: dry baguettes crackled in huge, dry hands as she crushed her palms together. She sowed the water with the crumbs, which floated like little boats. The head of the fish shook from side to side, great whiskers poking the sky, whipping up a muddy bubble of blackness. The head was the size of Chrisnelt's head, attached to a long, snakelike body. The fish seemed to know the woman in the way a dog knows its owner. Only tame fishes lived in this part of the river now: the edge of the feral was clear. The drum danced with the lone fish, the frogs and the trees of sleeping birds. The mist was long gone.

From behind them all – Chaminda, Chrisnelt, Peter, the lonely woman and the river-things, the bushes and the row of high, black trees that had begun to sway in peroration – the sound of taxi-cars had started to squeeze the day at them like piss. Chrisnelt could feel the River pushing him toward the sound of the street. He could feel its strength, the great surge of its waters. The River was on an eternal journey from the Forest to the ocean, and it was an important journey, connected to his tree. But he knew that in order to grow the tree he had to go to the centre of the City. And he had to go now.

'The River is coming for me, Chami, coming for my family – for my father it's already come; for all of us, for you too, it'll come. It's bringing this shimmering thing toward us.' He turned and looked at it come from the distance, between the Forest boundaries that were changing edges.

'It's been coming for everyone all the time, since the moment of the first clearing in the first Forest, since before then, when we looked from high among the leaves,' said Chaminda. 'Out of a heart shall flow rivers of living water!' – using the intonation of the priests of the churches he knew Chrisnelt had grown up with. 'But it moves unseen. Instead what people see is just a wide waterway, a high wall between peoples, a barrier.'

'The River will dance in words one day,' said Chrisnelt. 'It will give us trees of remembrance to be read like books and maps, the trees in turn will give us many answers.'

'Your father would have told you that,' said Chaminda.

Taxi-cars pushed into roads not far off. A common machine-gun rattled like an alarm clock. The City was waking up. Cooking fires pushed at the darkness in the distance. They looked at the wounded City lifting in the dawn light, crumbling into the mud.

'And it will take us to the sea, as it always has; then onward to other rivers far away, beyond the first sea, to other seas,' said Peter in English. Chaminda looked at him with surprise.

'I think of *Siddhartha*, which my father shared with me: a story of a great figure who watched his reflections in the river. So I see how you see this shimmering, the movement it gives the trees, the life of currents,' said Chaminda to Peter, knowing now that he spoke English. 'I see the strength and the sense of direction and the journey. I see the linking of all things in the world.' He checked himself. 'Shit, I sound like a preacher, like that damn Pastor.' He put his arm around Chrisnelt's shoulder; the boy smiled.

'We go to the centre of the City now, Chrisnelt.'

The sun wanted to come from behind the distant forest and change things. The two friends climbed back up the bank of dirt. Chaminda carried a plastic packet containing a small freshly caught catfish, given to him by the lonely young woman as a gift. Peter beat his drum just for them in the kindness coming from the woman, a kindness that rippled like water. Chrisnelt carried new thoughts of his tree, and the River, and the new seed he would soon get in the centre of the City. He was excited, and he was sad, but he was not scared anymore.

The deep cut in the bank – softened by the bushes and hidden by the row of black trees, the throng of American cockroaches, cosmopolitan larder beetles and smooth woodlouse from Europe – crumbled underfoot, the trees dripping blackness like blood, revealing a patient green. Birds stirred: a flock of white egrets spread into the sky, their sharp beaks pointing like black arrows toward the iron roofs and iron walls up ahead. The birds fanned, twirling into the wide shapes of white river lilies opening on air, all golden below, carrying the sound of that drum over the edge of the waters. The waters rushed as they had always rushed.

The centre of a thing always seems tight and full, thought Chrisnelt heavily. He closed a hand, his long fingers making a fist and a bone-cracking sound. Sweat stung a paper-cut in his palm. His heart was a ball inside him, dense like the middle of a tree.

They'd walked for hours, pushed on by the warmth of the air. It was still dim. Chaminda walked two steps ahead, his white shirt sticking to the line of his spine, his big feet flapping in sandals, arms flat to his sides because the pavement was now too narrow for people.

This is a shit place, thought Chrisnelt. No trees, just bloody cars. People don't live here.

All space was surrendered to the car, here near the core of the City. Remarkably silent, the vehicles moved with jerky certainty, squeezed together in the approaching dawn. They were largely taxi-cars: sedans of various models with scratched dark-green bodies and dirty-white hoods. The green finish appeared black, leaving the white parts to drift in strange detachment above the road, long rows of them floating on fumes. The yellow headlights nudged along as random pairs, independent of people, myriad tadpoles. The first hint of sunlight – now apparent in patches at the tips of the higher buildings – fought for attention with the tadpoles of the street.

The dust was now forsaken, overtaken by the omnipresent concrete and the glass. Chrisnelt could still smell dust in the air, though. He stopped and stood like one of the many steel poles lining the road, sweating in the heat. He breathed in blue smoke that made his eyes dance.

'Chami, wait. I can't walk anymore. I'm too tired. My lungs hurt.'

'We can rest for a minute, but we must get there before it gets too light.'

Chrisnelt wanted to cry, not from sadness but because of his weakness. 'I can't keep up with you. My legs aren't long like yours. Can't we wait for the sun – it'll only be a while? I can hear the birds waking on the roofs.'

'We can't.'

'What about one of these cars. There're all over?'

'Chrisnelt, I have no money. We should carry on now.'

The big glass shopfronts, with their electrified signage, shone in various corporate colours, and also the colours of government money. Some signs glowed high up on the building façades: the aloof names of banks and insurance companies. These were regimental, each letter forming its own square mini-sign, chunky slabs of light lined up into words. All insular, all removed from the street, rising on walls that climbed into the beginnings of someone else's morning in Europe.

One sign, bending petals of gold for a shop called McDonald's, buzzed in a swarm of lost bees, flickering as if to bait the waiting tadpoles stuck in the current. Another big sign in red and blue read 'PEP', the 'SI' just a dim silhouette of blown bulbs. Another expansive sign, the size of an entire building, was spot-lit from the opposite side of the street, as a superstar is spot-lit holding a trophy before a screaming crowd of illusions. On this particular sign was the image of a huge, clear plastic bottle that read: '*Mayo Ma Famille*!' From the '*y*' of the '*Mayo*' spouted a graphic fountain in bright blue lights.

'Imported water, next to the deepest river on Earth,' laughed Chaminda.

Chrisnelt was too tired to smile. 'I have to stop again,' he said.

'I can try and carry you?'

'No.'

'Lean on me. We can go together,' said Chaminda. He curled his long arm around the boy. He could feel that the boy's once crackling poem was wet with sweat; and there was a hum inside Chrisnelt, in his heart: a hum of conviction, like a continuous poem. They walked as one, and they talked. It helped the boy to breathe.

'I've never seen such a place, Chami,' he said. 'I've been counting these words and their letters as we've walked. They're like fire-writing in the sky.'

Chaminda looked at the signs above, pushing his thoughts forward as he pushed Chrisnelt. 'Well, instead of real words, all you have now in the City is a message made by the world.' He sighed. 'You see, this place of cars – it doesn't speak in the handwriting of people. It speaks in the writing of corporations that aren't even from here. Can you see?'

'Yes.'

'On my island far away, our letters – the shapes of the alphabet – tell a story before they even become words and sentences.' Chaminda leaned down as if to share a secret, arm tight around the boy's narrow shoulders. 'Our Sinhala letters come from ancient shapes,' he nodded. 'They're all very beautiful, made of soft, slow curves like the River, or the wings of wild birds. Long ago, when the letters of my alphabet were first written down, it was on leaves.'

'Leaves? Like the ones from the market?'

'Big palm leaves. The letters were curved, because the leaves would not tolerate straight, sharp cuts. Such lines would have torn the leaves and killed our language, leaving it in the past.'

'I'll only ever write on paper, soft paper that comes from trees – or maybe on your big leaves too,' said Chrisnelt. 'I can't stop writing – I like to feel my fingers move.' He twiddled them in Chaminda's face as they turned a corner.

'They move like your mind. Pity your legs don't do the same.'

'I write even more now with the dream of my tree.'

'You keep writing. Never stop. And never stop dreaming, too.'

'Okay.'

'But don't write like this!' Chaminda shook a finger at the billboards.

'Yes, Chami. Please can we stop again. I don't think I'm going to make it.' Chrisnelt breathed and swayed, gazing up at the twinkling words. His sadness fell back onto him from the high cliffs of concrete. 'I'm so scared of the darkness of this place, with all its lights. And that glass up there – all the small squares of it – it just reflects more darkness.'

Chaminda held Chrisnelt tightly. 'You're too big to carry, you know.'

'I'll try and make it. How far to go?'

'Not too far.'

The taxi-cars were so tight in the new street that Chrisnelt felt they were inside his lungs. The blue smoke chased him. He knelt down and rested, grabbing the pavement. A man tried to sell Chaminda a single shoe. Two men – one on either side of the street – tried to sell them the same newspaper, shouting in unison: 'The adverts are free!' Another man – who'd just opened a yellow glass sliding door – flashed scissors in Chrisnelt's face. 'You're in my way here,' he said. 'Go back to your shacks!'

Chrisnelt breathed loudly, looking about, fighting tears. 'Let's carry on. I think I'm rested now.'

'Okay, Chrisnelt. This is your show.' Chaminda helped

him up off the paving slabs, scattering bottle tops and cigarette butts that stank of piss.

They walked as one shadow, inside the vast new shadow of buildings, on that wide boulevard of pandemonium, in the deadness of that common street of commodities.

Bruised air sat in the colours of pain.
Thoughts tapped a shadow of rain.
And then a nod of my neck,
Because a scar came.

The poem leaked softly from the corners of his dry mouth. They walked carefully onward, in a straight line.

And the government district came in government buildings. A vast, wallowing herd of creatures made of concrete and brick: swaying elephants and buffaloes of steel and glass. These huge resting shapes stood next to each other, separated by dark carpets of lawn and fencing. Together they inhabited fields sterilised by idleness, staring with their eyes closed, chewing at the past.

'All the lights are off and nobody's home,' said Chrisnelt loudly, and Chaminda burst into laughter.

'Your father told you that? And if you work for the government you don't work. Nobody here yet, see. He was right.'

'Yes,' said Chrisnelt. It was still dark in the sky too. He missed his father so much he felt sickness in his mind. His stomach ached, as it had ached for days. He changed his thought to the Tree and the seeds he would soon see.

'This is where all the Departments are, in different

buildings. All with the same flag, but they might as well have different flags and speak different languages. The only thing that moves here are soldiers and machine-guns,' said Chaminda.

'And the taxi-cars on this road.'

'Yes, they move like blood in veins. And, can you see, they're all bloody empty.'

Chrisnelt had not noticed that before. It scared him even more. 'Just drivers, no passengers!'

'No money,' said Chaminda, 'just the hope of money.'

'How far now?'

'Not far.'

The high walls of these dead buildings broke the street with a snap, and Chrisnelt's view ahead became a dark corridor. Only the cars gave off a low, slow light.

There was more space between buildings though; such was the Government District. All seemed charred and smouldering, but starting to become green. The light poles became interspersed with tall palm trees, like he'd never seen, their bases painted white, stems and fronds uplit. The lawns that held the buildings and edged the boulevard shone. There were even colourful flower beds, in the colours of the national flag. Bushes, manicured like Mrs Malotika's fingernails, hugged the sculptures of military men with heads of bird shit.

'It's starting to get green here, in the glow of it all,' said Chrisnelt. 'Are we nearly there?' High street lights buzzed.

'The next turn, and we'll be there, past those rows of high buildings and flags. We must just follow the black-and-white curb lines to the Great Circle.' Chaminda's back was aching, Chrisnelt's full weight almost upon him.

'These curbs are like the legs of my singing mosquitoes,' said Chrisnelt.

'You know, that species is called the Asian tiger mosquito. It sucks blood during the day and during the night-time in much silence; it comes from my bloody home too. It's all over the world now. Maybe it followed me here!' Chaminda smiled.

'Stop,' said a soldier.

He stood some way off on a huge rectangular patch of lawn, beyond a gate of black steel rods holding golden daggers at their tips. His chest rippled with rows of bullets, his shoes shone like the black eyes of a snake, and he pointed a long gun. Small lights illuminated the edges of the lawn; they illuminated his gun and his teeth. As he shouted, he brushed the air with a free hand in a bright, white glove, tiny insects hovering like hair.

Another soldier, on the opposite side of the street, slept on a bench, in the bizarre camouflage offered by dappled dawn light. A high flag on top of a flat concrete roof fluttered unexpectedly, flushing purple pigeons into a puff of steam that hung alone and bright against the change of day. And the silhouettes of satellite dishes creaked within a filigree of antennae. Chrisnelt could hear little birds begin to call in a distant tree hidden in a courtyard somewhere. A cricket chirruped. Dew on the lawn glittered of moon things and the other memories of the departing night.

'You may not walk on that grass!' shouted the soldier. 'It does not belong to you. It belongs to the President.'

'Sorry,' said Chaminda, lifting his one arm. 'Just taking this boy to the Christmas Tree.'

'But Christmas has finished,' said the smiling soldier, lowering his gun.

'Not for him,' said Chaminda. Chrisnelt looked away.

They walked around that final corner, which was more of a slow and meandering curve, sucked by a gold and silver incandescence. Chrisnelt had retreated deep inside himself, looking for stillness, as he'd looked for it for so long. Stillness owned his limbs.

'A seed from the tallest tree. A seed for No and Tata, and from such an ancient tree; a tree with deep and wise roots, down to the River,' he muttered to himself, as in a dream. His heart stretched and his stomach twisted into a voluptuous knot. His thumbs were pale, his nails pink, almost red, squeezed in his folded fingers. His extraordinary eyes swelled bigger than they'd ever been. His upper row of teeth pushed down tightly upon his lower lip. His chin quivered. His large head throbbed toward a new hardness. The poem crackled in his groin, the roll of paper splaying like a fan, working its way out and up as he moved forward. The call of the last owl gave way to the call of the first crow of the new day. Nothing else moved then in Chrisnelt's mind, not even the flood of taxi-cars, not even the waters of the River, pausing like ice in his head. He stepped forward.

'There's the Centre of the City,' said Chaminda proudly.

Chrisnelt stood in silence, alone, light exploding before him, illuminating his shock. Convoluted circles of noise swarmed off taxi-car roofs. Around and around the traffic circle before him, in a whirlwind of headlights, as if tadpoles were being pulled into a great mouth, the world screamed in light. In the middle of that light was the Christmas Tree.

The Tree was like the powerful blade of a spear, razor sharp at the tip, piercing higher than all the buildings edging the central plaza, commanding the darkness. It rose up from an island of white marble that glittered as if water had puddled. And around this great circle – perfect like a halo – streamed a constant river of taxi-cars: six cars deep, all dark and devoid of dreams, the back seats filled with ghosts. From this circle, great boulevards extended at regular intervals, disappearing into the night in every direction like the spokes of a terrifying wheel.

The Tree was the brightest manifestation of energy Chrisnelt had ever seen; the sun reshaped into a cone, every leaf bursting forth in revolving eruptions and twisting hallucinations. At the base – as wide as a city block – the trunk of the mighty structure was hidden by the shimmering glow. The foliage was clearly divided into three tiers: the bottom, widest third shining with tiny red rubies; the middle third myriad blinking golden eyes; the top third – terminating in a delicate tip – a brilliant world of iridescent green dots that screamed to the fleeing moon. These were the national colours: not colours at all but illusions, illusions of light. And there at the tip of the Tree hovered a star of the most intense blue, swaying precariously.

'It's dead,' whispered Chrisnelt. 'It's a dead tree, burned by heat.'

For all these years, Chimanda had looked at the Tree as a beautiful manifestation of celebration, somehow giving him hope. But now – after walking with Chrisnelt through the night – he saw only servitude. Fear descended upon Chaminda, the boy beside him engulfed in tears. 'Just somebody's fucking billboard,' he said softly.

After all the struggles this poor boy has gone through, growing his little tree in the dust, thought Chaminda, hanging his head in shame. 'What have I done, bringing you here? Your father did not see it like this, or did he? What have I done.'

Chrisnelt pulled his hand from Chaminda's, stepping off the black-and-white curb into the ocean of taxi-cars.

'Stop Chrisnelt, stop!' Chaminda screamed.

The boy waded slowly, arms outstretched like wings, gliding across waves and rivers and lakes and seas. He curved his torso this way and that, the tears continuing to fall, gliding like a suicidal bird. There was hooting. There was cursing and jerking of brakes and squealing of rubber tyres, and the screaming of insults ricocheted off windshields. He pushed ahead. He flew on and then he fell. And stood. The slow, curving lines of taxi-cars absorbed him as he fell again. He was gently nudged by the cars as they shouted further insults, but he got up again. Finally, he crawled up onto the other side. It had been like a crossing through the strongest current. He stood there alone, in the middle of everything, the marble pavement holding him in the centre of the light, the dawn coming like a new idea, like a map of the past telling of the future. Chrisnelt reached out to touch the Tree, his long fingers spaced wide so as to expose every feeling, every nerve ending, and every thought to every glass leaf. His fingers reached out slowly, sacrificially, to the heat.

The taxi-cars had all speeded up now, the hooting intensified. Chaminda was helpless, stuck on the other side. He could only observe.

'Chrisnelt!' he screamed. 'I'm coming, don't you move!'

He would have to wait until the traffic lights turned red. It was like waiting for the sun on the longest night. The traffic heaved, as did his chest.

Chrisnelt stared closely at the construction towering above him. He stared practically, like a gardener would stare at leaves on a real tree. Concentric iron rings, resembling a billion bicycle wheels with a trillion spokes, rose steadily like circular ripples, getting smaller as they went, until they became the blue star – an emissary of Evil – in the distant sky. He touched the lowest wheel, the widest one.

'They are all fastened at the centre to a steel pole as if it's a trunk. And that's rooted in concrete like a gigantic stake,' he said. On each wheel, on its outer rim, rows of little electric lights blinked like eyes. 'These bulbs are hot,' he said. 'They're like beads from Hell.' He could see that it was just an old contraption of rust, welded together with crude, rickety joints. 'This is supposed to be very strong and powerful steel,' he said. 'It's like a god created it to last, but without real seeds.'

'Don't move, Chrisnelt.'

A taxi-car stopped: 'You want a lift?'

'Fuck off,' said Chaminda.

Chrisnelt looked at that whitest of white glows: terminal light, dying, like snow in the sunshine.

From the far side of his imagination came moths. Along the long straight lines of the boulevards, reaching back into the bending tightness and the curling pain of many histories, came moths; from the lone trees, trained and stained, scattered across Africa like captured animals in backyards, and from weeds in the forgotten graveyards, came moths; from a single garden shaped like a triangle came moths; from the distant forest villages beyond all other villages, where trees talked to people and people talked to trees, families sitting on grass mats at the edge of the sun, linked together as with songs and dances, came moths; from the pure peoples of great gifts, walking on tenuous gravel footpaths and loose sandy tracks far away from freeways and highways, came moths – wings bare and beautiful like bodies can be and once were; velvet wings like the softest souls. From the River and the River Trees, and from the green beyond came all the many moths in sacrosanct innocence. Moths came as missionaries, to a mission landscape of incalculable deaths. And they kept coming and coming.

The Tree, twinkling coquettishly, fluttered with moths, dancing at the end of the night: a tingling of busy bits of skin. Some moths showed wings of copper and some of bronze, grabbing yellows and oranges from the air. Some moths flashed staring eyes; some moths held hues like dust holds remnants of the earth; the largest hung like drifting birds of prey. Around each light-bulb was the heat of misunderstanding, of sad concupiscence before the burn.

A funereal breeze took the moths as they collapsed in smoke, tumbling shapeless and minuscule, plumed in wisps of the past. Chrisnelt shuffled his feet. Chaminda finally stepped up onto the pavement next to him, his bigger feet shuffling too on this bed of charred lives. The white marble pavement was thick with black innocence. The ground crackled like a poem. Chrisnelt knelt to scoop up the dead moths, and they drifted away again. 'They'll keep coming until the lights go out,' said Chrisnelt, thinking of his father's words. 'This was Tata's gift.'

Without breath suddenly, leaning on the shoulder of a concrete reindeer that had become a seat below the Tree, Chrisnelt began to write an extension to his poem, finding a way to a new ending. Silence gave him time; only serried cars moaned impenetrably.

Chaminda sat in a concrete sled wedged into the marble, one foot on concrete snow, a hand dusting away falling moths, the other resting on concrete holly – the peeling green paint sucked away in the tropical heat. Chaminda knew to be still.

Chrisnelt sat and wrote his words, and the sun came kindly to his face. At last he got up, and slowly slid the piece of rolled paper under the Tree, into the heart of darkness.

One day
the clouds might
drop singing birds
onto to the new trees
to be heard in between every home,
just in time for us:
spectacularly vast and visited hearts
leaping across streets
to touch
a private new body;
the gentle,
special arrangement:
the shadows of flutterings

warned of a world
that is in need of new wings.

He recited these words to Chaminda. 'Most of it was written by Tata, I just added a bit here and there, in the parts that reminded me of No and the tree I will grow,' he said.

They began to walk home, away from the thick crosses made by the roads that came to the Christmas Tree from everywhere.

Chapter Seven

It made a shape next to the black rock, which was still shining from mist. At first just the shadow of dust kicked by a breeze, and then a tight-feathered form: a small bird, with a long tail and a big eye, sitting alone on the rock, sharp and alert like daylight. The Blue-breasted bee-eater, new for his bird list (number fifty-two).

There are images that do not belong in photographs, or in paintings, or on the political posters rotting in the City, staining old and irrelevant walls, or hanging from telephone poles across wasted lands. Chrisnelt was sure of that. These images are of special beings, pure moments. They are images of birds. And one of these poems had alighted on the rock. Such a bird-landing had not happened before in front of Chrisnelt. Here was, simply, a beautiful feeling made of colour: blue fused to yellow and green and red, every map in the whole world becoming an explosion of ideas the size of a hand. Chrisnelt smiled loudly. 'At last, another bird. It's been a few years since the last new one.'

Then it was gone. Then it was back. Gone. Back again, as if it had always been there. A long black curve of a beak held a bee – although the Bee-eater was also known to eat dragonflies, butterflies and the mosquitoes with the black-and-white stripes on their legs. All the insects in Chrisnelt's garden fed on sunlight above weeds; now, this pair of big bird-wings danced with many tiny pairs of glass wings, lit up against the walls of glistening green.

He sat on the rock to watch. Such feasting had never been more important: the garden was feeding itself at last, as great gardens do. And Chrisnelt saw yet another beginning of a tree rising below the wings. He'd planted many saplings over these past years, but they had all died. It had something to do with the soil, he thought. 'When the roots get too deep, the tree dies. It happens every time,' he said to Chaminda, who'd just brought him another specimen from the forest. 'I'll use all these fallen leaves as compost again. A tree needs precious roots with lips at the tips, to drink the waters of the River in this City.'

'It's been many years, Chrisnelt. You'll grow it. I feel it in my bones.'

'I feel it in mine too – they ache, mainly my fingers.'

'Me too,' shouted Nipcia from the corridor. 'I feel it when you bring me that next dead tree for this fire, so I can sweat above this damn pot. Look at the blisters!'

'You're just rude.'

'You're lazy. You never go to school, and you never help in here. You just read and read and write stupid poems and things and draw stupid trees, and sit forever in that swamp of mosquitoes out there.'

'You're getting a bit old for this fighting,' said Chaminda. 'Come now. You should be proud of your brother, Nipcia. His garden is known all over the District.'

'It's just a waste of water. Five droughts in a row, and he keeps wasting water from the damn toilet,' said Nipcia. 'He should go and get a job like Divi did at the Church. There's no money since Tata went away like that into the Heavens.'

'I'll get a job one of these days, Nipcia,' said Chrisnelt.

He closed the bedroom door to the garden. He and Chaminda continued to plant things. He looked up into the sky, beyond the dust, to where an occasional cloud had paused, before being flushed onward by the birds. He traced its route toward the inner reaches of the Continent, to places far upriver, to mountains that were made like giant hands to squeeze water from the air for the world.

On the far side of the rock, the side not facing his bedroom, stood a new primeval tree, nudging at the rock's shade that kept it from the sweltering heat. It was tiny and alone below the feeding creatures. It was a time of diligence for the garden; that was how Chrisnelt saw it.

Chrisnelt had always noticed the shade from the rock each time hope arrived as a little tree. 'Shade is precious near the Equator,' he'd said. That shade always came running, pushed hurriedly by the rock. 'This one's young and strong,' he said, pointing at the tree. 'It's sturdy and lucid. From within the heart of the good leaves will come a new hegemony.'

Chaminda smiled, thinking back to that important Christmas-tree dawn, the river of cars, the mighty swim across the wide road by the brave boy. He understood Chrisnelt, as deeply as it was possible to see another mind. Keep growing. Keep growing all this stuff. A tree is on its way. A tree with the right roots.'

'I think this one will reach the River, Chami, these roots are the ones,' he patted the ground around the tree. Leaves rustled, and the garden swayed minutely. Things sparkled, as did his big eyes.

A high breeze brought seeds in the sky just then,

searching for a place, in the way a people searches. The seeds appeared captured, altered by the dusts of the new drought. 'Sometimes seeds grow in an illusion, forgetting the land, becoming nonsensical symbols. Sometimes seeds are so lost they can only grow in hate, occasionally escaping to settle waywardly. But occasionally seeds don't wander; they fall with purpose. Such seeds are both hopes and memories. Such seeds make other seeds,' said Chrisnelt. 'You know, Chami, I'm learning all the time, as I read the new books and plant the new plants. I'm really learning.'

'You're almost sixteen. Don't ever stop learning. It's the only road left in Africa, and the oldest road of all,' said Chami. 'Who knows, these white tufts that you call feather-seeds, one of them might hold a tree.' He jumped into the air, trying to catch one, but the air took it away.

'Jump!' Chrisnelt laughed.

'I'm too old to jump properly,' said Chaminda. He jumped again, missing the next cloud of seeds, their bellies curved like those of acrobats.

'I'm not tall enough,' said Chrisnelt jumping up off the rock, his arms high above his head, his fingers snapping shut, the seeds disappearing over the walls, and then over more distant walls too. So many walls; so many wasted seeds.

'Chrisnelt, bring me the wood from that last dead tree. I know you've hidden it,' said Nipcia, leaning on his bedroom door. 'There's no money to buy charcoal, thanks to you.'

As he slept that night, his mat crackling like a wild stanza, he dreamed of the newest tree, and in his sleep he smiled, watching roots push down and down and down into the freshest new earth, the old earth before the City came. A moth rested on his cheek, the softest legs of the singing mosquitoes rested there too, and no blood was spilt from their needle heads.

In the night and deep in a dream, the walls groaned in the heat, as did his face and his chest and his mat. The roots of the tree bent, twisting deeper like great, hot muscles, reaching the waters of the River: they drank. The smell was rich and sharp, sweet like the hottest fruits.

The tree grew very high. The fruits became sweeter. The roots drank more of the warm waters. The River fed the roots. The tree reached up strong. And deep waters flowed like a golden waterfall. Chrisnelt could hear them clearly. The roots dug deeper and the water was so hot. Down the roots went. Down. Warm, then hot, then very hot. The smell was as strong as the heat. The roots went down through caves of boiling heat, and down further to the infernos below, distant drums beating. And the heat came and came. It was so much heat that he could not breathe anymore. He sat up with a jerk, spluttering piss.

'Who's there?' he screamed, wiping his face.

'What's going on here?' shouted Divi, running into the room with Nipcia. (Mrs Malotika was again not there that night. She had not been there on many nights, in those difficult days.)

Chrisnelt spat. He stepped out into the garden, onto the soft sands and wet leaves, leaving the door hanging open. Outside, all was wet. The tree steamed, dripping golden piss. Golden piss in the light of the moon like leaking sun-drops, rancid and toxic.

Beyond, on the bending corrugations of the wall, the Nagasaki boys, the MacDonald boys, and one little Mohamed laughed as they climbed. The clamouring made the climbing plants tumble, a tall bush snapped, and the ferns wobbled and curled. All was wounded and wet. All was laid waste again in the laughter.

Chrisnelt fell into a ball, as he always did in darkness, and cried. Everyone else laughed. His poisoned tree was leafless, as it had been before, and it would surely be again, drowned in ignorance.

Many months later, a new small tree grew in the ground next to the rock. Chrisnelt was firmly of the opinion – carefully documented over many years, in hundreds of notebooks of formulae, in poems filled with geometric calculations, in graphs filled with poems, in number strings that made loops like rainbows, and on maps now so numerous they hung in banners from the ceiling – that a garden would be deemed nearly complete only once it began talking to itself.

On the planting of the latest tree, he was confident the completion of his work was at hand. He ran his fingers through the tall reeds that whipped the sounds of flutes at each other when brushed against. He jangled stems in chains of bending trumpets and tambourines, and he shuffled shrubs filled with bells of dangling fleshy lobes. He flicked and popped drying seeds on sprouting grasses, and tapped tiny drums on low, leathery fronds, releasing fireworks of laughter, and pulled at low branches that sighed like dogs do, stretching next to cooking fires. And there was the bush of frogs that came alive on golden-moon nights, hopping tunes, gurgling speeches everywhere, bubbling the dew of sticky games.

He looked out at his garden: an expansive ocean, a newly discovered valley without sides. Indeed a tiny place, yet its vistas contained the world. Daydreams and nightdreams, and life beyond the many distant lives of yesterday, and beyond the distant deaths of tomorrow, could be seen across the garden. The triangle of planted walls and floors and ceilings of leaves had become a room unlike any other in the City, a place of profound thinking, open and universal, as only abundance can be. Peering upward slowly, through the foliage, into the sky, all was revealed. 'What's at the end of a cloud as it wisps, if not the beginning of a new cloud of all the waters?' he whispered to the rock.

From on top of the rock, his attention fell back to his bedroom, tumbling vibrantly out through the doorway toward him. Newly donated cliffs of books stood there, high mountains of every shape and texture, forming a backdrop to the maps, the maps, everywhere becoming maps to maps.

And a bookshelf had emerged too. It was unlike Chaminda's little bookshelf or the shelves in the Government Library of Liberation – the only other bookshelves in the city – because it had no shelves. Chrisnelt preferred to stack his books on the floor, one on top of the other, each time he completed a journey through the words. He only ever read a book once, and always at great speed in the deepest silence. He would never need to read a book twice, memorising every word and every picture ever written. Most of the older books he'd given to the kind people selling fish down at the River, and to those who played drums at dawn, but some books he could not part with: they'd become part of him, intimate to the architecture of his mind; their many pages offered the crumbling walls of emancipation. These were the books about trees and the books about birds, some about both subjects, and one or two about the art of making Christmas trees out of plastic, concrete or other such things. And in that manner, the wall of books grew like the garden, pile after pile, until it was six piles wide, in a floor-to-ceiling aroma of knowledge: the best kind of dust. The best kind of wall, tight with titles.

Together, the spines of the books told stories connected to stories, essential like vertebrae: some gilded in silver or bronze words, one made of leather and interwoven feathers, many making little rooms for moths and dried leaves, all of them strong, bursting with tomorrow's divinations and the calamities of truth.

The spines of special books caught the sunshine, offering a busy horizon above the long grass at his feet. A wide shrub of mauve flowers, resembling a flock of resting butterflies, hovered in front of his sleeping mat, hiding it in complicated vibrations; the merest hint of his blue pillow emerged below the din in a lonely cloud. A row of tall, yellow bamboo fronds glowed in the light that often rested on the early morning floor. A butterfly came to tickle the folds of a map – recently donated by Chaminda – as it hung on one side, leaning onto the edge of the show, still damp from the mists of dawn. Everything sang. And on the ground at the base of his ideas, the garden ended (or perhaps began) in sparkling beetles and roots, feeding in a mattress of mosses and white pebbles. 'If ever a cool shadow is given the honour of offering a scent to the blind, it would be like this damp moss,' he said to the rock and the struggling little tree.

During this gardening time, while sitting on his rock, he would often lean to his right or left, almost touching the neighbouring walls of other people's homes, running outstretched fingers along the metal corrugations, playing them as one would a musical instrument. At those moments, when these side walls seemed to want to squash him flat into a piece of unleavened bread (not sold at Café Gourmandine), as walls were designed to do in the City, his garden walls seemed to unfold. They opened to the air, filling notebooks with tremendous space, rushing freshness upward in the stifling heat of the tropical drought.

He had his feet in the circular pond, on the sunny side of the rock. He looked down at the pond. The water had a face of stone. The rock looked like a black cliff in that light, the moving clouds rippling the image of the hard surface as if it had breath. Below, he watched little river-boats of insects gathering in rows on the pond like waiting barges filled with fish, fluttering oars made of shiny dragonfly wings; and the sterns and bows of bobbing frogs, all crossing freely from shore to shore, searching for the opposite bank, not realising it was all the same bank because it was a circular pond.

'When a rock is surrounded by an ocean, it becomes an island of life,' wrote Chrisnelt, right there and then. 'Without that water, it's only a rock.'

Occasionally, the orchid plant given to him by Chaminda gushed scent onto his head, thereafter dropping a flower of moonshine, which floated in foreign blacks and whites on the pond, looking for a home on the water, like a ship of chains from another world. Always, the orchid would make him think of Chimanda, the first friend his garden-making had given him – as happens with all ineluctable gardens of omen – who had become his best and most honest companion. And then he cried, as he often did, thinking further back in guilt, to the time of No.

'Tata, I *am* growing a tree for you and No now,' he said to the rock, and to his face in the pond. 'This garden is nearly complete.'

Quite apart from his perilous journey toward tree-making, in the months since he'd seen the Christmas tree, Chrisnelt had succumbed to a horrendous affliction. He'd awoken to it suddenly descending onto his face like a mask carved of pain. It was a private time of torture, and it occurred every morning and every night.

He faced it with bravery, the way he faced every new boundary. It was a case of terrible blinking: three hundred and sixty-five, point two-four-two-two blinks each dawn, and three hundred and sixty-five, point two-four-two-two blinks when he was about to go to sleep. His other obligation to this affliction was the involuntary chanting of a single poem that unsettled even the insects in his room: 'DON'T WASTE THE COMMONALITY OF RAINS!' he would start off by shouting, throat aching. Then would come the long poem, the poem of that walk with Chaminda in the dark streets, the poem that burned like No had burned, and like the Tree had burned the moths. He yelled it, the chanting and the yelling becoming an intertwined rhythm, a thing of writing shadows on the walls.

'Shut up, nutcase,' would come from Nipcia each time, as she slammed every door she could find.

'You're driving us nuts,' would come from Divi. This ritual happened every day. 'The Kingdom of Heaven is like a mustard seed. The mustard seed is the smallest of all the seeds. That's what Pastor says,' said Divi on one of these mornings of battle. And she threw a large nut at her brother, the brittle shell shattering against his bedroom door. 'Pastor says man sowed his field with it, and it grew greater than all the herbs, and became the most important tree, filled with birds. But your trees keep dying. I tell you, it's because of all this chanting and yelling. And your garden attracts mosquitoes not birds.' She scratched her itchy arms.

'Shut up,' said Chrisnelt from behind his door, able to speak again at last, the poem recited, the counting of the blinks complete, setting off the stench of burning flesh in his nostrils. It left him exhausted. The frustration of it all made him kick the door. All he could do was anticipate the coming of it again that night, and then again, and again, for all the mornings and the nights to come.

He looked outside at his tree. He could hear bells in the distance, sounding above the domes and inside the steeples. A single drop of rain came down in unction from a single cloud. The pond rippled a single widening ripple of silver as the drop landed. A man wailed from a minaret in the new light up the street. Another Christmas was coming. Chrisnelt wondered how it would pass; whether learning would come on the way to malediction, as it seemed to do the year before, and the year before that.

The garden stretched in preparation for the heat that was coming, the tree edging a bit higher than it had edged the previous day. 'Up to my head now, almost a tree,' said Chrisnelt. 'Only a tree when I can climb up into the branches one day.' He noticed a single flower near the top, resting between two big leaves. 'This must be a young Coral Tree. A Coral treeling. I know this flower from the books.' Chrisnelt found this discovery most appropriate: 'All trees should be named after creatures of the sea.' He noticed another flower, and another, all of the brightest red. 'Green feeding red and red feeding green,' he said. Bees buzzed, electric blobs. 'Bright red blooms, a sea of bugles playing to every bee.' The sand beneath his feet rustled in layers of old leaves, like the pages of every book ever written.

Chrisnelt had spent so much time in his garden, tending to the creatures he'd planted, that it now smelled of him, and he of it. Isolation held him like a wick holds a single flame in a lonely room, flickering and hissing, in the gaps between visits by Chaminda. Chaminda's life was pulled back and forth by a City that demanded charcoal. He had to go on long journeys, looking for trees to be burned. It was these journeys that formed sudden gaps in Chrisnelt's heart.

The memory of Chrisnelt's father grew enshrined and strong in the blossoming of the small tree, and the opening of the widest leaves began to open him too. Everything turned to follow the sun and the moon of mourning. The pond had deepened in questions as it settled into the ground, holding mirrors to the sky, filling the new leaves hanging above with mysterious, lacustrine light. Frogs kept the water clean in layers of metallic shimmers, allowing only occasional mosquitoes with black-and-white legs to rest at the edges, swaying on dark fronds that shook with tiny flowers. The edges of the garden had come of age too: corrugated-metal boundary fences lived as stretching hedges of great denseness, pushing a haze of insects up onto the air to inflict retribution on a sky that never gave anything but dust.

'I wish I could pray for rain, but that's part of a greater thing that belongs only to the River,' Chrisnelt said. Tendrils twisted and shoots curled in the communal dance of all the weeds of all the world. At night, the river mist visited, looking for seeds, lifting them to the stars like feathers.

Chapter Eight

A SCIENTIFIC PROJECT CAME to Chrisnelt as he was gently wiping leaves one day. Ideas had come to him before – many times – while polishing petals or cleaning dust from protruding tendrils, but this time there was a rush of brightness, accompanied by a song like that of raindrops dancing on glass. He'd been waiting for the tree to grow into a real tree. 'It's still very much a bush, in my book,' he'd said to Chaminda the previous week. 'The roots have not yet reached the River. It's not a tree, it's still a treeling.'

In the bend of one meandering tree-limb was the beginning of a small nest: a House Sparrow nest. Chrisnelt marvelled at the design emerging, neatly wedged there in the dappled light: dried grasses and bits of twig had coalesced to form a new thing, intertwined in a circular fashion, twirled with tremendous energy and clear purpose.

'No's sparrows have come home to roost,' he said, as he watched them flit back and forth across the garden, pausing in the eaves and on the boundary walls. 'They're singing for him. Perhaps this is *the* treeling, and it'll grow to hold me, and all the birds, high above the City and its sooty flatness.'

The House Sparrow was a small bird, now becoming common in every district. The arrival of these sparrows had been abrupt, unnoticed at first, and then incremental, as his father had told him and No – like the mango tree that had appeared suddenly up the street. The species presented a charming song of innocence, a swaying hymn, bathing in the dust. No once said that a sparrow's wings sounded like a clapping crowd in his head, and Chrisnelt now always listened for that applause.

He resolved to monitor the nest, recording its architectural story. It would be a story he'd want to read and read again, all the time thinking of No.

Nipcia appeared to warm to this new project. The nest was something she could see and touch, something manageable in the hands. It was like a little house to her: a home of curling branches, of swirls like the ones she made in pots of food on the fire, but a home nevertheless. She'd always been the loudest, and was the first to step forward after their father had disappeared. Mrs Malotika was not there much anymore, and Divi was always at church, singing in all the choirs. Home meant something different to her. The Malotika home had become her nest in many ways: her small world.

'Perhaps the first sparrows came here in cages, as pets, shackled to lonely dreams,' said Chrisnelt to his sister – their first proper moment of connection in all these years. They shared a seat on the warm rock, its blackness soothing their arses. 'Perhaps the sparrows hitched rides on boats that nudged the coast of Africa; or on the shadows of other birds, on a lightness of distance and foreignness. Perhaps it was a gentle suck of air that pulled them across the clouds, obeying the Earth as it moved the sun and the moon in illusion?'

Nipcia looked at him. 'You're weird,' she said.

Although she was intrigued by the little house and the movements of the birds, Nipcia was lost in the strange speeches her brother constantly proffered. Still, her arrival in the garden was good. It widened both of them, widened the garden in their minds. They were warm, a brother and a sister together, heart next to heart. Even in the uncomfortable heat of the City, warmth was good.

They dangled their feet in the pond, a black water-beetle crawling onto Chrisnelt's big toe like a castaway finding land at last.

'Look, the bird has not finished with the house,' said Nipcia, pointing, as the sparrow alighted next to a red flower with a long feather in its beak. The beetle now on his sister's big toe.

'No was onto something, playing with the sparrows,' Chrisnelt told her. 'He heard them. They'll want to stay when my treeling becomes a tree. That's for sure. Their first choice, long ago, must have been a tree.'

'The House Sparrow originated in the Middle East,' he explained, 'spreading alongside the people who were slowly planting a new world of green; they reached Europe, Asia, North Africa, and then the rest of the world. This little bird lives in many climates now. Some people say they always took to the air in twos: two by two into the future,' he said. 'Such soft little things, tossed into civilisation, an experiment of instinct. A civilisation of eaves, gutters, steeples, domes, minarets, parapets! Feathers scattered like bones and dice, holding ancient gamblers' dreams. What a thing! This bird has made nests on top of the highest buildings in the world, touching the sky; deep in the deepest mines, dug into lies. WHAT A THING! A bird of triumphs and failures. A bird dancing between wilderness and walls!'

Nipcia rolled her eyes.

'I must listen to you, like No listened,' he said to the sparrows.

The water-beetle had made its way to the far side of the pond, crossing its widest diameter. Nipcia scratched a mosquito bite and said: 'Now the other bird has arrived with a feather. It looks like a chicken feather from my kitchen.'

'They will line the inside with those, making the warmest mat on earth,' said Chrisnelt.

'A curved mat.' She made a shape with her hands.

'Yes, I guess so.'

'The smallest mat on earth?'

'Yes,' laughed Chrisnelt, still writing furiously, his wet feet shining under the sun. Nipcia lay on her back, curved backwards over the rock, looking a bit like a mat.

'Those Nagasaki boys and those MacDonalds better not come and piss on this nest,' said Nipcia.

'Yes.'

'I'll make sure they don't.'

The sparrows became a big part of the garden. Chrisnelt embraced these birds, spending much time watching their movements and reading of their important history of exodus. He jumped into his books, reading all about of the resilience of the House Sparrow. He adapted paragraph after paragraph, filling the gaps in his understanding. The words flowed like bubbling streams in his notebook, Chrisnelt sweating in all that heat, books open everywhere. The notebook said 'NO's BIRDS' on the black cover, the blue ink glistening in the light, as if the black cover were itself the night sky rising above a strange river made of words.

The books lay against him in his room at night. His fingers shook as he wrote about all the changes people had made on earth. He stood up, and with his ballpoint pen drew the routes of the sparrows across all his maps. He showed how they connected continents and oceans with their busy wings. In some places, he stuck their little feathers, one even on the very tip of Africa, just for fun. These allegorical birds of the street dust gave Chrisnelt many words – and quite a few feathers here and there, most of them collected by Nipcia – as they built the nest. He watched them constantly. Once or twice they flitted up into his bedroom, bringing the sun onto his highest books, resting, puffed, in decorations of silence.

'Get out,' said Nipcia. 'If you shit in there, *I'll* have to clean it.'

'Too late,' laughed Chrisnelt, wiping the wall with a finger. 'Good for the flies,' he said, transferring the deposit onto a leaf near the doorway, rinsing himself in the pond, attracting black water-beetles. 'Look, the ocean-going ships eat shit,' he said, continuing to laugh. Nipcia laughed too.

The notebook became a conglomeration of chapters imagining the times before antiquity, when little brown birds hovered above people who'd just begun to walk upright, away from the flat savanna trees toward today, from known truths into unknown lies, forgetting the sacred past: a message of a clear and lost connection with the natural world. Chrisnelt noted with concern that these house sparrows could no longer live in the wild grasslands; they could not live on the wild plains, or in the desert scrub. And they could not live in the air or on the water or within the ice. 'Instead they have come to find walls, high and long, and they have made a home alongside our desperation and mistakes,' concluded Chrisnelt to Nipcia. An unusual tear came from him then. He remembered how the sparrows fled the mango tree, before No became the highest branches.

The inability of the House Sparrow to penetrate the past, the primordial wilderness, danced in Chrisnelt's mind. He stuck sparrow feathers on every city marked on every map. On New York, Paris and London, he added tiny nests of twigs, on Beijing he added extra feathers. From some cities, the feathers fell.

He watched the birds, his eyes bent into intense shapes, especially when the birds sat still, dripping with the dew of oceans.

'These sparrows are a powerful link between a house and a tree,' he said. The birds came down to the ground next to his pond to feed on the seeds of his weeds.

Nipcia came down the corridor to watch them bathe. 'Any eggs yet?'

'No, not yet,' said Chrisnelt.

At sunrise the next day, having exhausted all his reference books, Chrisnelt commenced his scientific observations. He clasped a new notebook for the new work, determined to write revelations.

'I shall express clear data-capture procedures, noting modal and mean clutch-size information, with regard to the breeding biology. I will also explore incubation, hatching weights, fledging period and related climatic variables as the study proceeds. I will measure each egg. I don't have Vernier callipers, like the books say, but I'll use this blue plastic ruler,' he said to Nipcia. He flashed it around, having acquired it on the one day he attended school.

But of paramount interest to him – and the true motivation behind the observations – was that the nest was also the face of friendship: the smiling face of No. That face had become a mask inside his eyes, and when it was not making him blink it was making him think of his tree for the birds. 'I've missed recording nest-site-selection behaviour, a most revealing activity in a world with no free space,' he said, writing that down, the first bit of data, in the notebook.

'Chrisnelt, I want to do that,' said Nipcia, watching him measure with the blue ruler. 'You and No used those for sword-fighting. Now you're fighting with these little branches.'

'Well, if you hold the branch, I can measure the nest size. It'll help. It's bouncing all over the place.'

'Okay.'

On day one, Chrisnelt and Nipcia devoted time to interrogating the structure and shape of early nest-making and its component parts of obligate engineering. This was how Chrisnelt explained the job to his sister, the crisp plastic of the ruler flicking light up to the sky. She shook her head, calling out numbers, listening all the time for the birds that waited on the bookshelf. 'They squeak before they shit, Chrisnelt.'

With a pompous smile, Chrisnelt said: 'We shall call this nest design a vernacular tradition of natural selection.' The sun pushed the heat down onto every house and onto every slit between every house, the air shivering under the weight, walls swelling and sweating in the tightness. 'A good house is built on good foundations,' said Chrisnelt to Nipcia, although he was certain the houses of the City had no foundations at all, just a ponderous mass of cracks and hardness over ancient soils and forest footprints, tugged at by occasional rains and the dusty winds of failed prophets.

'I'm hot,' said Nipcia. She leant down, scooping up some water to cool her face.

'That's not for us,' said Chrisnelt.

'Sorry,' she said.

Chrisnelt began to sketch. It sounded like rain, the pen pitter-pattering about, the tip singing in circles. 'Nests are round because the Earth is round,' said Chrisnelt. 'It seems to me that a circular thing has great strength, unifying the forces of our world into a powerful vortex of love. Such is the shape of a raindrop before it becomes mud, and such is the shape of a nest before it becomes the tree.'

'Don't talk of water. I'm thirsty,' said Nipcia, now measuring the height of the nest from the ground, making an imaginary pole of blue segments with the blue ruler.

'The placing of the first, strong twig of a nest is an act I would one day wish to see. It's a thing of considerable creativity and hope, followed by commitment,' said Chrisnelt. The male sparrow almost sat on his head.

'Shut up and write,' said Nipcia. She called out the numbers.

'Every House Sparrow would undoubtedly find a place to make a home instinctively, but the moment of choosing the site is something beyond that, belonging to the realm of emotion: a profound interaction with a tree, the bird deciding a way forward in a world bathed in the aesthetic light of opportunity bursting through leaves, as if the leaves were little glass windows onto the future,' whispered Chrisnelt as he recorded Nipcia's measurements. He saw a nest in a tree as a place of shared ownership and voluntary cooperation, an exquisite landscape beyond walls. He blinked once, and smiled to himself. The mask of No's face smiled too.

A sketch of the nest was completed economically in seven or eight flicks of the hand, all the component parts interwoven on the page, a strange graphic record of the assembly of an enclosure for life. Chrisnelt wrote down the date next to his drawing, and next to that a list entitled 'building materials' in large, distinctive letters. 'A few feathers included early in the construction belong to the moulted wing of a Rock Dove. This is also not native to the City – just like the weeds, the foreign trees and the new languages,' he said.

'Shut up and draw,' said Nipcia.

Chrisnelt smiled and, in the pompous voice again, said: 'Even the sparrow finds a home, and the swallow has her nest, where she rears her brood besides the altars.' He wrote this down in big loops, quoting aloud further bits of a psalm from the region of his mind that stored such things.

'Shut up. I want to hear the birds,' said Nipcia.

Day two was a time of much activity in the treeling. Chrisnelt did not move from his position on the rock, toes in the cool pond of clouds, eyes on the movement in the leaves. The male and female sparrows – the male displaying a bright grey cap and little black bib of piousness, the female awash in quiet dust colours – owned the air of the Garden of the World, flying in and out on productive wings. Each item arrived like a triumph, joining the loose jumble of energy emerging. The branches of the treeling became a place of wonder: bark evolving into coarse grass stalks with seed heads, feathers, bits of cloth, fluff and crumpled newspaper columns. Some elements of the nest – leaves from elsewhere, folded and wedged – seemed to live independently; a single petal of luminous pink nudged its way into the hermetic formation. This nest arrived quickly indeed.

'I'm sick of measuring,' said Nipcia. She did not help on day three.

Chrisnelt observed how odds and ends from the neighbourhood had been brought together to make something new. He'd seen this before, when the River would occasionally give things to the shore: folding reeds, twine and plastic becoming temporary islands for terrapins, rafts for egrets and cormorants. He'd seen, too, how the rain pulled leaves and dust into the street furrows, accumulating mounds for beetles and lines of ants to cross. 'Memories of many places becoming a new place, the way ideas from all horizons can come together as a fresh commonality,' he said to his sister, with a fresh smile.

'Shut up,' said Nipcia from the kitchen. 'You sound like you're in a pulpit.'

The nest had risen from the widest branch (which was not too wide because the tree was still a small tree), and was interwoven with other, thinner branches. It was globular like an unusual head, with a tunnel-shaped side entrance of thinking shadows. It also reminded him of a squashed ball he'd once found, although considerably hairier and more interesting. (He'd never kicked a ball of any sort, deciding at the age of twelve that he never would, because balls looked too much like the Earth, especially when muddy.)

Just then, the sun floated through the clouds, and he sketched intently, showing how the branches holding the nest ended in myriad green leaves and red flowers, calling bees, butterflies and all the birds. He sketched everything in a frenzy of heat and shade. It was another very hot day.

'There is nothing myopic about the treeling, or any other treeling anywhere ever planted,' Chrisnelt said to the sketch. 'A treeling sees forever when it becomes the tree of sparrows.'

The male sparrow landed on his head, as did the female. Such was the tutelage of the nest-treeling and the treeling-nest.

Chrisnelt made important findings: the frequency of sparrow-calls was linked to the position of the sun in relation to the treeling, and consequently the sounds set the tempo of assembly of the various elements that became the nest. A low sun at dawn spoke to the treeling in silence, warming the leaves to bright green, releasing the beginnings of cheeping sparrows: one repetitive series of cheeps lasting a minute came from the male; single cheeps at ten-minute intervals came from the female. And in between the cheeps came bits of nest, added slowly in the moving shadows. By twelve noon, the sun held the treeling like a dancing marionette in full shimmer, the male sparrow now singing in constant cheeps interrupted only by the carrying of nesting material, the female cheeping here and there as she worked, the nest expanding in the lungs of all singers. And then, in the late afternoon, before the tropical stars floated out from behind dreams, the leaves dimmed to the tune of slow cheeps, silence came, and then silence gave way, and the moths came.

Chrisnelt, filled with vibrations, wrote in much detail about the silence between cheeps, regarding it as a time of reflection for the birds and the treeling above the glittering pond. 'In the natural world, periods of silence are more relevant than periods of sound.'

It was only when he heard the female making a short chattering call that he knew the nest to be complete. One morning, she opened her wings to the approaching male. Balanced on a branch, they performed the beginning of the act of egg-making in powerful silence.

Day three and four passed in stillness. Chrisnelt counted the hypnotic movement of butterflies and bees in the brightness. The little insects flickered bits of sun in the heat, playing with the treeling and the shadow shape it made on the ground.

'Living petals,' Chrisnelt said to Nipcia.

She'd spent that day sitting very still, watching her brother as he watched his world. 'You know, Chrisnelt, people think you're mad, always talking to yourself here. Divi says you've been mad for years. But I don't think so anymore. You're just talking to those that don't talk,' said Nipcia. She'd been standing there in the doorway for some time, a baguette for her brother in her hand, watching him watch.

He looked up at her, and the mask of No's face smiled.

On day five the first egg came. The black rock warmed Chrisnelt and Nipcia in incubatory thoughts. They both shifted delicately, then both reached up to lift out an egg for inspection, Chrisnelt's fingers usefully prehensile.

'Careful,' whispered Nipcia.

'It's white and it glows in fine, brown speckles against a tinge of distant green,' said Chrisnelt.

'It's hot.'

'Very.'

'It's like a boiling egg.'

'It's hotter than all the heat of the entire planet right now. So hot with life,' said Chrisnelt. The egg was like a rising moon in the hand. He began to cry: for its curved edges, for earthly circles and earthly hopes, and for the tiny horizon it presented to the future. He cried for his father and the gift this treeling had given. He cried for No: a gift of wings for tomorrow.

'Your face is like a mask,' said Nipcia, wiping away Chrisnelt's tears.

He wrote poem after poem, filled with numbers and the names he'd offered every leaf he'd ever known. He wrote like the rain writes, and he wrote like the rain sounds on the other side of blasphemy. An egg came every day for the next seven days, one for each day of the week. Sunday's egg was the biggest.

On that same day Chaminda came to visit Chrisnelt, stepping through the sea of books on the bedroom floor. 'You are growing birds now, not trees?' he said, noticing the feathers stuck to the maps on the ceiling. He handed Chrisnelt a forest fern in a Coca-Cola can.

'Where've you been, Chami? It's been weeks!' said Chrisnelt. 'I haven't needed replacement trees from you for a while, and look, this one's still alive. Not a tree yet, still a treeling. And it's got a nest in the middle of the leaves. It's stronger than any that have come before, and a little higher too.'

Every time he visited after a gap, Chaminda prepared himself for discovery, for something new. 'I feel like I cross a vast bridge when I come here, back into ancient lands,' he said.

'Nipcia and I have been doing some science,' said Chrisnelt.

'Yes,' said Nipcia proudly, holding up the blue ruler.

There was much chatter. The sparrows made circles above their heads. As they spoke, Chaminda looked around: a river of foliage in every green, a torrent of fecundity. The little garden was a remote patch of life in a sea of soot. Leaves surged, making Chaminda sigh: 'This is the Garden of the World now, Chrisnelt. And yet so small.'

'Yes, the moths have been waking me at night in the breeze, reminding me to keep watch over the treeling, and I've been diligent with the toilet water,' answered Chrisnelt. 'Many mosquitoes with the black-and-white legs have sung for me in the moonlight.'

'Yes,' said Nipcia shaking her head, holding her nose. 'Mr Stink has continued his work.'

'There's indeed much to learn, even in the midst of darkness, if you keep working,' said Chrisnelt.

'And much to learn about measuring and toilet water,' said Nipcia.

'This treeling has many lives within it,' said Chrisnelt,

patting the little trunk like it was part of him.

'You and the leaves, Chrisnelt, and the birds,' said Chaminda with a slow glint in his eyes, shaking his head. He looked back through the bedroom doorway, and down the passage leading to the front of the house, the street, and every street: 'You and the many leaves.'

Chrisnelt smiled. The passageway was filled with leaves. Tiny sketches inhabiting the walls, the floor, and the low ceiling: a tunnel of leaves drawn individually over week, many thousands of contemplations sparkling in an extraordinary fresco forest.

Mrs Malotika and the girls had noticed the appearance of the first leaf one night, in the dark hollow before Christmas. For two days it was a lone leaf on the wall near the light switch. Day after day thereafter, more leaves fell upon the walls. Divi and Nipcia went to their mother, filled with questions and concerns, until finally Mrs Malotika said: 'Leave him, girls. Your father would've said that we must leave him. Oh Lordoo. I pray that he'll share his thoughts with us one day before Hell.'

The drawings had taken many hours, each one carved with a pen of memories into the green paint, the blue ink tattooing the surface with fine-lined revelations. The astounding detail was botanically accurate, revealing the true nature of each leaf: primary veins, secondary veins, capillary veins, midrib, petiole, stem. The density, size and distribution of stomata were shown, dotted and patterned, giving the leaves breath. Bristling skeletons, bowing to the world of grace.

Leaf after leaf was a tombstone to him, planted in memoriam. Every leaf had been a friend, observed alive, delicate, stretching. Each leaf said 'Tata?' on an edge somewhere. Each leaf was framed by radiating lines of verse, telling of an individual life – No's life. Scratched words, pondered words, like the winding tracks through a forest.

'These are my tiny masks of green,' said Chrisnelt.

'The shade works just like the sun,' called Chrisnelt to Nipcia and Divi, rising the next day, much like a rooster. 'That's the heartbeat of a changing day.'

This he said below a new sun coming up, pushing fresh swathes of shade about. The girls had been preparing for the day, Mrs Malotika away at work before dawn again.

'That was a night of moon-heat,' he said to his sisters as he stretched. It had not been this humid for many years. He was wet. His mat was sticky. He'd had dreams that wanted to cover him like a corpse is covered. On finishing his blinks – he called them exercises now – he went into the garden to see how the treeling was coming along and to observe the nest project in its own magnificent heat. The sparrows sung from the eaves. And a murder of crows circled like shadows, long in wings and croaks.

'NIPCIA!' he screamed. 'I SMELL PISS.'

'The Pissing MacDonalds!' she cried, running from the kitchen, clutching the blue ruler like a powerful weapon.

Chrisnelt stood at the doorway, watching the burning tree, the nest to one side like a discarded gift. It gave off a little plume of white smoke. It was empty, stained and rancid. 'NIPCIA!'

'They've stolen beyond stealing this time,' she said softly to him, wise words on her lips, words she did not know she had had inside her heart, her eyes full of sadness;

the sadness more for her brother than for the eggs. 'The treeling?'

'Dead again!'

'They've burned it, and the little home. And more shameful piss!'

In delirium he fell, retreating into a ball. He began to sweat, searching for sanity away from the tears. As he shook, he became calm and detached. He whispered in his sister's ear, as she cradled his head: 'My latest observations yesterday showed the House Sparrow sits on eggs in twelve days of camaraderie. The male sits for a nine-minute session and the female for eleven. There is rhythm between the sexes, which is beautiful. Why have we lost rhythm in this City?'

'This shameful piss of foreigners.'

'Nipcia, at least one of the chicks had begun cracking its egg from inside – breathing the air of my garden!'

'Yes, at least.' Nipcia stroked his big head.

'Nipcia, I anticipated, in my calculations with temperature, and the monitoring of movements inside the nest, that the fledging period would be seven days. Everything is seven days. I've been haunted by the number of days that make a year, and now I'll be haunted by the number that make a week. Most unexpected developments are forming above in the skies of rain, much benevolence and much hatred. Life has flown the coop.'

'Foreign piss poisons the soil. More charcoal!'

CHAPTER NINE

THE KISSING BIRD, THE CROW – Pied Crow to be specific – was always around, high up in its habit of shining blacks and whites, shitting bones. 'It's the cleverest bird I know,' said Chrisnelt. It was full of melancholy, but a bird of games, too: he'd once watched a crow dance with a plastic bag in the way fish dance with jellyfish in dreams. He'd often follow the crows because their interaction with the City fascinated him.

'They make me dream of pain and happiness. They're white and black. One living thing of confused colours above the Soot of the World,' he said to Chaminda, while planting another tree. 'They're as determined as the small plants that wrestle the concrete kerbs, and they're as resilient as a mango tree.'

Pied Crows offered shade to Chrisnelt's head on hot days, hovering above in new thoughts, often bringing confusion; his face crinkled deeply each time he looked up into the blue and the dust. The shade of these birds moved like his mind. 'They kiss the prey before eating it,' was written in his notebook in thick, wistful, blue words. This he'd concluded after seeing a crow tap its huge beak against a small bird's head before the unfortunate creature disappeared into shreds and gulps and a bump in a white neck. He'd seen this behaviour repeated with all manner of other food items – lizards, geckos, leather shoes and once, even, an abandoned finger.

'It's a bloody finger!' shouted Chrisnelt, pointing up at the high bird flapping its slow wings. The people of the street just stared at him, even when a drop of blood fell onto the sand, continuing their business in the heat. Sweat was always blinding in the City, as was sparkling soot. Chrisnelt ignored his racing thoughts regarding the finger. It was just too hot. He walked on, head down, confused, muttering poems. It was so hot the dust burned his calves. It burned at the poems writhing in his brain, scalding his nostrils.

'No,' he said aloud. 'I need to find fresh soils in this City. That's what I've been lacking. It's so hot, blood is falling from the sky! A tree needs fresh soils.'

Chrisnelt was spending less and less time in his garden. He was losing hope with the latest treeling, the roots always rotting. And it was Nipcia who now tended to it, taking water from the toilet fourteen times a day, every time the sun adjusted the light. The garden helped too. It grew as did the heat.

The entire City sweated. Even the taxi-cars hid in the shade. Chrisnelt followed the crows now almost every day – and found another part of the City, above homes and ownership: the world of roofs. Roofs were drifting places, detached thinking places. They were – in many ways – giant nests.

He was learning to read the City like he'd read the books. He walked new routes along the tops of walls, searching these rusting corrugations that gave a mask of ignorance to the sky. Some iron sheets slid one into the other, some flexed sharp like knives, others sat flat, like sheets of dried river mud. Only shadows cracked the flow of the crows above roofs. And he could read the bumpy surfaces like a blind man reads brail: bleached valleys and ridges, every dent and twist a tale of rejection by the sky, the rusty lines a sad remnant of wet seasons from long ago. And all about waddled purple pigeons like bruises on old skin, flushed by the crows.

'From the sky, from up here, the City is covered by a veil of soot, and it has no eyes,' he said to a crow, hovering very high. Looking down in the sweltering heat at the gaps between the houses, he said, to a stranger who thought he was mad up there on the wall: 'Paths people make near the River and its trees meander organically, coming back to themselves inevitably, because they are created by the endless joy of instinct. Yet these fucking sharp streets of unnatural eaves end in corners that stop dead in dead sands.'

Chrisnelt stared with a frown at another stranger below – a man he did not know, a man carrying so much charcoal, his back creaked and his mouth dripped glistening spit. 'I think I'm losing it. Is it indeed normal to look up past the eaves, into all this sterility? And all I see are leaves inside my eyes.' A distant crow sliding in confession through the lies above his head.

'You're not right in the head,' said a lady, shielding her small children from him: an odd young man above her, his body covered in dust, his blue pen clicking in his hand, his eyes red in the heat, his long arms outstretched like a balancing acrobat. He staggered a little. He was not sure of himself anymore.

'Fishes in the River have skins of scales perfectly formed for water as they swim, yet it is precisely the water that has given them the scales,' exhaled Chrisnelt at a dog, glimpsing the River in the distance down a channel between roofs. 'And so it should be with roofs, made to protect us from the sun; yet they have forgotten they were once a canopy of leaves, filtering dappled rains.'

'Go home,' said a man, carrying a pile of rotting mangoes that attracted butterflies. 'You need to get out of this sun.'

'Instead of battling the sun as they do, roofs should embrace it, as the Forest once did. Now there is just rusting armour and shame.'

'Go home.'

'Yes, go home.'

'Why have roofs abandoned their past? They should be promontories reaching upwards, with the widest of windows and doors to greet the flying birds. Open for the air. Waiting for the rains to come to faces and calling mouths. Now they're just places on which people can climb, laughing at a garden, pissing on a tree. All of this is because of evil walls. Without walls, roofs would float like shade on the branches of trees,' raved Chrisnelt. He stumbled, sliding down a pile of mud bricks. He sat there for some time, staring unblinkingly at a crow that rested on the shimmering day.

'Roofs of lost affirmation!' he yelled at the boiling sun, scaring children who didn't know he was the Gardener of Dee Dee Street. He felt weak all over his body, but mainly in his brain and his heart.

He was grateful for the strong pull of the crows. They helped him walk forward each day. Perhaps they would help him find soil. They helped him search for tomorrow.

Yet, before leaving the house each morning, he'd always pause in his garden for a moment, running his fingers across all the plants, kissing the leaves of the newest treeling. 'My tree is for No's birds. It will never be complete without the sparrows,' he said to Nipcia, as he walked out the front door. 'And I'm learning from all of them, all the species, in fact, so that garden shall be welcoming.' Then he'd be gone, below the shadows of wings.

Careful observation also revealed much about what happened under the roofs: a dark place of surreptitious communications gilded in pathetic dreams. Television antennae grabbed at the sky with tendrils of every length; telephone cables hung in loops, spanning the vast distance between lost answers and forsaken questions. The loops from some cables hung disconnected and taciturn, hoping to find other lost families of cables, the copper ends just ends, not connections. Occasionally shiny gold domes, minarets, steeples and steel crosses pushed at the sun above the captured crowds, wailing in defiance of the distant call of the River. 'Under roofs of rusting skin is the rusting skin of minds,' said Chrisnelt to the pigeons.

Television antennae fascinated him: they had no TV at home, and he'd only ever interacted with one through shop windows or at Café Gourmandine, in wafts of simmering steam. The fascination was compounded by the shape of the steel-and-wire limbs, so attractive to sparrows and crows. An antenna looked like a little Christmas tree. But it was what they represented that intrigued him most: they were deliverers of penitential tears. All morning, every morning – except during the news bulletins and advertisements for plastic funeral bouquets – death notices would shine on the television screens. The notices shook in gold frames on the official channel: one after the other they filled the view, a persistent downpour. Solemn photographs of dead people in finest, final outfits, each lost face accompanied by a voice-over – the voice of Pastor Kadazi – raining borrowed auguries, reverential moans of solace that sounded like laughter. The gold frames were beautifully three-dimensional, glowing like the frames in government buildings that held the hallowed photograph of the Governor, nailed to his white marble walls. 'THESE MAD HANDS GRABBING AT THE SKY ONLY EVER GRAB DEATH,' he screamed in through a window at a family huddled before the news, before he was chased off, scuttling along another wall between houses.

'We'll call the police, madman!' said a man. Chrisnelt ran and laughed.

Here and there in the heat, Chrisnelt began to see the first few satellite dishes blossom – pop after surprising pop – on optimistic roofs daring to reach further, past the clouds and the shameful lines of this City and its sovereignty. The tropical sun gave each foreign form a certain brightness; and against the corrugations on top of the City, the sea of rust began to flower, eloquent and oracular, grasping the radio waves that wandered the skies of the world.

One day at noon, Chrisnelt walked into a big, red box. He'd been watching a crow that appeared keen to make a nest. Birds always had a way of showing him things. (These crow-days had added another ten species to his bird list.) The red box was hard and metallic, and because he had been looking up all the time, he had not seen it, kicking it with his big toe. The box echoed. It was filled with people.

The lofty crow had been teetering below the sun. It was bigger than normal, an expanding shadow across everything. A long strand of bent wire – a treasure – dangled from the beak as it glided. The crow landed on top of a high column of steel triangles, standing as a tree trunk might have once stood: a gathering place. The column rose from the street and the dust, displacing the pavement. Near the tip was a nest of barbed wire holding a second crow.

Chrisnelt had never seen a crow's nest made of steel before. 'A crown of thorns,' he said. 'A crown of steel thorns at the end of a mighty steel column. This thing's like a Christmas tree without branches.'

'Actually, it's a communication mast,' said a young man, appearing from within the red box. 'We've just erected it.'

Next to the mast, below its nest, the red box glowed in the heat. Its front face opened onto the street, a giant door hinged at the top, hanging open and horizontal, held by the hot sky, under which a shop hummed in an electric buzz. This was something new.

Chrisnelt's toe throbbed in pain. 'I think I've broken it,' he said to the man. 'I was following crows and looking for good soils.' He bent down to rub his toe.

'This is the first of our shipping containers to arrive,' said the man.

'Like packages from the post office?' said Chrisnelt. 'I see the postage stamp there: EXCLUSIVITÉ AIRTEL!'

The man laughed. 'All the way from Europe, just for you.'

'For me?'

'For all of you,' said the man. 'Actually, for all of Africa.'

'Some foreign parcels are bigger than others,' said Chrisnelt. 'I'm used to Coca-Cola cans.'

The man smiled. The heat was new to him. Metallic flies ran across his white forehead as if it were a snow-covered football pitch.

'Our continent is a place of foreign parcels now. Our cities are parcels too,' said Chrisnelt to the white man and the crow. 'So much has been delivered. How these big names have come in giant gift boxes filled with contradictions! I've seen many other boxes like these come on trucks from the coast, filled to the top with other parcels: our reed baskets now arrive readymade in blue plastic, clothes shimmer like plastic trees, and our old food is new food, wrapped in cooking instructions that nobody can read.'

The crow sat and looked at him from the sanctity of the nest of nails. The white man looked at him too, silent for a moment. 'Who are you?' he asked. 'You talk like you've had too much sun.'

'Chrisnelt.'

'Chrisnelt?'

He'd been told by his mother to be proud of his name, to stand straight, defying shadows. His was the forty-seventh most popular name in the Country. He was grateful not to have been named Chrisphy, which came in at number forty-nine, Chriscovitch, fifty two, or Christ, which was number one, carrying with it too much hope and responsibility. 'Chrisnelt, the Gardener of Dee Dee Street. I'm looking for soil.'

Chrisnelt followed the man inside, as did a flock of flies – all living things wanted to get out of that blistering sun. A long table at the rear of the container displayed four computer monitors with keyboards. Seats in front of each station were occupied by patrons, intently clicking away in a new dance. Lots of questions were being asked. The screens of the monitors sparkled and sang like a forest filled with birds. On the inside walls were posters: 'MOBILE MONEY; SEND MONEY ACROSS THE NETWORKS; PHONE THE WORLD; KING OF THE BUNDLES; SURFING THE INTERNET.'

The young man sat on a high stool to one side of this rectangular space of heat and premonition, out of the direct glow of the sun. He possessed a powerful stare of responsibility. His feet dangled in patent-leather, many-toned shoes – little patches forming a jigsaw puzzle of all the countries of all the world, thought Chrisnelt.

'Who are you then?' asked Chrisnelt.

'Ásbjörn.'

'Asbjorn?'

'No, Ásbjörn.'

'That's a new one.'

He was originally from an island in the far northern Northern Hemisphere, a place owned by ice that trapped the bluest sky ever made. Ásbjörn took this new job of his extremely seriously, watching the street of heat as it moved about, cooking up ignorance. His shop was in the only quiet corner, perched like a pet on a pulpit.

Chrisnelt had a way of getting to know people of importance. On observing the man's difficulty with the local language of the City, he'd begun speaking to this well-dressed manager in French, then quickly switched to English. He did not try Lingala, or any of the many other African languages that hid behind the old French walls, for the simple reason that Ásbjörn was so very white. In fact, he was the whitest person Chrisnelt had ever seen, and he'd grown up with quite a few of them. Ásbjörn was so white, Chrisnelt's eyes ached when he looked at him. He was whiter than a cloud in full sunshine, or the whitest feathers on the neck of the cleanest crow, or those on the cleanest chicken before it was plucked. He was even whiter than a free Christmas tree.

Ásbjörn was a translucent man, his skin silky and hairless, and as wet as the breast of a fish. His glowing whiteness offered clear glimpses of blue and green veins every time his heart pumped ideas through his limbs. Intermittent red hairs shone on a narrow head like nylon filaments, and his fingernails were more orange than pink, holding a permanent sunrise. He'd come to live his life in the tropical splendour of big trees because of an intense dislike of frozen sea-ice. He'd permanently lost his brother to a slab of it one winter morning near his home town – his brother had been pissing on the ice, dreaming of fire. His name meant Divine Bear in Icelandic, which was strange in itself, as he was such a small brittle man with no fur. Chrisnelt looked at him with immediate concern: the slightest breeze might snap him in two – and what if he slipped off the high stool? The sun had already made itself at home on his face – a remarkable blush that would soon swell into a single memorable blister of biblical proportions. The flies seemed particularly attracted to him, and they continued to play football on his face.

'This is a most unusual shop,' said Chrisnelt, leaning against the metal wall and rubbing his sore toe with a dirty foot. He was slightly distracted by the buzzing of the many flies. The shade of the roof scared away the heat temporarily. 'A roof can be like a tree, they say, providing shelter from the heat and many unwelcome insects. In exchange, the tree must demand the fellowship of tribes inside the tightness of its room,' said Chrisnelt, looking out onto the bright street, his words designed to stimulate much talk.

'Thanks for speaking English. Not many people do around here,' said Ásbjörn, 'and it's all I really have, apart from the language of these screens.'

'What's your home language?'

'Icelandic, but it's melted under this bloody sun of yours!' said Ásbjörn, with a laugh of despair tempered by delight. His words fell like snow: 'How old are you?'

'Seventeen.'

'You've got six more to catch me.'

'My friend Chaminda says I'm more like a hundred.'

'I think it's the damn sun!'

'I'm always in the sun, looking for soil.'

'Ah, the gardening.'

'Yes, I'm trying to grow a tree as a tribute to special memories. I've tried many species in my garden, but the sun isn't too kind. And neither is this City and its soil.' He kicked the dust.

'Well, there aren't any where I come from, just ice! So I'm no help.'

'Africa's the place of trees and the growers of trees.'

'And heat.'

'I also watch birds, they help me think,' said Chrisnelt, pointing up at the crow. It dipped up in an arc, croaking like a frog.

Stuck to the inside wall of the red box, behind Ásbjörn, stretched a vast map of the world. It was unlike any map Chrisnelt had ever seen. A blizzard of black; a map of deep blackness filled with stars glittering eternally; a map that opened the side of the bright container into the darkest, most spectacular night Chrisnelt had ever touched.

'This is the strangest map I've ever seen,' said Chrisnelt slowly, fluttering his long fingers across its shining surface. 'And I collect maps!'

'Actually, it's more like a photograph-map,' said Ásbjörn.

Such a map had been hinted at only in Chrisnelt's dreams, and in between raindrops on the sepulchral window of the Bedroom of the World: alive only when the rain came, lit by the moon. To behold raindrops chasing raindrops on pilgrimages to the ground had been Chrisnelt's private dance of numbers and equations; the formulae for the intimate festivals inside his big head; the way to finding No. Now it was here for all to see, in this red box of public screens, flies and heat. 'What a parcel this has turned out to be,' he thought. 'A black world of sky, filled with glittering raindrops!'

Ásbjörn laughed loudly when he saw Chrisnelt's dancing eyes. Shifting on his stool, he turned to face the map, joining Chrisnelt on his discovery, as new friends do. Flies ran across the blackness, following Ásbjörn's turning cheeks. 'Yes, this is quite a map; it really tells a story of a planet. A photo of the Earth at night, actually. You can just make out the edges of the great ball, the black on the deeper black: no mountains, no valleys, no oceans and no lands, just this. Openness. And all those stars – they're the glowing lights of all the networks worldwide that are interconnected to form the Internet.'

'And you can't make out the countries, all that's here are these stars like wandering peoples. This is the landscape of the future, glowing here. It'll link every home and every family member in every home,' said Ásbjörn, spitting at a very big fly that had crawled too close to the side of his mouth.

'Stars are linked to stars in the beautiful black,' said Chrisnelt.

'You've had too much sun, man,' said Ásbjörn.

'Stars inside minds,' said Chrisnelt.

'If you say so, Mr Gardener of Trees.'

'Glittering stars in the truth of the night. Look at Europe and North America, they're shining. And look at Asia and its reflections ...' he paused. 'Africa still waits for your stars? Perhaps it's a different blackness here?'

'Well, I'm here to sell the Internet in the heat and the blackness.'

'I can promise you heat. AND blackness. At night, this place only talks in charcoal fires. It's hot then too.'

'I've seen the smoke.'

'And these stars of yours' – Chrisnelt darted his finger across the plastic surface of the map – 'of internet, are like the night-fires at forest gatherings long ago. That's another kind of ancient heat that's often forgotten.'

'I came here for the heat, actually,' Ásbjörn laughed, 'and the fireside chats too, I suspect, even if there's a lot of smoke! I came to share these beautiful stars.'

Chrisnelt had read about the internet. He understood the broad concept of it, even much about its algorithms, yet here he saw it laid out like a poem. And for the first time, tangible screens flickered for his fingers. Ásbjörn sat him down at a computer on the far end of the long desk where there was a bit more space, below a high corner that had gathered an immense spider web, sparkling with dead flies that looked like diamonds in the buzzing fluorescent light. Chrisnelt looked up into the delicate shimmer holding yesterday's street dust in silken strength, and felt the gentle shadow of a canopy, as if he were inside a forest.

In the evenings that followed, Chrisnelt learned much about the Tree he would grow for No. More than he'd ever dreamed. Doors opened. Windows opened. And all was a gushing river made of leaves and clouds of escaping moths. At the computer screen, Chrisnelt spent much time – days, nights and months – with his back turned away from the dust. He would find every book ever written and every image ever drawn. He would see numbers in every form and poems in every language. On that first day alone, he learned to speak Icelandic and sing Icelandic songs, while listening to the calls of every bird in every sky that loved heat. He emailed many people he did not know, new people with new ideas. Many of the one billion emails sent that day around the world were his, he dreamed.

He read about the gardens of the moon, the flowers that bloomed in the ice of isolation. He read of gardens on the sun; green after tumultuous green. He read of trees falling, inspiring the falling of others like bodies on battlefields.

He read of trees that stood alone, wanting only to stand with others once again. And he saw trees calling, wanting to touch the branches of other trees, beyond the hopelessness of countries and the sickness of sovereignties.

The internet, it seemed to Chrisnelt, was the distant future, on the very edge of evolutionary boundaries, illuminating the other side of the walls of perdition: all the way back, long before Belief, walking along a spoor-line, to where everyone began on the plains, at the extremity of the first forests of birds, dancing with the grass. A canopy of pixels, a new roof for the brilliant world of thoughts on the far side of the City. A roof of windows in that red box on the dusty street. A digital sky; the smiling new mask of No.

Chapter Ten

Mr Nagasaki had recently come back from a short trip to Japan, quietly bringing with him his aging wife and their ailing daughter Amaterasu. He'd waited many years to fetch them. The home – sharing a common wall with the Malotika home – was now ready in this 'City of the Deepest River on Earth', as he always called it. (Although it would be more accurate to now call it the 'City of Communication Towers and the Deepest River on Earth'.) His catfish-farming business down at the dock was good, even though it attracted exceptional swarms of flies that could not be removed, not even by a sermon from Pastor Kadazi that only stopped traffic. His two sons had grown into their jobs stirring the fishponds next to the barges, and selling cellular-phone airtime coupons. And it was time for the Nagasaki home to become a family home in the traditional sense.

Nipcia had kissed one Nagasaki boy once and never again. Divi had kissed the other boy once too. Mrs Malotika had given up trying to teach Mr Nagasaki how to bake croissants. And Chrisnelt had long since forgiven the boys for pissing on so many of his treelings. Calm had come to Dee Dee Street, much like that before a storm. And to the calm was added hope: a new treeling was starting to become a tree. Another family of sparrows were settling in the garden, and the crows had left Chrisnelt alone, allowing him to linger there.

It was then that he heard her laugh from the other side of the corrugated fence. A storm thundered in his head. It was immediate. He sat on the rock, toes in the water. Out aloud, he said: 'No.'

Chrisnelt would always remember the evening they arrived: Mr and Mrs Nagasaki and a girl his age. His treeling had begun to release red flowers into the air, the branches just high enough to catch a breeze sifting over the roof. As the five Nagasakis stood in their especially prepared courtyard at the back of their especially prepared house, inspecting the space of new opportunities, red showered onto them from next door, and Amaterasu laughed. And then she said, after reflection: 'Look, they're like little flags from home!'

That night, she bathed. In the confines of his bedroom, Chrisnelt lay on his mat and listened to the gentle splashing she made up against their shared bedroom wall. The wall was warm. In the liquid movement and gently rocking sound, she became water to him: cycles of water across the earth, regenerations and slow metamorphoses from ocean to cloud to rain to river and to ocean, again and again. She was gushing water-pipes, dripping taps, flowing drains and culverts. She was the mud stain that fanned wide in his garden. She was simply 'Amaterasu' and Chrisnelt loved her because she bathed with bees.

Bees had made their way into a crack in the wall that divided their rooms. The bees had been busy in this wall. At first they'd come to the garden, from all over the City. Determined visitors, inquisitive migrants from the forest. Over many years, they came like small gifts of light, and then they came to stay, belonging to the flowers, reaching for the fresh pleasures of life in Paradise. Then they came, like the sparrows: a vast hive filling the space in the old wall of ancient mud, breeding and swelling in numbers to fill further spaces between the bricks and the built-in, iron Nagasaki bath, until the bees became the wall in a soft and private hum.

Amaterasu ran her bath late into that first night, and every night thereafter, in that quietest time of owls and bats. The cold water tumbled out of the tap, tight up against the wall. Then she'd fill the bath with hot water from the kitchen fire, pouring it on to the cold, chanting blessings to little flames, closing the bathroom door; and then she'd float still in the steam. Every night the warm water would hold her, as it held the bath and the wall, releasing an aroma of mulled honey. The sweetness would fill Chrisnelt in his bedroom. It filled his maps, his dangling feathers, the drawings of carved leaves, his books and his entire body. And it filled him as a man is filled. And it filled her too, in the silence of intoxication.

There'd be a pause, and then the warm water would come in a surge, mulled, twirling down the long drain to his garden: cloudy water with intermittent hairs, soft curls of a woman's rain. Every night Chrisnelt lay on his bed, pressed against the continents, mountains, forests and rivers, facing the baptismal drain into his garden, his back to the wall in the heat. He'd watch the flow, pushed hard by the vibration of bees, swelling the green, a treeling in a little river: wide, slow, intimate as wilderness.

Chrisnelt never did speak to her, never did see her, only knowing the call of the bees, stirred by her bathing.

Nipcia said Amaterasu's language was Japanese spoken

only by the eyes. 'She's very shy, and she runs away when she sees any of us at the door,' said Nipcia, reporting back to Chrisnelt the next day.

Amaterasu was mute on most days, except for the early mornings, and when she spoke, it was as if the heat of the sun spoke, as if the silence of shade spoke from behind the fence, which was now a fence of the most beautiful big leaves that looked like hearts. A soliloquy of shapes, like those made by fluttering eyelids and swaying hands, like those made by trees. Chrisnelt glimpsed her once through a slit of sunshine, her skin of silk, exotic yet endemic too. 'Water of flowers,' he said to Nipcia. 'Water of flowers.' She walked like only a tree can walk: swaying and yet always still. Her taste was that of water. Her smell was that of water too.

'She is one of the people of the raindrops: unstoppable freedoms moving around the world as a single, living thing, continuous in flow,' said Chrisnelt to the drain outside his bedroom door, watching it swirl gently, deep in the night, as she bathed. He simply could not sleep anymore. That spewing drain, the smell of Amaterasu, the obligatory blinking exercises. He was becoming crazy again.

'I need to get some sleep, Nipcia,' said Chrisnelt. 'No time for this, only time for my Tree. I need to find good soil.'

'I *have* been telling you for years that you need a job,' said Nipcia.

'Yes.'

'Divi is already a pastry manager AND head of the choir.'

'Yes, yes.'

'I'll speak to Mama next time she's home early. She always leaves before I wake up. Maybe there's good soil at the church yard.'

'Thanks Nipcia.'

'What about the soil from Mr Warnakulasuriya's vegetable garden that you always talk about?'

'That's only good for shallow carrots and onions that make you cry. No tree could ever grow in that. I need to find good soil for the very deep roots. I'll dig down next to the treeling, and feed it at the very bottom as it searches.'

He was sweating like never before, deep into the night. He gazed up at his maps on the ceiling, a single sparrow feather coming loose and dancing about to the tune of the mosquitoes with black-and-white legs, and the rattling American cockroaches, cosmopolitan larder beetles from Europe, and smooth woodlouse, also from Europe. 'Long ago a primordial island lay in waters of the world ...'

He turned on his side.

'... and from the distance, near the stars, all was a flood of blue, floating above potential browns, blacks, whites and many other communal colours, held in clouds of apocryphal considerations.'

He turned again, this time onto his back.

'From islands come pondering islands; our world has always been held in islands of every size, adrift in miraculous seas of connection.'

Now he lay face down, his nose squashed into the mat. He mumbled.

'Every island is on the move; such is the story of rain. The African island – like the others – is changing at the sacrificial edge of waves longing for leaves.'

He sat up.

'Africa is made by water like a painting is made by a frame.'

He reached for a pen. He wrote quickly, all these words, these big thoughts becoming tiny lines on his long fingers, the unsettled tap dripping outside. And then he said with a breath: 'And a Japanese island has arrived next door in the heat of it all.' He sighed. 'I need to get bloody good soil. And fresh air.'

'Hello Mr Nagasaki,' said Chrisnelt on a quiet day, and with a big grin. 'How's the House of Bees?'

'Ah, you speak Japanese now,' laughed Mr Nagasaki.

Chrisnelt had indeed learned considerably more than just a basic greeting, having prepared for any encounter with his neighbours, especially after Chaminda and Ásbjörn jokingly suggested he should call Amaterasu 'Honey' if he were to meet her in person.

'Yes, we have beautiful bee because of your red little tree. And far away from this tree, on my island we have another tree, native to Kyushu, with feather for leaf, and it fly with the bee to make best honey in the world!' He laughed again.

'The bees are a part of my garden,' said Chrisnelt, staying modestly with English. 'I'm relieved you are happy for them to be part of our wall.'

'This tree grow nicely, Chrisnelt.'

'It *was*, yesterday, but today the leaves are starting to fall.'

'I sorry to hear.'

'Yes.'

'You not give up, not even in this new heat. Whole street with you.'

'Yes, Mr Nagasaki.'

'*Whole* street!' he pointed up and down the dusty street. Even the taxi-cars were covered in dust, moving along like lost river crabs.

'It's the *hole* I'm worried about. I dug it as deep as I could this time, and Nipcia and I got the freshest soils we could find. The soil is dead in this City. Pure soot down there now. No place for roots. I'm looking for new soil now.'

'Tree will find water.'

'Maybe the walls go too deep.'

Mr Nagasaki bent forward with a smile: 'Your father told me: "The Bee, it sing, not buzz." This wall of ours is one of the good walls: it sing. And you know, many bee become a single bee of cooperation. That what bee do. My family pray for you when we see sun.'

'Thank you, Mr Nagasaki, and thank your daughter for me too.'

'It I who thank you. My daughter sick. It your tree that make her feel better. She call it tree of flags. She sit outside and wait for flower to come on wind and also leaf. She say leaf is green flag of whole world.'

'Perhaps all leaves are.'

'She say it every day, same thing. That her sickness.'

'It doesn't sound like a sickness to me.'

'It terrible sickness. She forget each day when sun go down. New day she see for first time, each day. *New sun bring same day.* And she sit and look at flower and floating leaf, *always for first time.*'

'Hers is a pure day.'

CHAPTER ELEVEN

STRINGS OF WORDS MADE CURTAINS for him against the heat of
the sun. What shaded Africa, if not the trees? The grid of
the City streets filtered light into muted greys, hiding the
deep cuts from the new light. Chrisnelt had often thought
of these shadows as the bars of a prison cell, making
crosses and lines of penance. Roosters crowed incessantly
as the blizzard of sunshine came straight down onto rust,
and concrete dust found windows.

'This is the hottest day I can remember,' said Chrisnelt
to Nipcia as he walked out the door.

He made his way to the internet shop – as he did every
day after a morning of writing and counting and planting
– to ask questions of the world in many emails; and as
he went he looked for birds and weeds that might show
him new soils, the garden and his mind always needing
nourishment. The sun made straight light, leading him
down the street toward colour and fragrance.

A street can become a window on a good day, but
today the air shakes so much with heat that all is a bloody
blur, thought Chrisnelt.

Ásbjörn's many-toned shoes were crawling with
beetles, attracted to the patent-leather patches: mirrors of
black, white, pink, purple, green and blue, dancing in the
sun like spotlights. The tiny beetles, iridescent and hungry,
scurried relentlessly across his feet in their hopeless search
for anything that resembled flowers. Ásbjörn sat with one

leg crossed, swishing flies in the air with a foot, talking to a tall man who was trying to sell him a cell phone. The tall man, with loquacious eyes, was transfixed by the glowing shoes.

'They are magical things,' he said, pointing, as Chrisnelt approached.

'All the way from Italy, via Iceland,' said Ásbjörn.

'I only wear imported things,' said the tall man. His body was draped in an immaculate blue suit that looked like it was woven from glass. On his head was a small straw hat, tilted to one side, boasting a white chicken feather dancing above an auburn strip of ribbon, waiting for music to make it dance higher. 'I am La Mame, the most famous *sapeur* in the City. The boss of colour. The god of clothes. The pride of all the areas!'

'A *sapeur* is a member of *La Sape* – the Society of Ambience-Makers and Elegant People,' Chrisnelt told Ásbjörn.

'Yes, I'm the proudest and most famous member,' said La Mame.

'I can see,' said Chrisnelt. 'I love the colour combinations. And your pink socks with the sequins remind me of the stars inside raindrops before they fall.'

'My socks are from Paris. They sleep curled inside my shoes when I'm barefoot because they're so precious.'

'I wish all raindrops could sleep nearby, waiting for me,' said Chrisnelt. 'You are most fortunate that your raindrops are so close.'

'Yes,' said La Mame, looking confused.

'It's the heat,' said Ásbjörn to La Mame, 'he always talks like that. He thinks like that too!'

'He's a wise man,' said La Mame.

'Well, good-quality socks are just as important as good-quality shoes,' said Chrisnelt.

La Mame wanted to swap a bouquet of flowers for the shoes. They would surely win him any competition on any stage in the City, fulfilling his dream of one day being crowned king. 'I have another hat, with feathers the colour of a rainbow bug, which will match these shoes,' he said to Chrisnelt in French. 'I want to offer this beautiful bunch of flowers to your friend – a fair trade of delights. What do you think?'

'I think it's a fair trade,' said Chrisnelt in English.

'Hey, my shoes aren't for sale,' said Ásbjörn.

Chrisnelt stared at La Mame. Then he recognised him: 'You're the guy who steals flowers from the graves at the cemetery to sell at funerals.'

'Yes, it is me!' said La Mame. He was as proud about that title as he was about his suit. 'And it's not stealing. It's giving life to abandoned blooms. Flowers go on an important journey with me, you see. I take them to sad people.'

'The only journey is the one money takes down your pockets,' said Ásbjörn.

'Plants are not for the dead, they are for the living.'

'I agree,' said Chrisnelt.

'And I recognise you too. You're the young man who collects weeds,' said La Mame. They laughed.

'I'm Chrisnelt.'

'I'm La Mame.'

'I'm Ásbjörn.'

La Mame's route was carefully crafted across the

City. Every corner was his home, every alley of dust an extravaganza of loose coins and dirty bank notes. His eyes did business with the dear and departed. Chrisnelt had watched him for years: the impeccable clothes, the impeccable timing of the pilfering. Bodies were not even cold, the sand still moist with tears, and the fresh flowers would be gone, sailing down the street, darting left and right as La Mame floated on before the crowds, wrapped in his strange music: the clattering of his big shoes below the graceful tipping of his hat, and the waving of his ceremonial handkerchief.

'Yes, La Mame with the green fingers!' said Chrisnelt. 'I always wondered how you got over that high cemetery wall, and how you never got caught.'

La Mame laughed and shrugged: 'You have to go in the mornings. No funerals in the early mornings. The preachers are all asleep.'

'And what about all the plastic wreaths along the wall? Why don't you steal those instead? No climbing. Recyclable too!' said Chrisnelt.

'There's nothing good about plastic,' said La Mame.

'But the flowers you pull out are dead,' said Ásbjörn, 'they're just flowers on stalks. No roots! No difference?'

'A flower is alive, in my book, until the petals fall off.'

'I agree,' said Chrisnelt. 'And even after that, when it becomes the freedom of pollen.'

'You smell very fine' – Chrisnelt sniffed at La Mame – 'is that the call of flowers, or is it yours?'

'It's the scent of Europe, *Bleu de Chanel* – the finest eau de cologne in the world, to match my handkerchief, and these cuffs. The scent is good on black skin. It gets the girls' eyelashes going,' said La Mame. He posed like a king.

'I know it,' said Ásbjörn, 'Made in France, via Iceland.'

'Reminds me of mangoes,' said Chrisnelt.

'Just one squirt on this blackness,' said La Mame with a grin.

'I need two squirts on my skin,' laughed Ásbjörn.

'The City seems to only want the things that look foreign – and now it wants to smell foreign too,' said Chrisnelt. In the packed shop, computer screens shivered before many big heads, sitting in front of other heads, standing in front of more heads and shoulders and pushing bodies. 'The world is now a foreign crowd.'

'These clothes make me feel clean and give me courage,' said La Mame, striking another pose, this time with his fingers, cuffs glinting in the bright sunshine, shaking flowers, bending cultures. 'Helps me get my petals.'

'You know, out there on the edge of the River, in the distant green of our beginning, my books say the wild flowers grow by instinct, pure instinct. They grow out of corpses like they've always done. They can be smelled like they were always smelled. Now the foreign crowds have come and we smell in the way of strangers,' said Chrisnelt.

'Perhaps if your friend does not want to trade, I can post a letter for you? It's my other service, and with my talents, I can also draw the stamps on the envelope myself. I always make them look like flowers. I only do local postage, just in the City. It will definitely arrive in the hands of the intended recipient, as I'll use these feet, these hands and these reliable fingers. I can't do international. Those are different kinds of flowers altogether,' said La

Mame, pointing to the sky, where a high aeroplane made a white line.

'Those green fingers of yours speak the truth, La Mame,' said Chrisnelt. 'In every country in the world there's supposed to be at least one flower that's found nowhere else.'

'In Iceland I think ours is the Mountain Avens, a white flower. Our national flower, actually. Also known as "Thief's Root", La Mame, because long ago it used to grow in abundance below the place thieves hung when dead,' said Ásbjörn. He laughed and Chrisnelt laughed.

'That's not that funny,' said La Mame.

'Ours is the Hibiscus,' said Chrisnelt to La Mame.

'I've never seen one,' said La Mame.

'Me neither,' said Chrisnelt.

'I've seen many in Iceland,' said Ásbjörn.

La Mame lived on a red-and-green couch splattered in a weave of pink palm fronds that turned purple when wet. It had no buttons, and the faded circles where the buttons had once been fastened hissed air when prodded. Whenever a guest sat on the couch – he had many guests – it would gush with howling voices. La Mame called it the singing couch, and he laughed during these serenades, his big teeth shining with delight. The three-seater with cushions, surrounded by colourful plastic buckets filled with flowers of the world – sat propped against a wall of relaxed rubble busy with lizards, below a roof of three boat-planks that rested in dust near a street junction not too far from the River and the morning mists. Chrisnelt visited La Mame often, as it was La Mame who'd given him a bucket and the idea of collecting River Mud.

'Your bunches of flowers look like giant colourful buttons in this sunlight,' said Chrisnelt. 'You could sew them onto your couch!'

'That stuff looks like shit, and it has a strange scent,' said La Mame as Chrisnelt arrived with his bucket of sludge.

'You say that every time,' said Chrisnelt.

'I just can't get used to the smell,' said La Mame. He always said that, and they'd always smile and shake their heads, and talk about his cologne and the new smells that mixed with the very old ones.

'Well, it seems to be doing the trick in my garden, although the treeling is not responding as I'd hoped,' said Chrisnelt, sitting on the couch of songs. 'It's a smell I love. *My* scent. Every morning it arrives fresh, just for me, on those cabalistic shores.'

La Mame shook his head again. 'I hear your tree is leaning over to one side. Chaminda came and told me yesterday. And Ásbjörn told me the same thing this morning, on his way somewhere to collect something.' They'd all become friends, drawn together by the making of a garden. 'They're both on their way here now.'

'Yes, I know.'

'Oh, I thought it was a surprise.'

'Not in *this* City.'

'You see the River,' said Chrisnelt, changing the subject for a moment. The Great Dancing Road was busy that day, silver in the heat, wider than on most days, scattering little mirrors of itself to the far bank, upon which shimmered another City that was – in many ways – the same City. Barges floated like giant twigs, piled high with containers of blue and red and many whites, and on top of the containers slept men that looked like flat black postage stamps. The longer barges strained in the immense waters, the current forcing blue smoke from the smokestacks, smoke that snaked like vipers biting the air. A lone gull cried in a hopeless white dive for food. To the left, at a great distance, could be seen the green tips of a quiet forest that waited.

'Yes. How can I miss it! The thunder of the cataracts down there keeps me awake. Deepest on earth, you know.'

'Our River, right.'

'Yes.'

'It's a river because it knows it has come from the clouds, and will return to them again one day. It has a memory of its past.' He dug his hand into his bucket of mud. 'See *this*?' said Chrisnelt.

'Yes. Your scent!'

'*This* is the memory of my garden. And my garden has forgotten it.' The mud dripped onto the couch. 'Now it's remembering, as I mix it deep below the treeling. But I think I'm too late!'

'My couch will remember it.'

'An open space can only become a garden if it finds the memory of its past.'

'Hello,' said Ásbjörn, arriving from the one street, carrying a red box.

'Hello,' said Chaminda, arriving from the other street, carrying a hat.

'This is the couch of convocation,' said Chrisnelt.

It was the day of his eighteenth birthday, and La

Mame had arranged a little gathering. The friends sat silently for a moment; friends don't need to talk straight away. Sitting on the couch made them feel very hot. They fanned their faces with their big hands. Ásbjörn used an actual fan, a branded thing he'd received as a promotional gift. Chaminda's khaki clothes seemed bleached in the brightness, washed-out like the sky, and he fanned with more speed than his friends. The air shook like water. Silence was cooling in the heat. Chrisnelt sweated and his arse stuck to his shorts. The sweating made him think of fire and of No, then of his father, and then his thoughts drifted to Amaterasu.

Of course he'd wanted to invite her, but instead had tossed a red flower over her wall. And he would do so again tomorrow, and every day thereafter. That was a birthday promise to himself. In a strange way, it was a gift to himself too: he had never seen her; he would never see her; yet he felt he saw her more clearly than she could ever otherwise be seen.

They'd all kicked off their shoes: part of the cooling process. La Mame sat on an upturned bucket, his dark feet spread, toes splayed and broad, nails flat and wide: the open, grinning toenails of a past without shoes. Chaminda's toes were similar to La Mame's, but a little narrower and smaller. They were toes that could swim, and they'd learned much during their walk across the world. Ásbjörn's toes attracted flies – glistening green-blue beads chasing each other across the whiteness, and two big ones vibrated, stuck together in sex – and his soles shone orange-pink, displaying swelling veins. His toenails were a pale blue at their bases, each one arched like the shell of a tiny scorched tortoise. These were feet that had never been unwrapped, tight feet of Europe and the ice.

Chrisnelt thought of unwrapping things, and of gifts, and plastic. He fanned. And he thought of Amaterasu's feet, and how soft and small they might be, how the nails might sparkle in the bathwater, and how they might flutter like leaves, smiling like delicate eyelashes, even in this heat.

'Toes are like fingers,' said Chrisnelt.

'What?'

'Nothing,' said Chrisnelt.

'It's the heat,' said someone.

La Mame's living room of dust, made of pieces of broken city, creaked in a slow tropical stretch. A fishing net above them – a gift from the Nagasakis that had come via Chrisnelt – hung as a ceiling of tiny, framed skies, rocking gently in a new breeze. La Mame had worked hard that dawn making this roof, in honour of the birthday visit. A bird flew from windowsill to windowsill on the opposite side of the street, which was also the far side of a lounge, gleaning insects from grooves, tapping panes of glass, reaching across the illusions of the earth. It was a Collared Sunbird of the brightest yellows that bordered the brightest greens.

'BIRD NUMBER SEVENTY, and on my birthday!' shouted Chrisnelt. They all clapped, and the bird flew away before Chrisnelt could enjoy it more.

'Here,' said Ásbjörn.

'Thanks,' said Chrisnelt. 'It's a cell phone?' He opened the small red box.

'No.'

'It's a hand-spade and a hand-rake,' said Chrisnelt.

'For my garden.'

'Here,' said Chaminda, handing Chrisnelt a big, blue, floppy hat. 'It's to protect that brain that belongs to all of us.'

'Thanks.'

'My gift is this announcement,' said La Mame, his teeth bigger than ever before. He rose slowly, his big feet digging into the dust. 'The three of us have got you a job,' said La Mame.

'What?'

'Yes. Pastor Kadazi asked me to ask you to come and see him. And the three of us agree that you must go. It's our joint gift,' said Chaminda.

'He wants a garden, Chrisnelt, a great garden,' said Ásbjörn. 'He'll pay too. And only half day, so you can keep growing your tree.'

'My Tree!'

'Apparently *he* wants trees,' said Chaminda.

'And lots of big plants.'

'Maybe that soil is different?'

'A Great Tree?' said La Mame. 'It can be anywhere?'

'It can be where it must be,' said Chaminda.

'Anywhere where the soil is right.'

'Where it finds its memory of its past!' said La Mame, looking directly into Chrisnelt's eyes. 'As you have sometimes said yourself.'

'Time falls from the sun on days like this to bless me before the rains,' said Chrisnelt. 'So much dust.'

Chapter Twelve

Pastor Kadazi preached in loud words above the congregation about the coming of his garden, a most foreign idea in those parts. He stood on a wooden stool on a wooden stage, in a vast structure that was corrugated metal of the most porous kind, the scattered bullet holes on its sides, sending tubes of light about in a shimmering lattice, piercing a stench of sweat. The great shed shook, as if it were a giant river-fish stranded in a drying pond. And up in the high rafters, purple pigeons clattered every time he wailed his biggest psalms. His white suit and the white feathers from the coat on his shoulders puffed every time he raised his arms. His white boots squeaked, and the white gloves on his hands flexed like the tongues of snakes. Giant steel fans on long stands hummed either side of him, making his fat cheeks ripple, sending jewels of water from his forehead in little missiles that splashed onto a hedge of plastic flowers that edged his tropical pulpit. The microphone in front of him swayed, as did the squashed crowd, especially the front row of professional criers who wailed to the tune of a single pianist. The black piano – borrowed weekly from the Government School for Orphans – gleamed with sprays of white bird shit.

'The Garden of Eden is coming,' he shrieked. 'I have had a dream that a Garden is needed to lead us out of dust. I have had another dream that we have forgotten the sanctity of this City, because of the heaviness of crowds.

And my third dream has told me that we have forsaken the glory of Paradise. My Garden will rise to remind us of the power of the Glory. We will pray, and we will pay.'

'He went on and on, Chrisnelt,' said Divi that night. 'He wants to hire you, and tell you about his vision. Mama even fainted in the front row, and they had to carry her to Pastor's house. He has spent much time speaking to Mama about it all. Very exciting, Chrisnelt. It's a great honour for our family. He has chosen you. You are chosen.'

'How much is he going to pay him?' said Nipcia.

'I don't know,' said Chrisnelt. 'I don't know about this.'

'What don't you know?' said Divi.

'Yes, you bloody well know everything,' said Nipcia.

'I've only ever made my garden.'

'You make one; you make another one,' said Divi.

'Yes,' said Nipcia.

'I don't know.'

'Tata would be proud,' said Divi.

'And you can try and grow more trees! He has money for any trees or any seeds or any bloody stinking soil. Maybe new birds too,' said Nipcia, as she took some toilet water down the passage to feed the leaning tree.

'If this one dies, maybe Pastor can bless a new one for you in his garden,' said Divi. 'Oh Lordoo.' (She had begun to form in the shape of her mother.) 'Oh Lordoo!'

It was a step beyond his imagination, this tightness of minds, these infernal realms of separation. Such was his view of churches and church people. All a church had ever done for him was howl. All it had ever done was be there like lightning when pain arrives. 'Perhaps I just need to get used to the stench, finding light in the cracks and fleeting gaps in this City's lugubrious shadow, especially when it's a place of stagnant dust between breaths of soot that forms crusts on my brain,' he said to his sisters, who looked at him blankly. 'I'm unhinged in the heat.'

'We need the money.'

'Yes,' said Nipcia from the end of the passage.

'Money,' said Divi, rubbing her fingers together.

He preached to himself the whole of the next day, tapping his lips together like a bird, and the following day, and the day thereafter, and all he saw was a face holding a lot of fat, and the disturbed convictions of sanctity. Much wobbled in Chrisnelt's head.

'He scares me, okay?' he said, walking away from Nipcia. It was only with her he could share such a thought in that house. 'Divi and Mama are never here. They're blind with the Love. We need the money. But the walls are too close together, too high everywhere.'

'We really do need things. I will watch this tree,' said Nipcia. 'Me and the sparrows.'

'"Something new in the City!" that's what Pastor Kadazi said, hey? I'll make something new in the City. *I've been making something new in the City for bloody years,*' said Chrisnelt. '"A high garden of exaltation, beyond a plundering spirit of undeniable desire, all for my chickens." That's what Divi has written here for me, these are the notes, the instructions. I'll make that, if Pastor Kadazi says he wants that. But why did Pastor not tell them all about what really inspired him: MY GARDEN! Why this thing about a recent business visit to Europe, and a "revelation surrendered from a poster that was fixed to a tall tree on the Champs-Élysées"? Why the long story of, "the tree spoke to me, reaching high on the pavement of a grand boulevard, leaping in an arch to the Glory"? That's what Divi's written! And why the "powerful garden of a great European tribal palace that teaches us to be tall and wide"?!' Chrisnelt paced about, ferns brushing against his thighs, a tulip bending, and three ants on a leaf rising up on hind legs to avoid his heat, like patient old friends. 'This is all like the making of a bloody Christmas Tree.'

'We need the money!' shouted Nipcia from the kitchen.

A new garden became animated in immense grandness in Chrisnelt's head. He attacked his books, raved across his maps. He did not sleep for days. He curled into ball after ball on his mat. Not even the bathing of Amaterasu soothed him in the dead of night. He started blinking again, and this time his mouth blinked too.

On the final day, Chrisnelt knelt in his garden, staring at the sun, looking for answers. Tremendous warmth screamed onto him then, punching his ears and his eyes, as if it had been vomited by a dragon from someone else's fable. His head ached and his tongue swelled. He could see the dragon. It was so hot it burned his mind. It was of steel, covered in vines that ate insects and breathed the reddest fires, and its legs that were roots shooting into the depths of the earth: great harpoons looking for water. It had a tail of every flower he'd ever read about, and its ears were bird wings and its face was the face of a giant sparrow.

'He wants an "architectural garden" too, it seems.

That's what it says here. He wants it to be "regal" and "royal" and of an "imperial world of knowledge". He wants an "exquisite dance to give lessons to his chickens", does he? I will give him a living wilderness, holding the clouds and the leaves and the birds in a garden of such exuberance that no one has ever known.'

It was true that Pastor Kadazi was only impressed by ornate things made on other continents. They were images imprisoned within him, as was the image of his god. He always walked in some sort of glow: a sheen of fabrics capturing peoples' souls, like his hat of plumes capturing the moonlight. It was indeed true that he was seen clasping – in a flat gold frame of flickering glass – the photograph of the most ostentatious garden possible, waving it to the people in the streets as he drove by. And he was heard saying to all who listened: 'I want to have one of these expensive-looking, foreign gardens.' His attitude was of a man who reaches and eats only to fill himself, without questioning the origins of a thing and the place that made it.

That was Chrisnelt's view, after days of quizzing Divi and his mother, after reading the instructions in the note.

'I will transform something into something else, if only to set myself free, even if it's only an idea that flies to the stars in the end, searching for No,' said Chrisnelt to Nipcia.

Pastor Kadazi's house made a wide shadow, and the shaking and shouts of his sermons fell on top of the people in Dee Dee Street and many other streets beyond. He spoke to them regularly on the personal subjects of religious and financial matters of the heart. He did this with a loudhailer too, on the very wide streets, from the back of a white truck. It was on such a day that he remembered Chrisnelt's garden. It was the only thing in his midst that was beyond his control. And it was a notion triggered by a large green leaf that had fallen from the sky, getting entangled in the feathers on his head. That garden was an inaccessible realm. It was still alive, and yet it was beyond his rules.

It was a recollection brought back to him, too, one afternoon when his need for a garden reached Mrs Malotika's ears. She said to him intimately, on a quiet corner, as a worshipper does to the worshipped:

'Gardeners aren't known in the City, my Pastor, are they? I think they are very rare, my Pastor? Chrisnelt is fragile, as you know. He has such a thin neck now, and his body has become shorter, his legs are longer, and his fingers have turned green. They sway in the breezes, you know, Pastor, and he enjoys the company of flowers and birds more than that of most people. He does wonders with weeds, and he can make dust into mud in these dry seasons. He has read all the books in the City, you know, my Pastor. And he will make you a well-researched garden, like the one you have told us all about in the Great Hall. Oh Lordoo, yes he will.' She hugged Pastor Kadazi's one leg as he stood above her in the turmoil of her incantation.

Chaminda had seen this act of faith; he'd been sharing the same shade, his khaki making him invisible in a low cloud of dust, and he'd saved it in his mind to tell Chrisnelt, as he always told of all the things he saw. And it was then that Pastor Kadazi approached Chaminda, quite spontaneously, to order him to tell Chrisnelt of the job.

And Chaminda had saved all of that, as some sort of good news, as a birthday gift he would give to his friend.

'That Pastor Kadazi is now the richest man in the region – a great deal of his considerable wealth, much of it in cash, coming from selling chickens and the charcoal needed to cook them,' Chimanda elaborated. 'And he now wants to be the first person to have a great garden.'

'I know of his wealth, Chami,' said Chrisnelt.

'Well, you can't miss it. Look at that damn house. It's a palace.'

'Yes.'

'So tall it commands a shadow that seems to last all day; even at midday, it defies the sun!'

'Yes. I've seen it. And I've rested in it too. It's how I imagine the shade from a mountain to be.'

'He calls it Africa House.'

'The words are in golden letters that swirl in devotion; the grandness will glow when I've finished that garden.'

'He wants to invite the Governor, and even the President, when you're finished!'

'La Mame says the people at the River have been told by the people at the churches in all the districts that this garden is for them to come to, and to feed in. That it's all for Pastor Kadazi's flock of wonderful chickens,' said Chrisnelt.

'A garden is a piece of ground adjoining a house, used for growing plants,' continued Chrisnelt, quoting a dictionary. He walked in the dust, head tilted down, hands in pockets, a finger releasing a clicking sound from the end of a ballpoint pen: his thinking sound. Chaminda walked silently at his side.

The brightness of the brownest dust was cut into slabs of shade, the rhythm of the blue swathes set by gaps in the high walls, in the pauses of ownership between dominions, creating a pattern of light that spoke to Chrisnelt like the lyrics in birdsong.

'This dry season has become the colour of my skin, Chami,' he said. The light flashed on and off from the sky onto their faces. They stepped from shadow into light and then into shadow again. On and off it went, the light and the thinking, like the beating of distant drums. They walked and they talked. Yet again, Chrisnelt pondered the meaning of a garden. This would be a new garden of a new day and a new night. This new garden would need to be calm like a lullaby, he thought, sending him into daydreams, growing ideas that stuck to him like sweat. He would need to be strong. He would need to fight the blinking, and he could no longer afford to curl into balls. The day rusted in the brown heat.

'It's one week before you go into Pastor Kadazi's house for the first time. That's when he gets back from China,' said Chaminda – finding shade in the heat of noon made him think with new energy. 'New worlds ahead. And now a new garden to talk to your new dreams, my friend.'

'Like that walk we did in the dark streets, and how you showed me that finding the centre means first finding the edge,' said Chrisnelt.

'Yes.'

'Okay.'

'I work for him too, Chrisnelt.'

'I'll figure out his edge and his centre,' said Chrisnelt. 'We need the money. And I need a better place to grow my tree. Bloody soils!'

'Read what he reads, or what he thinks he reads,' said Chaminda.

Chrisnelt searched across the City for days, from one fire into another, and much sweat came. The French Tome in the library of the Roman Catholic Church of hissing wooden seats down the road did not satisfy him. At the old wooden hall of The Church of Jesus Christ of Latter-Day Saints, the blue-and-gold Portuguese Books sighed in lights, pretty cartoons and creaking walls, not expanding his understanding at all. The Italian Resource, in Latin, at the new Franciscan church-school for the deaf and dumb – a place that vibrated to the touch, serving sweet cakes on Sundays apparently – was not of any further help; neither was the English Book at the Anglican Church of brass bells and dancing quails, nor was the Arabic One rolled up at the small mosque of praying dawns and wandering moons. The Hebrew Scroll at the synagogue-kitchen, which gave away free, dried dates, the small, brash Russian Document in the cool office of the Church of Sinners, and the orange Gujarati Sheets at the tiny, new Buddhist Temple – recently noted for its beautiful bodhi tree, which had been grown from the branch of a tree planted in East Africa in 1920 – did no more to assist. The Mandarin One, at the place with the rattling roof of geckoes, Confucianism and Taoist gatherings, possessed of an enchanting cluster of motifs covered by lace curtains, added nothing. The Japanese One, at the house of candles, alongside the Shinto shrine with the shiny arch of plastic panels, the Spanish One he'd been told about and couldn't find, the Tamil and Sinhalese Ones he'd borrowed briefly – none did in any way contribute to his enlightenment. The local Lingala One at the police station – old and water-stained with remembrances of flooding mud on the frontispiece – did not even have the word *garden* in it, and there was nothing at all in the Others. All was most frustrating, the fruitless search drawn out and out and out like the heat and the dust and the never-ending shimmer of corrugations that went on and on and on.

'Nipcia,' said Chrisnelt, on the morning he was to go to work, 'Pastor Kadazi does not read.'

'We need the money. And anyway, your leaning tree is now firewood.'

'Bye,' said Chrisnelt, opening the front door.

'It's still dark.'

'I want to think. And so, a long walk first.'

'Bye.' Nipcia wanted to say be careful, but it was all just too big a thing to see him go.

Perhaps it was the colourful mural on a congregational wall that shone in the security lights through barbed wire loops, figures dancing like acrobats around mangers and piles of straw; or simply a little painting on a solitary windowpane of coloured glass in one of the outer walls of one of the many religious precincts, that first showed him the answer. He wasn't certain. Perhaps it was an otherworldly inspiration, spawned like ejaculate from a tremendous thrust of Nature that came pouring from the escaping moon, as it was being showered with the kisses of cavorting bats playing with lost moths in the chants of dawn. Perhaps it was the worship-filled screams he heard as he passed through the streets, fleetingly mingling into one scream from many Beliefs, making one Belief. Perhaps it was the generosity of spirit offered to him in food and tidings – and free advice – by a beggar, who extended a piece of meat before feeding his blind dog. Perhaps it was the blinking eyes and fluttering eyelashes of Amaterasu and her bathing tides that had settled in his heart. More than likely, it was a combination of all of this, coupled with his many visits to all those good intentioned, devout people, and a synthesis of their blessings, that fed the wonderful epiphany, greater than every birth ever conceived. And it was certainly, ultimately, all of these, plus his formulae, poems and the numbers of raindrops that he held in his head. In the end, whatever and however it formed, his idea unfurled like a stem, and in madness. It was certainly not found in the pages of any book. That was for sure. What he was most certain of was the quickness of its coming, and the eventual fecundity it secured. It flowered completely, owning him, controlling his way forward that morning of the job.

There it came, right away, like the clumsy flight of a chicken across a dry street: 'A tree *begins* with a garden. A garden *does not* begin with a tree,' he said to No.

'The World Tree,' he continued, looking for a face to speak to. And he found a bird: a bird, high in the sky, smiling like No. An awakening crow had been calling above him, form hidden against the blackness, the sound of the big bird translucent like his dreams, and its wings casting muted shades. The dawn sun of rich gold was coming.

'A central tree in the middle of it all,' he continued. The bird cocked its big head, looking at him with eyes the size of planets. He described the tree with his arms in the air. The bird hovered: a floating umbrella of blacks and whites, head and tail heavy like thunder, attached to a white body that might have been an escaping cloud. 'No, I see you, No,' he said, reaching up to the bird. 'You know, Crow, you fly up there with the two big colours, and yet between the tips of your wings and in the middle of your heart are all the greys waiting to fall on me like shit! You are like the Mango Tree. You are like the ash from a falling fire.'

He cried as he had not cried for some time. He cried joyfully, in the clarity of his new way ahead, toward his friend, holding his father's hand as he walked: the hand of the tallest, strongest shadow.

'When I plant this special new tree in its waiting garden, it will bear every fruit of the world. And do you know, Crow, there once was such a tree? I feel it in my heart. It swirled like all the currents of every ocean into a twisting mountain, pulling continents as one island rising from the blue, reaching up into a vast place of bark and branches. And from this, a canopy breathed out – on the other side of the clouds, beyond the river mists, beyond the heat of the sun, stretching to the stars; and leaves of all the greens glittered like rain. That tree became a new world, Crow, one place for all of us, Edenic, without walls,' said Chrisnelt.

In the light of the coming sun, he sketched a picture of a tree in sand that was so soft and warm, a big toe making broad scrapes of pink, a finger scooping to indicate leaves of orange, and with the point of his pen he prodded a sky of raindrops in the sparkling dust.

Vernon RL Head

'In ... distant ... parts ... of ... the ... mind ... certain ... gardens ... are ... created ... alive ...' – as each prick of his pen made rain, he said each word out loud – 'In ... the ... heart ... of ... these ... are ... trees ... captured ... by ... hope ... and ... skies ... of ... rain ... that ... never ... end.'

He looked up into the space above his head, the wide ceiling of bursting stars, searching for the heating sun. He anticipated the garden Pastor Kadazi would pay for: the exoticness of it all, the expense. 'A garden cannot be owned, even by Pastor Kadazi.'

Just there, squeezed through a crack in a dried mud wall to the left of him, on the boundary of the street, was a woody weed: a short plant covered in grit and heavy with age and time, the old curves of bark bent and frowning, stunted through lack of opportunity: a lost colour calling up to the heat. Covering the weed was a transparent plastic shopping bag, ensnaring it like a spider-web, taut and tense. Chrisnelt looked at the weed behind the plastic. He stood back for a moment, and was reminded of gardens in bondage. He saw a separateness that was sad. He leaned down and pealed off the plastic. Dust sprang off the leaves as the plant breathed. Chrisnelt was exhilarated – he'd never freed something that was alive before. He looked up at the crow and walked on, clicking his pen furiously in epiphanic thought: 'A garden inside the heart of a house, or inside any building for that matter, is not a garden. No garden can be isolated,' he said to a nearby fence, running his pen along the metal slats in a tune of shadows: 'A garden needs to be part of the garden next door.'

Click-click ... click-click ... click-click, the pen spoke to the fence. White birds carried the sun above him, gliding the light toward the River, and his eyes looked for green things. A purple pigeon pontificated, its throat expanding into a bubble of iridescence that beat like a heart, and a dirty chicken clucked and shat.

Click-click.

CHAPTER THIRTEEN

'Good morning, Pastor,' he said. 'I am Chrisnelt, we met when I was quite young, but I never really introduced myself then.' He took a step backwards, to the very edge of the marble step, before it became the dust behind him. 'Yes Pastor, I am Chrisnelt. My mother says I must work for you?'

Pastor Kadazi shook his hand slowly and carefully, in the ceremonial way one might shake a new possession before using it; his huge, fat hand engulfing the boy's delicate fingers.

'A gardener is a privileged person, who fashions bridges of leaves between people,' thought Chrisnelt, looking beyond Pastor Kadazi, through the doorway of the house to a distant light, imagining what lay at the other end of that interlinking passage. He thought of Chaminda then.

The day before, the City had felt immensely tight, like a vast skin. There'd been no place or time for gardens. On the street, he'd seen a steel frame making the outline of a stall – as if it had been drawn in the air with thin pen lines. The skins hanging there glistened in the sunshine, some fresh from antelope and still covered in fur, some curling slightly, shimmering in flies; some flat and hard and faded white, like ivory. Some had made their way onto a wooden plank and had become belts and purses. One had become one shoe. The rocking skins reminded Chrisnelt of the bats in the eaves at home. And they also made him think of the tight City, and of his pending job.

'Stinking black and brown skins,' he said to Chaminda. 'all of them cooking in the air. We're all just skins.'

'*Aaaaaaaaah yaaaaaaaaah!*' The scream reached up into the brittle sky, cracking a line of drifting birds into a burst of feathers.

The stallholder whipped around. The screamer was behind him in the dust, staring up at the sun, his mad eyes wide, unblinking, his hands hanging at his sides. He was naked, his black curls bleached orange on his head, his skin caked in river mud. He stared up at the heat. His scream had no obvious cause. It was as if he needed to scream, as if he only felt safe when screaming.

'The sun is driving people crazy,' said Chaminda.

'He looks like he's come from a cave,' said Chrisnelt. 'Like he's seen inside the Earth!'

'Space and shelter have been traded for this place of soot,' said Chaminda.

'Even caves are getting filled with soot.'

'You'd be surprised at the amount of soot there is in places across the world, and some places don't even know this kind of fire yet,' said Chaminda. The screamer screamed again, drooling a long strand of spit. And he continued to stare, unblinking, at the burning sun.

'I sometimes think that No and Tata are in those caves of yours, the ones made by the first rivers, the ones with the dancing people and the dancing crocodiles on the walls,' said Chrisnelt. 'Caves were homes once, like trees were homes, and now we have houses that are not homes.'

Swaying on the marble landing, Chrisnelt looked up at

the face of Pastor Kadazi's house. The Pastor, too, loomed above him. It was a very hot Monday morning near the end of another dirty June: the City should have already been cleaned by the sky, but the rains had not come. It had not come many times. The Palm Swifts – number eighteen on Chrisnelt's bird list – flew higher than ever, looking for rain in a deeper new haze of searches and expectations.

The house was even bigger and whiter than he remembered. It was known by the people of Dee Dee Street and surrounding districts as the White House, although the Pastor himself called it Africa House. It was four storeys high, which was three storeys higher than any other house. The construction was solid and fortified – at least, that's what his father always told him when they walked past. Five white marble steps descended abruptly to the dusty pavement from the front of the house. Above the steps was a grand portico, with a row of white, fluted columns, a pointed, triangular gable like a strange steeple, and a pitched roof scaled in white tiles. All of which was lighted at night like the glow of a foreign mask.

Everything about the house was white. Its whiteness shone more than most white houses do because it was cleaned twice a week by many people. On most days, after school was out, children could be seen giggling on the low window ledges, cleaning the panes of the ground floor in exchange for stale croissants that Pastor Kadazi scattered like business cards. The upper floors were strictly out of bounds. This was known by all who visited. Those tall, tinted windows were cleaned only by his staff of big men. Above all of it flew a white flag on a long white pole, emblazoned with a gold cross that was always bending in the breeze, making people feel uncertain. Next to the flag, a great white satellite dish had recently been added, often a roost for purple pigeons.

Chrisnelt decided the real reason the house was so white was because all the other houses were so black. It was generally agreed in the street that there was no point in keeping homes clean on the outside anymore, as the mud and the rain were great friends, and they were not to be defeated. In any case, there was nothing more patient, or more persistent, than the dust.

The only other colour on the White House evident from the street – apart from purple pigeons and purple shadows – was a rippling, shiny gold, like melted bullion, found predominantly on the front doors: two gilded timber leaves like the cover of a giant book. They'd been carved by skilled men from a distant forest, who understood the nature of wood and the gifts hidden deep within the highest forest tree – a tree too hard and precious for charcoal. The doors were very heavy. Chrisnelt knew this because they made the sound of creaking walls as they waited for him. The golden doors were set centrally on the face of the building like questioning eyes, each containing four glass panes: smallish and shining, as if mirror sunglasses had been fashioned for this face.

Ladies, carrying children, baskets of fruit, peanuts, small crocodiles, dried worms, catfish and crates of bottled water, sometimes paused when passing, to admire themselves tentatively in the glass. Together with the panes, their plastic water bottles made much flickering of buoyant shards of light down the bumpy-busy street, below the diaphanous clouds.

Men carrying bags of charcoal, bags of dust, rolls of plastic cloth and sheets of corrugated iron also passed by, as did men pushing wheelbarrows of wood, mud bricks and stacked crates of chickens. And then there were the men who passed clutching high towers of free blue plastic chairs. Everyone carried a cellular phone: a thing that had become part of a face. And all of them bent forward in a morbid bow as they hurried past, in the hope of a glimpse behind the glass.

Dogs sniffed at themselves in the lowest windows of Pastor Kadazi's White House, pissing yellow puddles that became sticky, trapping flies. Sparrows came on quiet days, some hovering in front of imaginary foes, others hopping forward, tapping at the glass, before plucking at the flies.

Chrisnelt looked at Pastor Kadazi's face that morning; it was the first time he'd seen it properly, in the honesty of daylight, in the truth of a fresh morning. And all he saw were teeth. Pastor Kadazi had many teeth. *More than I have ever seen on one person*, he thought. *More than I'll ever see in my little lifetime.* Chrisnelt was scared of teeth. He thought of No's teeth, and the shocking resilience – the brightness of white on charred black – of dead teeth. He became very hot. He sweated unnaturally, his temples dribbling onto Pastor Kadazi's white marble tiles. He was nauseous in the heat of his vulnerability. His stomach throbbed. He wanted to curl into a ball. And it was still early. Everything was early.

He looked at the teeth in front of him again. They were very big and white, and the two front ones were golden, appearing to absorb the energy of the sun. The great hole of the open mouth shimmered with so much heat that it might have been the source of all the City's tormented fires.

His mouth and his teeth match his house in every way, he thought. They were dangerous teeth: chiselled by time, delicately jagged like broken pots. Such tips, so sharp. *Does he chew on bones like a dog?* And most frightening of all were the gaps: between the teeth was impenetrable darkness.

I CAN'T MAKE THIS GARDEN. I DON'T WANT TO MAKE THIS GARDEN, screamed Chrisnelt deep inside himself. MY TREE WON'T GROW BEHIND THAT WHITE FACE OF HIGH BRICKS!

'Chrisnelt, your mother works for me,' said Pastor Kadazi. 'Your sister works for me. Your friends work for me. Now you will work for me. Right?'

'Yes, Pastor.'

'Good.'

'I'll just do all the windows? No charge. Then I can go?'

'Have you not been told about the garden?'

'What garden, Pastor?'

Chrisnelt had never lied before. His stomach hurt, and he wanted to fall into the smallest ball. In his hand was clasped his big, blue floppy hat, and in a little sack were wrapped the hand-rake and the hand-spade. *Please don't grab this from me. Please don't open it, Pastor.* Sweat fell again.

'You're not stupid. I remember your garden. Now it's your chance to make mine.'

'Yes, Pastor.'

'I will give the money to your mother. It will be extra money for her.'

'Yes, Pastor.'

'You can start now.'

'Isn't it better to get the gardening from the people making the new airport, Pastor? Maybe I can just prepare things for you today. Those people have made great lawns. Before, it was just concrete, now it's bright green, with flower borders of many colours for the tourists that are starting to come. I hear they're going to do the same near the palm trees of the Governor and the President, and along the boulevards between the hotels; all the routes the tourists will take. I hear they are the ones to make things appear green.'

'Listen, they've not seen what I've seen. You will start today.'

'Yes, Pastor. Today.'

'Now.'

'Yes, Pastor.'

'And if you do a good job, there will be extra money, just for you.'

'Yes.'

Chrisnelt followed Pastor Kadazi through his shining front doors to begin his new job, the swing of the wood bringing in a soft flow of heat at his back; then the street disappeared with a thud, as did the heat.

His mind was a sea of loud thoughts. 'A big day in the heat,' his mother would say of his new job, if he were so lucky as to see her that evening. He didn't think he would ever see anyone again, such was the coldness of the space inside that house. He looked up. The interior was wider than a normal house and many times higher. The mirrored glass panes of the front doors still shook slightly, long after the giant doors had shut. The hardness of all the surfaces scattered a sharp echo. 'It feels like ice must feel,' he said very softly to a wall, touching it with his longest finger. 'White and bloody freezing. This is a fever like I've never known.'

Chrisnelt followed Pastor Kadazi quietly and obediently, like a hungry little chicken. His stomach gurgled deep within. His arsehole vibrated in a bizarre spasm – the same spasm he'd witnessed in a dying chicken. He turned back briefly toward the door and the waves of heat outside. The mirrored windows, not yet awake to their maximum shininess, gently blinked at the new day, staring at the street, throwing morning about. The doors shook again, this time under the bright, interior lights of the white hallway. Everything buzzed in white marble.

The house was designed to make people gasp. Chrisnelt gasped. High up at the top of the hole hung an extraordinary light fitting with silver branches and glass leaves of tinsel and tiny baubles that twinkled: a white tree growing away from the heavens, reaching down to him with its sharpest point. 'It's growing from the sky to the ground. And all those lights at the tips of the branches!' he said aloud.

'What?' said Pastor Kadazi.

'Sorry, Pastor, it's the first chandelier I've ever seen in the flesh,' said Chrisnelt. 'Very beautiful. Very expensive. Like a tree of ice crystals coming from the sun.'

'Follow me.'

'Yes, Pastor.'

On either side of the vast hallway of ice, a stairway climbed to the floors above: two arms of white. Steps of marble like a folded cloud. Slits of light shone below each step.

'Fire has been trapped inside the ice. Everything's floating in incredible desolation,' said Chrisnelt. He longed for the heat of home.

'What?'

'Very beautiful, Pastor.'

White lacquered balustrades cast a pattern of shadow ribs across the white floor and white walls. Peering past Pastor Kadazi in desperation, his head tilting sideways for a moment to see where he was going, Chrisnelt could see a long white corridor terminating in all that ever was white. 'A cave without dancing people,' he said.

'Hurry up, Chrisnelt.'

'Yes, Pastor.'

New echoes played with the smoothness and the hardness, again and again, to the song of Pastor Kadazi's shoes. Chrisnelt's head began to ache like his stomach, and the cave of cold stone burned his bare feet. He hopped across the marble surface on tiptoes. He'd never walked like that before – it just seemed to come to him. He tucked his hands deep into his shorts, pressing his chin to his chest to find warmth. *This is for Ásbjörn, not me*, he thought. 'Perfect for his skin,' he said aloud.

'What's going on, boy?'

'Sorry, Pastor,' said Chrisnelt, 'my legs are stiff. I'm freezing.'

'You sick?'

'No, Pastor, it's just that I've never been cold before.'

It was for him like climbing a marble mountain; he was lost in the deepest snows. He shivered for the first time – he had not known his body possessed such a trick. He had no control over the violence of the air. 'International jetliners cutting lines of white ice in the heavens,' he muttered, his lips shuddering in his face, his body raging with the coldest fires. 'No place for people of the trees.'

Pastor Kadazi had disappeared around a corner. Chrisnelt looked at the ceiling above his head; great showers of icy air poured from it like river mist. It all hummed and burned: the walls, the floor, the ceiling, his limbs, his face. In all the marble that enveloped him, he noticed fine grey veins making cracks and patterns like he'd only ever seen on tombstones. The snows hit his chest and he coughed from a deep place within him owned by oracles. The house was like the sheer cliff of the world with a hole cut through.

'The core of the planet is not molten rock, it's ice,' Chrisnelt said. 'Impenetrable flames of ice have come to Africa in this house.'

A tall, black man – *Much blacker than me*, Chrisnelt almost said out loud, *blackened by all this whiteness, I imagine* – ushered him hurriedly around the corner, through a set of clear glass doors into yet another room of white, this time exploding with bright lights and warmth. Before him, things melted gently, loosely, like hands and fingers of flesh.

The room had three white walls, making it seem bigger than it really was, the light bouncing naturally in every direction, flooding into the room. A rooster clucked nearby. The fourth wall was wonderfully absent, defined only by five thick marble posts, elaborately carved in swirls depicting water currents, or perhaps surging waves, supporting a white marble beam that was patterned like the jaws of a river fish beached by the tide. The marble grain was evident everywhere, the posts leaking cloud shapes determinedly.

The ground lay bare beyond. Before he even built the house, Pastor Kadazi had had a great white wall built around his entire yard, along each boundary. He'd said to his congregation: 'Great walls make great lands of the Lord.' The wall was a storey-and-a-half high. On its top surface gleamed the coloured teeth of glass shards stuck into cement.

Chrisnelt looked out through the columns onto the hot dust. He'd seen patios like this attached to the fronts of government buildings, but never one that was part of a house. 'What a big white veranda,' he said softly.

Pastor Kadazi sat slumped in a large white rattan chair of many silver pillows, his back to the corridor and to Chrisnelt. Above him, a high ceiling fan clattered. Glass coffee tables with gold legs shone, surrounded by golden-satin-upholstered lounge suites cupping voluminous pillows that caught the light unusually. Fantastic smells of perfume rippled up his nose, leaking from little sticks that glowed in silver pots.

'A place for entertaining and doing big business deals in much comfort,' said Chrisnelt.

'What did you say?' said Pastor Kadazi. The fans rattled above, sending mosquitoes with the black-and-white legs into the corners of the veranda.

'Yes, Pastor,' said Chrisnelt.

The very black man stood at his side, holding a tray of tools.

'Come here.'

Seated across from Pastor Kadazi, hunching forward

but hidden from Chrisnelt by the big pillows, was Georges Feti: the owner of Grace's Private Burial Home, lucratively situated in the middle of the City near the government hospital, and recently elected Governor of the Province. The two men continued their conversation of laughs, sifting through things on the table that looked like small piles of diamonds.

After a few minutes, Pastor Kadazi said again: 'Come here' – adding, to the surprise of Chrisnelt: 'blessed child.'

'Yes, Pastor.' It was then he saw Governor Feti.

'Your task is indeed sanctified, blessed child,' said Feti.

Chrisnelt recognised the Governor without hesitation. He was on every poster. He was on sacks of charcoal and on toilet paper rolls, on tickets for the stadium, and on stickers that found their way onto taxi-car windscreens, front doors, many walls and almost every streetlight pole. He was also well known because of his noisy, white Mercedes-Benz: the only car, apart from that of the President, with windows that looked like mirror sunglasses. These tinted windows were bullet- and soundproof, according to La Mame. They were never cleaned unless the Governor was attending a funeral or important meeting, and people in the streets had learned to read his windows and their dirt like his diary.

The Governor always entered his cemetery grounds from the back, along a discreet gravel track behind walls and tree stumps, far from the wailing people. Like Pastor Kadazi, he was determined, always in a hurry to find things that belonged to poverty, selling stale baguettes, unwashed cloth and contraband cigarettes from the coast to the poor at a huge profit. He was an owner of the deep holes dug by desperation and much foreignness. He never seemed to be alone; men always followed him, one with an umbrella that never opened, one with a permanent smile that never closed, one with a machine-gun dangling in beads. His vast cemetery, which he always referred to as a 'burial home', was the only open space of any significance left in the city – apart from the Pastor's yard, which had always been open, and the City garbage dump. Chrisnelt had regularly – and secretly – gone there to collect plants for his own garden, under the guidance of La Mame, following in his friend's exquisitely skilled shadow.

Chrisnelt looked at the eyes of the Governor, those unassailable eyes behind mirror sunglasses. And he remembered how La Mame had shown him the art of vaulting over the most treacherous walls.

All manner of exotic flora kept springing up at different times of the year at Grace's Private Burial Home, a veritable park sewn by the hands of mourning. Life from all over the world was brought here, in the many fertile bouquets – the ones that were not plastic – accompanying coffins, and the big fertile wreaths – the ones that were not plastic – leaning up against headstones. The flat openness of the place, with its rivulets of sewage in the low inundations between displaced clods of sand, released profound nutrients, bubbling up into a special cocktail. This 'marvellous mixing', as he called it, carried seeds freely into a delta of borders and beds of the most colourful sprouts in the universe. And in these times of dryness, the soft breezes sprinkled things further, tossing the daffodils of Europe with the lilies of South America, the daisies of the Far South with the begonias of the Far East. It was a new kind of wilderness, perhaps a new world. Chrisnelt had no problem taking from this bounty: 'A land of life made from a land of death.'

It was very dark. He'd just flown over the high stone wall of the cemetery. 'Step into my hands,' La Mame had said, moments prior.

La Mame had made a foothold out of his fingers, locking them together to form a stirrup. With a great thrust of his arms, he sent Chrisnelt into the early morning air. Over he'd come, landing and rolling on the little hills of buds. La Mame had followed, as if tugged up and over by the dawn.

Ghosts sat on each of the little hills that pock-marked the flatness, icy with their slabs of marble. Chrisnelt read: 'Lord James Holmes of Canterbury, born 1897, died 1897.'

'He had a short stay in Africa,' said La Mame.

'ALONGI ODONGO, born 1918, died in the year of our Lord 2008.'

'That's a life of this place,' said La Mame. The marble was wet with the mist. 'And lots of flowers.' He bent down to pluck the tallest stems.

Chrisnelt wandered the mounds, kicking plastic wreaths as if they were footballs. He was after unusual plants he hadn't seen before, the ones that had come from distant hothouses. The ones that would help his treeling become a tree. He sat on a tree stump. The air was cool but the wetness from the stump was warm. A low flock of birds came from the River, fanning a little gust of dust. The birds cried. White egrets, many white egrets.

The lights of the Governor's Mercedes-Benz rose like yellow suns up ahead, and a line of tree stumps burst into momentary flames. Chrisnelt realised the stumps had once been an avenue of trees. A few scattered headstones glistened; others absorbed the sweep of light into sooty, gaping mouths.

Men spoke. Some men spoke harshly, and some dug. A silent man sat very still in the sand. Chrisnelt and La Mame lay flat.

'I thought you said no funerals in the early mornings,' whispered Chrisnelt.

'This isn't a funeral.'

'What is it then?'

'It's a burial.'

'With no weepers.'

'No wailers. No grievers.'

'A political disagreement,' said Chrisnelt, his pockets fat with seeds, his hands clasping new little bushes that shook. 'Pallbearers of freedom.'

'Chrisnelt, come here child, this is Governor Feti,' said Pastor Kadazi, after some moments.

'He calls you,' whispered the man who was much blacker than Chrisnelt, still holding the tray of tools, the silver of the tray making the tools float in a suspended pond of sunshine.

'What.'

'Come here, blessed Chrisnelt,' said Pastor Kadazi, raising his voice above that of the fan and the mosquitoes with the black-and-white legs.

'Yes, Pastor,' said Chrisnelt, still lost in the skies

revolving around the fan; in his head, La Mame still leapt through flowers in the wind, tugging at roots, flitting over the little beds of the dead. 'Yes, Pastor.'

Pastor Kadazi was much taller than Governor Feti, who was a tall man. Even when seated, Chrisnelt could feel the great physical strength of these men of shining pillows. The pillows popped from either side of huge thighs. The armrests creaked as the wide torsos leaned back. Someone farted luxuriously. Both men smiled lightly. They'd just resumed counting the three small piles of stones: dancing auguries on a black velvet cloth, exploded constellations, throwing light about in busy sparkles like the mouths of fire-eaters. Chrisnelt had never seen such a dance. It was how he imagined the river bed in a forest to dance. Governor Feti continued the counting. Pastor Kadazi cleared his throat as he always did, preparing to speak.

Governor Feti separated each stone from the next with the blade of a knife, his grin that of a child making a slow shit. His concentration was like physical exercise: he sweated in an austere bit of shade cast by the Pastor's head, the whining fan filling the gaps between everyone's thoughts. He slowly pushed the stones into a little sack. And the knife wobbled on the glass table.

'Look at my garden, look how big,' said Pastor Kadazi.

'It's a very big area, that's for sure, Pastor,' said Chrisnelt.

'Very big,' said Governor Feti.

'Yes, the biggest.'

'Yes, Pastor.'

'My problem is that it looks dead,' said Pastor Kadazi, flinging his arms apart, the pillows singing like

La Mame's couch. The biggest pillow, with the biggest silver reflections, tumbled to the floor and skidded across the marble, sending the rooster into a noisy leap, and the mosquitoes with the black-and-white legs left the wall, circling in the heaviness of the heat. 'It's a dead field.'

'It's very big,' said Governor Feti.

'It's dust. I've kept it like this for too long. I was going to bring many chickens.'

'It would have stunk like my burial home.'

'It has a few good bushes here and there, Pastor,' said Chrisnelt. 'I can work with those.'

'I want a big, shiny garden. Big shiny bushes. High!' Pastor Kadazi's arms waved, and more pillows fell. The rooster hopped into the air again.

'That would be very impressive, like at the hotels. I wish there was a hotel near my burial home, and a bigger hospital.'

'I want people to sit here and see it lit up at night, too.'

'And in the middle a fountain?' asked Governor Feti.

'Yes, I want a marble fountain in the middle, and big leaves everywhere, and a pond, and trees.'

'And one of those Chinese bridges that always go over the pond.'

'Yes, one of those. Very good, Governor.'

'Yes, Pastor,' said Chrisnelt. 'I will make it very green, with the bridges and the ponds too. And a tree for the Pastor.'

'Yes. Trees.'

'Yes.'

'It will be a very important garden.'

'Yes, Pastor.'

Governor Feti remained very much in Pastor Kadazi's debt. It had been Pastor Kadazi who had seen the need for a private cemetery. And it had been Pastor Kadazi who had loaned him the money to build the high wall around the plot of land. It was the cemetery that had made Feti famous, indeed it could be said that it had made him Governor of the wealthiest province in the country. The days of public-run cemeteries were coming to an end in the City. They may have been cheaper but they were not well maintained, and on top of that, they were overcrowded. At \$300 for a tomb and \$1700 for a marble headstone, Governor Georges Feti's private offering was doing very well. Pastor Kadazi had been right. Having presided over many funerals, he had long ago observed that there would never be a shortage of clients, as God was his witness. Governor Feti prayed hard in agreement most Sundays, and in speeches too.

Chrisnelt watched the men and his head filled with marble walls, marble corridors and marble headstones. Marble was best left far away from human beings, uncut, undisturbed in a distant world; a rock lying quietly in a mountain, clasped by the roots of a great Tree.

'So you know what to do, hey?'

'Yes, Pastor.'

'I give money to your mother every evening when she comes here to see me.'

'Yes, Pastor.'

'You use the side gate from now on. The men will let you in. You walk that way. No more in my house.'

'Yes.'

'And here are your tools,' said Pastor Kadazi. The very

black man gave the tray to Chrisnelt. On it was a pair of secateurs, three hand-spades of various shapes, and a few small bags of seeds with beautiful pictures on them of rolling fields of flowers that seemed to want to burst out of the picture into the dust. In between the flowers stood windmills like trees.

'Thank you, Pastor.'

'And I will bring you many plants. I have already ordered some. I asked for the shiniest and biggest ones.'

Mr Feti pointed at the rooster pecking at the pillow sparkling in sunlight. 'He is pecking like a madman, for nothing but his lust.'

'He has many hens, like me,' laughed Pastor Kadazi. Both men laughed, and there came another luxurious fart.

Chrisnelt walked with the tray. He stepped off the patio into the glare of dust. His mind began to fade like the colours that had once been in that wide space.

'This is wasted space,' he said to himself. 'The world can't afford to waste space. What will I make here? Will I find the deep soils and the deep waters of the River? Will I find the beginnings of my tree?'

Out of the corner of his eye, he watched Governor Feti close the black velvet bag. The rooster flowed in radiance behind him, dropping a feather, jerking and laughing at the heat.

The knife that was on the glass table flickered and the fan rattled to the tune of the mosquitoes with the black-and-white legs. Governor Feti said to Pastor Kadazi: 'I will be selling those Pink Passion Wreaths from Beijing soon, and the Rainbow Wreaths with the plastic flowers that glow in the dark. It's a new idea over there. They arrive in a big container on the River next month, even smell real, and they don't bother dying.'

Chrisnelt thought of all the plastic flowers, and he thought of all the plastic seeds.

Chapter Fourteen

He worked in the sun for many days. The substantial shade of the house fell on the street side, a mountain of bricks and concrete separating him from that shade. The flag with the loud gold cross could be seen from the street and from the yard in which he worked. The flocks of white birds circling the cross were the same birds for everyone.

Chrisnelt moved about slowly, followed by the rooster, which was regularly chased away from the house when Pastor Kadazi was away, along with a few white hens. He dug aimless little holes all over the yard, testing the colours of the soils, seeing how they might mix. 'It's a difficult thing to begin a garden when the soils don't speak,' he said. 'When will Pastor's plants arrive?'

He shook sand through a flour sieve that he'd obtained from Café Gourmandine. Making a beautiful and important garden would be hard work indeed, but the Café had some good tools that were seldom used. The sieve – when tapped vigorously, while singing – yielded wonderful bounty: seeds of every description shone in the midday light. The big brown ones looked like nuts. Tiny bronze ones gleamed. There were waxy ones, shrunken like raisins. A flat one with wings fluttered in the birdsong. Several coiled ones bounced on springs. A red one leapt, leaking like a ripe tomato. A green one rested patiently in his hand, in a shadow cast by his fingers that looked like a tiny tree.

Fluffy lanterns caught the sunlight, drifting as words on the breeze of heat, making sentences, holding facts. 'These sky-seeds are looking for a home,' he said.

He'd been provided with a long hose, and he began spraying the dust with water. He prodded wet clods of earth with a toe; the patches that he could not reach, he flicked with the hose. He'd always loved earthy toes: they held the stories of his youth.

'The very nature of the soil and its geological history is revealed by the length of time taken in the drying process on the toe,' he told the rooster. 'The resulting tones and textures spread like a litmus test on the skin, clearly elaborating composition.'

He liked how the soil dried, cracking in lamentation, changing colours, telling stories. 'Soil can have the colours of flowers and the colours of sunrises and sunsets. Soil can have the colour of fires, hey, No?'

He remembered how the two of them – best friends in all the best mud – had rolled and rolled, and how his mother had chased them with a bucket of water and a cloth, always shouting: 'DON'T COME HOME UNTIL YOU'RE THE RIGHT COLOUR!'

He missed his friend terribly. He dreamed of the tree he would grow. He had to grow it soon. He said to the rooster: 'Time is pulling at me like a disease. These soils need to speak soon.'

And the rooster scratched and shat, shuddering its neck feathers.

Another week passed, as if pulled by the heat across the sweltering sands. But still the seeds did not grow. He longed for the coolness of his bedroom, and the coolness his feet felt in the waters of his circular pond. The dream of a growing treeling – of it climbing to the stars – drifted further from him and his heart.

'What if I can't grow my tree here? And the soils are like all the soils of the damned?' he said angrily to the rooster. The heat was violent that day.

A dry weed crackled as Chrisnelt pressed it with a thumb. He turned a yellow leaf over. It became a piece of parchment, revealing a poem. 'A message in a bottle, that's a curled-up leaf,' he said to the rooster, his sweating body shining like feathers. His energy was slipping from his limbs. He studied the stains on the leaf, the fading circles and lines filled with answers. The world was very hot. The blue floppy hat was not helping his brain. Before him rocked another leaf, also curled, on the ground, telling clearly of how it had died and dried: there had not been any rain for so many months.

'Only the screaming fires descending miraculously from above,' said Chrisnelt. He was dizzy. The history of how the water had left that leaf spoke to him: 'I have bled the water out of me so I could feed the River and help it on its way to the coast,' said the leaf.

'I AM BLEEDING TOO!' shouted Chrisnelt.

The rooster rattled its head. A dead white hen lay in the dust, covered in black ants.

'Now I am a skeleton,' said the leaf.

A vast fan whirled above Chrisnelt's head. It was a fan of pure heat, the size of the sky, and silent. It went from bright light to darkness and then to bright light again. It burned, stinging his toes. He screamed: 'WHEN THE

SUN COMES INTO THIS GARDEN OF DESERTS IT NEVER LEAVES!'

The rooster ran away then, back to the patio and the silence. Chrisnelt collapsed. The curve of that single leaf was shattered by his fall, and he lay in a fixed curl, his spine brittle and bright. The dust settled on top of him. He shone with sweat, his skin growing darker in the sun. He lay next to his hat. 'I'm blazing in a scorching storm of fire,' he said weakly, wiping his mouth: 'Where's my tree going to grow?'

It was only the nausea that stirred him. He was alone. It was dusk. A soft breeze had gathered dry leaves against his side, along with sand and ants. The ants were hungry. Mosquitoes with black-and-white legs sung. The leaves crumbled as he rolled onto his back. Looping circles of colour filled his eyes. He cried. He vomited up the past: green, orange, yellow, yellow-orange of mango, brown then black, black into fiery red, and then the whites of ash sifted across his mind.

Silence comes like death in the Tropics when day shifts into night; the call of birds pauses, transmuting into the call of frogs. There is always a single star somewhere up there, like a tiny pond of hope. Chrisnelt sat up. The dusk smelled soft and sweet. And the weeds had started to come up toward him and his pleading eyes.

'Weeds! Wild herbs springing up where you are not wanted!' That was the meaning of the word he'd learned from his copy of the *Pocket Oxford Dictionary of Current English*, eleventh impression (with his own corrections, which he would send off to the European publishers in a long letter).

'Weeds,' he said again, dusting ants off his chest. 'Beautiful refugees from other lands! You are like me.' He stood up. 'You are the first to come, and together we will build this into a bloody garden. You weeds are wanted here! You are all I have in this beginning.'

Although some of the weeds might have looked emaciated in the dust, like the skinny, tired bodies of the old, they had not been forgotten by Chrisnelt. He was of the view that weeds might very well be the most important things in the world, each one bearing a message from somewhere special, from a unique place in which their particular species belonged to a deep history.

And so the weeds became his first clues to reading that place of desolation. How elegantly they moved about, telling a tale of possibilities from every continent, he and the weeds in the shadows. He could start to think clearly again now. Coolness had washed clarity across his eyes, like water taking away dust.

'I am not lonely here. I have you weeds. I have the first green languages of my garden,' he said. He ran back and forth across the yard, watering everything that swayed on the sands, however small. The moon helped him, as did the waves of bats coming from the River. 'I'll work all night. That's what I'll do.'

'This night, a real garden will bloom,' he said to the bats. 'No barriers for me, no borders to this yard. I am making a new island in this island. I am changing it into an island of life. I am coming, No.'

Clouds curled in the shape of rib bones in that morning sunrise. Flocks of birds had replaced the night's bats, coming from the River in the familiar colours of the new day. Chrisnelt was still gardening. His arms and his hands and his fingers had worked all night, the brittle sounds of his breaking fingernails sharp, the hollows below his tired eyes deep. And he was covered in soil. Seeds stuck to him: the texture of friendship on that bit of land, intimate and strong. He was coming to know it.

A low film of dust hung in a busy blanket. The walls of the house shook. He glimpsed the very long truck. It was not a dream; he knew this because of the fresh scent arriving. In the gap between Pastor Kadazi's house and the house next door, all he saw were leaves, sliding in on the rumbling back of the truck.

'POTS AND POTS OF PLANTS!' he shouted.

Then men came through the side-gate and down the ally, carrying plants, pot after plastic pot, the bushes and shrubs shaking above the men. Many plants of many shapes came, and some were indeed very shiny. And with the pots came three fibreglass ponds each the shape of a heart, and then came two Chinese bridges made of plastic to span the ponds.

'Where do you want these?' said a man at the back who was not carrying plants. He held a clipboard, and he shouted instructions at the men.

'Over there,' said Chrisnelt, pointing, his fingers dripping all the colours of all the soils, seeds falling from his face. 'Put the plants in rows next to that high wall. I'll take it from there. And you can put the other stuff in front of the patio for now.'

The man looked at him and shook his head. 'You don't look good,' he said.

'I've been working all night.'

'Digging a hole?'

'Working,' said Chrisnelt, pointing at the scattered stems of delicate weeds, each in its own brown stain. The weeds looked bright.

'They're just weeds.'

'Not for long. And anyway, there's no such thing.'

'We're bringing more plants tomorrow. They come from Paris, you know.'

'There used to be plants here once. In this bloody City.'

'These ones are European.'

'Yes.'

'I don't know why you grow weeds.'

'I am a gardener,' said Chrisnelt. 'Walls and weeds: this is what I have to work on here; walls and weeds.'

Things stood where they needed to stand. Rows of shiny bushes and little shiny trees waited to be planted: it was all set out for the future. 'Nothing can be more relevant a design problem than walls and weeds and rows of bushes and trees, waiting to work together,' said Chrisnelt. He wiped his face, the sweat coming again, the big shadow of dawn rolled away by the dust, which always gained new life in the heat.

After all the peering down at little plants, squeezing long fingers into holes, and looking sideways at dirty neighbouring walls, Chrisnelt began to see a plan. He looked at the walls: 'From the sky, they must look like jaws, snapping at the clouds. I will plant bushes, and trees, and I will grow climbing plants. And they will turn those jaws into a mouth that speaks to everyone, in kissing languages.'

He began to see out and into the distance, beyond the

walls and the dust. Pastor Kadazi's land dropped away slowly from the house: an ever-so-gentle rolling forward of earth on an uncurling tongue, long and wide like that of a hunting chameleon. In the heavy air, the land glinted with waking flies. If Chrisnelt stood on his tiptoes, he could even see the edge of the City, the ragged line of corrugated roofs, sleeping between plumes of cooking smoke rising – a sad burning. Domes, minarets and spires paused like watchdogs over the City. In the far distance, in the blue retreating mists, was the Softness: the Great Dancing Road and the Forest. He breathed privately. He rested his hands on his hips. His breath held him as a friend holds a friend. This site was to be a garden. 'I will make it *my* garden,' he said to the weeds. 'A garden for *my* tree.'

'If I can raise the land to the height of my waist, at least in the very centre – at its highest possible point – I will be able to plant that special tree. And it will grow higher than any other. It will be seen from every road, from every street, and even from the distant forest paths, and from the barges on the River, and from across the River, from the other city. And below it, I will place a seat to wait on before I climb to the very top.'

The rooster, flushed from the patio by the servants, pecked at his toes. He said to it: 'Next to the magnificent seat, I will build a birdbath for pilgrims from the sky. When the early morning is just right, the sun will catch that water and hold it still, fitting bits of the garden together like other people's prayers: pieces of sky with pieces of cloud, pieces of tree with pieces of other tree, pieces of green and blue and white and all the browns, together into the single language of the past. And then the birds will come, one by one, the rainbows on their feathers swimming in the water as I have swum in my maps, in my books, and in the splashing raindrops inside my head, whispering of No.'

CHAPTER FIFTEEN

WEEDS CLUSTERED INTO GROUPS of bright colour. Some patches looked like emerald mountains, some like ruby seas; some were vast swathes of all the yellows on all the summer plains of the world; some had the shapes of continents in greens that faded into more greens; some were very big and wide like oceans of aquamarine, white coasts bursting at their edges. Most looked like escaping maps wanting to find their homes in the real sunshine and the real air. All things flowered with much ebullience.

One group of weeds was filled with poetry: the bed of irises. 'Is such a thing named for the flower or for the plant?' Chrisnelt asked the rooster. The big bird with its cocked head, often looking at him sideways, had become his new friend. Working so hard, he'd not seen Chaminda, La Mame or Ásbjörn for many months. He'd only glimpsed his sisters, and he smelled his mother once. He'd felt Amaterasu's warmth every night, but that did not count because it was contact from another universe.

And so he'd struck up this good friendship with the listening rooster, who he named Rooster, and with whom he shared his lunch. This was provided by the kitchen in the house, always placed in a tin box on the marble step of the patio. Here he sat, eating such a lunch, wondering whether he planted flowers or whether he planted plants.

'Rose is a rose is a rose, they say in the books, but when is it a rose*bush*, Rooster?'

Rooster lowered himself into the last bit of dust and made a private cloud of brown. He disappeared in feathers and flailing wings for a minute or so, then settled, squat and apparently content, waiting for the heat.

'Or is it only a rosebush when it is devoid of roses?' asked Chrisnelt as he dug a nice, wide hole for one of the new, shiny bushes.

Chrisnelt had seen many of these weeds he now nurtured, on many graves, during his past adventures with La Mame. They always looked lost there; now they had come home. He stared at the irises again, his eyes intent with thoughts. These deep, red ones were luminous, translucent, turning into floating goblets of red crystal like the ones on Pastor Kadazi's patio table. Each iris offered up a drop of sacrificial wine. Adding to this – completing the hallowed arrangement of ceremonial inflorescence – was a show of church dancers, jugglers and acrobats: the cavorting teams of insects, drunk in the humidity of the midday show. Some of the flowers reminded him of wailing church choirs, some of rioting crowds. Some even looked a bit like floating plastic wreaths. One or two rose higher than the rest, like prophets and presidents. They seemed dangerous in solitude. Captured, and yet now becoming free.

Chrisnelt measured the general width of his garden (it was his in his heart and in his dreams and in his hopes): fifty-nine paces from side wall to side wall, including an extra skip and a slow hop for extra flexibility. The length he estimated about three times the width, sloping ever so patiently down and away from him and the house of deliverance. Many new bushes sat scattered in between old bushes, all of differing heights and levels of forsakenness – a few even high enough to start wanting to become trees. Some were of a sickly green like somebody's sin. One or two were dark green, wanting to jump with grasshoppers into the heavy blues and grasp all the secrets in the sky, such was the joy of growth. A couple of densely leafy ones were round, like the huge tortoises that once hid here, pretending to be small hills. There were pointy bushes, like spears or carnal flames. One bush shook like a prediction, because it threatened to grow extremely high.

'When does a bush become a tree?' pondered Chrisnelt aloud to Rooster. 'When is that magical moment of change?'

These questions spoke to him of transition in Nature, fundamental to his way of seeing, creating rich and deep connections to every delicate leaf. Special answers came delivered, wrapped in leaves, by the Forest he'd never seen with his fingers. 'Trees are big and bushes are small, but there is a place in between, where bushes – certain contemplative bushes – can see their way forward, toward the world of trees. It is a shady place, hovering under the lowest line of the oldest leaves, in the shadows of the future,' he said to the dust below Rooster.

'How extraordinary, the transition, when a dragonfly moves forever from the water to the sky; or when pollen becomes honey inside a beehive wall; or when a bright flower stretches into a bright fruit. How extraordinary a thing, when black sand pops up into a white mushroom, or when rain on the hot metal roof turns to steam like a sneeze of life, or when a bird up high stops flying because it no longer has to, resting within the lungs of clouds, becoming harmony. How extraordinary and magnificent the shift from one thing into another, the continuity of it all,' he said to the soil on his hands, as he dug deeply with his crackling nails. 'And I wonder how many trees it takes to make a forest. When is the moment of that *final* individual tree, when it becomes the first tree of a forest, grasping upward?'

'I need to observe more bushes becoming trees,' he said, 'especially the Special Bushes, and they are particularly uncommon.'

Chrisnelt and Rooster raked the earth with their feet. 'The first thing to look at is the stem; see if it has become woody and hard over time,' he wrote in his notebook after wiping the sand from his fingers, underlining 'see'. 'Once this stem is located, it is often textured and crinkled, has begun to develop significant girth, hinting at strong roots below and sturdy branches above. It hints, too, at a structural truth: preparedness, and a consideration to steady itself, seizing the earth, ready to rise higher than the rest, ready to reach up to the levitating birds. This stem, if examined closely with the eyes of a gardener, is on the verge of becoming a trunk. In addition, the Special Bush has special leaves of the very darkest, sincerest green, hidden from the sun for much time, situated at the very lowest level of time, hovering just above the ground and the world of the fallen dreams.'

He wrote further, on pages patterned by dust, drawing a sketch, making notes for a poem and capturing a few calculations and earthy hues. 'The layer of dry leaves resting below the Special Bush carries the shadows of warning, the tiny shadows, the brittle shadows, the breaking shadows.

It is those very low, old leaves that reveal the past; some hang stained with dust, and the spattering of dry mud, like blood, held long after rain. They are the leaves of memory. They will stay behind, because they belong to the ground; a world that lives further and further away from the sun because of the gift of rain, as the new tree grows onward and upward and becomes sanctified.' Sketches filled the pages, made with numbers and letters shaped like leaves. 'The bottom of the Special Bush will tell of its top one day,' he declared to Rooster. 'And the top will tell of forests.'

For Chrisnelt, the place under a rising tree was the pupa of the moth: an intimate part of one thing, unfolding into something new. 'Decay is life,' he said. 'From below comes flight to the sky.'

With all his hard work, Chrisnelt awakened the garden. He sunk the propitious hand-spade into the sand, twisting the earth thoroughly, loosening trapped twigs, pebbles and every half-hidden leaf. The energy released with each plunge was subtle, often filled with escaping moths. The ground absorbed the blows gratefully, like a massaged muscle, waiting to stretch and flex with new living things.

He worked day and night for many weeks, often sleeping under his bushes. Rooster slept with him on those nights of deep exhaustion, when he was simply too tired to walk home. In time, he opened up the soil to the air, helping it breathe in and out in the rhythms of the Earth, finding its salvation, rising in awakened moths. He got to know every plant. He got to know when a flower was to come, and when it was to go away into the sky as seeds. He watched the growth of leaves carefully, and when he saw a struggling stem, he relocated it appropriately, or nursed it back to health, banishing all putrefactions and irrelevances that hindered growth. He pushed sand this way and that way. He discovered black river boulders under the sands and he freed them, polishing them like the River used to do. Once or twice, he unearthed old stems of giant trees; they would crumble in his hands and his tears, as many little mice and resting snakes and lizards scurried away. He apologised to these creatures that had found slumber within these majestic cathedrals of yesterday. If he were fortunate to unearth the ancient shells of forest snails deep inside the darker soils, he collected them in a bucket, so as to scatter them about on completion of the garden, in their brilliant whiteness becoming a celestial sprinkling of little hollow churches and chapels.

And – in addition to the many shiny plants that kept coming on trucks – he brought many plants from all parts of the City. He searched indiscriminately in the corners of warm nights and the flatness of flaming days. He spread the word to people who owned long boats, and to the strong quiet people who carried baskets of chickens for trade. He requested plants from across the many districts and beyond. He waited for plants on the wind and those that fell from birds. He followed lost bees to new petals and concussed butterflies to new stems.

He asked Chaminda to search in the back-country of his high hill of cans, unravelling forgotten plants growing in the garbage of the City's lost chances. He asked Ásbjörn to summon seeds from the internet, and La Mame to collect the envelopes filled with these requests. He brought plants in his dreams, too: the blessed plants waiting where the River turned to the East, widening – as Great Dancing Roads do – into sacred selections and holy collections of untold beauty. He beat a baptismal call for plants on a stainless steel pot, like church bells sounding from the highest roof. He beat and beat and beat that drum. He did all of this; and his work lasted many months, almost a year.

And when the rains finally came, he told himself, he'd be sure to beat the mud; he would jump and stamp and beat, calling every earthworm – the tremendously long ones that blink, the ones sleeping deeper than ever before known. In those rains, he would be sure to summon so deeply that worms would come from beyond continents, from the place of tremors and shifting worlds, well below the oceans, on the other side of the unfathomable, where it had rained only at the beginning of time; and the worms would bring with them a universal freshness. And on that day Chrisnelt hoped to awaken the garden to its fullest potential, and it would begin to grow in a new and most unusual dampness; it would grow a tree.

Chrisnelt plunged the hand-spade into the earth with much love, twisting thoroughly. Cracks made zigzags along hard surfaces; loops and parabolic arches leapt across soft surfaces; dust tumbled and loose loam rippled in little waves; the spade twisted, flipping everything about. During a brief pause, after hours of churning the land, he sat next to Rooster in the shade of a wall – a wall now a vertical garden reaching to the sky – and the swaying shadow of a passing crow, the spade at his side filled with debris. After a moment, he heard the hiss of a rivulet of sand falling from the spade.

The hissing stopped. Protruding from the edge of the spade was the tip of a finger. The nail hung bent, twisted yellow cracked in fine lines, muted purples of old blood below, the bone still clinging to torn dried skin. The finger lay suspended in time, oddly frozen by the drought and the fineness of the dusts. A big, green fly circled, moving from his nose to the finger, his eyes following it, the insect's sheen illuminating the scene of demons. The finger toppled off the shovel. 'Shit,' he said to the Rooster and the fly.

He picked up the finger, a precious thing, and blew on it to chase the fly away. The crow shuddered in the sky, drifting away, following an escaping cloud. Chrisnelt pulled a wooden wedding band from the middle of the finger, and with it came a piece of hardened skin. He curled into a ball of terror, the bright white sun hotter than it had ever been in any garden.

CHAPTER SIXTEEN

CHRISNELT ABANDONED THE GARDEN. He walked out the side gate, leaving it swinging in the street dust. His crotch was wet, crawling in flies. He vomited in the middle of the street. He vomited and he tried to walk. And he vomited again while walking. The rooster walked after him, and then it walked off into oblivion.

He clasped the finger in his sweating hand, the wooden band lying deep in his pocket. He walked into his home without speaking and he went into his own garden and he lay next to the circular pond under the shade of the warm Rock, his head on the fallen leaves. He lay there for two days. He did not speak. He breathed softly. The singing mosquitoes with black-and-white legs sang all day and all night. The beetles on the water made constant ripples across the sun and the moon. The butterflies flew at night and the moths flew in the day. Sparrows came and went like never-ending dances of pollen. Crows sat on all the ridges of all the roofs. Plants grew and grew and grew.

Nipcia fed him as she fed the sparrows and the plants. She did not ask him what was wrong. She'd stopped doing that long ago. The very black man from the White House came to ask after Chrisnelt, and his sisters said he was sick. Pastor Kadazi phoned the church from his hotel suite in China, and Mrs Malotika told him her son was not well in the head. Pastor Kadazi said he would pray for him, but he wanted his garden finished on his return the following week. The garden at Africa House was silent, but it also screamed.

When he finally sat up, covered in moths, having been mistaken for a sleeping log, his eyes were swollen and red. He did not blink. The moon was in the middle of the darkness, its silver light was in the centre of his heart. The moths lifted, shining like Christmas decorations sucked up into the night, on a journey to the Centre of the City.

'I know what I must do,' he said to the Rock, his cheeks raw, sticky with the worst tears, the ones that come when you sleep and truly see the world. 'I will finish his fucking garden. Then it will be ready for my tree.'

He took the finger and the wooden wedding band and he placed them delicately inside the letter from No's funeral day, rolling the paper very slowly and with much care, tucking the parcel under his sleeping mat. And he thought of fingers, writing:

'Most of us have fingers, yet we do not know this precious gift sleeping in our hands. They are like opening doors: ten miracles touching the world, changing everything all the time. Fingers are like feet: offering a way forward and a safe route home. They are like eyes, like the tongues of the greatest cooks, the great noses of the world, resounding with flavours of discovery. Fingers find a place for us to grow. Just as words are crippled without the power of my pen, so knowledge will die without fingers and their dance. It is not possible to change the world without fingers. And these can only ever be the fingers of those that work for our hope.'

Of fingernails he wrote:

'Fingernails grow constantly as they move forward on

the fingers. But is it growth or is it death that is happening at their tips? It seems to me nails are on an inevitable journey to a vast precipice at the very end of it all, searching for the sky above and the wet earth below. When fingernails grow in pink, and then finally the white of splinters and screams, they change like the shit that is shat in life. Fingernails need to be trimmed into an epiphany, through the hard work of hands that will give life to a tree.'

Chapter Seventeen

A Special Bush always stands in a fixed pose: an impatient creature, waiting for the hand of the forest. Chrisnelt looked at the large bush directly in front of him. It was how he had left it. They were all as he had left them. They'd done what he'd expected them to do. They had grown. And the garden shone for him, just as a flame shines for a moth. He'd carefully spread these Special Bushes all over the garden, one here and one there, a process that had required constant diligent observation.

This one Special Bush stood before him like a friend who'd waited for him. It was bright in the sunlight, and he imagined it would be bright under the moon too. It offered a bouncy shadow on that new morning of determination. It had become an idea – the notion filled his notebook in the heat. It shook, it seemed to call out.

It does indeed want to become a tree, he thought. *It's perfectly situated to become the great tree of my garden. It will require a lot of water and the best soils.* The shaking continued. He opened the bush, as a surgeon would the chest of a troubled patient, parting branches and clusters of thick leaves, his hands and fingers tingling at the touch. The spongy interior presented a quivering bird: a leaflove. 'Like a pounding heart!'

The Yellow-throated Leaflove – number seventy-one on my bird list – is to the tree what the albatross is to the sea, he imagined. If ocean waters had wings, they would fly in the form of the albatross, and so it is with this species and the trees of the West African tropics. If the trees could only lift, they would take to the air as leafloves: birds of all the greens, part shadow, part light, part tail, part wing, part pointy beak, part branch, part frond, part flapping leaf.

'If a person is lucky enough to glimpse you, all that's revealed is a beating throat, heart-shaped and full; a lonely glow seen through leaves, yellow like a window at night,' said Chrisnelt to the quivering bird. 'More often than not, all that's observed of you is your call: a creaking sound, as when a stem bends in song, the tree owning lungs for a moment, letting loose a delicate breath.'

Chrisnelt knelt like he had not knelt for quite some time. He untangled the small bird, its leg tightly caught in twine and a twig. All was soft and warm. He'd never held a wild bird before. He'd never even seen a Yellow-throated Leaflove – until that morning had only ever observed it as a shaking, squeaking bit of canopy, high up in lone trees, near where the River currents touched the City in warning.

It cocked its head, looking up at him sideways, and the wildness that came from the pale eye held focus. Chrisnelt had always seen eyes as a pair: one thing made of two, together giving expression to a face, any face, whether human or animal. Eyes to him had always been a gaze or a blink, a singular act of unison, like the two wings of a bird in flight. Yet here in this side-on eye of the leaflove, staring directly, was a new kind of dream. Perhaps it was the newness of seeing an eye by itself, alone and out of context of the full face, like seeing a single finger. Perhaps it was the chance to be so close to the concentric circles, the glistening curve. Chrisnelt looked again into the deep centre of the eye: far in the distance, he could see the natural world, and within the watery translucence burned lost light.

He opened his hands. Momentarily startled, the bird sat in a pause, bright green and warmed by a white, sepulchral sun. A quick fluffing of feathers, and then – just like a dream – it was gone; a tiny piece of tree ripped away. Chrisnelt stood for a long while squinting down and out at the faraway River, a little dazed at the suddenness of the encounter, the hotness of the day coming onto him.

'CHRISNELT! Blessed child!' shouted Pastor Kadazi. 'I am back with more ideas for my garden. Come here, blessed Chrisnelt.'

'Yes, Pastor, I'm coming,' said Chrisnelt, turning to face the house.

Pastor Kadazi stood in a gleaming new white suit, an entourage of thirty or forty guests a short distance behind him. Some carried plants. From between the legs of the guests scurried many hens, and a new rooster. Chrisnelt looked down into his left palm, at the white-and-green smear of shit, shining with fear.

'We have brought many orchids.'

'Very good. Thank you, Pastor.'

'I see you have been very busy.'

'Yes.'

'So you have healed your head.'

'Yes.'

'You have planted all my bushes?'

'Yes.'

'And this plastic bridge, I like it. It looks good over this pond. And that too. I like the heart shape of the water.'

'Yes.'

'And the other pond in the ferns. Good. I like the shiny stones around it.'

'Yes.'

'And I like all these flowers. You have collected many flowers. Very good. Many colours everywhere now. Many shapes.'

'Yes.'

'I see all my walls are green now? Very green.'

'Yes.'

'Everything is very high on the sides, and down there at the bottom. High bushes, high leaves. Very high and green. Yes. It's like a jungle. It's like a great shiny jungle. Very good. Just like the photographs I was sent. Just as I had been told!'

'Yes.'

'Your mother's been paid a lot.'

'Yes, thank you, Pastor.'

'And this hole here. What is it you are making? A great lake? For my fountain and the jewelled fishes?'

'No, Pastor. This is for a tree.'

'What tree?'

'I don't know.'

'What don't you know?'

'The tree.'

'It's a landmine hole!'

'I will get a tree.'

'It's a terrible hole.'

'I will get a beautiful tree for you, Pastor.'

'Fill it in.'

'There is a tree.'

'Fill it in now.'

'Yes, Pastor.'

The crowd of followers came out, flexing like dangerous creatures escaping from an alien zoo. Men in black safari-suits with silver pinstripes and pointed shoes of patent leather, glowing with toxic smoke like burning twigs. Fat ladies in golden taffeta dresses, and others wafting kaftans dotted in pearls, unfolded onto the front lawns. Cell phones shone, as did eyes, faces crackling as if the people were escaping fires. In the heat, many of the heads appeared to bear sharp horns. Earrings everywhere, dangling like Christmas decorations. People smoking red-coaled cigars trampled through the fern garden, thinking – due to the simple greenness and the large black boulders that lay quietly – that the area was still under construction. Metallic headdresses on two small women flickered above the leaves like anger, or pain. They laughed a sick laugh of excess. Fronds snapped. All these captured people pulled and peered at the ponds. A young man in a green army jacket, medals gleaming, stood on the Chinese bridge and called to his friend on the other Chinese bridge, pointing at the fishes that shimmered like bars of gold between the floating white lilies.

Governor Feti called to the guests: 'Come and look at what I have brought for Pastor Kadazi's patio!' The crowd turned.

Chrisnelt stood on the far side of the limitless hole, at its edge. It was deeper than he'd remembered, and filled with echoes. He could hear the drums from ancient caves, the caves that showed dancing peoples on the walls.

He felt sick. His stomach ached and he wanted to dive headfirst into the depths, so that he might never be seen again. He wanted to curl into a ball of pure ash, far down at the very bottom of the world. His head sank into his neck, and his ears buzzed. He stood there with his back deep in the softest leaves. Africa House glinted above the crowd, reverberating with the noises of Pastor Kadazi and his people from within its whiteness. Chrisnelt pushed at the rich soil with his feet and it started to crumble, sliding back down into the pit. It would take him days to fill. It had taken him days to dig.

'The roots were going to come to you. Somewhere down there you are waiting, River, for the roots from my tree. I am sorry, No.'

From the garden, the patio set into the white façade seemed to howl, the bustle and murmurs of the guests amplified; lights from the phones flashed on and off as photographs flew into the sky on the wings of pixels.

'Look at the beautiful plants,' shrieked a man from the throng of busy guests squashed onto the patio. He was taller than the others, and on his head was the hat of a general. It was a very bright hat, filled with authority. The smells of canapés filtered out across the lawns.

'Well done, Governor,' said a man of vast weight, smoking a cigarette, his face glowing. 'What a lovely gift.'

'Thank you, Governor, praise God,' said Pastor Kadazi.

'Hanging silk orchids from my factory in China. They never have to be watered. They give life to this patio, and to this House, as Pastor gives life to us,' announced Governor Feti, to loud applause. 'My people have hung them everywhere for him. On all the walls.'

'Well done, Pastor!' cheered the crowd in unison. 'Well done, Governor Feti! Such a patio has never lived. Such a house of silk flowers and leaves has never been seen in Africa!'

'Well done,' said a soft voice, parting the faces. The crowd stepped to either side of the small man.

Ten soldiers walked out onto the lawns, with machine-guns on their shoulders and helmets on their heads. They were green, like the lawns; their white belts and white boots shone against all the green. They looked across the garden. Behind them stood other men in black suits and black sunglasses: they shone like the shining black rocks in the ferns at dusk.

'Your Excellency, welcome,' said Pastor Kadazi.

'Thank you for inviting me, Pastor Kadazi.'

'Thank you, Excellency. Praise the Lord.'

'Sorry I am late.'

'It is an honour, Excellency.'

'So *this* is Africa House. It has a spectacular garden. It carries a great responsibility.'

'Thank you, Excellency.'

'What will grow in that hole?'

'It will be filled, my President,' said Pastor Kadazi. 'And on the open land we will place a sculpture of our Founder.'

'It should be filled with a big tree from the Forest,' said the President.

CHAPTER EIGHTEEN

THE EXPLOSION OF THE ammunition depot made the sound of a trillion hideous choirs: a deluge of the loudest order, reverberating within an almighty cave without light. Many thousands of people were part of the screaming dust and darkness of that day. Many died instantly under walls: impenetrable tombstones of crumbling rubble. Some were buried in the skin of others, their bodies mingled. It gave the sky a physical dimension; some people said afterwards that the air killed people. A plastic bag high in the sky suffocated a crow.

Ásbjörn's internet shop rocked subtly; spiders fell from the ceiling, their interconnected webs of silk adjusting their loops, draping paying customers in the carcasses of dead flies and extra fees. While lying on his hill of scales, the crumpled remnants of tin and waste, Chaminda watched mushroom clouds rise through concrete, pushing heat against the distant mists. The chaos made Mrs Malotika work all day baking even more bread and croissants, shaped like yesterday's smiles; and the Nagasakis prayed for tomorrow, as did the MacDonalds and the Mohameds, and every other family of different languages and ways.

Chrisnelt counted the blasts, his fingers pushing into the deep soil each time. There were twelve at irregular intervals, the last being the biggest, the reverberations continuing intermittently until one o'clock that afternoon. A square kilometre of the City was flattened, right down to the riverside, windowpanes crumbling to sand, roofs crumpling like giant leaves, streets evaporated. The River current surged into new clearings, creating a fringe of mud. The River deepened and swelled.

The Minister of Defence came on the radio to say that it was not a *coup d'état*. Television sets suspended the gold-rimmed-death-notices programme. Governor Feti said: 'This is indeed a terrible act of Hell! The Burial Home will provide free body-bags to the poor.' Battalions of green soldiers gathered on both banks of the River to assure the opposite bank that it was only a calamitous accident, again. (There'd been a similar event a few years previously; that time, only sixteen tonnes of arms had been wasted, with many live gun bullets and big tank shells retrieved intact from holes. This time, too, the cause was a fire from a short-circuiting wire, also from a toaster.) 'The punishments will be the same as last time,' said Governor Feti. All military camps were moved to the new outskirts beyond the old outskirts of the City.

Pastor Kadazi was away on business again, in a very high aeroplane. Chrisnelt looked up from the garden to see if he could see lines of ice on the sky. He did not want to be surprised again. All he could see above Africa House was the smoke from wild fires, deep and thick and black from escaping rivers of fuel and melting plastic. In the distance, the cry of birds came scattering from the River. He shuffled his feet and pushed his hands down into his long pockets. They clattered faintly with many bleached finger bones. He'd collected three or four a week, for many weeks, and over many months, and that week was no different. He knew what to do. He would take them home, as he'd done with all the others, to let them rest in secret below the leaves of his own private burial home.

As the plumes of smoke rose, they faded into a sunset backdrop of orchid-pinks and pigeon-purples beyond the White House. The house appeared whiter than ever, the white roof tiles glowing like never before, the white columns, arches, walls and window-frames whiter than snow. Even the shade shivered white in the heat, and brown sparrows darted, escaping the horrific music.

With the next explosion rising in his ears, Chrisnelt shook his head and said to the soil: 'Governor Feti will smile under this sunset of putrefaction.'

It had been a further month of planting and replanting, of searching and carrying, of digging and more digging. Before leaving, Pastor Kadazi had said: 'Dig that hole twice as deep and twice as wide.'

Chrisnelt had dug it even deeper; and a little wider too. Now he stood on the edge and looked inside, the land bending down into the brownest, most fertile soil he'd even seen. 'A deep valley in my garden for my tree,' he said to the new rooster. And he patted the little mountain of earth next to him. It smelled sweeter than the sweetest croissant.

At the bottom of the hole, two bubbles popped out of the earth, one by one, and the beginnings of water seeped gently upward in a slow moan that was more like a chant. The tiny current swirled, and then it settled and was still. A very small pond glittered shallow and fecund.

Deep inside, within every cavity of his mind, a powerful surge of juices swirled; the muscles in his cheeks shook as never before, and he wasn't sure if his eyes would burst forth in tears or his mouth gush in the brightest birdsong. He stared at the ground. His hands clung to his face. 'It's my River Mud. It's the River – you've come! I've dreamed of you all these years. You've found the hole. You've been called by the imminence of the Tree,' cried Chrisnelt. 'Those bloody earthquakes must have opened a way for you. It is a miracle, No!'

The sun was going and the moon was coming. The house was changing into its usual blue. A long row of sparrows, crows and purple pigeons sat on the ridge line of the roof in silence, a last stop before heading to their roosts. Flocks of white egrets arrived and went like low clouds. Swallows of various species circled, as did a single aberrant gull. Chrisnelt fell back into the sand of the hill. It cupped him like a cool, soft couch. He thought of La Mame's couch. He thought of all his friends. He thought of his sisters and his mother. He thought of his father. He thought of people and their delicate bodies, and their limbs becoming trees. His head rested, the first time in many years. He gazed across his garden, his face scanning what he'd made, his eyes wide, his view wider. It was the world.

In it lived plants from all the continents. The many scents became a single scent, and he breathed in long, certain of what he smelt. Even a flat and hardy moss that came from Antarctica had found a space, making its way in on a pebble, abandoning ice forever.

'From every valley and every hill ever explored and named anywhere have come plants in pairs to breed in my dreams. Seeds have arrived from the sky. They did not fall. They *arrived*!' Flowers bloomed continuously, reflecting upward everything that was good. 'Flowers are now making the other flowers bloom. The seeds are making seeds,' he said.

And, being a garden made of many islands, there was water, the water of wilderness, linking.

'Not those big fibreglass ponds below the bridges. Not the stream in the curving concrete channel that came in pieces to be assembled, cast with glass pebbles. Not that new slope there, trickling down in all those tiny waterfalls to that bench at its base, fuelled by a noisy pump. Not that sparkling stream there, so clear you can see the mosaics of all the angels. Not the sound of the water on that shoreline of marble chips, vomited from that sculpture with its marble wings and its marble crosses. Not any of that anymore for this garden.' He lay back and closed his eyes. 'Now the real waters, from the real tides of the Planet,' he said softly.

Crashing waves soothed him, as did the lapping streams. He drifted, flowing in cool mists, and in the warm spray from the heads of whales. Sifting currents took him in a song through a world of divinations, toward wild chanting continents, each one a sea of high trees. The melody was so soft in the calling leaves, and laced in the deepest roots that penetrated to the other side of every home and beyond. There was only space for life now, for a clear recommendation by the insects and the frogs. It was time for the birds, and for every edge to become every other edge: the dissolution of boundaries.

Chapter Nineteen

'I HAVE ARRANGED TO GO upriver,' said Pastor Kadazi.

   'Yes, Pastor,' said Chrisnelt.

   'I have been told of a special tree.'

   'Yes, Pastor.'

   'Have you been upriver before?'

   'No, never, Pastor.'

   'I need you to tell me if that tree will grow in my hole.'

   'Yes, Pastor. I will tell you.'

   'And you'd better not be wrong.'

   'Yes.'

   'No more shit in your head?'

   'No, Pastor. No more shit there.'

   'It's a long way by boat,' said Governor Feti, sitting on one of the huge patio couches that hissed, fiddling under a fingernail with his knife. Once again, he was sifting through the little stones sprinkled on the black velvet cloth. Behind him, silk orchids made all the walls bloom, and on them rested mosquitoes with black-and-white legs.

   'I must go past one of my chicken farms on the way,' said Pastor Kadazi. 'A helicopter can't land there. So we go by boat.'

   'I would come with you,' said the Governor.

   'No need.'

   'Okay.'

   '*He* must be there, though.'

   'Yes.'

'Yes, Pastor, I will be there,' said Chrisnelt, trying not to look at all the rich stones, or at the knife.

There'd been no speaking for many hours in the inferno that came down from the sun near the City. The flatness on the River simmered from the time they pushed away from the pier, as if it had been raining on banks of fire. The heavy gurgle of the engines fought with the hot breeze, the clouds searching for beatification beyond.

Humidity only chases those who sit with searing flies, thought Chrisnelt, his shirt sleeves rippling in the air and the crisp openness. Trees lined the banks in tight clusters. Seen from certain angles, a cluster linked with a cluster in an illusion of endless leaves, a memory of a Forest. A flock of egrets lifted brightly, mingling with a flock of Sacred Ibises, then with a flock of Lesser-striped Swallows. All the sizes and shapes understood each other, a patterned wave of life held by the pull of the River.

'Look at all these birds, Chrisnelt. I know you like birds,' said Pastor Kadazi.

'The most abundant bird in the world is the chicken, Pastor. There are twenty-four billion of them,' said Chrisnelt.

'You get hungry when you see these birds?'

'No, Pastor. I'm just saying there are lots of chickens in the world.'

'There can never be too many!' Pastor Kadazi spluttered and shook. It was the first time Chrisnelt had ever seen Pastor Kadazi laugh like that, the mouth staying open for a long time, the spittle exploding from the fat face.

'Three times the global human population,' said

Chrisnelt loudly, trying to prolong his apparent joke. Talking was all he could think of doing in the confines of the speedboat. He felt nausea deep down inside his gut. His head ached as the world bounced. The sun slapped him in the face constantly, and his cheeks stung. He'd never sat so close to Pastor Kadazi before. The sweat of the men and the perfume from Pastor Kadazi's wet neck hung in his nostrils.

'Very good for me,' said Pastor Kadazi loudly, above the sound of the engines. He continued to laugh.

'Second is the Common Pheasant,' said Chrisnelt. 'One hundred and seventy-three million.' Nobody laughed. Pastor Kadazi had lost interest.

The speedboat moved fast against the current, away from the City, away from the crowds and the desperation; so many memories packed together on this ship of greed.

'Chicken is the best white meat in Africa,' said Pastor Kadazi suddenly, rubbing his fat thighs. 'Better than crocodile, or all the other kinds of expensive white meat I've tasted in the far south of this continent.' He laughed. 'Sweeeet meat that, lots of perfume on that, there, better than the little white meats of Europe too.' The men laughed. 'Chicken and charcoal,' said Pastor Kadazi, patting the expensive canvas seat, 'good for business.' His white silk shirt fluttered, as did his eyes.

'Yes, Pastor,' said Chrisnelt, tapping the stainless steel railing.

'Chicken and charcoal,' laughed Pastor Kadazi, 'veeeeery good combination!' The men laughed again; many laughs became a single laugh.

Chrisnelt sat sideways in the speedboat so that he

could look at the green bank and the many birds. Pastor Kadazi sat next to him, his back to the sun. The spray carved by the sharp prow threw up fake rain and fake mist and a fake rainbow of colours. Pastor Kadazi stared at the winding trail of white bubbles, an effortless road left behind on the brown river. 'It's like fresh chicken shit,' said Pastor Kadazi from under his dark sunglasses.

'It does look like shit, Pastor,' said Chrisnelt. All the men agreed.

'Like when I catch a bird with my hands around its neck,' said Pastor Kadazi. He laughed again loudly, a wail Chrisnelt hadn't heard before.

A Goliath Heron lifted from the faraway reeds – number seventy-seven for Chrisnelt's list – and it glided in the shape of a delicate, rusting leaf, brittle to the touch.

The River broadened into a field of water hyacinth as the boat of men came around a bend. More trees appeared in isolated clusters. The current seemed to dive down to great depths there, sucking the water surface into a vast indentation – a plunge deeper than that of any river on Earth, perhaps like that of knowledge – hiding itself, taking the light to see the dark, the day borrowed by the caves for a time, sending plumes of mud up in eddies and swirling bubbles. Chrisnelt looked into the water between patches of floating leaves that had stuck to the bubbles. He saw stars, a distant moon playing with the sun within a single, vast raindrop. He thought of his hole and his tree.

The hyacinth had made temporary rafts for water insects, some as wide as outstretched arms, some just tiny discs spinning endlessly, together in a journeying sea. They seemed to be wild places adrift in a home.

'The River is a road, but it is also a home,' he said under his breath. Pastor Kadazi stared at him. Chrisnelt looked down at the water again. It looked cool. The air hummed.

He'd been aware of the water hyacinth; it had become a living border between the City and the River. He thought back, remembering: *This plant moors itself back there, at the Edge of the City. Its long green skin runs the length of our bank. So very long. The final boundary, the furthest it dare reach into the Pristine, I guess, is here. And the current's always tearing at it, taking it through rumbling boulders and waterfalls, then off it goes again, on its way down to a coast of futures and pasts. A weed in its own simple equilibrium.*

The speedboat slowed, the prow swelling into glassy ripples. 'As wide as an ancient ocean all of a sudden: these mercurial waters have made a bay,' said Chrisnelt quietly.

Pastor Kadazi stared at him again. 'What, Chrisnelt? What are you saying?'

'Very hot today, Pastor. We are going very quickly in your boat.'

'Why do you not wear that big, stupid blue hat?'

'It fell into the hole, Pastor.'

'You growing hats now, hey?' All the men laughed.

'No, Pastor.'

'Maybe you shut up and watch your birds.'

'Yes, Pastor.'

The speedboat stuck to the deepest channel, somewhere near the middle of everything. To his left, Chrisnelt looked for new birds, the shoreline a distant horizon. Pastor Kadazi continued to stare at him. The islands of hyacinth heaved.

Chrisnelt fixed his gaze at the water, and he frowned. In the enormity, and of the pause given by bays to rivers, the islands of leaves had all come together into a single, shining mat. On it scurried thousands of birds of every description, in immense diversity of strategies and convictions.

Jacanas jerked along, iridescent copper shapes with splayed toes like elastic bands; egrets froze in ice sculptures, only to explode into charging spears; herons rocked below heavy beaks, glinting against the humidity; ducks swayed on the wake of the speedboat, one large duck shuttling its young in between hundreds of mauve blooms that sent bees about; crakes flicked their tails; and others, too busy to be identified, tapped small fish against their feet. Tall and short, fat and thin, they moved. Feathers of every colour and every creed ducked and dived, dodged and fed, calling and crying, bowing and bending, kneeling, scraping, freeing sparkling stories with wings that made mirrors of the sky. 'There are more bird species here than I have ever seen. No walls, just floating places of freedom. No hegemony can ever find a foothold here. The world was once such a river of islands,' said Chrisnelt to himself, not moving his lips.

'This tree will make me famous,' said Pastor Kadazi. 'You make sure it grows.'

'Yes, Pastor.'

'Those flat leaves are united only in temporariness,' muttered Chrisnelt, taking advantage of a loud hum from the engines as they rose above a wave, the propellers spluttering. He adjusted his position on the sticky seat next to Pastor Kadazi so that he was not quite so close to those sweating thighs. 'When a mat of hyacinth reaches that bend it'll become small islands again, and then it'll crumble, returning to the sea, to start all over again.'

The tall man at the steering wheel turned on a small radio wedged against the backrest of his seat, unfolding a silver aerial into the sky, as he had unfolded a machine-gun earlier that morning into the mist; the searching sound of DJ Yama's City Beat – an incoherent mixture of Kituba, Lingala and French, communicating with timber drums across a divide like a cave of echoes – blared into the stillness, bouncing above the wake of noise.

Thousands of birds lifted in primordial forms, and others scurried like tiny boats of mayhem. The islands of hyacinth became smaller and smaller still, until just a handful of leaves bobbed past; on one lay an empty Coca-Cola can.

New islands approached: the first barge was as long as a football field – actually four barges tied together lengthwise with cables. The barge was made of the oldest metal, becoming dust, and the oldest paint, becoming painted dust, pushed by an old tugboat of blue smoke. The deck was a street, or perhaps a town: scalloped corrugated-iron shacks and rows of bright factory fabrics and metal rods, giving homes to travellers who sold food and dreams and promises to other travellers. Little charcoal fires twinkled in tin drums, and a single hoot was accompanied by the chatter of bartering. Tiny flags on long wires made vibrant lines above all the shouting and selling. This long line of filigreed commerce was a destination on its way to another destination. People at the back pissed and shat. People at the side spat white toothpaste like ridiculous jokes. People near the front dreamed in the sharp tears of a breeze. The City downriver waited for these people to crawl under its tight skin. Other barges came past looking just like billboard signs: some longer, some shorter, some wider; all unstoppable in the pull of the River and the ocean waves of commerce, far away.

In the lulls between barges, tents of straw popped up on the wobbling surface of tree trunks: low, triangular habitations prodding the sky, lashed on top of the fattest trunks. Men with tall poles hopped about there, and at the back, a pirogue containing a sitting man seemed to nudge the trees. One tree at the end rolled like a carcass.

The River sucked silently at this flat forest sliding by. Many different islands passed Chrisnelt, in all sizes and with many different attitudes; one was just a plastic bag from Harrods of London.

'My chicken farm is up ahead,' said Pastor Kadazi, turning toward the bloated sun and pointing, parting the breeze with a single finger. His nails, manicured tips of indolence, never failed to shine. The nail on the end of the smallest finger of his left hand was yellow and long like a blade, cut to appear elegant, and yet it served to clean his fat ears with a rattling motion. The cutting of the engine made the boat shake and swing sideways, drifting toward a wide dent in the bank. The hull, immediately grabbed by the current and pulled, rocked toward a pockmarked shore of dried mud trampled by myriad footprints. Barefoot little children – at least a dozen boys and girls without shirts or opportunities – glistened and laughed and clapped, running down to greet the men.

'Look at my beautiful blessed chickens, look at the smiles for the Father,' said Pastor Kadazi, laughing.

After the sudden bump of docking, he handed out paper money – small denominations – to the many outstretched hands. The ritual was one of obedience rather than generosity, the money meaningless, the tiny smiles hungry and uncertain. Groping fingers don't lie like wide eyes keeping tears away. Chrisnelt had never seen such swollen eyes.

Pastor Kadazi walked up the bank of dust on a carpet of children in a cloud of floating bits of money and noise. Behind followed the men, the silver aerial protruding from the side of one man's head. The sound of Harry Belafonte's 'Island in the Sun' blared.

Chrisnelt followed, and behind him followed more dust in the loose shapes of angel wings under the brightness. It was hot on the land and flies came from everywhere, even from the cool edge of the River.

A small village, once dead, had grown up again around the chicken farm and the chicken shit, in posthumous jerks: five huts with loose roofs of dried palm fronds, pointing like old hats up to the heat, floating on gentle walls of clay that had begun to disappear in green tangles and bushes. The green was low, tight and thick like hair, impenetrable to the mind of any visitor, and treeless, except for the mango trees filled with mangoes of every mango colour. Chrisnelt could see how no helicopter could land in such a cramped mess.

This village of aggregations rested against the closest of the long, narrow chicken sheds that stood perpendicular to the river. Regimental shadows leaned down to the water. Chrisnelt counted twelve of these structures, and behind them another row of twelve. They were the lowest buildings he had ever seen: low walls of concrete block topped by low walls of wire mesh, below low roofs of corrugated iron, held in place by scattered rocks and hope. Between everything was red dust and red earth of the hardest kind, baked by the sun.

'It's flat, like a fried egg,' said Chrisnelt to the man with the machine-gun. The buildings sizzled with white hens; it was the hottest day he'd ever known.

Under a mango tree, a man stood up from a stool in the shade and came toward them.

'Hello, Geoffroy!' shouted Pastor Kadazi. 'The first time this year that I see you? You have not brought men to talk to me in the City for much time. No one behaving badly anymore?'

'Hello, Pastor. Welcome in all the blessings,' said Geoffroy.

The two men walked off to discuss business under the tree.

'Scrambled eggs,' said the man with the machine-gun quietly to Chrisnelt. They looked at the mass of hopping birds, feathers tossed about, heads and necks of white shaking the heat, shit spraying across feet, and smiled. 'Those ones at the back are for the chicks that are grown to a great size, and the ones here are for eggs of an even greater size!'

'That's a lot of chicken,' said Chrisnelt.

'Our City and its Brother City across the River have nineteen million mouths, all hungry for Pastor's chickens. There are no more fish like in the old time,' said the man, pointing to the River with his machine-gun, spitting a cola nut and a notion.

'Maybe the fish are hiding. This is a very deep river,' said Chrisnelt. 'The River needs fish, not chickens, but I suppose chicken shit is good for fish, when the current comes.'

Chrisnelt could clearly imagine what a barge of chickens might look like, afloat: white feathers coming together in one gigantic wing, flapping below an unreachable sky toward the madness, on its way from the beautiful darkness into the terrible light on the other side of the golden doors of Noah's Ark.

Another man, half-naked and shining, carrying a plastic bucket, approached Chrisnelt and Machine-gun Man. His bucket reminded Chrisnelt of La Mame. He was one of Geoffroy's feeders, not possessing enough fingers to be one of his egg-gatherers. He opened the low wire door to the closest shed, wading into a blizzard of white.

Chrisnelt followed him, the finely meshed shade running across their bodies. Both men floated in feathers. Hens scurried like children. 'What happened to your fingers?' asked Chrisnelt, as the man tossed food from the bucket, singing softly above the hiss and the stink.

'These hens have sharp beaks,' said the man.

A rooster crowed just then, a crow swooping upward like some sort of raised flag. And then it appeared, striding down the alley between the mesh walls of the two sheds, a copper-green sheen glistening, red skin on its head shivering, as if about to cast itself in brass under the heat of the sun. The eyes offered hard blinks, sharper than the beak or even the spurs on its legs. Those alleys were the streets of its city. The powerful bird scratched the dry mud, dust smoking like little fires. The rooster's toenails cut lines in the dried mud, delicate scars that seemed to bleed dust. The scales on its toes reminded Chrisnelt of monster-skin from internet films. He had visions of this great rooster, ten storeys high, pecking at the golden flag above Africa House, before settling into the garden's big hole for a bath in all the sands of the City. Flapping its wings into a storm of black soot, screaming above the call from every mosque, church or synagogue, summoning hens that were twice its size; and they'd come like clouds, trampling across the wasteland of corrugations with diamond eyes of powerful brilliance, making terrifying scratching sounds, like iron bending, that would cause every dog ever known to howl.

'Are these your women, or are they your children?' said Chrisnelt to the rooster, pointing a long finger at the hens and making a clucking sound.

The man with the bucket grinned pathetically.

'He is so important he can probably walk on water,' continued Chrisnelt, scattering some feed. Both men looked out through the mesh of the great cage at the River.

Pastor Kadazi was still under the mango tree, shaking his arms about. He gesticulated to Geoffroy, hands high in the air. Geoffroy responded with his own strange pose, arms held parallel above his head, gesturing convincingly to the heavens. Chrisnelt found himself alone in the cage. The water fiddled new glitterings like revelations. And the tiny mesh squares framed the light for Chrisnelt to see clearly the lies of men among chickens, and his own lies, as he scattered a palmful of diamonds. Wandering among the white hens, sewing just feed.

Pastor Kadazi grunted sharply: 'We must go!' He

handed Geoffroy a fistful of money. 'Chrisnelt, this man says that up ahead – not too far – is the tree I've been told about. He won't lie, because he has killed many chickens for me.'

'Thank you, Pastor,' said Chrisnelt, rejoining the group. They all made their way back to the speedboat. Again he was at the back of the queue; again the dust was behind him, following like a dancing friend. A little naked girl tugged at his pants, then she gave him a big, white hen feather. The girl smiled, the rest of the bloody wing in her other hand: a toy from a morning of games.

Chrisnelt remembered the plastic doll Nipcia had once lost, and that he'd found in Dee Dee Street, having stood on it by accident in the dust of a culvert. The head popped off with the sound of a cork leaving a bottle, releasing a gush of breath and sand, as if tiny brains had dried up inside. He looked at the girl and he remembered the doll's shiny nylon hair, the big blue eyes painted in a foreign stare.

'Chrisnelt, you like my chickens,' laughed Pastor Kadazi, as he climbed into the speedboat. He patted the seat next to him. 'Come and sit here. You want to eat them.'

'Yes, coming Pastor.'

'You want to put them on your bird list.'

'It's okay, Pastor.'

'Come and sit. We find a tree for my chickens now,' laughed Pastor Kadazi, and the men in the speedboat laughed, as did the men on the bank of the River.

'Chickens run wild somewhere,' said Chrisnelt, pushing his luck.

'Come.'

'Yes, Pastor, beautiful birds.' said Chrisnelt. 'Important for that charcoal from the trees.'

'Now you've made me hungry, Chrisnelt,' laughed Pastor Kadazi.

The pedagogical angels of the waters touched the speedboat in many thousands of little transparent wings.

'River flies,' said Pastor Kadazi, swishing his hand in front of his face.

The riverbanks on both sides of the world rocked. Banks that were always just limbs of one body, touching like parents touch children. The banks had been changed, separated, and would need to be changed back again one day. They were of one tribe, of a single language, yet they were two countries. Sovereignty had spoken pointlessly, and too much wasted time had passed inside dead nations: clucking chickens in separated sheds.

On the speedboat, Chrisnelt felt for the first time strangely free, in between the two countries, his mind weaving in the wake of the engines. He said softly: 'Illusions define neighbouring illusions.'

'What?' said Pastor Kadazi.

'Beautiful birds. I'm thinking about your tree, Pastor. I can see it in my head below the beautiful birds. It's very clear to me.'

The moabi tree arrived as roots, the speedboat coming around into another spreading bay. First those powerful fingers that protruded out over the bank, dipping into the water, grasping the River's edge. Such ancient fingers came up and into view. Free roots, free enough to come to the surface and show their hidden selves to the sun. The sight of such roots held the world in that moment.

The stability of them, and the security of their grip, settled Chrisnelt's heart into a beat of powerful serenity; at the same time, it unsettled his mind. To see such wide, hard and weathered roots was to know – with pure truth – that not all roots stay inside the earth. Some roots reach up to the sky, and guide the waters on a route that shapes every cloud. 'Those are the roots that work inside the deepest river on Earth,' said Chrisnelt.

From the roots, the trunk soared upward, thick and strong and old. It was straighter than a streetlight, taller than the tallest communication tower and more powerful than any Christmas tree. 'It is determined to reach beyond the world of people,' said Chrisnelt.

'It's higher than I had imagined,' said Pastor Kadazi. Everyone in the speedboat agreed that it was the highest tree any of them had ever imagined.

The base was a continent, a mountain range; eyes ached just scanning its folding girth. 'And that great width rises unchanged, until it reaches those high branches that in turn reach out sideways to the light, as if they are new trees searching for new lands up there,' said Chrisnelt. 'Like a forest in the sky.' The canopy bounced in the sun's brightness. 'It's as if the leaf clusters have become green clouds.'

'It looks very high,' said the Machine-gun Man, surprisingly. He'd put down his gun and was leaning forward with a mooring rope, anticipating an approaching root that was bent like a huge hook. Many of the other roots bent upward too, seemingly wanting to become trees.

The sun was hidden from view now, bursting out

here and there as the speedboat drifted closer. The tree's shadow lay across the River, rippling wide and long on the endless current. It had made its way onto the far bank, becoming a great field of the softest and deepest blacks. As they crossed the shadow, Pastor Kadazi blinked. He rubbed his eyes.

'It's a moabi,' said Pastor Kadazi. 'Nobody told me it was a moabi.'

'It's probably the last remaining moabi in the province,' said Chrisnelt. 'I have read that this species makes very good wood and oils.'

'I have not seen a moabi since I was a child,' said Pastor Kadazi.

'You will see it from across the City,' said the Machine-gun Man.

'There was such a tree in my village when I was a boy. It was surrounded by all the huts then. It was under such a tree my father gathered me and my brothers,' said Pastor Kadazi. 'It was under this tree my father told stories of the City.' His voice was soft. He spoke aloud, but he spoke only to himself.

'You lived here, Pastor?' asked one of the men. There was a long pause, the engines spluttering as the speedboat drifted. The prow bumped against a big root, bumped again.

'I lived on the other bank,' said Pastor Kadazi, pointing across the River. 'In that country, further upriver, before the wars. This same tree used to grow up there.'

'I will have to make the hole deeper and wider, Pastor,' said Chrisnelt.

'Yes,' said one of the men. 'Much deeper.'

'Yes. Deeper, Boss.'

'Much wider!'

'Yes.'

'It is the right tree for me,' said Pastor Kadazi. He stared at Chrisnelt. His eyes seemed angry, and for the briefest moment they flickered with memories. The current released bubbles from the muddy bank. Old plumes of dust slid down into the water and lay big curls on the surface. Then the dust was sucked away, and it was lost.

'It's the most beautiful tree I have ever seen,' said Chrisnelt, loudly.

'The world is a Border Town now,' said Pastor Kadazi, thinking of his life, changed long ago. There was silence for a minute.

'The most beautiful tree,' repeated Chrisnelt. 'A high thing on flat land rises in a singular moment of sharp penetration of the skies: a spire launching up, the sound of great bells lifting in a wave of wings.'

Pastor Kadazi stared at him. 'We get out,' he said.

Hundreds of African Green Pigeons swirled on a fresco of tropical heat, scattering the shade. The men climbed out of the speedboat. The sky was heavy. The green pigeons swirled and swirled above. The moabi was alone: a single tree from long ago. It grew in loneliness, left behind by a fleeing forest, thought Chrisnelt. It did not want to be in this openness of low brush and grasses and leaking dusts.

Even Pastor Kadazi would have agreed, should Chrisnelt have shared his soft muttering: 'It stands there like a crucifix.'

The men walked silently. Pastor Kadazi was in front, his white silk pants shimmering. The man with the biggest machine-gun of all was at the back, humming the Harry Belafonte tune. Flies stuck to sweating shoulders. Insects on the ground shivered like glowing coals.

Ancient drum-beats shook inside Chrisnelt. His legs wobbled. His lungs seethed each time he breathed. The primordial fire-dancers of the forest sparkled in his eyes. The Great Dancing Road swelled behind him, pushing him away from the tree. He glanced back at the waters, which had become dark under the great shadow. 'It's like the bluest-blackest ink from my notebooks. It's all I've ever written, like the current is dancing in magical words and numbers surrendering answers, taking them down to the City, and perhaps past it.'

'Hurry up,' said the man at the back.

'That is the greatest tree ever known in the world of people,' said Chrisnelt to the man at the back. A gap had formed between them and the man in front, who was now tight up against Pastor Kadazi and the Machine-gun Man, one man pushing another man forward, all wanting to follow, no one ready to be first on the thin line toward this unknown. The squeaking of rubber shoes was loud on the sand. 'Not because of its height, but because of its importance.'

'It's very important.'

'Yes.'

'Very.'

They were climbing the slight incline up to a cluster of huts. 'This moabi,' said Chrisnelt loudly, panting as he walked, 'will need to be pruned, both the roots and the branches. We will need many men, a crane and many ropes, and much burlap.'

'I must first speak to this village,' said Pastor Kadazi.

'Yes, Pastor.'

'Praise the Lord,' said the man behind Chrisnelt, his machine-gun across his shoulders.

'This is the home of Queen Makoko. I will request a price for the tree,' said Pastor Kadazi.

'It will be a good price, Boss,' said one man.

'I'd hate to know the cost,' said Chrisnelt to the one man at the back, who spat and shook his head every time Chrisnelt spoke.

'Big.'

'Every village used to have such a tree,' said Pastor Kadazi, the sight of the village up ahead bringing back more memories.

'Every village lived near *this* tree. The shadow must have walked on the waters of the River in every tongue and all great dreams. That shadow crossed all the edges everywhere, like a prophet,' said Chrisnelt to the man at the back, who spat again.

Pastor Kadazi was lost in the distant glare – he had paused, was faraway in the light – and then he appeared again. An apparition of shining whites, his big teeth hidden, eyes focused beyond.

The village was small. The mud walls of the small huts were bright red. Next to each hut rose a mango tree, and so each hut sat in its own shade. In each shadow sat small groupings of men and women. Naked children ran from shade to shade. The sun was a playmate, and it chased them as they giggled. There was much smiling. One group, under a big shadow of spiky edges, clapped their hands rhythmically; the men, sitting on bleached wooden benches, swayed and sang to the call of the day. There were many mats upon which small fishes dried, and red nuts, and other things that looked like tiny faces made of clay. Little low hedges of sticks sheltered crops of green fronds and bushes in rows. One tall adolescent boy kicked a Coca-Cola can to another, both of them bare-chested, sweating red mud.

Pastor Kadazi laughed, another uncontrollable laugh. He remembered the game of children running between shadows. He remembered being an adolescent and kicking things, and the game of watching the men talking, hiding from the midday sun. He walked into the clearing. A man approached from the shade on the far side, waving a cellular phone. He shouted: 'Welcome, Pastor! We've been expecting you.'

'I will organise a very long and wide barge with two cranes, and you will make sure it lives, Chrisnelt,' said Pastor Kadazi softly to the line of men behind him. The man at the back spat, then hummed like Harry Belafonte.

CHAPTER TWENTY

'I HAVE HEARD THERE ARE too many countries in Africa now,' said Queen Makoko to Pastor Kadazi, her red robe intermittent against the red walls and red floor of the hut, in the way a crow flickers against a dark sky. 'There can only ever be one country, like there can only ever be one tree.'

Pastor Kadazi clapped his hands twice, as was the custom, before nodding, although he didn't understand what Queen Makoko was talking about. His nod was a political nod. His nod would facilitate other nods, he hoped. He planned to nod often that afternoon: this was the ritual he'd anticipated.

He glanced through the doorway at the moabi tree in the distance, the River behind it a shining line of silver, the branches reaching shadows of the deepest black toward him and the village. Beyond the far edge of the River, on the furthest bank, and even beyond that, many other borders waited, as did the memories of his youth. He'd been granted this audience with the Queen – ruler of the Bateke – in order that he might negotiate a price for the tree. It had taken much planning in the City. Governor Feti had phoned many people. And Pastor Kadazi had already paid large sums of money just to be received in this dust.

Chrisnelt watched from the very back of the hut of Belief. He sat very flat, pressed against the wall, the warm mud making his back red. He'd been the last to be allowed inside, the last to be seated. He'd had to sit outside at first, until he'd been summoned to sit at the back. The heat was intense, as if wild heat had been captured and forced into the room. It made him nauseous. His stomach ached, as it always did, but this time with excitement. The room was redder than any room he'd ever seen. 'I am inside an ancient fire. It's as if I'm inside a burning tree,' he whispered to the wall. He rubbed the surface behind him with his hand. It felt like bark.

The room was filled with men, sitting on the mud floor in a low cloud of red, legs and arms crossed and their bare feet red. It was only Queen Makoko who was elevated: she floated above them all on her creaking wooden chair. She sat in it as if she were winged and feathered, sitting at the edge of a hole in a great tree. It was the first carved chair Chrisnelt had ever seen, made of a single piece of old wood, with a high back and high sides. He wondered if it was made from a fallen branch of the moabi tree: one of those limbs that is given in a storm. It gave off a sweet smell that filled the air above their heads.

The queen was very old, moving like a tiny beetle now, her smallness made up of many sharp points and bends. Her red robe was a red cotton blanket; Chrisnelt had thought it was made of glistening red plastic, until it began to hang differently, crackling like twigs. Her skin lay in so many deep folds, he thought it might be part of the robe, textured like the skin of the moabi tree.

Queen Makoko sat surely, scanning the crowd. The way her arms rested on her big knees made him reconsider her as she spoke. He listened more carefully. Every time she leaned her little shoulders forward, he leaned forward too. Her head rocked. His head rocked. It was her big head, wrapped in red cloth shrouding her eyebrows and her wisdom, that drew him the most.

Chrisnelt counted the creases under her chin, the creases running down her cheeks, and on her forearms and on her fingers. He counted the stars flickering in her eyes. Here teeth were perfect, and small in big wet gums. Her tongue was athletic, sending spit in slow arcs in between her words. She also had athletic fingers and athletic ears that twitched, dangling shining copper earrings the size of mangoes, resembling Christmas decorations. Her words hung in the air like birds making sentences on the sky. He thought to himself: *Old people shout time at us like a warning: each day is an exceptional place, a vast room, a wilderness, where we search for faces that understand the fecund clock of growth.*

In the red ash of that world, in the vermillion warmth, he found himself thinking of a Christmas, and of flames in trees. He said the word 'No'.

It was then that the green pigeons landed in the mango tree next to the doorway: swooping down in shuddering silence, only the sprinkled shadows revealing their presence. And it was only he, nearest to door, who felt the wings. Their quick gush cooled him. The mango tree rattled and a ripe mango rolled into the dust and the light.

'Dangling and laughing in feather-tails and feather-wings of liberation on every branch,' whispered Chrisnelt to the wall upon which his head rested. 'That's the way of trees, when birds carry their canopies across the sky.'

'Sir, this tree has been here since before there was a village, and before even the land of the Bateke, when the River spoke to the world without speaking. Why should we sell it to you?' said Queen Makoko.

'Yes,' said all the men of the village in unison, as if they were singing a hymn.

'Yes,' said Pastor Kadazi. He clapped his hands twice, nodding.

'Why should we sell it to you?'

'I have bought all the trees between here and the City. I have done so over many years, my Queen, for charcoal,' said Pastor Kadazi, after he'd clapped. 'I have always paid the right price to your people.'

'I have heard this.'

'Yes,' said the men again in song.

'I have made many people very rich,' continued Pastor Kadazi.

'The River and the trees have made you rich,' said Queen Makoko.

'Yeeees.'

'I am very grateful to the River and the trees, my Queen.'

'It is good.' The chair creaked.

'Yeeees.'

'I will give a lot of money, and I will send many chickens.'

Queen Makoko looked over the silhouetted heads of the men, into the light, and into the heart of the distant tree. 'It is not for sale,' she said finally, and very softly, her big gums glistening, her eyes the colour of raindrops in the clouds of Chrisnelt's imagination. She waved her hand; the copper bangles jangled and her fingers and fingernails shone red.

Chrisnelt stood up in the sweltering humidity that sat

on all the heads, clapped his hands together gently and bowed his head in a slow stoop, as he had seen done by others who'd spoken. 'My Queen Makoko, I am Chrisnelt, please may I address you,' he said, his voice trembling, his throat dry, the red dust all about him in a haze. Pastor Kadazi glared at him.

An old adviser was sitting on a very low stool next to Queen Makoko, facing the crowd. Chrisnelt had not noticed him from the back of the room. Now he waved his hand at Chrisnelt. 'Kneel, and you may then speak,' he said.

'Yeeees.'

Chrisnelt knelt and said: 'Please honour us with this tree. It is alone for a reason. It is Africa's Tree. It has been waiting for me. It must travel in many different and important ways. It must travel as the Mango Tree has travelled from across the oceans, all the way from Asia via Europe.' He pointed to the two Portuguese cutlasses hanging behind Queen Makoko on the red wall in a cross of conquest, leaking red rust down behind her. 'It must travel as the Christmas Tree has travelled across all of Africa. It is true that there is only one tree in Africa. There is only one tree in the whole of the world. Because a tree is a forest, and forests should have no end.'

'Who is this?' asked Queen Makoko.

'He works for me, my Queen,' said Pastor Kadazi, apologetically. 'I will deal with him later. Please allow me to pay whatever you want for the tree, my Queen.'

There was silence. Chrisnelt was terrified. He pressed his back against the wall and slid slowly to the floor, his shorts smelling strongly of hot piss. Pastor Kadazi stared.

After some time, Queen Makoko put her hands on her knees and slowly lifted her stiff body out of its wooden hollow. She stood high, on her left the cutlasses, on her right a wooden mask staring with primordial eyes: wooden eyes, carved before the time of knives. She sighed, breathing deeply, beatified by age. She pointed to Chrisnelt. 'If you get me a flower from the tree, it is yours.'

'YEEEES!' shouted the men of the village.

'Stand up, young man,' said the adviser, who had also stood.

Chrisnelt rose slowly. He slid up the red wall, hands at his sides scraping lines in the mud, legs shaking, his toes curled into balls. Everyone could see the piss dripping from his shorts. He stared at Queen Makoko. He stared at Pastor Kadazi. The Machine-gun Man looked down in embarrassment. All the men in the village watched. Pastor Kadazi looked at Chrisnelt unblinking, his white silk shirt shining like his white eyes and his white teeth. Silence held the red dust in blood-curdling heat. Sweat burst off Chrisnelt's face. And he ran.

He ran out the doorway into the sunlight that was hotter than it had ever been. Green pigeons exploded the silence into wings. He ran across the wide clearing, his bare feet kicking up the dust in a long, low cloud. He ran in and out of the blue shadows of the many mango trees, past the many round huts. He ran and he continued running down the hill toward the River, the dry shrubs shaking and the dry bushes bending. Dust followed him, hanging at his ankles. He ran and he ran and he ran, his long arms flapping in a desperate attempt to keep him from tumbling; he ran like he'd never run, perhaps like he'd always wanted to run. He ran like he ran in his heart's dreams, grass-blades stinging his legs, away from one pain and toward another. Grasshoppers leapt from below his pounding feet, as did a single screaming white hen. He ran down to the water, to the edge that glittered like it had never glittered. He ran to the very end of things and the very beginning too. He ran to the tree, and to No.

The men of the village poured out of the room like water. The red dust was strong, as if the room of heat had coughed a violent breath from the centre of the Earth. They flowed out into the wide clearing, and then they parted, like a sea. Queen Makoko walked down the middle of the parting, her adviser at her side, Pastor Kadazi behind her, his men behind him. And they stood and looked down at the River and the tree. Nobody talked, the only sound was that of the screaming hen, and the occasional clicking from the legs of lost grasshoppers.

Chrisnelt put his arms around the tree and he cried. His body shook. He pissed and sobbed. He was there for some time; it felt like the sun had gone away. He breathed softly into the bark. It was cool, the shade was wet. The trunk was itself covered in leaves: vines and other plants that had made a home in the vast shade. The deepness of the shade and the freshness of the green leaves took the heat from his shaking body. He breathed more calmly. The tears stopped. He looked up. At least twenty-six storeys, he thought. He grabbed onto the vines with his long fingers; his toes lifted from the dust. And he began to climb.

The crowd in the clearing gasped. Queen Makoko sighed.

Chrisnelt heard the sound, drifting up to him in a

strange moan shuttled by dust, and to it was added the whispering song of the fire-dancers of the River, the stars on the watery shoreline. He looked at the River rushing steadily down to the ocean, and to all the other oceans beyond. He looked up again, into a darkness sprinkled with tiny lights, and he pulled himself up with his long arms into the leaves, his fingers finding the tendrils. 'I'M COMING,' he screamed.

Many hours passed. It was late afternoon, and still he climbed. All the people in the village had come out of all the huts. The clearing was filled with men, women and children, sitting in unimpeachable silence. All the faces watched the stranger in the tree, the tiny figure inching upward; patches of leaves shivered in cryptic jerks and pauses as he made his way toward the heavens. Queen Makoko's chair had been brought to her from inside the red room, as had the stool for her adviser. Pastor Kadazi and his men had found shade under a mango tree. Nobody talked.

Another hour came and went. And another. Green pigeons erupted from the top of the great tree, lifting as one huge body of emerald green, circling against the deepest of shining blues that had started to radiate across the dusk sky. The people gasped again. Chrisnelt disappeared from view, absorbed by the canopy.

'Make a fire,' commanded Queen Makoko. 'Make it a big fire.'

'Yes,' said her adviser, and he waved his arms at some of the village men.

The fire was high, its tongues hissing in many languages; it roared in oranges and reds and yellows, higher than even the tallest hut. The men of the village fed it from below, pushing long, twisting branches deep inside roared, throwing straw that sparkled into drifting puffs of grey smoke. The heat reverberated on the many faces in the darkness. High above the gathering of village people, bats danced in between the stars, owls glided and moths soared. Everyone hummed and clapped steadily to the tune of the fire. Pastor Kadazi and his men sat to one side, still under the mango tree. Queen Makoko glowed crimson in her red robe, watching the blue path that led down to the River and the tree.

'Quiet,' said the adviser.

'Yeeees.'

The slow shape of the boy surrendered a long shadow under the dark sky. His heavy breathing was broken only by a faint cough of exhaustion as he walked toward the clearing. He stepped into the light. His clothes and his body green like the brightest leaf. Tears fell from his cheeks. With quivering fingers, he handed Queen Makoko a single flower. It was so small and pale: a rare greenish-white, its centre faintly red like blood. She took it in her open hand as she rose from her chair of wood.

'I could not make it to the top. I could not get all the way, but I got high enough to get the first flower I could find in all that darkness,' said Chrisnelt, between tears.

'This flower never falls from the moabi tree. It only comes down to us as a gift,' said Queen Makoko.

'Yeeees.'

The village men clapped and sang, as did the village women, and the children ran to sit below Chrisnelt. His wet cheeks flickered in red and orange and yellow. One of the smallest children, a boy with adventurous eyes, offered him an opened mango, dripping sweet and fresh.

'The tree is moabi: of the darkest woods, of the greatest variation, of purple veins and red veins and green veins that beat thick inside a heart that holds the Leaves. It will live with you, young man. You will take this tree for no money, and the River will assist you with your great weight,' said Queen Makoko.

CHAPTER TWENTY-ONE

PASTOR KADAZI AND HIS men left at dawn. The line they made as they walked through the grasses was deathly quiet, except for the man at the back humming Harry Belafonte. Chrisnelt was left behind with strict instructions to prepare the tree for its journey. Much money had been dispersed as gifts to all the people in the village, except Queen Makoko, who stayed in her red room, in her chair, below the Portuguese cutlasses from long ago.

Chrisnelt spent many days below the moabi tree, waiting for Pastor Kadazi's return. He spent nights there too, sleeping against the trunk, soothed in the warmth of fallen leaves that softened his dreams. The notebook he'd brought along – he'd had space for only one; the one that housed his bird list and some of his most important ideas – was all he had to remind him of home. In it he read thoughts. He read the words Chaminda had once spoken: 'Liberation for Africa is liberation for a single tree.' He thought of Amaterasu as he watched the night River surge past in an almighty gush, the sound never-ending. He thought of La Mame's smile when the people came down to the River to wash with laughter and dances. And when he looked up at the leaping stars, he saw the white face of Ásbjörn, particularly when one shot across the darkness in a flash of white light.

Each morning he read some of his shorter poems aloud to the tree, because in the mornings the sunrise gave the bark the mask of No. The village children gathered there to listen to him, and also to the tree. Chrisnelt smiled when he overheard an adolescent boy telling an old man that the poems were very odd: 'His words are in a foreign language, and we only understand the parts that are about raindrops, because then he points to the clouds, telling us the power of numbers and the many times water returns to the sky.'

When Pastor Kadazi returned, he brought with him many crates of white hens, and he released them in the village as if they'd come to take over the shade below the mango trees. Some hens ran into huts and would not come out. Some disappeared into the thick grasses and never returned. And some laid eggs straight away next to fallen mangoes.

'I HAVE COME WITH MORE GIFTS,' shouted Pastor Kadazi that day. The village clapped. Queen Makoko stayed in her red room.

After Pastor Kadazi's arrival, which was triumphant, like a conqueror's, the other boats followed. There were many. One was seven barges long and wider than the village. On it rose two steel cranes that looked like escaping communication towers. Hundreds of men came ashore then, and many cheered when they saw the tree. Other smaller boats moored like dried leaves against the side of a circular pond. Chrisnelt watched as they all came. 'Ants,' he said to a child. 'Ants and foreign insects. And they are stained, like soot on the walls of the world.'

'Hello, Pastor,' said Chrisnelt. 'Welcome back. I have been preparing your tree. We have dug a deep hole all the way around the base. The roots that are not critical for survival have been cut. As you lift the tree, we will unearth the deeper ones. I have explained this to the diggers who have been working very hard.'

'Good, Chrisnelt,' said Pastor Kadazi. He'd brought his own chair, and one of his men placed it next to him so he might sit and watch the extraction of his tree. He'd been sure to bring the biggest plastic chair in the City. It was shiny and of the bluest plastic, and his cushion was of the whitest silk. He had come wearing his plumed hat. He carried a white fan acquired in China, on which were painted many orchids. It fluttered like a wing. The feathers on his head rustled in the breeze that had begun to slide across the River, turning it from silver to grey.

Chrisnelt said to a boy, pointing surreptitiously at the puffed shape in the white suit on the chair: 'Pastor Kadazi is the biggest and most powerful Chicken in the City.' The boy laughed, and then continued to kick his rusty Coca-Cola can.

Huge steel cables unwound from the tips of the cranes, making wailing sounds. Some children cried, others fled back to the village, and others watched, captured by the unknown. Steel hooks hooked into other hooks that hooked chains. Loops were made into more loops. A woven lattice of cables formed a spider web in the sky, tightening around the tree. Burlap bandages protected the branches and the trunk. Huge wet sacks were wrapped around all the clusters of leaves. Men teemed all over the tree, devouring its green serenity.

'This is a flying tree,' said a child, before scampering away in terror.

With a creaking noise, the tree was pulled like a

precious tooth from the dusts. Sand fell and hissed. A hole gaped. It swung out and over the River, the vast shadow making night-time fall temporarily, an eclipse of the sun. As it was lowered on its side onto the long steel platform that floated in the middle of the River, the green pigeons came over it for the last time. They scattered and then they scattered again, offering a cacophony of wings.

'The dust is lifting beyond the clouds,' said Chrisnelt to one of the workers.

'It's so much dust, it'll probably stay in the air for days,' said the worker. 'Maybe you will even see it from the City?'

'It smells sweet,' said a child.

Then Chrisnelt said, carefully: 'That's not dust, it's flowers. Millions of tiny, falling white flowers.'

More clouds gathered, suffused with purple and grey, holding the scent of all the blooms. The entire village waited in the silence of the falling flowers; even the sun stayed low behind that impenetrable shower. And Queen Makoko looked down at it all from inside her red room. And Chrisnelt cried privately for his father and for No, and for all the people who had ever stood like tall trees.

'Wrap all the roots in wet burlap!' he shouted to the workers, who shouted to the other workers on the barge. The tree groaned and the barge whined under the weight of everything. 'It will rise again in the City,' he said to himself. 'It will rise,' he said to a child, as if to comfort him.

'Wrap all the roots.'

'Wrap the roots.'

'Good,' said Pastor Kadazi from his distant chair.

'Be careful,' said Chrisnelt to the workers near him.

'Good, good.'

'Don't let anything snap, or we'll lose the tree to the River,' said a man with a machine-gun.

'Good, very good.'

'Slowly.'

'Careful.'

'Good.'

'Bless the Lord.'

'The burlap. Gently with the roots.'

In his head, Chrisnelt watched leaves drifting between the flowers. He counted each one in his heart. Then it happened, fracturing the air like a miracle:

Two golden swallows glided from inside the tree, up and out, below the gleaming clouds. Tails glittered, long, twinkling gold; the two delicate bodies mottled in browns and blacks like the scales on a fish. These birds were truly wild, new to any place of tribes, pristine to science, pure. It would never be confirmed if they came from holes in the roots or from cracks in the bark of the trunk, or perhaps if they'd been within the leaves, unwrapped by the breeze; but they came nevertheless, rupturing like fire, molten and bright from inside the earth. They shone exorbitantly, swooping fast over Chrisnelt's head in powerful curves. Number one hundred for his list would simply read: Tree Bird.

The golden swallows flew across the village, then back down to the bank, out across the barge and the resting tree; and then they disappeared, diving into the River, becoming the current on its way to the coast. Just then, a breeze strengthened into a wind that came upstream, as if the River were following its own spoor-line back to its origins.

The wind held the heavy scent of salt and of the rumbling ocean waves. Behind it rolled more clouds. 'An ancient squall,' said Chrisnelt. And it began to rain for the first time in many years.

Chapter Twenty-Two

'A WOODEN TABLE HAS NO LEGS, only stumps,' said Pastor Kadazi solemnly, looking down at his immense thighs through the glass surface of his new dining-room table, fashioned for him from remnant branches of the moabi tree, vestiges that had become unavoidably detached on the long journey down the River. It was an unusual thing for him to say, but he was in an unusual mood. He'd spent a great amount of money. He was tired. He was unsettled, uncertain of the impact of the tree on the City, and the response that would surely come. This city displayed like a rooster, loudly crowing its desires without ever trying to truly fly.

'Acolytes nailed to acolytes, slaves in submission!' Chrisnelt had said of the table legs, as he hammered them together the previous day with the longest, sharpest nails.

A tall dining-room window had been commissioned by Pastor Kadazi in response to the spectacle of the tree, a suggestion proffered by Governor Feti. Through its bevelled panes, through the gentle raindrops that roamed steadily on the glass, the tree flickered concatenations of light down into the room. The whites of the walls becoming tumbled and blurred, whites becoming blacks under this new shadow from upriver. Outside, green soared upward forever. The roof of Africa House sat under new shade, permanently compressed by the past. The huge tree and its huge reach covered the entire house, so that it was no longer a white house but deep blue, like storming waters. And dust began to turn to mud in the City.

'My house has changed colour,' said Pastor Kadazi to Governor Feti. 'My beautiful white house has turned dull grey and blue. Africa House has gone dark. It's not shiny anymore.'

'It's the tallest, widest tree I've ever seen,' said Governor Feti. 'It's very impressive, very powerful. It will give your house the feeling of a palace.'

'The tree has made a damn shadow of my house.'

Chrisnelt looked up at the blue walls that tilted, at the high façade and the high windows and gables, at all the columns, at the vast patio. He flexed his back and rubbed his neck. His stomach ached. The sway of the walls made him feel sick. He thought of the falling flowers and the golden swallows. He knew he needed to climb to the top of the tree, the very top, the final tip, and then he knew to wait for the rains. They were coming. He felt the drizzle already, soft on his face. He stuck out his tongue and the dance was cool and kind. He smiled slowly. He would climb very soon.

His plants swayed in the opposite direction to the walls. They swayed in all the opposite colours, rhythmically, and with considerable life. Inside the leaves of all the plants, insects sang and many feeding birds buzzed, darting in feathers of many colours. 'So many birds have been drawn to the tree,' he said. Frogs rattled and sleeping bats swung in the warm moistness of that deep shade; it had not been humid like that for a very long time, not since before the City had come, before even a village, before a clearing in a forest. All was now a moving world of darkness and light, rocking harmoniously to the song made by the falling rain. In the fine, constant drizzle, even the earthworms slept under the sky, as did all the moles. The green world he had grown around him. His garden had waited for the tree, and now it was there, a powerful limb soaring up to the clouds, the rain coming down to meet all the leaves and all the ululations. The shade so extravagant now, Chrisnelt swam in his daydreams.

He turned his body, as if he were turning the pages of an important book, as if these pages had gilded edges, framing psalms of Nature. On the walls of the house that faced onto the garden, the windows rested on dense leaves, leaves stretching against the house, making a profound forest footpath to the sky, all linked to the great tree. Roots held roots everywhere.

Chrisnelt sat on the lawn, resting briefly. He had been caring for things all morning: pruning only with his eyes and his heart. He gazed at the many reflections in the new dining-room window, capturing the ancient clouds gathered in the highest leaves. He reached for his hand-rake. The earth above the roots of the moabi tree was soft and filled with much energy. Leaves had stopped falling from the tree. The tree had settled into its new place, was beginning to sprout new buds and root tips, crossing edges. Chrisnelt could smell the scent. Little furrows filled with water looked like sentences of silver on the edge of the lawn, against the base of the tree. The rain was steady and sure. Chrisnelt patted the trunk as he'd patted his mango tree long ago. The final hole had been filled in the earth. The final plant had opened its lungs. Growth had begun to find growth, linking all the journeys made by rain.

Chrisnelt closed the side gate, making his way home. From the street, the tree gave a dark background to Africa House, making it bluer than the deep curves of the shifting clouds, bluer than the veins on screaming faces, bluer than the skin on dead fingers. He rubbed his pocket; more fingers clinked. Gone was the white of snows in his head, draping the whitest of worlds. Gone was the whitest of virgin cloths, in the brightest of white vestibules. Gone was the white ash he'd carried in his heart. He walked with these new fingers, and he smiled.

Some people of the pavement – inspired by their children, who seemed to see more clearly – had remarked that it was as if the great house had at last been given a bush of vibrant hair above its contorted face. One man – the lead driver of the convoy of trucks that had come up the roads, thundering below the sleeping tree in transit, while it lay stretched, dripping river waters from its stem into every culvert and drain – said that the shadow of the tree at dawn now reached across the entire City, to other cities beyond cities. He did not quite say it like that. He said: 'This tree is bloody huge.' But Chrisnelt knew what he meant.

Even in this new rain, the tree could indeed be seen from distant districts across the City. It could even be seen from the other side of the River. It stood patiently in the sun-filled rain for all to see. The heat parted the raindrops so the new leaves could be seen from every direction. Even from the end of the runway at the airport, on the far side of all the roofs and all the walls, from within an aeroplane carcass that lay scattered in weeds, from a dead army tank that was now covered in political posters, through the dirty rows of porthole windows in barges and boats that had died long ago, it could be seen.

La Mame said that when he sat on his couch he could see the tree, all the green pigeons circling above it like the most beautiful dust. Chaminda, too, could see the tree from his shining hill. That tree had made him see all the trees that had ever been in the City, or so he said, especially the ones Chrisnelt had given to his imagination. Amaterasu had seen the tree suddenly, and she would continue seeing it suddenly like a brilliant idea every day; this is what Mr Nagasaki said. On the first day she saw it, she screamed with translucent joy; on another day, when she screamed again, Mr Nagasaki asked Chrisnelt to pick her a leaf so she might chew it and dream of Japanese blossoms. Ásbjörn commented to Chaminda that the tree had gone up surprisingly quickly, and would in fact make an ideal aerial if summited by an electrician with a long cable of love. Mrs Malotika proposed to the choir, and to all her baking friends, that the River had brought the tree, and that the City had received it like the breaking of bread in the rain.

'It *is* a very impressive garden,' said Governor Feti to Pastor Kadazi, who sat at the far end of the dining-room table. 'Maybe you should have a light shining up at the tree at night, then you can look at it from in here when you eat? The President would like that, I'm sure.'

'Not a bad idea.'

'And I'm very glad you like the silk flowers in here.'

'Yes, very nice, very impressive. And I see you have had them placed in all my bedrooms too. Wonderful flowers for me.'

'I imported more for your entrance lobby last month. Just like the ones on the patio. Beautiful silk. Big and bright. They're selling well too, the more the people hear that they're all over Africa House.'

'Yes.'

'What do you think of the ones that now hang from your chandeliers? Those were a surprise for the arrival of the tree.'

'Yes, impressive, especially with the lights on. And I love the ones in the pots at the entrance. They can glow in the dark.'

'I hope they will complement your finished garden.'

'Yes, yes. They finish it all off. They give it life.'

'And no water!'

'Yes.'

The two men smiled. 'It's now the finest garden, and the big tree was a good idea. Very impressive indeed. Bless you, Pastor, and your tree,' said Governor Feti, high on his chair. 'Now, with all this, what do I do about the chicken problem?'

'Yes.'

'Some of our stones are gone.'

'Geoffroy says many hens are shitting gems at the farm upriver,' said Pastor Kadazi. 'In this City, sons own thieving fingers, just like their fathers.'

A few days passed. Chrisnelt was invited to the inauguration of the tree. It was an evening event, and he was to be introduced to the President. He was to wear long pants, and he would be collected in the white Mercedes-Benz. He would be paid overtime.

He spent that day at home. He prepared for the big evening. He watched his sisters cooking at the family flames in the kitchen of memories. He listened to the laughter coming from pots, contemplated the glow of smoke and the long, leaking bag of charcoal on the floor. He smiled a lot at the grey dust.

The living room remained empty of church converts. He was uncomfortable in the shoes and long pants he'd borrowed from La Mame. His crotch itched and the socks made his feet sweat. He walked quietly down the corridor of poems, adding a stanza here and there, in special places. He sat next to his pond, rolling the socks off with much relief, and dipped his toes in the water. They twinkled for the beetles and the mosquitoes with black-and-white legs. His gaze channelled through the flowers, back to the Bedroom of the World, and beyond to the wall of maps and the ceiling of more maps, the oldest one an image of the world as a new island, just a land of blue floating in a sea of green. Above him, sparrows chattered, gathering like clouds. Crows searched for new nest sites in the highest places. On the horizon, flocks of white egrets flew toward the River in the direction of deepness, interrogating the twilight. He looked at the empty falling spaces inside the clouds, sucked by the swelling flow.

The rain continued. He looked up through leaves of every shape, his face wet and shining, the water bouncing in stars off his tight curls. He did not care about being wet. The rain danced in slow descent, delicate and constant, as it had done for many weeks: sometimes just a light mist, sometimes heavy, but all the time immutable of purpose, on a divinatory journey down to the ground. He counted the raindrops like he'd always done.

He leaned against his first flower, which was now a resting bush, and said to it: 'Skies of sharp glass cut gaps between trees, culminating in great columns, domes and spires, hard and high in the sun. Our City – as it is with all cities – takes its shape from that light and from its sparkling birdsong, instinctively. And leaves have bent into rafters. Yet pews and mats have forgotten their branches and their roots. We were once so wondrously wooden and warmed in boundless forests, shaking our wings in gatherings under the first bells and songs. Now, in this City is a single white thorn pointing up like a finger from the dusts of a new kind of cremation. Above and beyond its polished doors and plastic things has risen my Tree, linked to a distant place, green of rain and the flowering hymns of Africa. Tomorrow I shall climb it, I suppose.'

The white Mercedes-Benz shuddered in the mud. He climbed inside. Through the tinted windows, he saw night in the day and day in the night. The rainstorm had given time an in-between meaning, on the edge of light. The chrome rim framing the glass made him think of the world as a computer screen; he pressed the doorknob down like the 'Enter' key. Raindrops sparkled in a trillion pixels, running down toward the earth on a journey to an almighty connection. The ancient link between sky and land had always been water. He counted and he counted, and he counted some more. Each raindrop carried a message, racing toward the inevitable River.

How the land must look like a tree of water from the sky today, thought Chrisnelt on the seat next to Governor Feti, who was dressed in a spectacular suit from Paris, a silk flower in his lapel. 'How it must all glitter from high above in a synaptic dance.'

The car pulled away, and the raindrops ran sideways in straight lines parallel to the street. Chrisnelt could just make out the top of the moabi tree in the distance, as they approached Africa House. It was wider than he had remembered. Behind it stood other trees, much smaller, but growing, and beyond them everything was shimmering faintly green in the rain.

The car paused at the stop sign. Chrisnelt looked at the tree up ahead. He smiled. 'Look, Governor, all the birds settling on the top. Time to sleep.'

'Very impressive job,' said Governor Feti.

'Lots of work,' said Chrisnelt.

'Yes,' said the driver, nodding.

'Yes,' said the man sitting next to the driver.

'Still much to do,' said Chrisnelt.

Through the raindrops on the windscreen, the tree looked like a million trees, and the sunset made each one shine and leap in clean oranges and fresh reds, like fruits.

Then the world flickered. The sun and the moon collided in a thunderous roar of light that rippled through the car. The driver slammed his foot on the brake and everyone jerked forward. The brightness entered every raindrop on every window, scattering fireballs, ripping sight from all eyes.

'I AM BLIND!' shouted the driver. He rubbed his

face with a hand. The car jerked again and stopped. Taxi-cars hooted everywhere. People on the pavements dropped their wares and dogs howled. A rooster crowed somewhere close by.

'The world is golden outside,' said Governor Feti, with a slow smile. The street was lit by a horrific sunrise, the kind that only comes at a time of damnation.

'IT IS LIGHTNING!' shouted Chrisnelt. '*Lightning has struck the tree!*'

The window buzzed and the glass pane lowered with a hum. Governor Feti had pressed the button. They looked out through the lines of silver rain at the tree. It was on fire, burning in a voluptuous glow of tiny lights of every colour. They twinkled. So many little glowing lights. The entire tree shone. The entire district shone too. The heat was immense, and Chrisnelt shielded his face, the rain pouring all over his shirt. He could just make out the flocks of terrified birds, their delicate wings turbulent and desperate as they fled.

'The City is burning,' said Chrisnelt.

'I'm getting wet,' said Governor Feti. He pressed the button that pushed up the window. 'Pastor has a magnificent tree. If he keeps those lights on, there will be no shadows over Africa House in the daytime either.'

The car moved quickly. It did not stop at Pastor Kadazi's front door.

'Too many people there now. We'll come back later,' said Governor Feti, 'when there's space to park my car.'

Chrisnelt collapsed back into his seat. He wanted to curl into a ball. Tears fell from his face. He closed his eyes. And the street became a path:

Very narrow and soft underfoot, it curved down to the bank, textured with butterflies and hoof-prints – remembering duiker, forest buffalo, river hog in this night-journey of dreams. The yellow sun balanced the mist, lifting orange and purple scents of fruit and warm mud above the River; all was breathing in a clearing of people fluttering skins and sweet twigs ... An old man in red scraped Bateke patterns on clay. An old woman swept crackling red leaves. Young men and women lay on mats, talking and wriggling in laughter; some fished, plopping little cages into the shallows. Some fanned around a fire of secrets, some appeared and disappeared like playing children, growing like green leaves in murmuration everywhere, and the earth seemed to fold silently at the touch of joy. Long grass huts stretched and rested in between the people, huts not owning walls, curving grass roofs that simply became the ground; the roots of the past held on the wings of the birds.

The car turned into a wide corner and the street became a dream of memory:

A route down to the water's edge, which was no edge because carved logs made constant bridges to the other side, like effortless stepping stones on a silver pond. The fishes gave themselves to the birds then, offerings of abundance. And inside that village of leaves, the land gave itself in many ways: routes invisible to the eye, routes connected to other routes; wandering through the high forests, across the grassed plains and into the hills that led to the coasts, from the dark into the light and the light inside the dark; always these routes came back to the village, which in turn would lead to other villages under the steady sun of life and trade: embraces across a continent.

The car slowed as it went around the traffic circle in the centre of the City, pausing below the flickering lights and moths, and the street became a terrible sign of burning:

In the centre of that village stood the last moabi tree. Below sat a man of great age on a leopard-skin mat, patterned with scratched finger-circles of white river mud on his black skin, legs crossed, arms crossed, palms crossed, forehead frozen, twisted under a blizzard of lies, showered by tropical snows. These were the snows of men from faraway, snows that had come on ships. A wooden staff lay before him, polished yet out of reach; to his right was a thick, new, foreign blanket for the cold, to his left a wooden casket on gilded legs, containing a treaty of cession of territories and futures, all in the shadow of a world of walls.

The car made a grinding sound, pulling in through the gates of Grace's Private Burial Home, and the street and the dream came to a blasphemous end:

Wounds too deep to possibly be healed by the sap of bark, too late to be cured in time for the summer flowers, too wide and gaping to be knitted together. No healing the bones of forgiving souls torn from the Forest. No soft massages of ancient fingers, no dances in masks at the fires of life. No growing of things in sacrificial devotion; no birds. No Great Dancing Road. All that lay ahead was a plethora of sacramental thrones, evil sermons screamed, sovereign lines become absolute; and the digging of a pit of black.

'NO!' shouted Chrisnelt.

The white Mercedes-Benz made private mist, the air-conditioning unit spitting ice like bits of dead teeth.

I SPOKE TO CHAMINDA IN A forest of concrete trees, in the constant tropical heat. Years had come and gone, and the Monument of Languages had been photographed by every kind of pilgrim from across the world. Like others before me, I'd flown to the City to write about the trees, and about Chrisnelt.

There were ten or maybe twelve trees, the trunks reaching fifteen metres tall, each tree's branch-tips gently touching those of the next. The trees had been made carefully with chicken mesh and cement, wire branches clutching the air or stretching into the light like great wings. Feathers were tied in tight clumps to the delicate twigs, fluttering constantly; some branches held small brown nests. The thick grey trunks of the powerful trees flexed, beautifully textured: poems were carved in waves of words, in every language ever known, and between the many stanzas protruded the finger bones of people, pointing like thorns, white and bleached.

Chaminda laughed: 'Can you believe it, we are now the first country in Africa to celebrate the National Day of the Tree! The President says it's better to vote under a tree than inside the dark rooms of instability.'

I smiled and took photographs of the unique forest, a forest I'd travelled from across the world to see with my own eyes and touch with my own hands. This place was the most famous monument in West Africa now. Ásbjörn had made sure of that, with his particular dexterity with Google, Facebook, Twitter, Snapchat. 'Long shall they dance,' he had said, pointing to the sparkles in his left eye with a pale finger. Ásbjörn's one eye had turned from blue to green, the day after it all happened. 'It will always be green now. Waiting for the other one now.' According to Nipcia – who now sneezed in her sleep due to devotion, brought on by loss, she said; and who was always to be found on the hill near the Monument when the shadows started – this was due to his unusually large tears.

Earlier, we'd sat in Chaminda's strange house eating fresh fish, deep in conversation. Ásbjörn, Chaminda and La Mame all talked at the same time, excited at the prospect of a little fame. The idea of an article about Chrisnelt appearing in an international magazine was a good ice-breaker. Then we'd walked slowly up to the Monument from Chaminda's house, along a path cobbled in Coca-Cola cans and carpeted in weeds.

The day Chrisnelt went and never came back was a day of diluvian clouds, apocalyptic rains; the River flooded.

'The air moved in giant waves,' said Chimanda. 'Surf was thundering constantly on the shore. Never before had the Great Dancing Road breathed like that, flexed with such conviction. And if currents ever had purpose, that day they showed it: leaking into every crack in every wall, up every street, against every window, below every shivering roof and doorway. The wetness was thorough, and patient. Only the higher areas of the city protruded: islands within a single sea.'

'There was so much water here for three weeks, and not much food,' said La Mame.

'When I was a younger man, the Earth pushed the ocean up to the sky, and it came over my home in our bay in Sri Lanka, racing across the world, taking my wife and my children,' said Chimanda. 'Such is Nature, in truth: it always settles in the end, after the storm. Everything returns to the sea, you see. After that great wave of pain, a thing became clear. I looked around in the mud – so much mud – and all that remained were trees. It was as if those trees remembered ancient salt waters, for they stood when every building around them fell. So it was with this place, here, in the middle of West Africa.'

'We found strange fish, all sizes and shapes,' Ásbjörn added. 'Glowing white, from the greatest depths; whiter than snow. They came from such darkness, they had no need for eyes, yet they had eyes of a new kind: fins that flexed into fingers, seeing the land with touch, like they'd once lived beyond the river.'

'That's how Chrisnelt would have described it, if he'd been here,' said La Mame.

'Streets of fish,' said Chaminda. 'Then, as things dried, these streets below us became beaches, and those near the cemetery cracked into pieces. Beaches of bones.' He fluttered his fingers.

'This was all an ossuary' – Ásbjörn waved his hand at the horizon of the city, as if it were a strange new ocean – 'spewing every mistake and deception up out of the ground. I lost all my computers and phones.'

'It was like the bones came from inside the Earth, like the call of those ancient drums in their deep caves,' said Chaminda.

'A lot of people died then,' said Ásbjörn. 'Many

buildings collapsed, many families were taken. Thousands were homeless. In the areas of Makélékélé, Mfilou and Mougali, every wall disintegrated, and every poor soul had to be relocated to a higher place to begin again.'

'Across the scattered islands of this world moved many boats,' said La Mame. 'I've never seen so many pirogues – they were like bridges, like stepping stones made of people and wood. They stretched from this City right across the river to that City and back again.'

'The Congolese Red Cross provided much assistance to victims, providing shelter kits and planks, kitchen sets and tarpaulins,' said Chaminda. 'It was remarkable to see! So many red crosses everywhere! The Swiss Red Cross helped, providing nails and wood and other building materials, as did the Austrian Red Cross, the Monaco Red Cross, the Swedish Red Cross, the Canadian Red Cross. Then there were the Americans, the Belgians, the United Kingdom, and the Norwegian Red Cross too. Crosses everywhere. Mountains of Crosses. Islands of crosses, helping other islands in a vast sea beyond empires – that's how Chrisnelt would have put it.'

La Mame laughed. 'Beyond misunderstandings, beyond all the other chicken shit, that's what he would have said.'

Now we stood within the sanctuary of trees. Chaminda looked up into the strange canopy. 'People do not die because it is Ordained. People do not die because they choose to. People die like falling leaves, surrendering the future to new branches, blessed by the rain.'

Old garbage heaps can smell sweet, I thought as we stood there, the breeze not a breeze, but rather the soft risings of strange old gases from the ground below. It all smelt just like fruit. Ripe fruit. Chaminda's house of many windows shone down there, the sun pushing a glow of heat through the many-coloured panes of glass. His front door stood ajar.

He caught my gaze and he said: 'I will never close a door again; doors are made to hang open. A doorway is just that, a door and a way, a way from one place to another, especially when it rains. That's what Chrisnelt would have said.'

Chaminda and I looked down the hill, through his transparent house, toward the sun. One particularly green beam of light, laced with blue glimmers, illuminated his vegetables: lines of carrots, potatoes, *bok choy*, tomatoes, *pimiento*, cucumbers, *luffa*, beetroot, *ngayi-ngayi*, beans and *mfumbwa*, so much roaming *m'fumbua*. I commented on the health of the vegetables and their apparent wildness of spirit. I'd never seen such bright chillies, afloat like butterflies. Chaminda said this was nothing, and that I should see the many gardens in the city. In fact, I should look now, down below, between the roofs; and indeed, lone, high trees glittered in all directions in the heat.

'Those are the flags above our many gardens,' said La Mame.

'It was the Japanese girl who first took down the corrugated iron, allowing Chrisnelt's garden to stretch, finding a future. And she did it every day, in revelation, until out of pity her neighbours stopped putting it up again. And trees became more trees when the ground began to open and dry,' said Chaminda.

'And with the opened spaces came flowers, and moabi

seeds from the sky on wings,' said Ásbjörn. 'It was like a blizzard.'

La Mame handed the envelope to Chaminda who silently handed it to me. I opened it carefully. From inside slid a single, folded piece of old paper, crackling and warm to the touch, releasing a sleeping moth. I scanned it. 'It's a letter of considerable age from a father mourning a son?'

'No's father, yes,' said Chimanda. 'Chrisnelt kept it always.'

'But look on the back,' said Ásbjörn.

Written in sharp blue ballpoint ink, a string of numbers and shapes were held together by bridges of pluses and minuses, brackets and equal signs, dashes and symbols, squiggles and commas playing like fire-dancers of the mind. Pointing out and away from the central equation, beyond the crisp edges, teetering in a geometry of Belief, were four delicate arrows: one pointing up, one pointing down, and one each pointing left and right. In between the numbers – perhaps part of them – came the words: *We have always existed as unitary emanations of water and its dust.*

'In the evenings, the air sings up here, and I have to stop watching television for a little while. I can't even cook or answer my phone,' said Chaminda. 'The world is filled with thousands of sparrows coming home.'

ACKNOWLEDGEMENTS

I THANK MY PUBLISHER Bridget Impey. You opened a path for me under the most glorious trees: so many words and branches and seeds.

And just as it is with trees and the way of foresting: thank you to all at Jacana Media. Kindness is tangible in a home of books.

Henrietta Rose-Innes, you are magnificent. A simple truth, just like the clouds and the seas and the rivers.

I am grateful to Richard Beynon and Jo-Anne Richards for gently elucidating on the merits of story. You are wise.

Thank you to the birdwatchers (in alphabetical order – as it is with lists) who remind me how to try and see in different ways: Annari van der Merwe; Anton and Elaine Odendal; Alvin and Flick Cope; Adam Riley; Brian van der Walt; Callan Cohen; Claire Spottiswoode; Clyde Carter; Cliff and Suretha Dorse; Darryl Earl David; Dave Hoddinott; David Letsoalo; Davie Chamberlain; Dennis Cope; Etienne Marais; Gillian Barnes; Ian Sinclair; John Maytham; Johan and Joy Schlebusch; John and Greta Graham; Mel Tripp; Mark and Tania Anderson; Mark Brown; Niall Perrins; Peter Sullivan; Peter Steyn; Peter and Colleen Ryan; Richard Dean; Rob Leslie; Rob Little; Ross Wanless; Simon and Stella Fogarty; Silvia Ledgard; Otto and Sandy Schmidt; Sam Woods; Trevor and Maggs Hardaker; Warwick Tarboton; Wendy Flanagan; And I think of the late Anne Gray, Barry Rose, Ilona van der Walt, Kirsten Louw, Margot Chamberlain, Phil Hockey and Rob Martin. So many varied connections to wilderness – I often see Andrew and Heather Hodgson as they photograph Amazonian frogs and the secrets under leaves.

To Hugo Jankowitz (the South African Sapeur), Steve Moore and Charles Chabell, thank you for your comradeship as we explored the Congo River.

Thank you to my sister Binda, for her support and her understanding of family – a link to Dad. Thank you to my brother Nangamso.

And to my beloved and beautiful wife Kathleen, my son Tristan and my daughter Jess: I love you.

ABOUT THE AUTHOR

VERNON RL HEAD WAS BORN in 1967 in a bungalow near the sea and the gulls. He is an architect – winning national and international awards for design and creative thinking – and when not designing strange buildings, he travels the world watching the rarest birds.

He is past chairman of BirdLife South Africa – one of Africa's most influential conservation organisations – and he serves on the Advisory Board of the FitzPatrick Institute of African Ornithology (UCT). He is author of the critically acclaimed best seller *The Search for the Rarest Bird in the World*, long-listed for the Alan Paton Literature Prize. His first poetry collection, *The Laughing Dove and other Poems*, is described by PR Anderson as "of audacity and wisdom ... penetrating, a quite startling vision." He has twice been long-listed for the Sol Plaatje European Union Poetry Award.